BLACK HILLS BLESSING

MARY CONNEALY

BARBOUR
PUBLISHING

Buffalo Gal © 2008 by Mary Connealy
The Clueless Cowboy © 2008 by Mary Connealy
The Bossy Bridegroom © 2009 by Mary Connealy

ISBN 978-1-60260-800-9

Cover design: Kirk DouPonce, DogEared Design

Published by Barbour Publishing, Inc., P.O. Box 719, Uhrichsville, Ohio 44683,
www.barbourbooks.com

*Our mission is to publish and distribute inspirational products offering exceptional
value and biblical encouragement to the masses.*

Member of the
Evangelical Christian
Publishers Association

Printed in the United States of America.

Dear Readers,

I have always been fascinated with buffalo. I'm not sure why, really. I just love to stare at them. The longer you look at them, the weirder they look. Massive shoulders, head low to the ground, narrow hips; shaggy in front, short-haired in back. I always think God was just having a good old time when He created them. So setting a book around a buffalo herd was something I'd been thinking of doing for a long time, and I was thrilled when Barbour Publishing gave me my chance. The first book in this series, *Buffalo Gal*, is particularly focused on the herd and some of the weird mannerisms of the big beast.

I've been told that what is unusual about my books is that I tackle difficult topics with humor. I hope I accomplished that in this trilogy as I explored the strife between a vegetarian and a cattle rancher in *Buffalo Gal*, the conflict between a city boy and a country girl in *Clueless Cowboy*, and the struggle of a tyrannical husband with his wife to achieve a healthy marriage in *The Bossy Bridegroom*.

Thank you so much for choosing my book. I know you've got a lot of choices when it comes to reading, and I'm honored that you picked up this volume. I love talking to my readers, so e-mail me at mary@maryconnealy.com and stop by my Web site www.maryconnealy.com or any of my three blogs: www.seekerville.blogspot.com (about writing), www.petticoatsandpistols.com (about western romance), and www.mconnealy.blogspot.com (my personal blog).

Sincerely,
Mary Connealy

BUFFALO GAL

Dedication

Two people are really responsible (or to blame) for me writing. Wendy Connealy and Janell Gatewood Carson. Wendy, my daughter, was ten or eleven when she wrote this very short book about the Bermuda Triangle, and it was really good. I'm still in negotiations with her to steal her idea. So far. . .no way. Janell, my kindergarten classmate, interviewed all the WWII veterans in her area (not while she was *in* kindergarten) and got a book printed to sell in the local county museum. It was really well done and a fun, fascinating read. I was so impressed with both of them and thought, *If they can write a book, maybe I can, too,* and fired up my computer for the first time. Thank you both for being an inspiration.

Chapter 1

B uffy Lange had been at her new job for fifteen minutes. It was going to take a miracle to last out the hour.

"Don't let him through that gate!" She sprinted toward the fence.

The buffalo hit the metal panel with a clang of horns on steel. A dozen wranglers started shouting and rushing to support the slipping barrier between a buffalo and freedom. The young bull stubbornly refused to pass through the alleyway of metal panels. The massive brute swung his head, snapping a hinge holding the gate in place.

Buffy, coming from inside another pen, grabbed the top of the fence, vaulted it, and beat the wranglers to the action. Snatching the slipping tubular steel, she shoved her shoulder into it, closing the gap.

Two thousand pounds of cranky bison rammed the wobbling panel.

Her shoulder was no match. Buffy fell backward into the mud with the gate on top of her.

The buffalo's legs tangled in the open spaces of the slatted panel, and it stopped.

With the wind knocked out of her, Buffy looked eye to eye with the frantic animal who snorted hot breath in her face. The bull swung his horns, and adrenaline sizzled through Buffy's veins like an electric current.

The crushing steel gate rang and shuddered from the blow, but it blocked the goring horns. One sharp hoof scraped between Buffy's arm and her stomach. It ripped her sleeve and scraped off some of her hide. One last enraged snort and the beast plunged forward and was gone, its hind legs missing her by inches.

Screams and shouts echoed in the ranch yard.

Buffy prayed for that miracle.

Needing direct intervention from God to keep her hired men alive and herself employed looked bad on a résumé.

The panel was wrenched off and hands ran down her arms and legs. She opened her eyes, and Wolf Running Shield, her foreman, crouched over her. His black braids, shot through with gray, slid over both his shoulders and dangled over her head. "Are you okay?" His bottomless ebony eyes flashed with worry. "Did he land a hoof on you?"

Her abused lungs started working, and she dragged in the hot July air. "I'm fine."

"Mommy!" The bloodcurdling scream came from Sally, her three-year-old niece, supposedly confined to the house until the buffalo was safely penned.

Everyone around Buffy vanished, running to the rescue. Buffy jerked her arms out of the mud and scrambled to her feet.

A man, rigged out like a cowboy straight from the old West, raced his horse between the buffalo and Sally.

"Hiyah!" the cowboy shouted and slapped his horse's rump with an open hand. He thundered down on Sally a split second before the buffalo and snagged her by the front of her pink overalls. He swung Sally up in front of him, still at a full gallop.

The buffalo changed course and went after the horse and rider.

"Where's a tranquilizer gun?" Buffy noticed Wolf dashing toward the nearest barn and hoped he was getting one.

The horse headed right toward a cluster of scrambling men gathered to watch the buffalo join the family. The rider, with inches between his horse's heels and the lowered horns of the buffalo, wheeled his mount away from the crowd.

The buffalo's horns hooked at the horse. They missed by a hair breadth.

The cowboy held Sally, still screaming, perched high in front of him. His horse danced away from the charging bull and began zigzagging across the open yard to avoid people. The man moved with his horse like they were one creature.

The shaggy beast lost interest in the horse and rider, whirled away, and charged toward the prairie that surrounded the Buffalo Commons Ranch.

For a split second, the adrenaline and the beauty of the buffalo made Buffy feel like she could fly.

The great shaggy beasts were meant to run free on the boundless South Dakota hills and prairies. But these hills and prairies had bounds, and her buffalo was out of them.

The cowboy yelled again and kicked his horse, galloping toward the ranch house. He set Sally down beside Jeanie. He took two seconds to speak some words to both of them that made Sally fling herself against her mother's legs and Jeanie cross her arms and scowl. He pulled a rifle out of a stock on his saddle. Yelling, he bent low over his saddle horn and took off after the disappearing buffalo, his intentions lethal.

"He's going to shoot Bill." Buffy whirled away from the angry man on his charging horse.

Wolf ran up beside her with the tranquilizer gun. "You drive!"

They dashed for the pickup, hooked up to the trailer that only seconds ago held the prize bull. With quick, efficient motions, Wolf unhooked the stock trailer while Buffy jumped in the driver's seat. Wolf threw himself into the passenger's side. They tore out of the yard and into the grass that stretched for miles in all directions in this fertile valley circled by the peaks of the Black Hills.

The buffalo appeared on a rise then vanished.

"The land seems so flat," Buffy muttered, her foot shoved all the way to the floorboard.

The rider appeared, closing the gap between himself and the buffalo. Buffy lay on her horn, but the rider didn't look back. If anything, he leaned down farther on his horse's neck, trying to get more speed out of the big bay quarter horse.

"It's deceiving. There are low rolling hills right up to the mountains." Wolf loaded the rifle with able efficiency.

"He wants to kill the bull before we get there," Buffy yelled. "I can't believe this. The man can't possibly intend to shoot down an animal as valuable as that buffalo."

"That's Wyatt Shaw," Wolf said, shaking his head. "He's the second-biggest rancher around here, after our boss, Leonard. He hates buffalo, and he hates what we're doing. I think he's been looking for an excuse to put a bullet in a buff ever since we moved the first head onto the ranch."

Shaw raised his gun. There was a sharp *crack* of rifle fire.

The buffalo swerved in a different direction but charged on. He seemed unhurt, but a buffalo could run a long time after it had been wounded.

Buffy tried to coax more speed out of the truck. They roared up the crest of one of the endless swells of land and were airborne as they came over the top and dropped down. They gained on Shaw as Shaw gained on her buffalo. She jammed her foot more firmly on the accelerator.

Shaw took aim. Another report cut her eardrums.

The buffalo swerved sharply, now running at a right angle to Buffy. She cut across the angle, hoping to narrow the gap and get there first. Bill gave her a glance and swerved back the way he'd been going.

The cowboy, still running flat out, turned and glared at her. Even from this distance, she saw straight into hazel eyes that shot sparks of golden fire at her. There was such fury burning there she wondered if her buffalo was the only one in danger.

Shaw looked away and aimed his rifle. He fired.

The buffalo turned. Buffy veered across prairie, trying to cut it off.

Wolf caught her arm. "Don't do that. Keep going straight."

"Why? We can beat Shaw to Bill."

"Do it," Wolf snarled. "Straighten it out."

Buffy didn't like it. She was the boss, had been for almost thirty minutes now. But she needed to keep her eyes on the dipping and rolling prairie. She did as Wolf said just to keep things simple.

Now Shaw and Bill were running at a ninety-degree angle to her. Shaw raised his gun and took careful aim.

Wolf lifted his gun from the cab of the pickup. They were nearly within range.

Shaw fired. The buffalo swerved away from the gunfire.

"It's almost impossible to hit anything from the back of a running horse or the cab of a bouncing truck," Wolf said. "Stop when I say."

"Okay." Buffy gripped the wheel with white knuckles. Her blood pounded until she heard it in her ears and her temples. Her arm burned from Bill's scraping hoof. Her body felt like a time bomb vibrating before it exploded.

Wolf nodded. "Keep going straight. That buff'll keep to the low ground when he gets to that rise."

Shaw almost lay down on the back of his horse and steadied the gun across his arm. He fired. Bill stumbled.

"He hit him," Buffy said through her clenched teeth.

"No, he didn't."

"He's going to kill him before we get there," Buffy raged.

Her truck hit a rut that launched the front end into the air. They landed and bounced, and the underbelly of the truck grated against the ground.

Bill ran steadily, as wild and beautiful as buffalo had been at God's creation.

Buffy tried to gain every second she could, even if it meant her rig was destroyed. That buffalo was more valuable than this shiny, new Ford.

Bill took the low ground, just as Wolf had predicted. That turned him until he was headed almost straight toward them.

Wolf shouted, "Stop!"

Buffy wrestled the rig to a halt, tires skidding on grass.

Wolf leaped out, graceful even with deep wrinkles cutting lines into the corners of his eyes. He braced the tranquilizer gun against the hood of the truck and settled his finger on the trigger.

A whirl of dust caught up with the truck and swallowed them. To Buffy, everything suddenly seemed to be in slow motion. Sitting in the cab, her heart pounded, her nerves screamed, her blood coursed, pushing her to action.

Wolf looked down the barrel of his gun. Bill charged closer, hooves drumming until the prairie shook.

Shaw raced behind Bill, his horse's hooves thundering along with the buffalo.

Wolf sited his gun.

Shaw leveled his rifle. Buffy knew he wanted the buffalo dead.

That's when she remembered to pray. She'd already asked God for a miracle when Sally was in a direct line between Bill and freedom. When she'd prayed, there, instantly—Wyatt Shaw.

This buffalo hater was no answer to her prayers. She stifled her resentment at God. One more thing she needed to control.

Bill closed to within a hundred yards, and still Wolf waited.

Shaw charged behind the bull; he was close enough now that he couldn't miss. Not even on a running horse. Buffy saw his cold fury and shuddered.

Wolf waited, waited. Buffy almost saw Wolf's Native American blood flowing cool and steady in his veins.

The buffalo was a hundred feet away. Then fifty.

Wolf exhaled slowly, held his breath. He fired.

A bright red flag marked the dart's direct hit on Bill's densely furred chest. Bill kept coming, his hooves rolling with the steady beat of distant thunder. His horns gleamed with the sharp danger of lightning. He showed no sign of being drugged.

Wolf held his ground.

"You can't shoot him again," Buffy yelled as she swung her door open. "He can't take that much sedative."

Shaw was almost on top of Bill. He could have leaned forward, and slapped him on the rear end. He leveled his gun forward, and Buffy saw him cock the hammer.

Buffy slammed the truck door and ran to the front of the truck. To protect her bull, she'd tackle Wolf if he decided to shoot again.

Wolf gave her one enraged glance. "Get out of here."

Buffy shouted to Shaw, "Don't shoot him. We've got him under—"

Suddenly Bill was on top of them, and Wolf vanished.

Buffy stumbled backward, bumped into the truck grill, and barely missed those sharp, curved horns. Something tightened on her neck like she was being strangled, and with a speed that made her stomach swoop, she was airborne.

She landed with a *thud* on the hood. Bill turned and smashed his wicked horns into the truck where she'd been.

Wolf had her by the collar. He released her with a look of disgust. "Crazy woman."

Bill whirled away from the truck then charged again. He slammed into the front fender and shook the rig hard enough that Buffy slid sideways to the ground. Bill turned on her.

Shaw's horse burst past the buffalo, and he gripped the front of her shirt in both his fists. As if she weighed nothing, he hoisted her into the air and set her down facing him, her legs straddling his saddle, her face pressed against his chest. He set his horse to dancing and dodging just as he'd done with Sally.

Wolf yelled, "It'll take affect in another couple of minutes, Wyatt."

Shaw said, with a rage so icy it chilled the back of Buffy's neck, "Great. I've got nothing better to do than keep this fool woman alive."

11

Buffy glanced up at the man who'd just saved her life. While Shaw was freezing her with his voice, he was burning her with his eyes. Buffy's head was spinning from the pivoting of the horse and the snorting of the grouchy buffalo and, just maybe, from the scent of a strong man wrapped in leather and sweat and rage, holding her.

For one second, she felt safe. She tightened her arms around Wyatt's waist and held on tight as she wondered how long it had been since she'd allowed someone else to keep her safe. Then she remembered how strength could dominate and how that domination came larded with disrespect. She worked with men like that. She'd grown up with a man like that. She didn't need to sit in the lap of a man like that.

Bill stumbled to a halt.

Buffy spun around to watch and whacked Wyatt in the face with streamers of muddy hair. He spit mud out of his mouth. "You're as shaggy as your stupid buffalo." Something her father would have said.

Bill staggered, panting, still on his feet. Buffy held her breath. Bill sank to his front knees.

Shaw shoved his rifle back in its sling.

Shuddering with relief that Bill was sleeping and not dead, Buffy collapsed against Shaw's strong chest and let herself be held for a minute. "Thank you."

Shaw snorted.

Buffy remembered Bill might have a bullet in him. The adrenaline was still roaring through her veins, and suddenly it exploded with nowhere to go. The whole mess caught up with her—being crushed under the gate panel, Sally's screams, the wild truck ride and the blazing gun, her near miss from Bill's horns, and this cowboy's grubby hands all over her.

She grabbed the front of Wyatt Shaw's black leather vest. She jerked him down. He didn't bend, so she ended up lifting herself until they were nose to nose. "Are you crazy? Shooting at my buffalo like that?" She shook him like she'd seen a cat shake a rat. He didn't budge, because he was twice her size and made, apparently, of forged steel, but she shook him anyway.

"Did you hit him?" she demanded. She let go of one side of his vest because she needed her hand. She jabbed him right in the second button of his blue chambray shirt. "If that buffalo dies because of you, I'm going to have the sheriff haul you in to—"

"Shut up," he spoke in a voice so grating it left rasp marks on her eardrums. The tone froze the words in her throat. "If I'd wanted him dead, he'd be dead. So—just—shut—up! Your animals are a menace."

Buffy leaned away from the rage.

Shaw leaned closer. "I've got a right to defend what's mine."

His nose touched hers. "I rode over to meet the new boss and ended up saving your daughter's *life.*"

He must mean Sally. Sally wasn't her daughter. She'd have pointed out yet another way he was wrong, but he wasn't done talking.

"I saved *your* life."

Her life? Huh! Bill had been seconds away from collapsing. She'd have been just fine. Of course, a couple of seconds with a buffalo stomping on you was a long time.

"But the thing that *matters* is—"

What did that mean: matters? Her life mattered—

"I saved my herd from having a bull buffalo running free in it. If I hadn't been here to head him off, he could have spread disease to them. I could have lost a year's income while my cattle were quarantined. And that's not the only damage he could have done." Suddenly his face turned red, and his fiery hazel eyes blazed like wildfire. *"Your daughter isn't the only little kid out here!"*

She ducked quickly and began mentally swearing out the warrant for his arrest once she got a doctor to diagnose her whiplash. And then she'd sue him for every penny he had.

"I oughta sue you for every penny you have." With a swift, reckless motion, he lifted her off his saddle horn. He unceremoniously plunked her onto the ground. "If I ever catch one of your buffalo running wild again, I'll kill it, and then I'll be at your place with the sheriff." He wheeled his horse and took off at a gallop.

Buffy opened her mouth to yell all the things that had been boiling inside of her.

Wolf stepped between her and Shaw.

"What?" she snapped.

"I'm trying to turn your temper on me, which might save us from a million-dollar lawsuit."

Buffy looked for Shaw. He was just disappearing over a nearby rise. "Why shouldn't I yell at him?" She decided to take Wolf at his word and aim her temper at him. "You heard the things he said. You saw him shooting at Bill. That buff is worth a fortune. He's got the bloodlines the Commons needs. He's practically irreplaceable."

Wolf looked over his shoulder in the direction Shaw had gone. Good, he seemed to be finally figuring out what Shaw had almost done.

Wolf jabbed his thumb toward Shaw. "I reckon he thinks they're irreplaceable, too."

Two young children, accompanied by a woman, stepped up so Buffy could see them against the expanse of South Dakota sky. They were right where Bill had headed when he'd taken off. Shaw had said Sally wasn't the only little kid on the prairie.

"They must have been out riding." Wolf crossed his arms as he studied the small group. "There's a wetland over there with a lake. The Shaws go picnicking right after church most Sundays. When Wyatt saw the buffalo tearing that way, he figured his twins were goners if he didn't do something drastic."

Buffy had to stop scowling and admit she was wrong, in every way, right down the line, which made her mad and set her to scowling again. She stared at Shaw, who pulled even with the children and swung himself off his horse with the graceful motion of a healthy animal. He turned back to look at her, and even from a distance that by now was a hundred yards, she could see him fuming. The woman took the horse's reins, and the boys grabbed his hands.

One of them hollered, "Did you shoot the buffaler, Dad?"

"Did you blow it into a million pieces of steak?" the other one asked.

The foursome dropped over the horizon.

"And he wasn't trying to kill the buffalo. He shot alongside it to turn it. He was herding it toward my tranq gun."

"That's why you told me not to drive straight toward Bill." Buffy glanced at Wolf. She'd only met him when she'd introduced herself as the new boss and arranged a crew to unload the bull she'd brought. But he had a reputation that was unrivaled when it came to buffalo. "You knew even then what he was doing?"

Wolf shrugged. His braids swung slightly against his beaded vest. "I thought maybe he had that in mind. It didn't matter if he was herding it toward us on purpose or by accident. Why get in his way?"

"He could have just missed," Buffy pointed out. "You said yourself it's nearly impossible to hit anything from the back of a running horse or the seat of a moving truck."

"That's me. That's most men. But Shaw, now there's a man who hits what he aims at. Oh, he was mad enough to kill the buff, and I thought at first he meant to. He'd've been within his rights."

Buffy heard an engine behind her and turned to see a rig, pulling the stock trailer they'd left behind, coming out to help. "The legal right to do something doesn't mean you should."

Wolf gave her a long considering look that set her back a little. His eyes were the bottomless black of his Sioux ancestors. His battered brown Stetson with the brightly beaded hatband was part of him, just like the buffalo and the land.

The solidness and wisdom of his gaze helped Buffy get hold of herself. She had been overreacting from the minute that buffalo had slammed her into the ground. She could still feel the adrenaline humming.

"You aren't one'a them that puts an animal's life on an even keel with a human's, are you?" Wolf asked with cool interest. "I'm all for raisin' buff. I like

14

the sight of them on this land, and it heals something in my soul to tend them. But if you think he should have let that buffalo hurt his children rather than shoot it, then I need to start job huntin'."

Buffy blanched. Wolf Running Shield had been here from the beginning. She had the credentials and the education to put a scientific face on this experiment in creating a buffalo commons in the Midwest, but she was just here for three months to work on her doctoral dissertation. Wolf was here for the duration. He was the man who ran this place. Without so much as an hour of college classes—and some suspicion about his years in high school—the man was a legend for his skill in handling buffalo. Leonard was calling Buffy the director of the Buffalo Commons because her advanced degrees put a shine on the place, but everyone knew Wolf was in charge.

If she had lost Bill, she'd have been fired. If she lost Wolf, they'd send her barefoot down a thorny road back to Oklahoma. They'd have her Doctor of Veterinary Medicine degree rescinded. They might assign her to study buffalo in another country, one where women had to wear veils. And she'd deserve it.

"I can't believe you said that." She sounded frantic, which she was. But she also meant it. Since she still had adrenaline coursing through her veins, she snapped, "Of course I don't think such a thing. I was just upset, and I didn't know his family was there. I'd have shot the bull myself before I let it touch one of those children."

"That's quite a hot button you got there, girl. You got any control over it?" Wolf asked, crossing his arms.

She took a couple of deep breaths and unclenched her fists. "I think having a buffalo run over me kind of overloaded my circuits. I'm sorry. And I shouldn't have yelled at Shaw either."

Buffy looked back at the now-empty horizon. "I suppose I owe the man an apology."

"And a thank-you," Wolf said.

She narrowed her eyes at the horizon. "I'd better hand that over, too."

"Yeah, Mr. Leonard is a stickler for community relations." Wolf mentioned the big boss, the one whose money was propping up this whole experiment.

"Besides that," Buffy muttered, "if I don't, I'm a coward and a lousy human being."

"Good point." Wolf walked away to kneel beside Bill and pull the dart out of his chest.

Buffy looked at the rolling hills of grass that looked level but hid swell after swell. It apparently also hid children and ponds, buffalo, and heavily armed ranchers.

The Commons truck pulled up. A cowhand climbed out. "We've never had one get away like that before. Wonder what riled him up?"

15

"He's a buffalo," Wolf said, as if that explained everything.

Buffy decided it did.

Wolf nodded and turned to Buffy. "Might'ez well go on back to the house. We can handle this."

Buffy didn't like it. Wolf was testing her. Did she pass the test if she stayed to the bitter end? Or did she pass the test if she left the buffalo in his capable hands?

She didn't know—which was probably the real test.

Bill was as still as death. She went over and knelt beside him and laid her hands on his chest. It rose and fell steadily. He was strong, even lying here. He didn't need anybody. If someone pushed him, he pushed back hard. She fiercely loved him and his kind. She prayed every day she could be just like them.

She headed home to clean up and get on with her apology to Wyatt Shaw. But first she had a few things to say to Sally's irresponsible mother.

Jeanie had been through a terrible year since her tyrant of a husband had deserted her. Buffy was glad to see the end of Michael Davidson, but Jeanie had let the man run everything. Without him, she was lost, and she blamed herself for Michael's desertion. She covered her sense of failure with sullen indifference and occasional outright hostility.

Right now Buffy's temper was still simmering, and it might not be wise to confront Jeanie. If Jeanie got upset enough to leave, what would happen to Sally? Jeanie barely paid attention to the little sweetheart. But Buffy had to go in that house. And Jeanie wouldn't let Buffy get past her without saying something that Buffy would take exception to.

Feeling the full weight of messing up her first day at The Commons, dealing with her sister, and atoning for her rude behavior to Wyatt Shaw, Buffy trudged toward the house.

Chapter 2

I'm leaving." Jeanie swung the door open before Buffy got to it.

Having Jeanie on a rampage didn't alter Buffy's plans to keep cool.

Jeanie was three inches shorter, all blond curls bought at a beauty shop, generous curves, and pink lips used mainly for complaining.

Buffy was lanky, with straight brown hair that would have been in her standard no-nonsense braid if she hadn't lost her rubber band in the mud.

"You should have heard what that jerk said to me. I'm not living like this. Get us out of here."

"What did he say?"

"He glared at me and said, 'I got cows who're better babysitters than you.'"

Buffy choked on a laugh. "I'm sure he didn't mean it to sound as bad as it did. A mama cow is a very good mother. I'm going over to see him right now. I'll tell him how upset you were and insist he never speak to you again."

A calculating look came into Jeanie's eyes. "He was good-looking, wasn't he?"

"Who?" Buffy couldn't believe the turnaround. "Shaw? The jerk?"

Jeanie narrowed her eyes. "I didn't say I liked him. I just noticed he was attractive."

Jeanie had to find a new man to run her life one of these days. Shaw might be the perfect answer, but Buffy couldn't quite squash her uneasiness. "I'm on my way over to see the good-looking jerk. He helped me catch Bill."

"Who is Bill?" Jeanie brushed her mauve fingertips through her blond hair.

"Bill." Buffy prompted. "The buffalo we just spent two days hauling across three states?"

"Oh yeah, him." Jeanie waved away the buffalo that was so dear to Buffy's heart.

"Anyway, Mr. Leonard is big on community relations. So now I need to face a very angry man and apologize. I expect him to hand me my head. If you want to ask him out on a date, I'll take my head and quietly hold it in my lap while you hit on him."

Jeanie sniffed. "I'll wait until he's not quite so mad. You go fix the mess you made, and maybe I'll drive over and see him in a week or so."

"Okay." Buffy nodded her head, and a clump of muddy hair came unglued from the rat's nest on her head and swung around and slapped her in the face. "I'm going to take a shower first."

Jeanie sniffed again, and this time Buffy was pretty sure that it was a commentary on how Buffy smelled.

Jeanie had cut ties with their parents when, over their father's objections, she ran off to marry Michael. Buffy had cut those same ties just because she had a functioning brain.

Now Jeanie had nowhere to go and no one to do her thinking for her except Buffy—not a job Buffy had applied for. She walked away before she could say any of the things she wanted to—about how hard work sometimes got a person dirty, and it was nothing to sniff at, and Jeanie should try it sometime.

—⁓—

"An' then you pulled your gun and blasted that nasty ol' buffaler right into a million pieces of steak, right, Dad?" Cody acted out the gunshot and fell to the ground in a poor imitation of a dying buffalo.

"You took out your gun, and you hung from the neck of your horse, holding the reins in your teeth." Colt snagged the collar of his T-shirt between his teeth and talked around the fabric. "Then you blew him away."

Cody started shooting his finger at Colt. Colt "died" with a lot of screaming; then he sprang to his feet and started shooting back. The boys ran in circles, shrieking and pretending games of horrible, painful death—all in good fun.

The house wasn't large. The upstairs family room had been converted to a makeshift bedroom for Wyatt's sixteen-year-old niece, Anna, for the summer. Anna had come faithfully every summer since Jessica had died. Wyatt didn't know what he'd have done without her for the last four years.

Wyatt turned the page on the Sunday paper and let the boys scream and knock over the kitchen furniture.

It kept them occupied.

He was sitting there when he heard a pounding on his front door. Once he noticed it, he had the impression that maybe the pounding had been going on for a while. He'd just chalked the sound up to thundering footsteps and falling bodies. He laid aside his paper irritably. "Who in Sam Hill comes to my front door?"

Wyatt had to go into a room he never used, although Anna had dusted it the other day. He went to the front door and had to fiddle with the dead bolt for a while, because he didn't remember which way to turn it. "I'm coming. Hold your"—he swung open the door on that little wildcat from the Buffalo Commons—"horses."

"What about horses?" she asked.

Something short-circuited in his brain. She looked a lot different when she wasn't covered with mud. A lot better. She was wearing a blue jean skirt that hung nearly to her ankles and a loose-fitting white blouse.

She had brown eyes, light like warm baked earth, and one smooth, fat braid draped over her shoulder that hung nearly to her waist. Without the mud and the bad temper and the mind made up to hate him, she was about the prettiest thing he'd ever seen.

He just stood there and stared.

And she stared right back.

Finally the gracious host in him kicked in. "What're you doin' here?"

Her eyes hardened.

What kind of nonsense was going on in her head now? He waited.

She glared.

His boys saved him. They crashed into him so hard he staggered forward, almost into her.

He caught himself; then he caught the two boys, one in each hand.

She looked away from him, examined each of the twins for a second, and smiled.

Rats, it was a great smile. And he'd gotten close enough to find out she smelled great, too.

She bent down toward his boys. "Hi, did you guys see that buffalo this afternoon?"

Wyatt looked down at the twins. Their eyes got so wide and serious they could have been watching Jesus come again and realized they'd yet to repent. After a stunned silence—a small miracle in itself—they started yelling.

Cody went first. "Dad left us to play by the lake while he went over to meet the new boss at the buffalo ranch."

"We saw the buffaler charge right over the hill." Colt bounced.

"We were running for the tree, but it's too high to climb." Cody waved his arms as if he'd considered flying to safety.

Colt added, "We were trying to save Anna when Dad came charging on Gumby."

She glanced at Wyatt. "Gumby?"

"Then he pulled his rifle and blew it away." Cody acted that out with sound effects and flailing arms.

"The boys named him," Wyatt said.

The buffalo gal said to Cody, "He didn't blow it away."

Cody nodded frantically. "Into a billion pieces of buffalo steak."

Wyatt noticed that Cody's steaks kept getting more plentiful. That could mean he was hungry.

"What are your names?"

Wyatt wondered if that was a sly jab at his lack of manners. Or maybe she just wanted to know their names.

"I'm Cody."

She stared at him with fixed attention for slightly too long, and Wyatt wondered what she was thinking.

"I'm Colt."

She gave Colt the same close examination.

Colt went into his favorite part of the made-up story. "He hung on to the reins with his teeth."

Dividing her attention between the boys, she said, "I'm glad you're all right. Your father saved you and Anna. He saved me." She laid her hand on her throat and crouched down so she was eye level with the boys.

The boys moved past him so they were between Wyatt and the woman, which struck Wyatt as a good idea. He didn't like her being so close.

She rested a hand on each of the boys' shoulders. "And he saved my niece, Sally, a tiny little three-year-old girl who was right in the way of terrible danger. Your father is a hero over and over."

Both boys were struck dumb. Another moment of silence—unheard of. They stared at her for a frozen minute then launched themselves at her, and each grabbed a hand. They started tugging her inside, and Wyatt had to step back or be run over. Or worse yet, smell her again.

She gave him a startled look.

He shrugged and stepped farther out of the way. "Come on in, I guess."

As they dragged her past him, she said, "I'm Allison Lange."

"Wyatt Shaw."

"Call me Buffy."

The boys quit manhandling her and stared in awe.

"Buffy, like in *buffalo*?" Colt spoke first, which was unusual. Cody usually talked for the pair, but he looked stunned.

Cody found his voice. "You're named after the buffalo?"

"I love buffalo, and I've spent my whole life studying them. The nickname sort of sneaked up on me."

Wyatt snorted. "Your whole life? What are you, twenty?"

Allison said severely, "Twenty-five."

"Well, 'scuse me."

"How old are you, fifty?" She narrowed her eyes.

The boys couldn't stop staring. Wyatt was having a little trouble himself. "No, I'm twenty-five."

She glanced at his six-year-olds and raised an eyebrow at him.

"I started young."

"I'll say."

The boys fell on her again and dragged her fully into Jessica's formal living room. Jessica had wanted a room just for entertaining guests. Trouble was they never had any guests except the ones who came in the kitchen door and plunked themselves down at the kitchen table. They more often than not had muddy boots on and wanted to talk about baling hay or castrating bull calves. So Jessica hadn't wanted them in her nice room anyway. Wyatt would have done anything to ease Jessica's unhappiness, and he was glad to let her do up this room all formal; in the end, it just reminded her of how disappointed she was with her life. Now this room existed as a kind of shrine to her memory and a sharp poke in the eye to Wyatt if he ever got lonely for a woman.

"How did you get named after a buffaler?"

"Was it one buffalo? A special one?"

"Dad had the teeth in his reins. . .I mean, the reins in his teeth."

"Colt, I never had the reins in my teeth."

"Do you want me to bring coffee for the lady?" Anna came into the room, her eyes lively with curiosity. Anna, dark haired like Wyatt and his boys, was as tall as a woman but still had the gangly figure of a teen. But she was mature and as smart as a whip. She had to be to stay ahead of Wyatt's boys.

Cody jerked his thumb at Allison-Buffy Lange. "Her name is Buffalo."

Colt chimed in. "She said Dad is a hero. He saved the whole town from a rampaging buffalo."

Cody shoved his brother and ran toward Anna, still dragging Allison. "Mrs. Buffalo fights buffalo just like dad. She shoots them and blows them into a zillion pieces of steak."

"Are you hungry, Cody?" Wyatt asked. That was a question that, in his son's whole life, only had one answer.

Both boys began shouting about how hungry they were.

"I want steak. Can we have buffalo steak?" Cody—of course.

"No! Cookies!" Colt shoved Cody sideways. "Anna made chocolate chip cookies yesterday."

"We ate them all, stupid," Cody sneered.

"I'm not stupid. You're stupid." Colt launched himself at Cody.

"I hid some," Anna announced. The teenager was wise beyond her years. "This way." She pointed at the kitchen.

Both boys quit wrestling, yelled, and headed out of the room, abandoning Allison and dragging Anna with them, telling her all about what Mrs. Buffalo had said, or rather their wildly altered version of it.

"Dad's a hero. He saved a hundred lives," Cody said.

Colt shouted, "That's more'n Spiderman."

"That's more'n Spiderman and Superman combined." Cody elbowed Colt and ran.

Anna glanced over her shoulder. "I'll bring coffee in a minute." She followed the boys into the kitchen.

His guest sank into a chair and stared after the boys.

Wyatt tried his best not to smile. Then he remembered who he was dealing with, and it was easy not to smile.

She turned to him. "Where do they get all that energy?"

"They tap it straight out of my bloodstream. I'm half dead by nightfall." He said it lightly, but it irritated him that she seemed so horrified by his children.

"My niece is a handful, but she can't touch the two of them."

He hung on to his patience. "Your niece?"

Allison nodded. "Yes, Sally, the little girl whose life you saved this afternoon, right before you saved your three children."

Wyatt's temper cooled a little. "Anna's my niece. She's staying for the summer to babysit."

"That's good. 'Cuz she'd've been born when you were about nine."

"She *was* born when I was nine. But my sister and her husband were doing the honors, so no one considered me too young." He was flirting. He ran into a mental brick wall as the idea bloomed to life in his head. He hadn't flirted with a woman since he'd fallen in love with Jessica in college.

Allison returned to buffalo talk. "You didn't just save Sally and your family. You herded my buffalo toward me so we could tranquilize him. Then you saved me."

"After Wolf had already done it once. Not to mention being nearly crushed under that gate when you let that beast get loose to begin with." Wyatt changed his tone, determined to push Allison out of his head and out of his house. "And I understand you're the new boss? Great."

"Only for a while. The permanent boss comes in a few months. I have the credentials Mr. Leonard wants for his buffalo ranch, but Wolf will still run the day-to-day operations."

"You've spent most of this day screwing up big-time, Allison."

Allison didn't react as he expected. "And it's early. I'll be half dead by nightfall. And call me Buffy. It's gotten so I can't remember being Allison."

"Well, Sunday is my day of rest, so from now on, you're on your own. . . um, Buffy." He shook his head. "I can't call you that. You look nothing like a buffalo."

She smiled. "Thanks. So there you were, saving people right and left. And by way of thanks, I shouted at you."

Wyatt felt compelled to add, "And strangled me, and poked me in the chest, and called me crazy, and threatened to set the sheriff on me, and—"

Buffy held up her hand. "Enough, please. I'll be here all day apologizing. Surely you want to get rid of me."

Wyatt thought how true that was, and he was poised to say so when Anna came back in with the coffee. "The boys said Uncle Wyatt saved your life. We were down by the lake when all this happened. We just barely caught a glimpse of the buffalo before Uncle Wyatt drove it away. Tell me about it."

So Buffy, instead of being politely but rapidly dismissed as Wyatt had planned, settled in to tell the whole story, complete with Sally screaming and her own near death under a gate. Then the grand finale, when she was snatched from the jaws of death—or the horns of death—by Wyatt's heroic action.

Wyatt gritted his teeth when his boys came in and listened with silent fascination to the whole tale, which Buffy recounted far more dramatically than Wyatt thought was necessary, casting him in a superhero role that easily outdid Spiderman and Superman on their best days. That's all he needed—more stimulation for the boys.

Buffy talked with her hands and did Wyatt's voice, almost echoing with valor, and Wolf's voice, wise and deep. She did herself, weak and terrified, in the very best tradition of a damsel in distress. It was alive and dramatic. Wyatt thought, with a little work, she could make it on Broadway. She glowed while she talked, every emotion vivid and full. He couldn't take his eyes off her.

When she was done, the boys began to act it out, with a lot more screaming than Buffy had included and way more shooting.

It broke the spell she'd put him under. Wyatt stood the racket and Buffy's pretty face as long as he could, and finally, when the boys had dashed outside so they could create their drama on a larger stage, he said, "Well, I need to get back to my day of rest."

He watched her looking nervously after his boys, and when she didn't take his hint, he stood, took her hand, and towed her gently but firmly out of Jessica's fussy chair. Touching her was a mistake. Her hand was callused from hard work, but the back of it was as smooth as silk. She was tanned almost as dark as he was. Everything about her said she was an outdoor girl who loved animals and the country, everything his wife hadn't been. He had to get her out of here.

He escorted her firmly toward the door and booted a rather surprised Mrs. Buffalo out of his house and left her standing on his front porch. He only let her out that way because he wanted her to be able to find her truck.

He was going to close the door in her face and hope that eventually she'd figure it out and go home. Then, because she had that strange look in her eyes like his boys had frightened her more than that charging buffalo this afternoon, a perverse streak kicked in. "You know, talk is cheap, Buffalo Gal. If you're not up to controlling that menace you call a buffalo commons, then get out and take your buffalo with you."

Her eyes focused a little, and he thought he saw something worse than a woman who didn't like his children. He saw a woman who didn't like herself very much.

That strange flash of self-doubt faded from her eyes quickly, and she replaced it with her sharp tongue. "What's your real problem with me and my buffalo? Today was bad, and I can't thank you enough for your help, but you were already angry with the Commons before Bill got away."

"My problem is, your boss is an arrogant city boy whose money is screwing up this whole country. His dream is to own every acre of land out here and let buffalo roam loose on it."

"He buys it. He doesn't steal it from anyone. Who cares what he does with it?"

"I care. He pays too much for it. He's so rich he doesn't need to make the land pay, so every time a piece of land comes up for sale, he outbids every rancher in the area, which locks out any chance for young men to get a start or for established ranchers to expand their holdings."

"Meaning you," she accused flatly.

"Yes, meaning me. I have wanted to add to my land for a long time, but I've butted up against Leonard everywhere. He practically owns all of the land in a circle around the S Bar."

"If he's willing to pay it, then that's what it's worth. That's how supply and demand works. Maybe you've heard of it? Capitalism?"

"And my taxes skyrocket because he's pushed land values up. This land doesn't return much per acre, because the watering holes are far apart, wells are expensive to dig and maintain, and the grasslands are broken up by the rugged foothills. But your boss comes in here and doesn't need it to pay 'cuz he's rich. It's the same as if someone came waltzing in here and offered to do your job for free. It doesn't hurt them because they're rich, but maybe, just maybe, you need that pesky money to feed yourself."

Indignantly, Buffy swung her braid over her shoulder. Wyatt followed the graceful movement of her head and tried to remember why he was yelling at her. She jammed her fists against her waist and reminded him. "This area once belonged to the buffalo. They are native to it, and it's more natural to have them roaming than your cattle. You're the newcomer here, not my buffalo."

"Newcomer? My great-great-grandfather homesteaded this land. Shaws have lived here since before South Dakota became a state. If I'm a newcomer, what are you?"

"I'm tending what is natural. If I had my way, this whole state and North Dakota, Nebraska, Kansas, Oklahoma, Northern Texas, Wyoming, and Colorado, all the way to the Rockies, would be part of the Buffalo Commons. You just said yourself this land barely supports a cattle herd. Mr. Leonard can't do it all himself, but eventually, with the help of a lot of well-intentioned people, we're giving this land back to nature the way God intended."

Wyatt knew this was at the heart of Leonard's Buffalo Commons. He'd always known, although no one ever admitted it out loud. He had a feeling Buffy wouldn't be doing it right now if she wasn't so upset. "Giving it back to God? You just displaced about twenty million people and wiped out eighty percent of America's beef supply. Where are we all supposed to live? What are we supposed to eat?"

"I'm a vegetarian, so I'll be fine, and as for where you live—"

She poked him in the chest, which took them right back to where they'd been this afternoon. Wyatt decided right then he wasn't going to be nearly as polite about her next apology—

"I hear there's a lot of empty space in Siberia these days. How about that?"

"A vegetarian?" Wyatt snorted. "I suppose you're one of those PETA freaks who are always vandalizing medical labs and posing naked on billboards protesting fur."

"I've got my membership card in the car. National, state, and local chapters."

Wyatt grabbed her hand to make her stop digging a hole in his chest and leaned down until he was right in her face. "There aren't any local chapters. This is South Dakota. We have a hunting season on people who won't eat meat."

And right when he was going to really let her have it, give her the full and final send-off—which he hadn't thought of yet but figured he'd just yell until it came to him—the boys charged around the corner of the house, shooting each other, of course.

She said tartly, "Maybe instead of a *hunting* season, you ought to try an *education* season to teach children shooting isn't a game."

Wyatt almost choked. His rage faded into something hard and cold and bitter. He'd been furious with her, but he'd had political debates with people and never went away mad.

Through clenched teeth he said, "I don't have to stand here and listen to an educated idiot insult my children. You may have college degrees coming out of your ears, but anyone who lets a buffalo loose in a yard full of people is either incompetent or stupid. I'm betting you're both."

He glared at her and saw her eyes widen. She lifted her hand to cover her mouth, glanced at his boys, and said from behind her fingers, "I'm sorry. I didn't mean to insult your boys. They're wonderful. I was upset, and I shouldn't have—"

His boys charged up to her. They looked at her with shining eyes and included her in their hero worship.

Wyatt wondered how much they'd heard.

"There's cookies left. And we're having buffaler steak for supper. Why don't you stay?" Colt grabbed her hand.

She bent over him and ran her free hand over his dark hair. "I'm sorry, Colt. I have to get back to my own place."

"How do you know it's me?" Colt's heart was in his eyes.

She said kindly, "Why, you're Colt." She looked sideways at Cody and brushed her hand in an identical motion over Cody's unruly curls. "And you're Cody."

"But no one can tell us apart. 'Cept Dad," Cody said in awe. "We even fool Anna all the time."

Wyatt saw both of them fall completely in love with her in that instant, and he wanted to scream at her for making them care when she held them and him and their whole life in contempt.

She glanced up at him and visibly flinched at what she saw in his eyes. *Good.* "I'm sorry."

"You're sorry you can tell us apart?" Cody said, confused. "Is that what an *educated idiot* means?"

So they'd heard that. Had they heard her make that crack about them shooting at each other? Of course, truth be told, Wyatt got a little tired of the constant shooting, too.

"No, I'm not sorry I can tell you apart," she said awkwardly. "I was telling your dad I was sorry."

"For what? What'd ya do? We have to say we're sorry all the time." Colt added in a deadly serious voice, "And we have to mean it."

She looked so sorry and was being so nice to the boys, but Wyatt had been married to Jessica too long to ignore the words that came out in the heat of the moment. In his experience, that was the only time a woman told the truth.

"Tell us again about what a hero Dad was," Cody demanded. "We want to hear the part where the buffalo stabbed you with his horns and was shaking you to death when Dad yanked you loose."

"I want to hear the part when Dad jumped on the buffalo's back with a knife in his teeth." Colt started chewing on his shirt collar again.

"Miss Lange has to go now, boys. You've already heard the story. Say good-bye."

She laid her hand on his arm. "Don't do this. Don't send me away without accepting my apology. You've got to forget I said that. I'm around buffalo too much. I've forgotten how to watch my mouth."

"Or you've forgotten how to lie." Wyatt grabbed both boys by the hands and pulled them, protesting at the top of their lungs, into the house.

They took off toward the kitchen, shooting at each other again.

"Wyatt, please. Wait."

He slammed the door in her face; then he clicked the lock on the front door so hard he felt it snap inside the door. He fumbled with it a second and realized he'd broken it. The door was locked for good. Wyatt looked around the room. His shrine. His reminder. Suddenly he knew he didn't need Jessica to remind him of how a woman could be. He had a new neighbor who'd be doing that better than Jessica ever had.

"Boys, how'd you like a bigger bedroom?" he yelled loud enough to draw them back from their wild-game hunt. . .or wild-cookie hunt probably.

They returned, still protesting the loss of Mrs. Buffalo, but the offer of more space turned their attention.

"Sure, Dad," Cody said.

How had she been able to tell the boys apart? They were so identical that Jessica had left their hospital bracelets on until they were nearly two, taking them in to have them replaced when they got tight. Little more than toddlers, they'd already learned to trick her all the time, right up until she died four years ago. They'd made a joke out of it, but he knew it had hurt them that their own mother couldn't tell them apart.

"Are you going to build on to the house?" Colt tugged on the leg of Wyatt's blue jeans.

"No, we're going to throw out this old pink furniture and move you in here." Wyatt swept his arm to erase all of Jessica's fussy, perfect details.

Colt and Cody exploded into hyperactive joy.

Anna came in to see what the trouble was. She got excited when Wyatt told her he was making the boys' bedroom into a room for her. "What brought this on?" she asked.

"I'd just about forgotten this room existed is all. I can't believe I've let this space go to waste."

"When do we start?"

"Right now," Wyatt said through clenched teeth.

Anna gave him a worried look.

"I'm going to hitch up the stock trailer and start hauling things outside." He glanced at the broken door and was suddenly furious that he couldn't open it. He'd have to take it off its hinges. He blamed that inconvenience on Mrs. Buffalo, too.

He heard a truck start up and drive slowly out of the driveway. Only now did Wyatt realize that Buffy must have stood in the yard all this time, probably hating herself for insulting his children, the one thing any parent—which she wasn't—would know was unforgivable.

A little voice in Wyatt's head whispered, *Nothing is unforgivable.*

Wyatt looked over at the picture Jessica had hung over the back of the couch. It was a radiant sunset. The stark silhouette of an empty cross stood black against the glorious sky. Across the bottom of the picture blazed the words, Jesus Is the Light of the World.

On this he and Jessica had agreed. They'd been at odds on so much, but they'd tried to accept their differences, sometimes with grim patience, and respect the commitment they'd made before God. This picture was the one thing he wasn't going to throw away.

He tried to harden his heart. He tried to ignore the picture. But he was wrong. Buffy had apologized, and she'd meant it. She'd been arguing with him mainly because he'd been hassling her from the moment she'd come here with her gracious apology and her exaggerated story of his own heroism—a gift to his children that they would cherish all their lives. Or at least until they were teenagers and figured out what a weirdo their dad was.

Yes, she'd said something rude when he'd pushed her to the brink. But she'd immediately regretted it. He'd seen that clearly in her eyes.

He listened to the fading sound of her truck and knew the truth, disgusting as it was. He needed to forgive her. Even more that that, he owed her an apology.

He stared sightlessly through the walls of his house across the miles to the Buffalo Commons. He had to go over there. It was his turn to grovel. At this rate, they'd wear out their tires slinking back and forth with their grudging apologies. Except hers hadn't been grudging; hers had been beautiful. She was beautiful.

He shook his head to clear it of the way she looked and smiled and smelled. He'd do it, and he'd get out before either of them could make it worse. And then that would be the end. He'd make it a point to never see that snippy little city girl again.

He said to his rioting boys, "I'll call the secondhand store in town in the morning and make sure they'll take the stuff. We can load the stock trailer now then move your stuff in. No reason you can't sleep in here tonight."

"Uncle Wyatt?" Anna said doubtfully.

"Huh?"

"Uh, the room is kind of. . .pink for the boys."

The boys froze as they studied the pink walls. They looked at their father in horror.

Pink! What had his wife been thinking? There were frills and flowers everywhere. She'd created a room so out of place on a ranch that no one could be comfortable in it.

Wyatt looked at his sons' faces, alive with dread that they'd have to choose between a new room with pink walls or no new room at all. For a man who was feeling sick from having to slither on his belly to tell a woman he was sorry for being a jerk, he almost smiled. It was just as well he did feel like smiling. He didn't think he'd be doing much smiling once the Buffalo Gal had her say.

"Okay. We paint as soon as the furniture goes. If the store can take this old stuff tomorrow morning, I'll run it into town and buy paint. We'll paint tomorrow afternoon, and you move in here Tuesday."

The boys resumed their joyful ruckus, and Wyatt thought grumpily of the helping of crow he was going to have to swallow.

Chapter 3

S omebody ought to lock me up." Buffy sat in the front seat of her truck, resting her forehead against the steering wheel.

"I can't believe I said that. God, why did I say that?" She'd been praying the same prayer nonstop since Wyatt Shaw had slammed his door in her face. She wasn't any closer to an answer beyond she was stupid and rude.

She'd always believed that when someone did something truly awful to her, she could chalk it up to "stupid or rude." It was a simple test that satisfied a person's hurt feelings because either answer left one feeling superior. Now she had to use the test on herself.

"Am I stupid or rude?"

God was silent.

She heard a snuffling sound and looked over at Bill nosing his little corral. Bill's nose poked through the massive timbers that stretched for miles across the prairie, penning in over a thousand head of buffalo in a 54,000-acre pasture that wound along the edges of the Black Hills National Park. She tried to absorb Bill's strength and let it soothe her soul.

Instead, she remembered telling Wyatt to move to Siberia. She had told him she wanted all the other people in South Dakota and the rest of the Midwest to go away, too. She'd driven past Omaha on her way out here. A million people living in the metro area according to the road map. Where in Siberia were they supposed to go? Instead of fencing buffalo in, she'd have to slap up a fence around a million people so a herd of buffalo wouldn't come stampeding down the interstate during rush hour.

When she'd heard about the Buffalo Commons, she'd looked at the map and the vast open spaces, and she hadn't really thought about these few little towns in the Midwest. Now she'd figured out there were ten thousand little towns, and where were the people living in them supposed to go? Somewhere. They'd move. Big deal.

She banged her head on the steering wheel. "Stupid? Rude? Stupid? Rude? Easy." She looked up at the roof of her truck. "You don't need to bother answering, God. It's easy. I'm both."

She tried to remember what else she'd said. She was sure she hadn't plumbed the depths of this afternoon's stupidity and rudeness. Of course, first, last, and always, she'd insulted his boys. He'd taken everything else pretty well.

He'd seemed to hate her no matter what she said or did, but besides that, he'd taken it well. And then she'd taken a shot at his children. She banged her head on the steering wheel for a while longer.

"Aunt Buffy?"

Buffy turned her head and looked through her open window. Sally, outside alone again. She hesitated, thinking maybe she was too stupid and rude to be this close to little children. In the end, she risked Sally's welfare and opened the door, because she needed a hug.

So that made her stupid, rude, *and* selfish. Buffy moaned.

"Are you all right?" Sally said with a little furrow between her brows.

"C'mere, honey." Buffy reached out her arms, and Sally scrambled up onto the seat. Buffy scooted over so Sally wasn't squished between her and the steering wheel.

"What'za matter, Aunt Buffy?" Sally laid her chubby hands on Buffy's face and held her head so she couldn't look away.

Buffy smiled at the little sweetheart. She was a mirror image of Jeanie, with her white blond ringlets and perfect pink cheeks and blue eyes that showed everything she felt.

"I'm feeling bad about letting that buffalo get away today." Suddenly Buffy remembered Sally's screams. Her heart lurched, and she clutched Sally tight to her. The image of Sally, crushed and dead under Bill's heels, was almost too much to bear. "I'm so glad you weren't hurt, honey. So glad."

She gave Sally a kiss on the top of her head and made her decision between stupid and rude. She knew exactly how bad it could have been. And she knew what she'd do to prevent it from happening again. She was *not* stupid.

That left rude. She decided that was better. A person could learn some manners, but stupid was forever.

With a hefty sigh, she knew she needed to go apologize yet again. But not tonight. She was too tired and frazzled. She'd probably just end up being rude again and digging herself in deeper. Besides, Wyatt might shoot her on sight.

Sally said, "Can we go inside, Aunt Buffy? I'm hungry."

Buffy looked at the darkened sky. It was midsummer, and the days were long. It had to be after nine o'clock. How long had she sat there talking at the Shaws'? She'd actually been having fun for a while. Then she'd come home, changed into work clothes, and done chores alongside her hired men, her conscience poking at her for being away from the job.

Because she didn't want to go in and listen to Jeanie whine anymore, she'd climbed back in her truck and sat, feeling sorry for herself. "Didn't you get any supper?"

"Nope, Mommy was tired after the long drive. She said for me to find something in the refrigerator, but there's nothing there."

Buffy slid out of the pickup with Sally still in her arms. She began walking toward the house. "Of course there's nothing there. We just moved in today. But we'll figure something out, or else we'll run out and get burgers."

"Is there a McDonald's around here?"

Buffy stopped short. She looked in all directions. She knew the main road led to a town, but it was tiny. No doubt the sidewalks rolled up at nine o'clock—if they had sidewalks. She shook her head and started for the house again. "We'll just find something here. We don't want to drive a long way this late at night anyway."

"Okay," Sally said with perfect trust.

Buffy carried her into the house, so tired and demoralized she was having trouble lifting her feet.

Supper ended up being a can of tomato soup—the only thing Buffy could rustle up from the bare pantry shelves. She started a grocery list and helped Sally with a bath. Then she found the room Sally was to sleep in with boxes piled everywhere and no sheets on the bed. She'd asked Jeanie to take care of this.

Afraid of what she'd say if she found Jeanie, she made the bed herself, digging for Sally's pajamas and ferreting out a set of sheets and a blanket. Sally was falling asleep before Buffy finished. Digging out the baby monitor, Buffy took it to her room, not surprised to find out she had to make her own bed. She took another quick shower to rinse the sweat off her body so she could sleep. She was near collapse when she lay down.

She assumed Jeanie had gone to bed without a thought to Sally's supper or sleeping arrangements, let alone Buffy's. She also knew it wasn't safe to assume anything with Jeanie, but she didn't check on her sister. As she adjusted the volume on the monitor, it hit her anew as she lay there that she'd insulted Wyatt's children. She covered her face with both hands and wondered if the moan was the Holy Spirit praying for her.

There was a Bible verse that said, "We do not know what we ought to pray for, but the Spirit himself intercedes for us with groans that words cannot express." She hoped the Spirit was praying for her now, because Buffy couldn't put it all into words, all that she'd done wrong today.

"Maybe I am stupid after all," she suggested to God.

She got an idea then. It wasn't a still, small voice or a bolt of lightning, but she thought it came from God all the same because it was 180 degrees from the direction of her thoughts. It was simple.

She was forgiven.

She'd start over tomorrow. She'd apologize to everyone, maybe even Jeanie for being forced to live a hundred feet from the end of the earth because of a buffalo obsession.

"God, what other choice do I have anyway?"

The turmoil in her soul settled, and she slept.

Wyatt felt differently about apologizing to Buffy by the time he'd tossed and turned all night, rehearsing.

She hated him.

He hated her.

It was a system he could live with.

Then Cody kicked Anna in the shin and told her she was an educated idiot. The fistfight that followed between his boys was their usual exaggerated reenactment of everything their father said and did, which meant he'd better start setting a good example.

Wyatt took the boys with him to buy paint and pitched in on the painting until noon.

While they ate, Wyatt said, "I've got to quit helping with the room for a while, guys. I've got to go over and apologize to the Buffalo Gal. I was rude to her yesterday, and when a man is rude, he's got to say he's sorry."

Cody and Colt looked at him, blinking.

Wyatt doubted they got the lesson.

Then they went nuts, begging to come, and started tearing around the room hunting imaginary buffalo.

"We want to see Mrs. Buffalo again," Cody kept shouting.

Colt rushed up to him and grabbed his hand then went back to attacking Cody.

Wyatt didn't want them along. They would open themselves up to more insults, and they'd fall further in love with that East Coast-liberal, PETA-freak, buffalo-loving neighbor of theirs, who would no doubt dress up like a carrot and picket his ranch on her days off.

"Please take them, Uncle Wyatt. They're driving me nuts with all their help," Anna added good-naturedly, holding up a paintbrush in the room, now so empty it echoed. "You two have got to quit shooting at each other all the time."

Wyatt didn't feel so much as a twinge of anger at Anna for the exactly same insult that he had refused to forgive Buffy for, so he was all the more aware of his need to grovel.

A cowardly streak Wyatt wasn't proud of prompted him to let the boys come. Buffy might not leave as deep of bite marks when she bit his head off if the boys were witnesses.

He loaded them in the truck, having to wage a war to keep them out of the back end and another one to get them in their seat belts. Then he took off to crawl on his belly.

—◦◦◦—

"Buffy, Bill came up lame this morning. You'd better have a look at that cut on his leg."

Wolf and three hired men were crowding Bill with a heavy panel until he stepped through the head gate, which snapped on his neck. There was a bucket of corn under his nose, and although some buffalo fought the gate until they were a danger to themselves, Bill just started munching.

Buffy climbed in with her vet bag and found a deep gouge on his hind leg. Bill did his best to kick her head off while she and Wolf tied the leg so she could stitch it. She gave Bill a shot of antibiotics and measured his height and weight on the underground scale he stood on, all data she needed for her doctoral research.

"Bill survived both the trip and his wild run across the prairie with no serious injuries and no weight loss." She flinched when Bill's leg slipped loose and whipped past Wolf's head, even though the buffalo never quit gobbling the corn.

"And no loss of his bad attitude." Wolf centered his hat back on his head.

Buffy peered around Bill's side, smiled, and checked her clipboard to compare Bill's vital statistics against the data she'd been given at the animal preserve in Oklahoma.

By the time she was done, she was soaked with sweat, Bill had slammed her into the fence a dozen times, and she'd eaten half her weight in dirt.

She moved away, and Wolf released Bill from the gate. Once he was free, Bill just stayed in the same spot eating until the corn was gone.

Wolf laughed as they climbed the fence. "Bill spent the last half hour trying to kill us, and now he's loose, and he doesn't even bother to run away."

Buffy looked down at her filthy clothes and sure-to-be-bruised arms; then she smiled fondly at the stubborn bull. "I suppose it makes me weird, but I love buffalo and I love this life."

"Me, too." Wolf leaned against the fence. Buffy stood beside Wolf and looked through the heavy wooden fence, listening to the quiet *crunch* of Bill cropping grass. Then Wolf got back to work. "We've already separated out the other old bull so it's safe to turn Bill into the herd. Bill has the makings of an alpha male, but he might need a couple of years to grow into it. The old bull will sense that."

"Yeah, they'd fight, and there's no reason to risk one of them getting hurt." Buffy made a few more notations on her clipboard; then she looked up at Wolf and smiled. "We'll ship the old bull down to Mr. Leonard's Oklahoma ranch and let him run with that herd for the next couple of years. It reduces the risk of narrowing the gene pool."

Wolf shrugged, and his leathered face almost curved into a smile. "I don't know about genetics, but I know it's not a good idea to let a herd get inbred."

Buffy handed the clipboard to Wolf, jerked her leather gloves off, and tucked them behind her belt buckle. She wiped the sleeve of her blue chambray shirt across her dripping forehead. "We're just putting scientific lingo to something any good rancher has known for centuries."

Wolf nodded at the herd of buffalo milling across the fence from Bill.

Resting her arms on the rugged boards, Buffy felt a slight breeze ruffling in the July heat cool the back of her sweat-soaked shirt. She and Wolf shared a moment of harmony as they watched the big animals.

"Listen, Wolf, I want you to know I respect what you're doing here. They call me the boss, but it's only on paper because Mr. Leonard likes college degrees on his staff. Even the guy who's coming to replace me doesn't have your experience. You run this place. You should have the house."

"I don't need it and you do. I'm happy in that fancy trailer Mr. Leonard pulled in."

"So I was told. But, well, we both know who's in charge. Don't doubt it. I know where I went wrong yesterday, not wiring those gates and working where the footing was wet, but I want you to tell me how you've done all of this before. I don't plan to change anything. The reports I've gotten on the Commons are too good. I want to document it. It's all going into my doctoral dissertation. I'm doing a case study of how to reintroduce buffalo to the wild."

"I'm not going to be a good sport about it if I hit one with my truck."

Buffy spun around at the intrusive voice.

Of course it was Shaw, come to hand her her head, no doubt.

She squared her shoulders, determined to take whatever he dished out and not say a word. Cody and Colt hit her with hurricane force, and she staggered back against the fence. She felt the hot puff of Bill's breath on her neck.

"Hi, Mrs. Buffalo."

"Hi, Colt." She smiled at his impish face. Cody tried to get out of her arms and run toward Bill. She sighed.

"You knew me again!" Colt shouted just inches from her face.

Bill snorted at the commotion.

"Cody, you stay away from that fence!" Buffy said. "Can't you look at Bill and know he's nobody you should be messing with?"

"Bill? This is Bill? The buffalo Dad chased across the open prairie while he tried to kill a hundred people?"

Buffy glanced at Wyatt.

He shrugged. "You're the one who made it into a stage production."

She had to admit that was right. "Yes, this is Bill."

"He's in the pen. He can't hurt me," Cody announced, squirming away from her.

Just as he slipped through her grasp, Wyatt caught him by the back of his shirt and hoisted him high in the air to settle on his shoulders.

"I want a ride, Dad!" Colt left Buffy and jumped on his father.

Wolf laughed.

Bill slammed his head into the timbers. Although the fence was rock solid and it would hold, Buffy hated to see Bill's head take a pounding.

"Let's go inside, shall we?" She snagged Colt halfway up Wyatt and swung him up on her own shoulders. She grunted as he landed in place. "You're huge!"

Colt leaned so suddenly that he almost tipped Buffy over forward. Colt looked her in the eye, only his head was upside down because he was leaning, vulturelike, over her. He was wearing a cowboy hat that was a miniature of his father's, and it didn't fall off. "You're strong!"

"Well, I wrestle big, ol' mean buffalo every day of my life. I had to get strong so I could whip 'em in a fair fight."

Cody said from his perch on Wyatt's shoulders, "You rassled 'em?" He spun his body around to look at Bill. He almost pitched himself off Wyatt.

Wyatt swatted him on his thigh. "Be careful up there!"

Colt leaned even farther forward until Buffy couldn't see past him. She stopped, afraid she'd walk into something.

"You really rassle buffalers? Is that how you got the name Mrs. Buffalo?"

"No, I got the name Mrs. Buffalo. . .uh. . . . That is, my name *isn't* Mrs. Buffalo. I got the name *Buffy* because I work with buffalo all the time."

"Can we ride a buffalo like Dad did yesterday?" Cody asked.

The weight lifted off Buffy's back, and she grabbed at Colt, thinking he was falling. She saw Wolf set him solidly on the ground.

"Stay put." He reached for Cody on Wyatt's shoulders and put him beside his brother, who hadn't moved or taken his eyes off Wolf.

"No one rides a buffalo. No one." Wolf pointed his gloved hand at Bill. "No one ever gets in the pen with a buffalo. They're not pets. Every single one of them will stomp you to death if you give it half a chance. The bulls, the cows, and even the little calves."

Wolf said it with such a hard voice that both boys' eyes widened with fear. Then they turned to look at the buffalo.

Cody said a little uncertainly, "Dad would save us."

Wyatt said, "Cody!"

"Didn't you just hear what Wolf said to you?" Buffy asked fearfully.

The boys looked past Wolf at Bill. Colt took a step toward the buffalo.

"You stand right there." Wolf had their undivided attention.

Buffy glanced at Wyatt to see if he'd take exception to this treatment of his sons. Wyatt had his arms crossed and was imitating Wolf's glare—at his sons.

Cody and Colt looked at their dad and saw no help there. They turned to Buffy, and a second slow but in time, she glared at them, too.

"Look at this." Wolf bent down and jerked one boot off; then he yanked off a long gray sock and pulled up the leg of his jeans. An ugly, wicked-looking scar appeared.

"A buffalo did this to me when I was six years old. I was in a park with my family where the buffalo roamed free, and I was told to stay away from them. They seemed so tame. They just stood around eating grass. Even when I got close to them, they ignored me."

The boys looked from that vicious red scar to Wolf's serious expression.

Wolf's voice was no more than a growl. "And then I got too close. A buffalo is like that. It doesn't pay much attention to things until something gets inside its danger zone."

Cody said fearfully, "Danger zone?"

"Yes. There's this range around a buffalo that it claims for its own. With some buffalo, it's just a few feet, but with others, it can be as big as this whole ranch yard." Wolf spread his arms wide.

"So you don't know how close you can get?" Colt asked.

Wolf leaned so close to them that his voice barely carried to Buffy's ears. "No, but you know what I think?" His voice fell further, almost to a rasping whisper. "I think they're waiting until you get close enough." Wolf shouted the last words, *"Then they get you!"*

The boys yelled and ran screaming toward Wyatt's truck.

Wolf pulled on his sock and boot; then he rolled down his pant leg and stood calmly.

Buffy raised an eyebrow and muttered, under the cover of the screaming, "That looked like a burn to me, big shot."

Wolf shrugged, "Buffalo, campfire, what's the difference?"

Wyatt said, "How'd you make them stand still like that?"

"It's a gift."

"Yeah, the gift of terrorizing children," Buffy said sarcastically.

"Bet they leave the buff alone," Wolf said smugly.

Wyatt rolled his eyes and headed for his truck.

Wolf followed along, and when the boys hopped back out, Wolf snatched Colt and settled him on his shoulders. Cody settled on top of Wyatt. They headed for the house.

Wyatt walked between Wolf and Buffy. The boys were bombarding Wolf with questions about the buffalo attack. Wolf was making up grim details that were guaranteed to keep the boys out of the buffalo pen—and probably give them nightmares besides.

Wyatt turned to Buffy, and although she'd have preferred to beg his forgiveness in private, Buffy grabbed her chance. "Wyatt, I'm—"

"I'm sorry."

At the same instant they said, "Last night I—"

They looked at each other and fell silent. Then at the same instant they said, "What did you say?"

They said nothing. The boys chattered on so there was no awkward stretch of quiet, just an awkward stretch of noise.

Buffy opened her mouth and saw Wyatt do the same. She lifted her hand, and he stopped.

"Me first, because I'm the one who was in the wrong. I came over there on a mission of peace, and I only made things worse."

"No, you were being nice. I gave you such a hard time you finally took a swipe at me. I know you like—" He glanced upward at his wriggling son. "Just fine. You were very kind to them, and I was rude, and I'm sorry."

Buffy was determined to apologize more than he did. She'd insulted his children, for heaven's sake. "They're just normal little boys. They're perfect."

Cody swung his foot and missed kicking Buffy in the nose by a fraction of an inch.

Wyatt grabbed the marauding foot. "Yeah, right. Perfect."

Buffy glanced at the boys, not wanting them to hear themselves being discussed.

They were still grilling Wolf. Wolf was talking easily about buffalo mayhem.

"For their age, they're perfect. Even a little advanced," she said.

Wyatt's mood lifted a bit. She could see him walk a little taller, which, considering he was over six feet tall, wasn't necessary. "Yeah? You think they're advanced?"

"I do!" Buffy said stoutly. "And I'll personally help you beat up anyone who says different. Including me."

Colt said, "Are you going to beat someone up, Mrs. Buffalo?"

"Her name's Buffy," Wyatt said.

"Forget it. I kind of like Mrs. Buffalo."

"And then I had to drag myself over to the campfire," Wolf said, "and stop the bleeding by branding my leg with a burning stick."

Both boys shouted with horrified glee at the grisly story.

Sally came running out of the house. "Can I go ride the buffalo now, Aunt Buffy?"

Wyatt looked at her with a cocky expression.

Buffy leaned forward so she could see Wolf. "You mind rolling up that pant leg again?"

"She's three," Wolf said dryly. "Her brain hasn't grown in yet. You've just got to watch her. No excuses!"

Sally jumped into Buffy's arms. Buffy wasn't ready for it, and a loud *oomph* got pounded out of her.

Wyatt said smugly, "Another perfect child."

Buffy shook her head as she swung Sally onto her shoulders. "We're hip-deep in 'em."

Jeanie stepped out of the kitchen door. She was wearing Buffy's only good pair of blue jeans. They were too long for Jeanie and about two sizes too small. She had on a blue chambray shirt, also Buffy's. But Jeanie wore it unbuttoned, tied in a knot just under her ample breasts. Her hair was perfectly curled. She had on the full array of makeup. Not a chip in sight on her nails.

Buffy had been wrestling buffalo for three hours. She no doubt looked and smelled like it. Buffy's teeth clicked together.

Wyatt glanced at her then focused on Jeanie. "Hello. We met briefly yesterday."

"Call me Jeanie," she purred. Then, like it was a question that had fascinated millions of people for millions of years, she asked, "And you are?"

Wyatt lifted his Stetson off his head. That showed good manners. He hadn't so much as doffed it for Buffy. "Wyatt. Wyatt Shaw. I'm your closest neighbor."

Jeanie came down the steps of the porch that wrapped all the way around the white two-story farmhouse. She moved with the graceful flow of prairie grass in a summer wind. Her eyes never left Wyatt. "And you are the man who saved us yesterday. You rode in here like a knight in shining armor and saved all of us."

Cody and Colt both overreacted to the reminder of their father's heroism. They started trying to climb down from their lofty seats. Wolf and Wyatt set them down, and they rushed toward the house, yelling the story back and forth.

Sally squirmed to be free, and Buffy let her go. "Wait for me!" She disappeared into the house after the boys.

Jeanie came forward and slipped between Buffy and Wyatt. Since there really wasn't room, she had to get really close to Wyatt.

Buffy had to back off or run her older sister over. She didn't make the decision lightly.

Jeanie looped her hand around Wyatt's elbow until his arm was hugged against her body. She said in a throaty voice that Buffy had only heard her use on men, "Come in and let me thank you properly."

Buffy stumbled slightly at the suggestive tone of voice and was left behind. As near as she could tell, neither Wyatt nor Jeanie noticed, although Wolf gave her a strange look.

Wyatt and Jeanie went into the house, and Wolf followed along.

Buffy had a stricken moment. She almost turned and went back to the buffalo. It was ten thirty. She had eight hours of work to do before noon. Then her day really started.

She crossed her arms and thought of her sister feeding Wyatt the coffee Buffy had ferreted out of the pantry and made earlier this morning. Not a box had been unpacked yet, unless Buffy had done it. She wondered if Jeanie could find where Buffy had put the coffee mugs.

If Jeanie found them, she'd look cool and competent, something Buffy hadn't ever managed in her life. If Jeanie couldn't find the cups, she'd look flustered and helpless. She'd give Wyatt her poor-little-old-me look, and he'd jump in to slay the pesky Dragon of Missing Stoneware.

Annoyed at herself, Buffy marched into the kitchen. She'd drink one cup of coffee, but that was all. She needed to get back to work. Mostly she just needed to get out of here.

Chapter 4

He needed to get back to work. But mostly he just needed to get out of here.

Wyatt clung to his patience. He needed just a few seconds to talk to the Buffalo Gal, say his pathetic apologies, and then he'd go. He had three days' worth of work to finish today.

And this little blond airhead wouldn't quit chirping at him.

Just when he thought he might implode, Buffy erupted from her kitchen chair. "I can't sit around here chitchatting all morning." She seemed to spread her accusation of laziness evenly between Blondie and himself. "Some of us have work to do." She stormed out.

Wolf got up like the oak kitchen chair had an ejector seat. "Yep, got work. Gotta go." He ran as if Wyatt was going to whip out a doily and insist they sip a cup of tea.

Wyatt stood and clapped his hat on his head.

Blondie latched both of her hands on his forearm and hung on with a grip that belied her dainty size. "No, don't go. I was hoping I'd have a minute to thank you properly for saving Sally."

Wyatt was ready to use straight force on her to get her to turn loose.

The boys chose that moment to race through the kitchen as they had done with extreme regularity. This time they skidded into Blondie and smashed her into him. She flung her arms around him, and just like that, the boys were gone, fighting some war or other, Sally hot on their heels.

Buffy was pulling her gloves off her hands as she came in. "I need you to move your—" Her boots clumped to a stop, and her jaw dropped open then snapped shut. He'd heard her teeth *click* like that before. It wasn't a good sign.

Wyatt pried the octopus off him. "I'll move it."

"No, really. You're obviously busy," she said coldly. "Just give me your keys."

He walked up to her, and she did some quick surgery on him with her laser eyeballs. He knew exactly why. He'd have been mad if he'd walked in on her with some man. And that made no sense, so he refused to think about it.

"The keys are in it. I've got to get going."

"Whatever." Buffy left the kitchen.

Wyatt followed, hot on Buffy's heels.

Jeanie caught up to him. "I'd love to come over and see what you're doing

40

with the boys' room. I'll drive myself over one of these evenings." She ran one hand up his sleeve. "Thanks for asking."

Wyatt recalled the boys shouting about painting the color of Sally's T-shirt over the ugly pink. Colt had yelled that it was going to be bloodred. Not true. He'd gone with off-white. Whatever she'd heard about the painting, he was absolutely clear on asking her to come over. . . .

He hadn't.

"Don't come without calling first. We're gone almost all the time." He unhooked her claws.

The boys dashed past him. He grabbed a couple of handfuls of them and towed them along screaming. He lugged both boys and saw Buffy was coming along.

"We're gone almost all the time?" She snorted and veered off toward that stupid, worthless buffalo.

He still hadn't had that moment alone with her. He couldn't let the boys go—he might never catch 'em again. And the leech in the kitchen might get him again. Finally in complete frustration, he yelled after Buffy, "You know I came over here to apologize to you."

That froze her in her tracks. She turned around and wrinkled her brow. "What did you do that requires an apology?"

Wyatt looked at his boys, avidly listening as they swung, one from each of his arms. He arched his eyebrows at her, hoping she'd get that he couldn't talk. "Surely I've done something you can think of."

Buffy smirked.

"You told me you were sorry last night," he said.

"What was she sorry for, Dad?" Colt asked, dangling from his arm and wrapping his feet boa constrictor–like around Wyatt's leg.

"I imagine she's sorry for almost every second she's spent in my company."

Cody walked up Wyatt's body until he was hanging upside down. The kid was one prehensile tail and an opposable thumb away from being a spider monkey.

"That's so true," Buffy said in a snippy voice.

"Sometimes I'm sorry I have to hang around with myself."

"I'll bet that's right." He caught a little smile on her lips.

Cody's feet swung past Wyatt's face. "I'm hanging around you, Dad. And I'm not sorry."

Wyatt wondered ruefully if she was having any second thoughts about insulting his boys.

Colt picked that moment to let go with one hand and try to pry Cody's hands loose from Wyatt's arm. Cody held on desperately and managed to kick Wyatt in the face while he was battling for his handhold.

Sally came screaming out of the house at that minute and slammed into Buffy's legs. Buffy hoisted her up and ran a gentle hand over her head. "I'm the one who should be apologizing."

Wyatt got kicked again and lowered both boys to the ground by crouching. He still didn't let them go. He looked at both of them wriggling in the dirt like a couple of sidewinders. "You asked me to forgive you, and like a jerk, I wouldn't," Wyatt said. "God gave me a little reminder later that He's forgiven me a lot."

"Oh, surely not." Buffy arched her brows too innocently.

"And I know I was being rude until I deserved to be slugged. A lesser woman would have been pounding on me by that time."

Buffy did smile this time; then she sobered. "Instead, I took a potshot at the most precious, innocent thing in your life." She hugged Sally tighter. "I've spent my life working with buffalo."

"You're twenty-five. What life? You're a baby."

"And how old were you again?"

Wyatt shrugged.

"I had my first summer job at a park when I was twelve. I cleaned out stalls that held injured buffalo."

"You hauled manure?"

"Yeah, pretty much. Did I mention they didn't pay me?"

"You hauled manure for free?"

"I'd have done anything to work with those buffalo. I was forbidden to get near them of course, but I did everything they'd allow, and they had a tight budget so they let me do a lot. I've been at it for thirteen years. The fire department lets you retire after twenty."

"Well, your buffalo aren't on fire, so you'll probably have to keep at it till you're sixty-five."

"I've taken every class, every job, every chance I could get to be around them. When I leave here, it's for Yellowstone. It's got the finest management system in the world. And I'm going to be in charge. You don't think they'd let a novice take the manager's job here, do you? I'm an expert."

"Okay, you've been working with buffalo almost as long as I've been ranching. I started almost as soon as I could walk."

"I'm better with buffalo than I am with people." She gave Sally a noisy kiss on her chubby neck.

Sally giggled.

Buffy smiled at her, and Wyatt had a hard time taking his eyes off that smile.

"I've got a long way to go in learning manners. The things I said to you about them"—Buffy glanced at his boys—"were unforgivable."

"You know, I had the same thought myself," Wyatt admitted. "Did I mention the little reminder? Of all I'd been forgiven? I wouldn't be much of a Christian if I didn't forgive you."

"If you really came over here for that"—she glanced past his shoulder again toward the house—"then you're a very nice man. I accept your apology and hope you accept mine."

"Already did," Wyatt said.

"I was going to drive over as soon as Bill had been turned loose. I thought we should give starting over one more chance."

"Yeah, well just remember who went first."

Buffy smiled again then hesitantly said, "My sister. . ."

"What about Mommy, Aunt Buffy? Did Mommy do something again? Are we going to have to move again?"

Buffy gasped. "No, sweetie. Your mommy's fine, and she never did anything that made us move. I don't want you to think that."

"But once I heard you say—"

Buffy laid her hand gently over Sally's mouth. Sally couldn't know that her mother had made some pretty shady friends back in Oklahoma, after Michael had run off. They hadn't made this move because of that, but Buffy had been glad to leave behind some bad influences.

She turned to Wyatt. "I'd better get back to work. Are we even on the apologies now?"

"Dead even, I'd say." The boys made a sudden concerted break for freedom, and only six years of hard-learned lessons kept Wyatt one step ahead of them.

"Then maybe we should never speak to each other again," she said.

Wyatt thought she sounded kind of sad.

"Quit while we're ahead?" he suggested.

"Something like that."

Wolf shouted from across the yard, "I'm ready to load the old bull. I can use a hand, Buffy."

"We'd better get out of your way," Wyatt said.

He saw Buffy look past Wolf to the buffalo, and he felt her attention drawing toward the big animals. Her heart wasn't in it when she gathered herself and turned back to him. She looked down at Sally and tried to be diplomatic, "Anyway, she's been known to. . ."

Wyatt saw the trust in that baby girl's blue eyes and knew Buffy still wanted to say something about Jeanie but couldn't in front of Sally.

Buffy was helpless against that look. She shrugged again and said, "Uh. . . over—"

Jeanie came to the door behind Wyatt. She'd lost that breathy, dumb-blond voice and now spoke in a tone that made the hair on the back of his neck stand straight up. "Buffy, when are you going to get some groceries? There's nothing in the house to eat. Why do I always have to— Oh, hi, Wyatt." The crooning voice was back. He heard her jogging down the porch steps.

Wyatt gave Buffy a wild look.

"She's been known to. . .you might say. . .over-depend." With the tiniest possible trace of malice, Buffy added, "I suspect depending on you will do as well as depending on me."

Wyatt shuddered at the thought. "Well, gotta go. We're late. Let's get out of here, boys." He scooped the boys up, one per arm, and held them like a human shield as he practically ran for his truck. He couldn't see any one of the three women for the cloud of dust he left behind. But as the road curved away from the Buffalo Commons, he saw Buffy striding toward the buffalo pen, tugging on her leather gloves.

Chapter 5

Buffy woke to the crack of thunder.

She jerked awake and was already getting dressed without taking a second to try and figure out what was going on. Whatever it was, she wanted to face it with her boots on.

The thunder rumbled again, and she was running down the steps toward the kitchen, when she heard Wolf yelling for all he was worth. The only word she could make out was "stampede." She didn't need to hear more.

She met Wolf at the back door. A ball of lightning split the night, and an explosion rang far across the black sky. A flare of fire could be seen in the distance.

Wolf turned away from the blaze. "That last bolt of lightning set a tree on fire. The herd is already running. We've got to get out there."

Buffy ran for her truck. She shouted at her rapidly moving hired men, "Someone take a couple of rigs around the outside of the fence. If you can beat them to the end of the pasture, honk and flash your headlights. That might head them off. If they hit that fence running this hard, they could knock it down."

"I'll drive myself," Wolf shouted over the howling wind. "We might need every truck on the place."

Buffy had the truck started and floored before she got the door shut. In just two weeks at the Buffalo Commons, she was on her second mad scramble across the prairie.

―――

Wyatt jerked out of a sound sleep.

He'd never felt an earthquake before, but he was feeling one now. Then a second later, he knew better. Stampede!

He yanked on his pants, jammed his feet into his boots, grabbed his shirt, and was already dressed and running by the time he was fully awake. He ran past Anna, who came stumbling out of her room. He skidded to a stop and grabbed her arm so hard he knew she'd be bruised tomorrow. "I'm going to get the boys. You stay up here. The herd is out. They're stampeding around the house."

"The cattle?" Anna asked. "The cattle have never stampeded before, Uncle Wyatt. And you don't have the herd on any pasture around here, do you?"

Bright flashes of lightning glared out the upstairs window. "The storm must have set them off." He was already down the stairs, his boots clumping on each step, his unbuttoned shirt flying.

Bodies crashed against the house, which shook on its foundation. The deafening noise drowned out everything.

He dashed into the boys' room in time to see Cody running for a window. Wyatt sprinted across the room, grabbed his son, and lifted him. Colt was only a step behind his brother, and Wyatt managed to grab him, too, then turn to the window in time to have it shatter in his face. He shoved the boys behind his back as flying glass slit his skin.

A huge head slammed through. A buffalo head.

The boys screamed. Wyatt staggered and backed away, clinging to his sons.

The big beast let out a strangled, roaring bellow. One front leg came through into the room. The animal kicked as if to tear out the wall and run all of them down. Then, with a plaintive bawl of pain, the buffalo pulled its head back and thundered across his porch.

Wyatt, with a son in each arm, ran to the window, his feet crunching on countless shards of glass. Another buffalo ran past his window so close he could have slapped it.

Cody reached out one hand, and Wyatt took a quick step back. The buffalo got past, and he saw more of them. More and more. Everywhere. His high-powered yard lights lit up a boiling sea of coarse brown fur and bobbing horns. He heard the bellow of frantic animals. Hundreds of them. Maybe thousands.

The three poles that held his yard lights began quivering as they took one hard hit after another. They began teetering then swaying. One at a time, in a shower of sparks, they fell. One landed on the beautiful old barn built by his grandfather at the turn of the century.

Wyatt watched in horror as flames began to flicker in the haymow. Forcing himself to look away from the destruction, he whirled and ran with the boys up the steps to Anna. "Hang on to them. None of you come down!"

He raced back to the living room and gripped the edge of the window to keep from running for the barn to fight the fire. Running out into that raging herd was certain death.

He saw headlights, still a mile away, following the herd. The car was coming out of a field, not the road. A flare of lightning lit up the yard, and he saw the fence around the horse corral trampled under massive hooves. Gumby ran wild with the buffalo; then, just as another blaze of lightning exploded overhead, the horse stumbled. Wyatt couldn't see if Gumby stayed on his feet or not.

"No, boys," Anna yelled. "Get back here."

"Dad? We want to watch." Cody came charging down the stairs. Wyatt realized the boy wore nothing but gym shorts. Colt was right behind him, running straight for the glass-coated floor in his bare feet.

Wyatt turned on his sons. *"Get back up those stairs and stay there!"*

Cody froze on the spot. Wyatt had never heard that sound from his own mouth. It was an order no one—man, woman, or child—would ever disobey. Cody and Colt whirled around and dashed back up the stairs.

Wyatt turned back to the window and saw the flaming roof of his barn. It stood away from his steel machine shed, but sparks raised to the sky toward his house. If the house caught fire, they would have to run outside. . . .

Wyatt began to pray. He felt as if he were falling. Sinking back into the past.

The herd came, and came, and came. He'd heard stories of buffalo herds on the prairie. Herds so large the whole world was alive with them. They spread from one end of the horizon to the other.

"Dear God, what's going on? Don't let anyone be hurt."

He thought of Buffy and wondered if they'd overrun her place first. He imagined Buffy crushed beyond recognition under thousands of hooves. He knew she'd never let this happen if she could humanly prevent it. What had happened?

"Dear God, let them be all right."

There were more homes on down the road. They weren't that far from the little town of Cold Creek. How many people might die before these beasts stopped their stampede? He thought of Bill. One buffalo, alone, running wild. He hadn't been easy to bring down. How did anyone ever round up a herd this size? They trampled everything, and still they came.

He fumbled for the phone, not knowing whom he'd call. Buffy? 911? The line was dead.

He heard the crashing and brawling of the huge bodies blundering through his farm equipment, his outbuildings. His barn was reduced nearly to ashes already, but nothing else had caught. A gust of wind whooshed over the barn, and sparks flew. Wyatt heard a soft *whumph* and saw his truck start to burn. A ruptured gas tank, maybe? A spark from the barn or a sharp hoof? Anna's car went next.

Then his own internal gas tank ruptured. He went tearing for the back of the house and his locked gun cabinet. He was so mad he couldn't remember where he'd left the key for a few minutes. He finally got it open, then had to load it, and then had to lock the cabinet back up. How had John Wayne ever gotten anything done?

He ran back to his broken window and—nothing. They were gone. The splinters of glass and the gaping window were proof they had been here. Choking dust filled the air and covered everything in the house. But only a rumble of faraway hooves marked their passing. He wanted to sit down. He wanted to collapse.

He wanted to shoot a buffalo.

He cocked his rifle and stormed out of the house. A wind that drove the storm clouds high overhead caught at his shirt as he ran down the wrecked steps of his porch. He couldn't drive after the herd because his truck and Anna's car were destroyed.

Buffy came flying into the yard in her rig. She slammed on the brakes when she saw him and leaned over to throw open the passenger door. "Are you all right?" she asked frantically. "Did anyone get hurt?"

Wyatt heard the needle-sharp edge of hysteria in her voice. "We're all right. My ranch is destroyed, and my livestock are all dead or run off, but the kids and I are fine."

He was as close to being in a killing fury as a man could be.

She took a wild look at his rifle as if she wondered if he'd use it on her then glanced at his face. "You're bleeding!" She scrambled across the seat and stood in front of him.

He looked down at his bare chest and saw rivulets of blood streaming down. He wiped his sleeve over his face, and it came away red. He did a quick inventory of his wounds then buttoned his shirt. "They're just scratches. A buffalo tried to climb through my living room window. It's nothing." His tone of voice could have burned a barn down on its own, no buffalo stampede required.

"It's not nothing." Buffy checked him over, her callused hands gentle on him.

He didn't want to like this female softness. . .but he did.

She dabbed at his face then pulled a handkerchief out of her pocket and dabbed some more. At last she was satisfied. "None of them are deep. You'll be all right. I've got to get after the herd."

"Don't move. I'm going with you, but I can't leave the boys."

"I've got to go," Buffy shouted.

Wyatt forgot all about her gentle touch. He grabbed her arm. "You owe me. You wait right here."

Buffy looked in his eyes then gave a short nod of her head.

"Buffy, this is Wolf. Come in. I've got the sheriff on his way, and I've called everyone I can think of to come help. I've got a shipment of tranquilizers coming by helicopter. Mr. Leonard is pulling out all the stops. No expense spared."

Wyatt nearly ripped the passenger's side door open and grabbed the handset of Buffy's CB radio. "That's because he knows he's going to get sued until his ears bleed."

"That you, Wyatt?" Wolf asked.

"It's me."

"What happened at your place?" Wolf sounded exhausted.

"We all lived. But they took everything on the place except the house. They're a menace, Wolf. I've been telling you that from the first."

"It's not the fault of those buffalo. If lightning stampeded your cattle, they could do just as much damage."

"They never have, and you know it." Wyatt dropped his head into his hands, trying to get hold of himself.

Buffy took the mike. "The buffalo are following Wyatt's lane out to the road.

The herd is running straight north. They can't run much farther without tiring. Call the rest of the men and tell them to try again to get ahead of them."

"When we first brought them into the country," Wolf said, "we held them in some pens just south of Cold Creek. That holding area is still there. If we could get them stopped, then maybe we could toss them some hay and lead them to it."

"You know how they follow your truck when you drive out and throw bales?" Buffy asked.

"Yeah, once they've calmed down, that might work. We could lead them into the pen and load them from there."

"How far to the pen?"

Wyatt was suddenly in possession of the CB again. "I know where it is. I'll give her directions. There'll be stragglers, Wolf. You'll never get them in one sweep."

"No, but we can cut the odds in our favor real quick."

"And the stragglers will be in every herd in the area. It might take weeks to round them up. Every rancher around here could lose their whole herd."

"Mr. Leonard will make it right, Wyatt," Wolf said quietly. "You won't be out anything."

"Money," Wyatt snarled. "That's your answer to everything."

Buffy wrestled him for the mike. Because he wasn't prepared, she got it. She clicked the TALK button. "Make it happen, Wolf. I'm going to make sure Wyatt's family is safe; then I'll follow the buffalo and keep tabs on them. Open up that holding pen. Get the hay you need. I'll let Wyatt yell at me while I'm trailing the herd."

"I can take it, Buffy. This has been between Wyatt and me from the first."

"I know. But you've got work to do."

Wyatt clenched his teeth until she hung up. "You don't need to talk about me like I'm another chore that has to be finished. If you think—"

"See to your family, Wyatt. Can Anna drive herself over to my place? She and the boys can stay with Jeanie and Sally."

Wyatt looked at the wreckage of his place. "What are they supposed to drive?" But even when he said it, he knew. "I'll be right back."

He turned and ran toward the house. He stumbled to a stop over the body of a baby buffalo. He saw it had been crushed to death, run over by the herd. He dropped to one knee even as he recognized the contradiction of the rifle clutched in his hand. He felt the compassion every rancher has for creatures who die before their time. He turned wearily to Buffy. "You lost a calf."

He heard her gasp.

He strode into the house. "Anna!"

Anna appeared at the head of the stairs. She and the boys were fully dressed.

"Are you hurt, Uncle Wyatt? You're bleeding."

"The cuts aren't deep. The bleeding has already stopped."

Anna accepted it better than Buffy had. "I saw it from up here. Is the old pickup in the machine shed?"

That was exactly what Wyatt had in mind. Anna had lived with him for four summers now. She'd learned to drive on that old truck. "Take it over to the Buffalo Commons. You can sleep there. I don't think the house is going to burn. The barn has died down."

"And my car," Anna added bitterly.

Wyatt looked again and saw tears had left tracks in the dirt on Anna's face. Dust covered everything and everyone. Wyatt couldn't imagine the effort it was going to take to clean up this mess.

"And the Buffalo Commons house is fine?" Anna asked, her voice laced with anger. "The buffalo didn't hurt their place?"

Wyatt didn't like the settled look of hatred on Anna's face. He wondered if his face looked the same. He tried to control himself for her sake and the boys'. "I just had the old truck going yesterday. It'll start up. Let's get you out of here."

Anna gave a tense nod of her head. "But I think I'll go over to the Swensons'." She mentioned an elderly couple who ranched about ten miles to the west. "I'd just as soon stay there."

"I don't want you driving that way, Anna. The herd may have fanned out in that direction. You could find out the Swensons had their own stampede. You could be walking from the truck to the house and get attacked by one of the big brutes. The one place we know the buffalo *are not* is the Commons."

"Fine," Anna said sullenly. "We'll go there. . .at least until morning."

"Thanks. I want you out of here before I leave, in case of fire."

They went out the door and saw Buffy kneeling beside the buffalo calf. Anna walked past the calf and Buffy without speaking. The boys, subdued for once, stared wide-eyed at the baby. Wyatt kept them moving.

When he had them loaded in the truck, he said to a white-faced Anna, "Be careful. The herd is past us, but there might be stragglers. Don't drive fast in case one would jump out in front of you."

"A little worse than that deer you hit last spring," Anna said with vicious sarcasm.

"If something happens—a flat tire or anything—stay in the truck until some-one comes to help you." Wyatt patted her awkwardly on the shoulder. "Your cell phone won't work out here, but you've got a CB in there, so call for help if you need it." He added, "We'll get your car fixed, honey. It's insured. It'll be okay."

Anna twisted her lips in something that was a horrible imitation of a smile. "And that makes it right? This nightmare?" Anna's voice began rising in delayed panic. "What if the boys had gotten outside?"

Wyatt knew she was right. Cody and Colt couldn't resist getting out to see what the ruckus was.

"They'd have been killed," Anna said in a hoarse whisper that Wyatt knew the boys, who were hanging on every word, had to hear.

"But they weren't, honey. Just go."

Anna nodded, clenching her jaw to keep from saying more.

Wyatt watched as the truck drove away. Then he turned back to Buffy, who'd returned to her truck. Wyatt climbed in beside her. "Let's go find your buffalo."

"Are you planning to use that thing?" She tipped her head at the rifle Wyatt still had clenched in his rigid hand.

"If I have to."

Buffy drove.

For a while, the silence in the cab was so thick Wyatt could barely inhale. But he wasn't going to apologize again. He was already over his quota for the year.

Buffy pointed straight ahead. "There's one of them." The buffalo was still kicking up its heels. It ran full out tirelessly, as if it could go on forever.

"How far to the pens?" Buffy asked.

"It's at least ten miles. If they decide to quit running, Wolf'll never get them to walk that far as a herd. They'll just start spreading out and foraging."

"Ten miles." Buffy sounded hopeless as they drew closer to the running animal. "They've already been running longer than that from the Commons. But buffalo can lope along for hours. They might keep going most of the way."

Wyatt could see more of them ahead.

"Are there any more ranch houses between here and there?" Buffy asked.

"None on a direct path. There's a country school about three miles to the east, but it's on the other side of Cold Creek. And there's a country church on past the pens, the one the boys and I attend. If we don't stop them, they'll probably ruin that." Wyatt watched more buffalo appear in the headlights. "But they'll miss both those things if Wolf can lead them to the holding pens. They'll need to be turned a little to the east after a while, but there's a steep bank along the creek if they keep on this course. That'll turn 'em, I hope. If they were still stampeding, they'd probably go right over it, and most of them wouldn't survive, but if they've slowed by then, it'll turn 'em naturally."

He heard the lift in his voice. He was getting involved in the project of recapturing the buffalo. That was the nature of ranching. If something got out, you got it in. If your neighbor had trouble, you pitched in to make it right.

With a resigned sigh, he knew he had no other choice. His rifle was useless unless they were attacked by a single buffalo. He'd calmed down enough to know shooting them wouldn't solve the problem. "A buffalo commons," he said coldly.

"What?" Buffy looked away from her prey.

"That was your plan, wasn't it? To turn the whole state of South Dakota into unfenced prairie? Give it back to the buffalo?"

"Well, it's the way nature planned it."

"And God had another plan, didn't He? He made man. He gave him dominion over the animals. Or are you one of those people who throw out the parts of the Bible that don't suit you?"

"I don't throw out parts of the Bible. I can show respect for the planet and still be a Christian. People who think animal rights are in conflict with human rights just aren't trying to adapt. Destroying one species after another endangers us all. And a person can live a healthy life without meat in his diet."

Wyatt turned on her furiously. "You know that might be true in America. This is a rich country, and we have a million options in our diet, but if it's immoral to eat meat here, then it's immoral everywhere. What about the people in Africa who have one herd of goats for the whole village? What if that's their only food. Are you really going to tell them they're sinners for eating that goat? Are you going to tell a man his children have to starve to death because an animal has the same right to life a human being has?"

"Don't try to compare—"

"So it's a sin here," Wyatt said sarcastically. "Animals have the right to life, liberty, and the pursuit of happiness in America. But in Africa, well, that's different. Eat up. Your ethics are pretty convenient for you. Sin is now a matter of geography."

"I don't know why you keep talking about sin. It's not about sin."

"I thought you said animals have rights. If that's true, then they have the right to life. I can no more eat a chicken than I can eat one of my kids."

"That's disgusting." Buffy dropped the speed of her truck again as the buffalo in front of her slowed.

"What's disgusting is you putting those dangerous animals on a par with human life. You know everyone talks about saving the tiger. They talk about how elephants and rhinos are disappearing from the wild. Well, let me tell you something, Buffalo Gal, I'd be a real poor sport about my son being eaten by a tiger. It's so easy for you to sit here, thousands of miles away, and talk about leaving large, dangerous animals in the wild, but the reality of living in a village that is in the hunting territory of a pride of lions is pretty grim.

"Do you think those poachers who shoot elephants for their tusks don't want them dead and gone? Do you think I want a herd of buffalo rampaging through my ranch? Do you think I want wolves and mountain lions roaming my land? Is there any way for me to relax and appreciate them when my children are at risk every time they step out the door?"

Wyatt rubbed his hand over his mouth to keep from saying any more. His other hand tightened on his rifle, which rested beside his thigh, the muzzle pointed toward the floor of the truck. He stared at the buffalo in front of them.

An occasional flash of lightning showed the earth, a living mass of movement in the distance.

Buffy said in a low, urgent voice, "There may be some fanatics who really believe a rat has as much right to life as I do, but I'm not one of them."

Wyatt raised his hands as if in surrender. It didn't look much like surrender with the rifle in his left hand. He tried to quit sounding like a madman. "I'm yelling at you, and I know this isn't your fault. And I know Mr. Leonard has tried. I've seen the efforts he's gone to. He's supported this area in a lot of ways. But that doesn't change the basic argument, does it? I'll believe in animal rights when I see a chimpanzee judge put a cat in prison for killing a mouse."

"Wyatt, now's not the time to talk about this. You're upset, and I don't blame you. I'm going to insist that Mr. Leonard raise the budget to include riders to patrol the fence night and day. We need a stronger fence. You'll see, we—"

"We won't see about anything. I won't rest until those buffalo get out of this area. You know, if you want to restore this area to its natural state and make a real buffalo commons, Leonard needs a predator for the food chain. He wants to reintroduce wolves into the area. Mountain lions. Grizzly bears. You think a wolf is going to face a buffalo when he can have one of my calves? But it doesn't matter, because I'll be long gone if Mr. Leonard has his way. What a harebrained scheme. What arrogance. What disrespect for me and my neighbors." Wyatt forced himself to be silent again.

"You know how badly I feel about this."

Now that they were close enough to hear the thundering hooves of the herd, he flashed back to that buffalo smashing through his living room window. He saw his boys running into that glass-strewed carpet. He saw his horse go down. He rubbed his hand into his hair, and glass cut his hand. He opened the window to shake off the glass. Dirt billowed into the truck, stirred up by the herd, so he closed it again.

Buffy drove along, tailing the stragglers. There was a kind of desperate stillness to her, as if she didn't want to attract his attention and start him yelling again.

Wyatt tried to let go of his rage. "I'm sorry. I know this isn't your fault. I know you've had as much harm done to you as I have with this mess." He didn't mean it, but he said it.

"We spend way too much time apologizing to each other."

"I've noticed."

"Look, they're veering off east."

Sure enough, they were. They were slowing down, too. The gravel road that led to the pens was the path of least resistance, and they followed it.

"They probably built this road on a trail left by buffalo," Buffy said.

"It's the low road. It winds around the hills and avoids the creeks."

"Just like a buffalo would."

Wyatt didn't respond.

The buffalo in front of them dropped from its ground-eating lope into a rugged trot. It moved along for a mile or so at that speed and then fell to a walk.

Buffy stopped the truck, and they sat, listening to the thundering hooves fade as the rest of the herd began to walk. Silence reigned. They passed through the dust kicked up by the running herd, and the air cleared as they drove slowly onward.

The lightning storm faded in the distance.

"We'll make this right." Buffy turned to him. "I promise. Even if I have to work at your ranch single-handedly until everything is rebuilt and replaced. I'm so thankful none of you were hurt." She'd pulled the truck to a stop in the middle of the road but left it running, and he could see her in the dim light of the dashboard.

She reached out and touched his temple and pulled away a finger tipped in blood. "At least not hurt badly. And no matter what I say about animal rights, the danger we put your family in is inexcusable. We're going to do whatever it takes to make sure this never happens again. You have my word on that."

Buffy was asking for his forgiveness. . .again.

The night closed around them. The whole world was silent. Not a cricket chirped. Not a frog croaked. They'd all been scared away by the monsters crashing through their territory.

Wyatt turned to look at the strolling herd, disappearing out of the beam of their headlights. His head dropped back against the headrest. "I believe you, Buffy. But I don't want to live with this kind of threat in my backyard. And I don't know any other life. I have to fight for my ranch, and that means the buffalo have to go." He remembered Anna's words. He wondered if she'd first heard them from him. "There are some things Mr. Leonard's money can't fix."

"And if the buffalo go, I go with them," Buffy said.

Wyatt hadn't thought of that. Buffy and Wolf and a couple dozen other hands at the Buffalo Commons. Mr. Leonard was one of the area's largest employers. He paid well, too. Full-time jobs with good benefits—something rare out here. Wyatt hired some help during the haying season, but otherwise his ranch was a one-man operation. Most ranches were.

He looked at her in the gentle light of the dashboard. Her light brown eyes glowed with regret. "Where would you go?" he asked.

"I don't know. I'm supposed to spend three months here is all. Then, when my doctoral dissertation is done, I've got a job waiting for me in Yellowstone. It's the premier buffalo herd in the nation, at least to my way of thinking. I want to spend a few years there, learning everything I can. Then I thought I might try to get on with Mr. Leonard permanently. He's doing the most exciting work with buffalo of anyone. Of course if this blows up in his face, he'll have to abandon it. He has ranches like this all over the country." With a sad little laugh, she added, "There's not a lot of call for a buffalo specialist."

"Who was your guidance counselor in high school?" Wyatt asked. "You could have used some career counseling."

"Actually, I'm a licensed veterinarian."

That brought Wyatt's head up. "A veterinarian? I thought you said you were twenty-five."

Buffy shrugged. "What can I say? I'm gifted."

"We could use a veterinarian."

"But I specialized in buffalo. I didn't learn much else." She rested her cheek against her headrest.

Wyatt knew she wasn't talking about buffalo. What she didn't learn much about were men, sitting too close to her in dark trucks. Then he saw his boys running for the window and his barn collapsing. There was always going to be a big, fat, ugly buffalo standing squarely between them. "Why buffalo? Whatever possessed you to be obsessed with those nasty, stupid critters?"

Just that easily, the spell between them was broken. But so was most of the tension.

Buffy leaned away from him and smiled. "They're no uglier than cows."

"Sure they are. Way uglier. A cow's a pretty little thing."

"That's why a woman is so tickled when someone calls her a cow."

"All the women I say it to are honored."

"Try calling one a heifer sometime and see if she likes it."

"Already have. I've had some luck with it."

Buffy laughed. "Well, that just goes to show. . ."

"What?"

She gripped the steering wheel. "An hour ago, when I realized that the herd was loose and headed for your place, when I realized you and your family could be killed by the buffalo, I was so scared I would have bet I'd never laugh again."

Wyatt heard more in her voice than the worry of a rancher for her neighbor. He heard the same thing he'd heard that morning two weeks ago when she hadn't liked finding him with Jeanie. The same thing he'd heard behind every insult and apology. There couldn't be anything between them. . .but there was.

Without making a conscious choice, Wyatt reached for her and pulled her into his arms. She looked startled, but she let him drag her over to his side of the truck.

Wyatt, knowing every move was pure stupid, lowered his head.

Lights in the rearview mirror jerked them apart.

Buffy scooted away from him so quickly, Wyatt thought she'd been snagged by a lasso and hog-tied to her door.

Before Wyatt could say anything, Wolf pulled up on Wyatt's side of the truck, and Wyatt opened his window in a night so full of dust he could chew the air.

"I'm just going to ease on through the herd." Wolf jerked his chin in a nod. "They usually let me drive right out among 'em. I'm hoping they'll catch the scent of the hay."

Seth called out from the back end. "If they don't follow, I'll throw out a little hay to bait 'em. The sheriff is already waiting at the pen. He'll have it open, and he's lined up every truck he could muster to form a wall, including several semis. We're hoping they'll all just walk right in; then we'll load 'em and take 'em home."

"Not all," Wyatt said.

"Nope." Wolf shook his dark head. "I already saw a few turned aside from the herd. I've been radioing their locations to the other hands, and they're darting them with the tranquilizer gun and picking them up. We'll get 'em, Wyatt. You know we will."

"I know you'll try. But how many of my cows will be pregnant with buff calves by then? It's the height of breeding season right now. And if your buffalo have brucellosis, my herd may have to be quarantined and slaughtered."

"We'll replace them if it happens," Wolf said. "It's the best we can do."

Wyatt's hand, resting against the open window frame, clenched into a fist. "It's not good enough."

"I know." Wolf began driving forward. He was the kind of man Wyatt could understand. Now wasn't the time for talking. Now was the time for doing. Wolf, like Wyatt, kept going forward because there was no other direction a man could go.

"You stay back here, Buffy. We need someone to bring up the rear." Wolf drove into the slowly moving herd.

Wyatt saw the buffalo perk up their heads as Wolf drove by. "They know him," he said with quiet amazement.

"He sings to them. Listen. It sounds like an old Indian chant of some kind."

He heard the low, guttural crooning of a Native American tribal song. The buffalo started falling into line behind the truck. Wyatt said, "They know their master's voice."

"We should all be so wise," Buffy said.

Chapter 6

That would be stupid!" Wyatt turned from watching the tenth semi pull away from the stock pens.

Buffy was sick of being called names. She jammed her hands on her hips. "We need to call the radio station. The newspapers. The television stations. We need to *warn* people, for heaven's sake!"

"The nearest paper is in Hot Springs, and it only comes out once a week. There's no TV station that carries local news. If Rapid City got the story, it would just be for the sake of gossip. What can they do? And as for the radio letting people know, we already did."

"Called the radio?" Buffy asked.

"Let people know. Wolf phoned everyone in the area hours ago."

Buffy nodded. "Makes sense."

"They're all taking precautions with their families, and they're riding out at first light to spot runaways. They'll start phoning in reports of buffalo as soon as they spot them."

"That's the last of 'em," Wolf said.

Buffy hadn't given much thought to Wolf's age before tonight, but now she noticed the gray hairs reflected by the headlights. His face was lined with fatigue.

Of course, she might have gray hair and lines in her face after tonight, too. "Did you get a head count, Wolf?" Buffy had stopped pacing for a while as she watched the buffalo load, but now she went back to it. She was running on pure adrenaline, and she needed to keep moving or start screaming.

"I counted every semi load, and we're putting each load in a separate pen back at the Commons. We'll recount there. We started this night with 1,462, including the spring calves."

"I didn't know the herd had gotten so big," Wyatt said with obvious disapproval.

He was the one she'd start screaming at if she cracked, so she kept her mouth clamped shut. He'd been growing increasingly rude. He responded to every comment with terse insults. She didn't know how much more of it she could take.

"I've loaded 1,241 on the trailers. We kept careful count."

"Two hundred and twenty-one buffalo missing." Wyatt bristled with hostility.

Buffy couldn't blame him, but that didn't keep her from wanting to stuff a cork in his mouth. And unfortunately it didn't keep her from thinking about him almost kissing her and, worse yet, her almost kissing him back.

"It's not that bad." Wolf lifted his brown hat off his head and settled it back in place. "I've had every extra man here scouting. Over a hundred of them returned to the Buffalo Commons on their own."

Wyatt jerked his head up and said sharply, "I sent Anna and the boys over there. Are they all right?"

"I've been in contact with them. Anna, Cody, and Colt, as well as Sally and Jeanie, are at the Commons, all sleeping like babies. Anna got the boys to bed and told me she was heading there herself."

"So only 121 buffalo loose," Wyatt sneered.

"Look"—Buffy turned on him—"I've about had it with—"

"I said we found *over* a hundred." Wolf talked over her, which was a good idea.

She clamped her mouth shut.

Wolf went on. "We got an exact count on the ones we loaded in the semis, so we're sure about them. Seth's taken the best head count back at the Commons, and he thinks there're more like 150. They're milling around, and we aren't firm on the number yet as a few more have wandered back in since they first found them. We've driven the ones there well away from the hole in the fence, but we've left the fence open, hoping more will come home."

"So only, say, seventy-five buff rampaging through my ranch. Great!" Wyatt was still holding his gun.

"Hey!" Buffy snatched the rifle out of his hand and stormed over to her rig and put it on the seat. "I'm sick of you stalking around with that dumb thing. You'd think you needed it to prove your manhood."

"Buffy, you're tired," Wolf said. "Don't start in on Wyatt."

Buffy waved her hand at Wolf. "I can't stand here and listen to him whine for another second!"

"Whine?" Wyatt wheeled on her.

She tilted her head up, way up, so she could meet his eyes. "If I have to listen to one more smart remark from you, I won't be responsible for my actions."

Wyatt sneered. "Not responsible. I'd say that about sums it up."

She realized she could see him. The sun was coming up. Wyatt was exhausted. She was exhausted. She knew he didn't deserve this, but her control was hanging by a thread. She tried to get away from him. "I've got buffalo to find." Buffy spun around on her heel.

Wyatt grabbed her arm, and she spun right back. He hauled her hard against his chest. "I've been working all night trying to clean up the mess you made." He shook her arm.

She jerked against his grip, and when he didn't let go, it felt like the top of her head caught fire. "You get your hands off me, or I'll—"

Wolf shoved in between them. "I didn't finish. There aren't seventy-five buffalo running loose, because quite a few calves got scattered. I've got men combing the area bringing them in. We've found twenty-three so far, and we've just started hunting."

"Th–there's one dead at Wyatt's place." Buffy forgot about Wyatt's grip for a second and felt tears sting her eyes. She had about fifty good reasons to cry, all of them still on the loose. Oh, who was she kidding? She had about 1,462 reasons. She looked at Wyatt's furious, exhausted face. 1,463.

"What now?" Wyatt yanked the brim of his hat low over his eyes. "Do I have to stand here while the poor little lady cries her eyes out? That's all I need!"

"It's getting light." Wolf pushed his hands out flat against their chests, and Wyatt let go of her arm.

Buffy had to step away from Wyatt or start fighting with Wolf.

"We don't have time for this. Let's get to work rounding up the rest of those buff." Wolf said to Wyatt, "I've got a half dozen tranquilizer guns in the back of my truck. I'll hand them out. We'll post guards around your cattle and every other herd around. We'll stay connected by the CBs."

"How many men do you think you have?" Wyatt asked cynically.

Buffy wondered herself. Wolf sure was promising a lot of manpower.

"I've got all I need. Mr. Leonard's Learjet is expected in with twenty men on board. They're all off-duty forest rangers he contacted in and around Yellowstone, so they're top men. They're used to working with buffalo. He's rounding up another twenty out of Wyoming. And he's coming out personally to make sure this whole thing turns out right. Having the Buffalo Commons succeed is important to him, and this is a major screw-up. He's going to take whatever steps are necessary to make sure it never happens again. We'll get them, Wyatt. By the time we finish counting the dead, we might find out we've got all of them already."

"Yeah, I'll bet," Wyatt said bitterly.

Buffy reached past Wolf to throttle Wyatt.

Wolf caught her hand. He said to Wyatt, "Grab a tranquilizer gun."

"For her?" Wyatt asked icily.

Wolf ignored him. "There aren't that many buff left to round up. Let's quit talking and start looking. You take Buffy's truck, and we'll head back to the Commons."

Wolf boosted Buffy into his truck before she knew what happened. She wanted to go with Wyatt. She had a few more things she wanted to say to him.

Wyatt tore out of the yard, leaving a trail of dust a mile high.

"Leonard looks like he's on top of the world," Buffy observed sourly as Leonard came out of the house to meet them. She hadn't been thinking clearly enough to send a truck out to the landing strip, but Wolf must have remembered.

"He loves it out here." Wolf pulled his truck to a stop and tugged a handkerchief out of his pocket, wiping dirt and sweat off his forehead. "The other times he's visited, he's always been excited like this. Of course, I get the idea he's running on a pretty high voltage all the time. And he knows about the stampede; I had one of the men stay on the phone in contact with his jet."

"He's going to start writing checks, I suppose. I don't like to think of what Wyatt might have to say about that." She almost hoped Mr. Leonard would just leave it to her to handle. Wyatt might insult Mr. Leonard so badly that she'd end up fired. She thought glumly that she deserved whatever happened.

Leonard came striding toward the truck as Buffy and Wolf climbed out. He extended his hand to Wolf and didn't so much as look sideways at her. Buffy felt energy coming off Mr. Leonard in waves. High voltage didn't do him justice.

She had never met him before now. She'd been hired for this job by his Buffalo Commons Department, or whatever Leonard called it. She'd received a congratulatory phone call from him once she'd accepted the job, but that was all. She'd heard he visited occasionally, not overnight and never with any warning.

"Wolf, it looks like you're getting things under control."

Wolf took a quick glance at Buffy, and she knew he expected her support in anything he said. "The buff are almost all rounded up, but there's been a lot of damage. They ran through our nearest neighbor's ranch yard. They destroyed two vehicles. A barn burned down. He's got some dead livestock, and his house is about half ruined. It's a mess, and it might be worse than that. His herd, if the buffalo get out with them—"

Mr. Leonard held up his hand, and Wolf fell silent. Buffy could tell Wolf didn't like it.

"I've got someone over there right now assessing the damage and making plans to set things right." Leonard talked like a machine gun, spraying his opinion at the world. "I've already talked with Shaw's niece. She's a very angry young lady. Apparently her car was in the line of the stampede. And I'm aware of the repercussions of my buffalo getting at his cattle. I hear you sent men to ride herd on all the cattle in the area to watch for buffalo trying to join the group. Good thinking, Wolf."

Buffy didn't bother to mention that she and Wolf had decided that together.

"I've got more men coming in. I've got aerial surveillance already underway. I've hired every local crop duster I could find, and they're being organized to fly a pattern over the whole area looking for buffalo. I've got a team of security experts coming in to make changes on the fence. I also want to put a dozen additional riders on the perimeter permanently. That's a dozen all the time, three shifts a day. I'd like to hire locals if you can find them. It pumps money into the local economy. In the meantime, I'm bringing in riders from outside. I'm committing an additional million dollars a year in salaries. Plus the expense for the fence. I want that fence to stand up to lightning or a tornado.

"That all sounds good, Mr. Leonard"—Buffy decided it was time to at least make herself heard—"but there's more than just money at stake. Mr. Shaw's children could have been killed. He's determined to get these buffalo out of here. If you'd talk to him, explain your commitment to endangered species, I think it would—"

"I've got business demanding my attention." Leonard looked at her for the first time, but he never quite made eye contact. He wrinkled his nose a little as if she smelled. He directed his comment to Wolf. "Flying out here from New York this morning wasn't part of my schedule. You'll have to handle community relations. When my assessors are done, they'll write Mr. Shaw a check. I'm going to add a quarter of a million dollars for emotional distress. That ought to take care of it. If he wants more than that, I'll hire an arbitrator to hammer out the details."

Buffy said, "It's not the money, Mr. Leonard. Wyatt's children were—"

When he waved his hand this time, Buffy almost jumped him.

Wolf settled his hand on her shoulder.

Still talking to Wolf, Leonard said, "I've got an associate who will be here tomorrow to begin restitution proceedings. Please relay any further damages to him." Leonard turned from them and began striding toward the Jeep that would drive him back to his flashy little jet.

He was walking so fast Buffy had to run to catch up with him. She wanted to grab his arm, but she was a little too intimidated to do it, which made her mad. "You can't just issue orders and walk away from this."

A uniformed pilot jumped to attention and came around to hold open the door to the Jeep.

Mr. Leonard turned for the first time and really looked. "You're Miss Lange, aren't you? You're supposedly in charge here?"

"That's right."

"I wouldn't have agreed to hire someone so young to fill in until the director I want was available if not for that 'Doctor' in front of your name and such impeccable references. I was led to believe you were a woman who could handle buffalo."

"I can handle them."

Mr. Leonard's lips curled in what could only be distaste.

She was filthy—she'd spent the night in a cloud of buffalo-churned dust—and she reeked. She'd earned this stink through brutal hours of hard work. Her hair was a rat's nest, and she hadn't even unpacked her makeup yet, if she had any Jeanie hadn't swiped. She had no wish to pass some sleazy test of beauty administered by Mr. Leonard, but still his disgust stung.

"I'll make any unhappy people happy, and you will do your job and keep your mouth shut. Refer any reporters to my public relations division. They're preparing to handle everything. If any quotes in the press come from you, you'll lose this job, and the people who work with buffalo are few and far between, Miss Lange. I'm a major supporter of most of the work that is being done with them in both the public and private sector. The wrong word from me could make you a pariah."

The pilot, deaf by all appearances, waited until Mr. Leonard finished threatening her and got in. The pilot slammed the door, climbed behind the wheel, and drove off.

"Santa Claus in a Learjet," Wolf said sarcastically, coming up beside her while they watched the Jeep disappear over the rise to the runway. "Ho, ho, ho."

"Did you hear what he said?" Buffy was still gasping from the shock.

"Every word. That's the way he operates. He didn't get to where he is by being a soft touch."

"No, he got there by being a ruthless dictator."

Wolf tipped his head in agreement. "All he lacks is a country of his own and some weapons of mass destruction."

"Right now Wyatt might think the buffalo counted as weapons." Buffy turned her thoughts from what could easily become the wreckage of her career. "I was sure Mr. Leonard would at least apologize to Wyatt in person. Although I have to admit, I was worried Wyatt might deck him. Now that I've met the man, I'm even more sure that's how it would have ended up."

"Oh, I don't know. He was pretty decent to me." Wolf's voice was droll, and the look he gave her told her he was waiting for her to explode.

She decided not to keep him waiting. "Who does that man think he is?" Buffy heard the jet fire up and watched to see if the noise made her herd stampede again. They ignored the noise. Then the plane disappeared into the sky. "I heard so much about community relations. And I thought this was more than a rich man's hobby. He's supposed to be a naturalist. How can he not stay and see if we get the buffalo rounded up? What about the environmental impact of this stampede? We could have damaged the ecosystem, destroyed wetlands, trampled nesting areas along the Cold Creek. . . . What can Leonard be thinking?"

"A more interesting question," Wolf said thoughtfully, "is why did he bother to come if he was only going to make a token appearance?"

"PR," Buffy said coldly. "If this leaks, the press will know he came. Mr. Sincerely Sorry inspecting the damage."

"Who in the press are we supposed to tell?"

Buffy said grimly, "Who indeed."

Wolf gave her a worried glance. "Buffy, you wouldn't."

"Actually no, I wouldn't. All we need is a bunch of reporters hanging around here."

"But you're tempted," Wolf said mildly.

"I'm tempted to do a lot of things I won't do. For example, I was tempted to knock Leonard on his backside for the way he talked to me. I didn't."

"Good girl. I was tempted to knock him down for the way he treated you."

Buffy jerked her gloves off her hands and tucked them behind her belt buckle. "Noticed that, did you?"

"Hard not to." Wolf rested his hand on her shoulder.

With Wolf's rugged support, Buffy allowed herself to feel the sting of Leonard's disrespect. It helped that Wolf had seen it and cared. "Let's go see how the head count is going."

Chapter 7

Wyatt sent the truck racing backward in time.

It was as if history were erasing itself as he barreled over the rough pastureland toward the hulking buffalo in the middle of his cattle. He was driving Buffy's own truck, near as he could tell. It had Oklahoma plates and her name on the registration. And Wyatt hadn't seen Wolf consult Buffy, so Wolf had probably not been in the right to lend it out, but Wyatt kept it anyway.

He raced his truck toward the buffalo and wished he had Gumby. He hadn't even been back to his place. He didn't know if Gumby or any of the rest of his horses were alive or dead. He didn't have time to go check, and besides, he couldn't stand to. Wolf had promised to send someone by and to take care of any injured animals. Wyatt had to see to his cattle.

He'd talked to Anna and the boys on the CB radio. Anna was still furious, but they were safe. He stuck his head out of Buffy's window and yelled, "Git out! Hyah!" He aimed the rig straight for the buff, and the big animal only raised its shaggy head and stared. Wyatt quit acting like a madman and stopped the truck so the buff was out the driver's side window about twenty feet away. He lifted the tranquilizer gun off the rack in the back window, took careful aim, and fired. The buffalo barely flinched, and that was more from the noise than the bright red dart stabbing into his flank.

While Wyatt waited for the sedative to take effect, he radioed Wolf. "It's a bull, and it's had plenty of time to breed with my cows."

"We'll be over with a stock trailer in fifteen minutes. We'll have him quarantined and checked for brucellosis and any other contagious diseases that could affect your cattle. If he's healthy, the worst that'll happen is a few of your cows'll have a calf that's half buff. This is the first one you've seen?"

"Yep. How's the head count?" Wyatt watched the buffalo waver and go down on one front knee and then the other.

"We've got twenty-five still missing. Now with the one you've got, it's twenty-four. We're hoping a few more will wander back to the Commons."

"Twenty-four buffalo running loose? We could be finding them for a long time."

"No, we're not letting up until we've got them all."

"Check along the creek. Grass is good. Lots of water. And there's tree cover, so they might be overlooked."

"I've already sent men on horseback along the river."

Wyatt sighed as he saw the buffalo's back end collapse. He lay with his head up, panting. "He's down. Are men on the way?"

"I'm halfway there already, Wyatt," Seth broke in on the CB. "Is there any damage to the school?"

"None I can see. What if this had happened a month later and the kids had been in school?"

Wolf broke in. "Don't go borrowing trouble."

"Yeah, I remember. I'm a whiner," Wyatt said acidly.

"I'm signing off." Wolf was gone with a *click*.

"I'm going to keep hunting, Seth. I've got five more pastures to check. You got enough men with you to load him?"

"We've come prepared. We appreciate the help."

"I'm not doing it to help you." Wyatt shut the CB off with a sharp *snap*. Seth didn't deserve to be barked at, but Wyatt didn't call him back. Instead, he drove toward his next pasture. He ran nearly forty thousand head of cattle on sixty thousand acres. He'd checked about half of them so far.

He found men stationed at the next two places. The men reported no sight of any buffalo. Midafternoon he found a year-old buff, injured but alive, hobbling alone miles from anywhere. After some concern with the dosage, Wyatt decided not to dart it. He called Wolf and stood guard on the calf until Seth showed up.

"Ten more have come home, and we found a small herd of them, eight in all, along the creek." Seth climbed out of his truck, his blond hair matted with dirt and sweat, exhaustion cutting lines in his face. "We should have them back on the Commons by nightfall. With this calf, we're down to four missing buff."

Wyatt sighed. "I've got one more pasture to check."

Seth reached behind the seat of his truck and dragged out a brown paper sack. "Got a sandwich and some coffee for you. Buffy packed it, said you probably hadn't eaten all day."

He hadn't. He took the sack gratefully.

The two men with Seth climbed out and started loading the calf. The calf was young and only had three good legs, but it was still a thousand-pound buffalo. He tried to kill them. They threw a lasso on him and held him cross-tied, but he didn't quit fighting.

Wyatt watched the two wrestle with the feisty little critter but didn't offer to help. He lifted his ancient black Stetson off his head and set it on the seat beside him while he ate the huge sandwich Buffy had sent out.

Egg salad. No meat, of course. But he was starving so he didn't complain. He'd save that for later when Buffy was handy.

He took a long drink of the hot coffee and let the caffeine ease into his blood. It was a brutally hot day, and Wyatt had been driving with the window open rather than running the air conditioner, afraid Buffy's engine might overheat.

"Thanks, Seth. The coffee helps." He felt the sweat beading on his forehead from the hot liquid, and his already-soaked shirt was dripping. A light breeze wafted over him, and his wet shirt turned cold.

"You look beat, Wyatt. Time to call it a day."

"It's early yet." Wyatt drank deeply again and started a second sandwich.

"Seven o'clock."

"That's early."

"I know, but not when you were up all night. You're all in. We'll finish checking the herd. Leonard arranged a cleaning crew for your house and boarded up the windows. He's got the electricity back on and your phones working. So you've got a home to go to."

Wyatt felt a little lift from the day's brutal tension. He'd wondered where he'd sleep. "I've got six hundred head of unbred heifers with my best bull. They're the last herd I've got left to check. Has anyone been by the Johannsons'? Emily and her little sister are there alone these days."

"We've been up there several times. No sign of buffalo, but one might wander in. We've warned her to be on the lookout."

"I'll pull through there. My herd is right on the way."

"We can handle it. You need a break," Seth cajoled.

Wyatt got the distinct impression that the whole Buffalo Commons staff had been told to give him anything he wanted to head off a lawsuit. He had no intention of suing if Leonard made things right. But he didn't want them to quit worrying just yet.

"I'll stop in. And I don't need you riding out to my herd. My herd. My job."

Seth didn't argue anymore.

The two men with Seth strong-armed the wounded calf toward the cattle trailer.

For a moment, Wyatt and Seth watched the mayhem, and Wyatt realized he was enjoying it. "They're beautiful critters in an ugly sort of way."

Seth nodded. "There's something, I don't know. . .majestic. . .about 'em. Working with 'em's the best job I've ever had. A'course they'd kill you soon as look at you, but I've learned my way around 'em, and it suits me. I'm sure sorry about the mess they made last night. I s'pose if you want it bad enough, you can shut us down over this."

"I'm not going to talk about that now. I'm still too mad to trust my own judgment."

The buffalo went in the trailer; a thousand-pound baby bawling for its mama.

Seth drove off with a touch to the brim of his hat.

Wyatt headed for the last herd, the one farthest out. After he was sure they weren't being visited by the buffalo, he would go home, assess the damage to his place, then get Anna and the boys. He shouldn't have left them alone all day. He realized he'd trusted them to Buffy's care.

He didn't know why he'd trust a little woman who had done her best to ruin him, but he did. He didn't intend to think of almost kissing her either, but the mind is an unruly thing. She had been interested. Neither of them wanted it, but the night had worked its magic.

The truck drifted across the gravel road into the soft shoulder. The bouncing shook him awake, and he realized he was nearly asleep, lost in his daydream of Buffy's soft skin and gentle concern for him and his children.

And she'd known his boys apart.

He forced himself to quit thinking about how comfortable it had been to hold Buffy. Comfortable and dangerous.

The truck started bouncing again. He got back on the road and turned his thoughts to his children. They'd been through a traumatic experience. Suddenly he was anxious to get done working and be a father.

He pulled onto the gravel road leading to the Johannsons'. The lights were blazing in Emily's house. A big beast of a buffalo cow was eating her front lawn.

Emily poked her head out the back door when Wyatt pulled up. He stayed in his truck. The animal was squarely between Wyatt's truck and the house. It didn't seem neighborly to sit in his truck and holler, but Wyatt had no intention of ending this awful day by having a buffalo do a Texas two-step on his face.

He contacted the Commons with his CB, and they advised him to dart the animal. Yeah, great advice. He'd have tried to hook her up to a halter and lead her home otherwise.

"Get back in the house, Em. I'm gonna put this big girl to sleep."

Emily and Stephie went inside to be well clear of the shooting. The buffalo looked at its flank, sniffed at the dart, and went back to munching.

The Johannson girls came back out.

"You okay in there?"

Emily nodded. "I'd already phoned. The Commons is sending a trailer to pick her up. How weird is this, a buffalo in my yard?"

Stephanie, Emily's little sister, smiled out at Wyatt and waggled her fingers in a wave. The two were a matched set. Long, straight brown hair and million-dollar smiles. They'd been living all the way out here alone since their father died. Emily had been adamant that Stephie not be uprooted. She'd given up college to be a lady rancher. The only one Wyatt had ever heard tell of.

"Are you all right? Any damage? Were you outside when it came up?"

"We've been hiding inside all day like a couple of houseplants. The hands from the Commons even did my chores for me."

"How's your herd?"

Emily shook her head. "Okay, I hope. It's a cow, so I don't have to worry about it too much."

"Did the twins get to see the buffalo?" Stephie asked. She went to the same school as his boys, and the Johannsons attended the same church as the Shaws.

They weren't close friends. Their ranches weren't far apart; the Johannson place was across a rugged stretch of land, and it wasn't often Wyatt came back this far.

The placid cow kept standing, so Wyatt stayed in the truck.

Emily asked about his place, and they chatted over the shaggy back of the buffalo until it dropped off to sleep. Emily invited him in.

"I've got one more herd to check before I'm done, so I'd better go."

A Commons truck pulled up with a trailer.

Wyatt had to wind around to get out of the hilly area surrounding the Johannsons'.

He came up on the herd and found a couple hundred young cattle surrounding the well nearest the road.

A man on horseback rode toward him.

"These are my cattle," Wyatt said. "Are you checking for buffalo?"

"Yep. Matt Grissom." The rider touched his hat politely. "Mr. Leonard had me fly in from his Wyoming ranch until we get the buffalo under control." The man had the same weathered, ageless look Wolf had. He wasn't an Indian, but his skin was deeply lined and baked to a deep brown; he also had the same wise, patient look in his eyes. Wyatt wondered if they got hired because of that look or if they started looking like that after they worked with buffalo for a while. "I haven't seen any sign of 'em out here, Mr. Shaw."

"It's Wyatt. Saves time."

The man nodded.

"I'm going to drive around. I've got a couple more wells on over the draw. This is only about a third of the herd."

The man sat up straighter. "I'm sorry. I thought this was the lot of 'em. I can ride out if you tell me which way."

"Nope, don't worry about it. I'd need to check 'em anyway."

"I'm going to radio in." The man jerked his thumb at a heavy-duty truck with a horse trailer on the back. He'd obviously driven himself and his horse out here. "I'm going to tell them we need more men to ride herd."

Wyatt waved and started driving.

Wyatt found another couple hundred head around the second well. He sighed with relief. He was one quick check away from quitting for the night. He wasn't doing a head count and knew that might be a mistake, but he was going to fall asleep at the wheel if he didn't get home. The cattle, especially young ones, tended to stay together. The one thing he had to make sure of was his bull. He hadn't been with any of the other heifers. He was about twice their size, and he stood off alone, often as not. He could be picked out at a glance.

Then he got to the next water hole, and it didn't even take a glance. He saw a bull dropping down off the back of a heifer—a buffalo bull. The buff moved on through the herd; then, at the sound of charging hooves behind him, the buff turned to face the enemy in the form of Wyatt's purebred Angus bull.

Wyatt watched as the two animals faced off, bellowing. Wyatt jammed his foot on the accelerator to get between them before his bull was killed. His bull had obviously been driven off once already, because there was an ugly gash the length of his belly.

The buffalo, a thousand pounds heavier and armed with slashing horns, raced toward Wyatt's ten-thousand-dollar bull. The Angus broke off the attack and ran. The buffalo charged after him until the Angus headed for the hinterlands. Then the buffalo turned toward his girls.

Wyatt had closed the gap between himself and the buffalo. He slammed on his brakes and drew the rifle. Taking careful aim, he darted the monster. The Angus disappeared over the hill.

Wyatt slammed his fist into the steering wheel and watched helplessly as his bull ran into some rugged land where his truck couldn't follow. He needed a horse.

He looked at the wavering buffalo and reached for the radio. Well, they'd told him he could have anything he wanted.

"This is Buffy. Come in."

"I've found another of your brutes. I've darted him, and he's going down. He was fighting my bull. My bull's hurt, cut up bad, and he's run off. I'm going to need a horse out here."

"We'll be out there as fast as we can travel."

Wyatt settled in as the sun began to lower in the sky. He'd only been sitting a couple of minutes before Buffy was on the horn again. "We're on the way. I'm bringing my vet bag so I can tend your bull."

"I would have considered darting my bull, but I was afraid the dosage in the tranquilizer gun was too high. We've only got a hour or so of daylight left. He was bleeding bad. If we don't find him before dark, we'll find him dead in the morning." Wyatt heard the exhaustion in his voice. His thoughts wouldn't move in a straight line anymore.

"Tell us exactly where you are, Wyatt."

Wyatt heard her talking as if she were fading away into the distance. "You've got a man out here. Matt. . .Matt something. Uh, he was watching my herd. He said he was going to call in for more help."

"Okay, we know where he is."

"I'm. . .I don't know. Near him."

"Wyatt, are you all right?" Buffy asked. "I'm not picking you up very well."

"That's a stupid question considering the day I've had," Wyatt said. "Of course I'm not all right." Then he wondered, without really caring, if he'd actually spoken out loud.

He tossed the CB mike in the general direction of the radio and leaned his head back on the headrest. He couldn't give Buffy any better directions. He was so tired he didn't know where he was.

Chapter 8

There he is!"

Buffy aimed her truck at the herd of cattle surrounding the huge black lump on the ground.

Bill.

Their last escapee. Caught for the second time in two weeks by Wyatt Shaw. One angry cowboy.

"Why hasn't Wyatt answered the CB? Could he be hurt? I asked him if he was all right, and he said, 'Of course not.' What do you think he meant by that?"

"I don't know what he meant," Wolf said. "Same as I didn't know two minutes ago when you asked me and five minutes before that and four minutes before that and. . ."

Buffy leaned forward until her nose almost touched the windshield and talked over Wolf's recital of her nagging. "You know, I see his truck, but I don't see him. Do you see him in the truck? What if he's not in there? Where could he have gone?"

Wolf's only answer was a groan; Wolf had put in a long, hard day, and Buffy knew he wasn't inclined toward idle chatter at the best of times.

Buffy pulled up to the truck—her truck—and saw Wyatt slumped low in the seat behind the steering wheel. She jumped out of the rig before it had come to a full stop and raced to the door. "Wyatt! Wyatt, are you all right?"

He jumped so hard he cracked his head on the roof. "Ouch!"

Buffy noticed he didn't swear, which was something she was used to—being around men so much. But he put enough feeling in "ouch" to reassure anyone listening he was furious.

Buffy yanked open the truck door. "Are you all right?" She laid her hand on his scowling cheek, wondering that she didn't shrink away from his anger.

"Yes, I'm all right!" His tone nearly left bite marks. "I just caught a few minutes' sleep. Did you bring me a horse? I've got to ride out and check on my bull."

"Yes, we've got you a horse." Buffy knew she should be trying to appease Wyatt because of Mr. Leonard's worry about being sued, but all she could think of was helping him because she wanted to.

"*That* bull?" Wolf asked softly.

They all turned. Wyatt's black bull, with the ugly wound, vicious red against his shining ebony hide, stood panting on a grassy hilltop about a thousand yards away.

"That's him." Wyatt stepped out of the truck. "Wolf, what about the dosage?"

"We reduced the dosage in one of our tranquilizers." Wolf produced the altered medicine from his shirt pocket. "Cut it a little more than in half."

Buffy studied the big bull. Nowhere near as big as Bill, now sleeping peacefully, but the bull was still a huge animal. "It might not even knock him out, but it will make him docile. He looks pretty nervous up there."

They watched the bull stomp his forelegs and bob his head. Every once in a while, the prairie wind would catch the sound of a deep bellow and carry it to them.

Buffy caught back the words of apology. Surely somehow, someday, something could pass between her and Wyatt that didn't require "I'm sorry." No one had gotten around to apologizing for that almost kiss yet. Of course, they'd been interrupted. They might have gotten around to it.

"Better dart him," Wolf said. "He's ready to run right now."

"I'll treat him out here if it's not too serious. If he needs more, we'll load him and take him back to the ranch." She took the red-flagged dart from Wolf and handed it to Wyatt. "Wolf said you're the man to take the shot."

Wyatt took the dart. He loaded his rifle without taking his eyes off his bull. "I can't get him from here, not with this gun. I'll drive a little closer. If I can get my truck between him and the buffalo, he might even come in for me. On a normal day, he'd walk right up and put his head in my cab."

"Well, this will never qualify as a normal day. I'll drive." Buffy climbed behind the wheel of her truck, and Wyatt got in the passenger's side.

"I've got a horse in the trailer if we need him." Wolf jerked a thumb at the truck he and Buffy had come in. "And an empty trailer on the way. I'll get things ready to load Bill when he wakes up."

Wyatt gave the sleeping buffalo a startled look. "That's Bill?"

"Yeah, your old buddy," Buffy said.

"Will it hurt him to be sedated again so soon?"

Buffy was amazed when he sounded like he cared. "It shouldn't. Did you check and see if he was breathing?"

Wyatt gave her a sideways glance. "I took a nap."

"Look, your bull is coming in." Buffy tipped her head.

"Pull the truck forward until the bull can't see Bill." Wyatt carefully settled the rifle between them, muzzle pointed down.

Once Buffy had the truck in place, the Angus eased his way down the hill. He seemed to be at full strength, although he made skittish movements.

"He's usually so calm," Wyatt said. "A lazy old lug."

Buffy watched the bull prance forward.

"Do you toss hay out of your truck the way Wolf does for the buffalo?"

"Yeah, so they come when they hear the truck motor." Wyatt stepped out of the truck so he had a clear range of fire. "We could bulldog him, but I think it's better if he's asleep."

"Good. I can sew up his side and check for any muscle damage. If we aren't satisfied with how he responds, we can take him in."

Wyatt raised the gun and took aim. His hands were steady as steel on the rifle. He lowered it. "You're sure this stuff won't hurt him?"

"We use it a lot with the buffalo. I learned the prescribed dose for cattle in vet school. I'm sure."

Wyatt aimed. The bull walked straight toward them, and Wyatt shot him. The bull jumped and looked at Wyatt accusingly.

"I know how you feel, old boy." Wyatt hung the rifle up on the gun rack Buffy had in her truck. "Betrayed."

Wyatt didn't look at Buffy, but she got the message. A motor drew her attention. Another stock trailer pulled up.

Wolf trailed after the truck on foot. He looked over. "They're here for Bill."

Wyatt turned back to his bull without comment. His eyes were bloodshot. He was still a young man, but the sun and wind had already begun weathering lines around his eyes. Those lines were deeper than they had been yesterday, and Buffy blamed herself for that.

He ran his forearm across his brow and lifted his black Stetson with one hand to shove some unruly dark hair off his face with the other. He replaced the hat to anchor his sweat-soaked hair.

She had to try. One more apology. Maybe she'd stop screwing up after this. "Wyatt, I'm sorry."

"I know," he said shortly.

"The words don't mean anything, and Mr. Leonard's money only goes so far."

"You know how long I planned for that bull there?"

Wolf split a look between them and went back to the buffalo.

Buffy wished he'd stay and let Wyatt divide his anger, which made her a coward on top of everything else. "I know a purebred bull is an extremely valuable animal. You've got a herd that's pure black. The Angus breed is especially valuable. He's worth a lot of money."

"Ten years." Wyatt stared at the bull whose head was now hanging low. The bull's legs wobbled. "My dad and I decided we were going to get away from the more exotic breeds. We had white Charolais mainly. I've got Simmental and Chianina mixed in. Those are big breeds. For a long time, it was the theory that you'd buy the smallest cow around—that's Angus or Hereford—and breed them to the biggest bull. The cow is cheap to feed because she's little, and the calf will grow fast and give you a better return, but we started having trouble calving."

"Those little cows giving birth to whopping big calves." Buffy nodded. "I was called in during my last year of college to do a lot of cesareans."

"Which costs a lot and is risky for the cow, and there goes your profit. So Dad and I started going back to straight Angus, but we wanted to do it right. There was so much mixed blood in the breed that we weren't sure what we were getting. We decided to get a purebred. A purebred Angus has really beautiful lines. They're a healthy, hardy animal that thrives in the conditions in the Black Hills. We probably didn't need to get one as expensive as that one."

Wyatt's bull wavered. He was standing about thirty feet in front of them. When he staggered sideways, Buffy got a better look at the ugly slash in his side. Blood dripped from his belly and ran down his legs. This close, Buffy could see smaller cuts on the bull's head and neck, and one leg was badly lacerated. It was obscene on the proud, beautiful animal. The bull dropped to one front knee. Buffy prayed that he hadn't lost so much blood the dosage she used would kill him. She told Wyatt nothing would go wrong, but the world played cruel tricks, or at least that had been her experience. She could have prayed all night and not covered everything that could go wrong.

"He was worth it," Buffy said as the bull dropped another knee. "He's magnificent."

"Dad was finally going to retire and have a little fun. He surprised me with the bull on the day I bought the ranch. Dad sold for a fraction of what he could have gotten from Mr. Leonard, but Dad had lived like a miser and saved a lot of money; he didn't need Leonard's cash. And his father had handed it on to him for a token payment, so he wanted to do that for me. Still, not every rancher in the area made the same decision for their sons. A lot of my friends who had hopes of ranching left when their fathers couldn't afford to pass up Leonard's money."

Buffy opened her mouth to give her usual automatic support for Mr. Leonard the naturalist, but she couldn't speak the words, not after his ruthless performance this morning. She no longer believed Leonard's motives were so pure.

"I could have paid market value for the land, because Jessica had just died and I got a life insurance payment." Wyatt pursued the subject of his wife. "But instead, here I am buying the place for a song, and Dad comes up with Coyote there as a present."

"Coyote? You named him?" The bull's back end sagged to the prairie grass, and Buffy reached into her truck and picked up her vet bag.

"Not really. He's got one of those million-dollar names, Marquis Blazing

Star Stewart. I think that's it. I just call him 'the bull.'" Wyatt got out, and the two of them walked toward the dazed bull. "But sometimes we call him Coyote after USD."

"After what?"

Wyatt gave her a look that was pure disgust. "The football team?"

"Your local high school?" Buffy thought that might be a normal conversation they could have. She'd gone to high school. . .for a while. She'd graduated early, and she'd taken college classes the whole time and spent every summer and holiday and weekend working with buffalo, so she hadn't socialized much. But she'd been to an occasional football game. Never cared for them, but still. . .

Wyatt snorted. "The University of South Dakota. It's where I met Jessica." He got near enough to touch the bull and carefully knelt beside him. He patted the bull's stout shoulder. "Sorry about this, old man. Bet you never figured on having to fight a monster like that for the girls, did you?"

Buffy ran her hands over the bull. The worst wound, the one in his side, had hanging flaps of skin. She'd be sewing all night. The bull panted steadily, and she breathed a sigh of relief. His neat, black head drooped like it weighed a ton.

"Let's see if we can roll him onto his side."

The bull went down flat without a protest. His feet flayed around a bit, but there was no strength behind them.

Wolf came trudging across the prairie carrying a cardboard box. "Bill's starting to wake up. We're ready to load him. This is everything you brought to tend the bull."

"Thanks, Wolf. Just set it here beside me."

Wolf laid the box down then knelt beside the bull so he, Buffy, and Wyatt were lined up down the length of his belly, Wolf nearest his head. "He's a fine animal, Wyatt. He's young and strong. He'll be okay."

"Yep, I think he'll make it."

"You could go back with Wolf, Wyatt. I'll be at this for a long time, and it's really a one-woman job." Buffy glanced at the setting sun. It had to be nearly nine o'clock at night. Would this day never end?

"I'll stay."

"I have the CB if I need any help. You look exhausted."

"I'll stay."

Buffy had known he would. The truth was she didn't want to be left alone out here. But she'd had to try. "Fine."

Wolf gave the bull an affectionate slap on the neck, and the bull started. It blinked its eye resentfully at Wolf as if it didn't want its sleep disturbed.

"Don't like lettin' anyone else be in charge, do you, boy?" Wolf got up with a grunt of exertion that told Buffy how tired he was. He walked back to the buffalo.

Buffy immediately began rummaging in her box.

"Tell me what to do, Buffalo Gal."

"I already told you it was a one-woman job."

"I can sew up torn skin as well as you most likely. We can be out of here in half the time."

Buffy pulled battery-operated hair clippers out of the box Wolf had brought. "I want to clip the area along the wound; then I'll disinfect and wash it. Then I'm going to pack it with antibiotic powder, and I'll start sewing."

"Let's get on with it."

Buffy gave Wyatt a long look. She saw his determination and gave up on working alone. She didn't like kneeling here beside him, shoulder to shoulder, his warmth seeping into her, his scent teasing her on the soft evening breeze. She clicked the clippers, and they came on with a tooth-tingling buzz.

The noise prevented them from talking, which was just as well. Between exhaustion and anger, she didn't think Wyatt had anything to say she wanted to hear. But the bull didn't need to be shaved bald. The skin along the big wound and several small ones was clear in a few minutes. While Buffy worked in the bloody fur, cleaning the wound, Wyatt cleaned beside her. She heard Wolf drive away, leaving her and Wyatt alone with Wyatt's herd and the big bull sleeping under their hands.

She'd just gotten comfortable with the silence when Wyatt said, "He bred at least one of my heifers. I wasn't quick enough to see which one. The buff calf'll kill her. My Angus are too small to give birth to a baby buffalo. Look at this wound on his back leg." Wyatt pointed to a cut with the blood dried to a hard black crust. "He got this cut hours ago. That buffalo has been out here all day. Who knows how many he bred."

Buffy examined the muscle wall under the cut for damage. "Bill hadn't really been accepted into the herd yet. While the rest of them ran together, he just wandered a different way. And this pasture isn't that far from the Commons as the crow flies. Yes, I'd say we need to figure he's been with this herd most of last night and all day today."

Wyatt never quit working. "All these heifers are the age to be bred. I could lose a dozen of them, and if Bill is carrying brucellosis or any other disease, the state has to quarantine at least this whole herd until they're tested and found healthy. If even a few of them are sick, I could lose six hundred head of my best young stuff."

Buffy shook her head. "Bill is healthy. He was checked carefully before we moved him here."

"And he's been with your herd for two weeks or so, right? Are you sure every buffalo cow you've got is healthy? Are you sure none of them has passed anything on?"

"No, that's possible, but not likely. Look, I'm sorry—"

"Stop! Stop with 'I'm sorry!' " Wyatt roared. Then he clamped his mouth shut.

In the deepening dusk, Buffy saw his determination to control his temper and the exhaustion that weakened his iron will. She was just as tired. She almost reached for him, but she knew that was exactly the wrong thing to do. She knew buffalo men, and Wyatt was cut from the same cloth. The refining fires of the West forged them into pure, unalloyed steel. She had a desire to comfort him that was purely female. She recognized it as a better part of herself. But she was also a woman who'd worked with mean animals and hard men all her life. She squelched her softer instincts.

"All right, forget sorry. Forget Leonard will make it right. Forget all of that. Just get over it."

Wyatt's eyes, drooping with exhaustion, popped open. "Get over it?"

"That's right, you heard me." She faced him. "Get over it! It happened. You'll do whatever you need to do to get through today, and then you'll get through tomorrow. That's life. This is an ugly mess, and it may get uglier, and you'll do whatever you have to do. Anything else you say about it is just *whining!*"

Wyatt's jaw tightened until she thought his teeth might crack. He glared at her with those blazing hazel eyes. It wasn't the first time he'd burned her with them. It wasn't the first time she'd accused him of whining. She almost smiled.

Wyatt was the strongest man she'd ever met, and she'd met some strong ones. If ever a man had a right to complain, it was Wyatt Shaw.

He breathed in and out. His nostrils flared, his eyes got hotter, and he rose to her challenge. "That's right. I'll do whatever tomorrow brings, because the sun will rise tomorrow, and I don't have any choice but to live through it."

Buffy was so proud of him she wanted to. . . Well, never mind what she wanted to do—it was a bad idea. "So you stay here"—she jabbed a crimson finger at the bull's belly—"and you survive as best you can, and I will, too. So I'm sorry—not because it's my fault—it isn't! I'm sorry because I know your life is going to be a complicated mess for a while. And then it will be over."

"My life?" Wyatt asked.

"No, this mess!"

"And what?" Wyatt sneered. "We'll all look back on this and laugh?"

"I don't see much chance of that."

Their gaze held a moment; then she went back to sterilizing the cuts. Out of the corner of her eye, she saw Wyatt's fist clench for a second; then he turned to his bull and began working alongside her again. It was almost companionable—in a demilitarized-zone kind of way.

Buffy sprinkled topical antibiotic on the wounds. "The bleeding has stopped. He would have been okay without our help if he could have avoided an infection.

The skin flap might have caught on something and gotten worse, and it would have left him with an ugly scar."

"Well, we wouldn't want him to be ugly, now, would we?" Wyatt said dryly.

Buffy threaded a needle and handed it to Wyatt then got one for herself. The big bull breathed in and out but was otherwise still.

"I don't see muscle damage." The bull's eyes fluttered open once in a while. "He's not really unconscious. He's just stoned out of his gourd."

Wyatt laughed as he sewed. "What is that stitch you're using?"

"It's a little more difficult than the one you're doing. I'm not that long out of vet school, so maybe it's something new."

Buffy showed Wyatt how to do it, and he adapted to her method. "I'll bet this would leave less of a scar."

"Oh, not really. Your stitch isn't going to leave a scar that'll show once his hair grows back."

"I meant on myself."

Buffy's hands dropped to her sides. "You mean you sew your own cuts?"

"Yeah, sure."

Buffy grimaced. She thought of scarring and pain and infection, and finally all she could say was, "That'd hurt."

"It hurts some, but usually you're already hurting like crazy, what with having a cut big enough it needs to be stitched. A few more pinpricks don't make much difference, and I'm a long way from a doctor out here."

"You've really done it?" Buffy was having a hard time imagining a man taking a needle to his own flesh.

Wyatt paused to unsnap his sleeve and shove it up to his elbow. A jagged cut ran the length of his left arm. "I did this one. If it'd been on my right arm, I might have needed to go in."

Buffy didn't like the looks of the nasty scar. "A doctor could have done better for you. You wouldn't have that scar."

Wyatt gave a rusty half laugh. "Yeah, I'm ruined. My dreams of being Miss America are over." He reached for the thread.

"Do you sew the boys up?"

"Of course. With those two wild animals, I'd be running to the doctor for stitches twice a week. I just sewed a cut on Cody's foot a few days ago. I wouldn't do it if I thought he was hurt seriously. I'd want a doctor to rule out any complications. But he kicked his bare foot through a window and slit the top of his arch."

"And he lay still for it?"

"No," Wyatt said, as if she'd lost her mind. "That kid has never laid still, night or day, in his life."

"How'd you get him sewn up?"

"I wrapped him up so tight in a bedsheet he wasn't able to move a muscle. The doctor taught me that years ago."

"You're saying a doctor knew about this and didn't demand you bring him in?"

"Who do you think taught me to put stitches in? Well, I mean besides my mom. A doctor gave me some good tips that improved my methods. The first time I did it, Cody was two years old. I wrapped him up, and Jessica held him down. He screamed the whole time, and I bet anything I've got hearing damage from it. And Colt thought we were killing him, so he screamed, too. It wasn't pretty."

"How could you stand it?"

Wyatt shrugged. "It would have been stupid to drive fifty miles to a doctor and make that poor guy listen to the screaming. And I'd have had to listen to it, too, in the doctor's office. It was our problem. We took care of it."

Buffy didn't want to ask about Wyatt's wife, but her mouth took charge. "Your wife must have been tough."

"No, actually she hated me for it the first time I did it in front of her." Wyatt laughed, and Buffy heard affection in his laugh. "Cody had cracked his chin and needed a couple of stitches. My wife cried the whole time, but she held him down for me. Then she fainted dead away when it was over, so I had an unconscious wife and two screaming kids on my hands. Long afternoon."

Wyatt sighed. "I had to call a neighbor lady to hold him when we took them out. He screamed just as loud, and it didn't hurt him a bit, and Jessica wouldn't speak to me for a week afterward."

Buffy put the last stitch in the bull's belly; then she turned to several lesser cuts on his head and neck. Wyatt began stitching on the back leg.

Buffy said, "She cried, but she did it. She sounds like a hardy woman."

"Jessica hated the ranch. She spent more time not speaking than she did speaking."

"But she stuck with you?" Buffy straightened and looked at Wyatt. "Even though it was a life she hated?"

Wyatt quit sewing and looked sideways at her. "Sure she stuck with me. We made a commitment to God and to each other. We both intended it to last for a lifetime." He paused then added quietly, "She was never happy, though. I was born to be a rancher. Never wanted anything else. But the year I graduated from high school, Dad was talking about retiring. I was born when he was older, and it was just too much responsibility for me. I wasn't ready for my whole life to be laid out and settled. I went off to college, thinking I could leave these Black Hills behind. I met Jessica while I was there."

"She wasn't raised on a ranch?" Buffy asked.

"About as far from a ranch as you can get. She was from a suburb in Connecticut. Her dad commuted into New York City every day to work."

"How did she ever get to South Dakota?"

"Oh, it's a long story. Something about a friend whose grandmother had spent her childhood here and always loved the country. How does anyone end up anywhere?"

Buffy thought of all the twists and turns that had led her here.

"She fell in love with the idea of the wide-open spaces ringed by these rough mountains. I'm sure I was homesick and talking about missing the land. She got excited about getting back to nature; then she fell in love with me." Wyatt smiled fondly.

Buffy looked back at her patient to distract her from an uncomfortable pang of jealousy.

"By the end of the first semester at the university, I knew I'd be miserable anywhere but out here. I told her I was quitting school and going home to ranch, and I asked her to marry me. She said yes."

"After only dating for a few months?"

Wyatt shrugged. "We were just kids, still in that first glow of new love. It all seemed like a miracle. I got out just long enough to find the woman of my dreams. She came all the way across the country to be an earth mother. We were going to have six kids and eat food out of our garden, and she'd sew our clothes and knit our sweaters. We eloped and came home for Christmas to tell my folks we were married and ask if we could have my old room. My folks were thrilled. Jess was pregnant by New Year's. By the end of January, she was stir-crazy."

"This is a beautiful place to live, Wyatt. But it's not for everybody."

"She sure wasn't suited to it. She wanted more socializing, more regular hours. Her folks had a lot of money, and she was used to traveling and shopping in stylish stores."

Buffy looked down at her sweat-soaked cotton work shirt and bloody Levis. "Culture shock, huh?"

"Big-time. The weird part of it was, her classy clothes and her urban attitude were the things I was most attracted to. So I was asking her to give up what I loved most about her."

"She would have adjusted eventually. All she really needed was time."

"Time just made it worse. She didn't like worrying about snow and drought. It wore on her. She cried a lot and yelled even more. She didn't want to live with my folks, but there weren't any other livable houses around. I might have bought us a trailer, but there were days her mood was so black I didn't feel. . ." Wyatt fell silent.

Buffy turned to listen more closely.

He cleared his throat. "I didn't feel comfortable leaving the boys with her. I wasn't sure. . .I wasn't sure what she might do. So we stayed with my folks. And about two years ago, she died in car wreck." Wyatt's voice faded to a whisper.

"I've often wondered when she died if it wasn't a relief for her."

"Was it that bad?"

Wyatt thought about it; then he turned back to his stitching, and Buffy thought he might refuse to answer. She started sewing again, too. They were nearly done. This horrible day might finally be drawing to a close.

The bull began moving restlessly as the sedative wore off.

"She never could tell the boys apart. Not even when they were older."

Buffy said incredulously, "They barely resemble each other. How could someone not tell them apart?"

Wyatt laughed. "Buffalo Gal, they look so much alike the teacher at their school makes me come in with them every morning and tell her which is which. They tried to trick her almost every day until we started doing that. It wouldn't have mattered much except the boys have a habit of fooling someone and then laughing like loons when they're done with their prank. It made the teacher mad to be lied to all the time, and it really made her mad to be laughed at."

"Haven't you had a talk with her? I mean, Cody's eyelashes are thicker, and Colt must outweigh him by quite a bit."

"Two pounds," Wyatt supplied.

Wyatt leaned away from the bull and groaned as his back cracked. "I know just what you mean, but the teacher doesn't see it. She suggested I put an *X* on the back of their necks in different colors of indelible ink so she could tell."

Buffy gasped. "She wanted to mark them? Like wild animals that have been darted and tagged by the Wildlife Service? That's awful!"

"Kinda struck me that way, too." Wyatt put the needle back in Buffy's satchel and reached for the thermos of hot water she'd brought. The bull stirred his legs, and Wyatt eased away from the big animal. Coyote lifted his head and moaned out a plaintive *moo* then let his head drop back to the ground.

"He's coming around. Give him some room." Wyatt poured warm water over first one hand and then the other. Buffy shifted her supplies out of the way of moving hooves, and Wyatt poured the water for her to wash. "In the teacher's defense, those two rascals were tormenting her. You know what they're capable of."

Buffy sniffed. "She sounds incompetent to me."

"Now, darlin', we don't go bad-mouthing teachers out here. We're still in that old-fashioned mode where if the teacher punishes you at school, you get punished again when you get home."

Buffy said aghast, "You really do that? You side with the teacher against your boys?"

"Every single stinkin' time, regardless of the circumstances. You've met my boys, right?"

"Even if they are active—"

Wyatt cut in, "And I've gone to church with Mrs. Rogers for twenty-five years. She was my teacher back in the day. I'd trust her with my life, and I trust her with my boys. Besides, I'm still kinda scared of her."

Buffy looked at Wyatt and tried to imagine him scared of anybody. She began to laugh.

Wyatt grinned. "I'm serious. She's tough." Wyatt leaned very close to her and whispered, "And I'll tell you another reason I side with her, but it's a secret."

They knelt inches from each other. He was too close. He had mischief in his eyes, and she could smell the hard scent of sweat and cattle and the prairie breeze on him. The metallic scent of blood was primitive like her reaction to Wyatt.

She should have moved away but instead she leaned closer. "What secret?"

With sparkling eyes, he said, "My boys run around shooting each other all the time. Drives everybody who knows 'em *crazy*."

"Wyatt!" Buffy sat back on her heels and swatted at him.

He caught her hand before she could do any damage. "You don't have any of those tranquilizer darts in a forty-pound dose, do you? Like two of them, maybe? To be administered at Cody and Colt's bedtime."

"Wyatt Shaw, don't you dare talk about your boys that way!" She tugged at her hand, but he didn't let go.

His voice was husky, and she barely heard him say, "This is so stupid."

Then he kissed her.

Chapter 9

Wyatt lost the battle, and the war wasn't looking good.

He pulled Buffy closer. The box of veterinary supplies was between them, and he shoved it aside and pulled her onto his lap. The shifting around gave him time to think, and he broke off the sweetest kiss he'd ever had. And that was a sad thing for a man to say who'd been married. He lifted his head, and she chased after him. He almost howled at the moon, he wanted to kiss her again so bad. Instead, he dropped her off his lap. "I shouldn't have done that."

Buffy's eyes were fixed on his lips. "I'll say."

Wyatt got to his feet and walked away from her about ten feet. He ran his hands through his hair and knocked his hat off his head. He clumsily caught it then tossed it aside on the dewy grass. He was far enough away from her that he couldn't see her expression. So he took a chance and faced her. "We both know that shouldn't have happened."

Buffy didn't answer. Instead, she rolled onto her hands and knees, turned away from him, and began packing her satchel with unsteady movements.

"Well, say something!" The bull's legs jerked when Wyatt yelled. Wyatt strode over to Buffy and yanked her to her feet. He gripped her upper arms. "It was stupid!"

"Very stupid." Buffy wrenched against his grip, and Wyatt had to hold on tight to keep his hands on her.

"Let go!"

Wyatt would never have let go if she'd fought him physically, but her voice, cold and angry, jarred him out of whatever madness had made him get this close.

He let go.

She turned and walked around the bull and crouched behind him. She was fussing with his eyelids, and she ran her hand down his neck. She reached for her vet bag across the bull's back in a way that made it clear she wanted to keep the bull between her and Wyatt. She fished around in the bag for a little bottle of medicine and with deft movements gave Coyote a shot of antibiotic. "I don't want to leave him out here unconscious. Why don't you go get some rest?"

"I'm not leaving you. You don't even have a way back."

"There's someone riding herd nearby all night."

"I thought you said Bill was the last. Why would someone still be riding herd?"

"Because we're doing a final head count in the morning, and we aren't going to let up on your herd until we've double-checked. You'll go right past him. Tell him to bring his truck over this way later and check on me."

"Forget it. You go. I'll stay."

"I'm the vet. And I'm the one with the escaped buffalo. This is my responsibility."

"My ranch. My bull. My responsibility."

"Okay, then go away so you can keep yourself from doing something as stupid as kissing me again!"

Wyatt had to give her that one. He did need to get away from her. Because now he heard the hurt in her voice and his own insult coming from her mouth. He knew the best way to make it better was to pull her back into his arms and tell her it wasn't stupid, that it was the best idea he'd had in a long time. *Years. Ever.*

"Buffy, you know I'm a Christian."

Buffy didn't answer.

"I don't kiss women to entertain myself." He planted his hands on his hips and felt the evening breeze ruffle his hair. He tried to drink in the cool of the night.

"Good, because that wasn't very entertaining." Coyote stirred, and Buffy got behind him and heaved when he tried to sit up.

Wyatt ignored that crack because he'd felt the way she responded to him. She'd been entertained almost out of her mind. Just like him. "So, I'm not going to kiss you again."

"Good. I agree. It's unanimous." Her voice could have taken bites out of his hide.

Wyatt knew the bull didn't really need her help, but she looked like she needed to keep busy. "And the opposite of kissing for entertainment is getting serious, and we both know it can't be anything serious, because you're headed for the job of your dreams, and I'll live out the rest of my life alone before I ask some woman to choose me over anything else."

"You're absolutely right: It can't be serious! Because I'd rather be an old maid than get involved with a man who thinks it's his right to dominate the whole world!" She yelled, but her hands were gentle as they ran over the bull's black coat.

Wyatt tried to remember Jessica ever touching any of his livestock like that. She wouldn't go near the cattle, not even the baby calves. She said they smelled bad. She was scared of the horses. Gathering eggs had been his job, too.

"So that's it. Nothing serious, nothing foolish. That leaves nothing."

"Nothing," Buffy agreed. She fell silent as she petted the big bull. Coyote shook his head and huffed a slobbery sneeze. Angus snot sprayed Buffy's neck and arm and the front of her bloody shirt. She wiped her neck negligently on one hunched shoulder with an *ugh* of disgust. Then she wiped her arms off on the bull's neck and slapped him affectionately on the shoulder. "Cut that out, you old coot."

She was filthy, and she smelled like a cow herd in July. She was soaked in blood, and she wanted Wyatt to stay away from her. But she kissed like a dream and knew his boys apart, and she didn't mind bull slobber.

Wyatt fell in love.

What jolted his body wasn't a timid feeling. It wasn't particularly joyful either, because it wasn't possible for them to be together. What it was, was real. It was a fully formed emotion that invaded him down to his cells and his chromosomes and definitely down to his heart. It was something that made what he'd felt for his wife pale and superficial. . .and heartbreaking.

Allison "Buffy" Lange was the most interesting, touchable, honest woman he'd ever known, coated with the hide and temperament of a buffalo. And he knew with an already-broken heart that he was going to love her for the rest of his life.

The bull flinched slightly when she slapped him and twisted his head to look over his shoulder at her.

"Sorry." Buffy patted more gently. "I know you've had a rough day. Why don't you get up for me, big boy? Show me some of that purebred heart."

As if he were listening to her, the bull lurched to its feet with a grunt. Buffy jumped to her feet and backed away, shouting encouragement. The bull stood, wavering a bit for a few seconds; then it began walking down toward the water tank that stood by the windmill. It walked out from between them, and Wyatt had to tense every muscle in his body to keep from closing the space.

He wanted to beg her to forget buffalo and all her years of education and come home and help him identify his boys. She'd only have to give up her life's work, her dreams, her future.

He estimated it would take about six weeks for her to start resenting him.

Buffy watched the bull walk away, and Wyatt used that time to get hold of himself. He turned, his muscles resisting his mind, and started packing up her medical supplies.

She had done most of it already, and it was the work of seconds to finish. When he was done, he trusted his voice. "Let's go. It's probably too late for me to see the boys tonight, but I'd like to get some sleep."

Buffy turned from watching the bull, picked up the satchel while Wyatt grabbed the box, and started for the pickup. "You'd better come back to the Commons and sleep with me."

"What?" Wyatt nearly strangled on the word. Then he hurried to catch up with her.

"Your house is probably livable, with the cleaning crew and repairs we've done. The carpeting was ruined, by the way. Anna gave the go-ahead to replace it with the same color. She said it was the color of dirt and you'd never keep up with anything else. Anna and the boys will be at my place. We've got plenty of room for you in the bunkhouse."

Oh.

Wyatt waited for the blood to start flowing to his head. "Okay. I'm too tired to look at my place anyway."

They drove back to the Commons in a strained silence that Wyatt couldn't breach, because everything he had to say was a big mistake.

Buffy pointed to the bunkhouse.

"I know my way."

"I had my men bring you a change of clothes, which will be on the first empty bunk in the door. Shower and come up to the house. There'll be some supper for you."

Wyatt wasn't going anywhere near her house, especially not if she was clean and sweet-smelling. He was so hungry his stomach had started gnawing on his innards, but he wasn't going in. "I'll pass on the supper. I'm dead on my feet."

Buffy didn't look at him. "Okay, then." She agreed so easily that Wyatt was sure she wanted to get away from him. He wondered if it was for the same reason he wanted to get away from her. And perversely that made him want to stick like a buffalo burr.

As she walked away, she said over her shoulder, "Tomorrow we'll begin damage assessment on your ranch. And we'll decide what we're going to do about your heifers having a buff calf. How long had your bull been in with them?"

"Just a couple of days."

"Okay, I've got a couple of ideas."

Wyatt nodded and began striding toward the bunkhouse. He wanted to look back and see if she was watching him. He wanted to so bad; only a lifetime of self-discipline, honed to an art form by marriage to a woman who was never watching when he looked back, kept him moving the way he had to go.

―∞―

Wyatt wanted to find a bed and fall face-first on it, but as he walked across the yard, a certain smell kept him on his feet.

Meat.

Wolf swung the door open to his trailer house. "Come on in and grab a burger. You've got to be starving."

Now Wyatt wanted to fall face-first on the food. He almost jogged into

Wolf's house and grabbed a bun piled high with a savory meat patty, tomatoes, and onions. He nearly swallowed it whole. He ate another one while Wolf doctored up three more sandwiches.

"I'm going to run over to the bunkhouse and grab a shower. If you're planning to eat all of those, tell me now so I won't get my heart broken when I come back."

"They're yours. They'll be waiting for you."

"I don't know if they're the best thing I've ever eaten or if I'm just starving to death." Wyatt swiped another one before he left to clean up.

"Both, I reckon," Wolf said dryly.

Wyatt was in and out of the shower and back at Wolf's place in minutes. He felt 100 percent better. "I didn't realize just how deep the grit had worked into my skin." He took another burger and ate it before he sat down.

Wolf put a plate on the table in front of Wyatt. He loaded two more burgers on it and a mountain of fried potatoes. He tossed an ear of sweet corn on the plate and set a dish of melted butter and a glass of iced tea on the table. He set a plate with more burgers in the center and brought along an empty plate for himself.

Wyatt was eating before Wolf sat down. "I didn't realize how hungry I was either."

"Tough day," Wolf said.

Wyatt chewed for a while, thinking of the day Jessica died. "I reckon I've had one that was tougher."

Wolf sat across the battered wooden table.

Wyatt felt Wolf watching him eat with strange intensity. "What is it?" Wyatt braced himself for more bad news.

"So, you really like the burgers. . . ."

"Yeah. They're great. Best I've ever had." Wyatt wasn't just saying that. Now that he'd finished three of them and half the potatoes, his starving belly wasn't screaming anymore. He could actually taste them. "They're different. What'd you do to 'em?"

"You mean you want to swap recipes, Mary Lou?" Wolf's black eyes sparkled.

Wyatt almost laughed. "That's about what I'm reduced to after today. Maybe after that, you can tell me if these pants make my butt look big."

Wolf laughed and grabbed a burger for himself. "It's a buffalo burger."

Wyatt stopped with his mouth almost ready to chomp the first bite out of his fifth burger. "This is buff? Really?"

"Yep."

A thousand questions ran through Wyatt's mind, and only exhaustion made him quit sorting around for the right one. He just said what was on his mind at the moment. "Does Buffy know you're eating her herd?"

Wolf started laughing. Unfortunately he had a mouthful of buffalo, and he almost choked to death.

Wyatt ate his sandwich more carefully.

Wolf finally was breathing right again. "That's not the question I expected, but I guess I should have known you'd think of her first."

Wyatt didn't like the strange tone or the sharp way Wolf studied him. He'd known Wolf ever since the Commons had popped up next door to him over ten years ago. Wolf had gotten along well with his dad, and Wyatt had always liked him, even if he didn't like his herd or what Leonard did to the price of land.

"You know," Wolf said thoughtfully, "Buffy and I have a very different idea about what a buffalo commons should be."

"The whole Midwest, empty of people and overrun by buff, just like in the good old days," Wyatt said sarcastically.

"Not exactly what I meant. I've known her a couple of weeks, and already I've learned that she thinks with stars in her eyes. She sees these animals and sees beauty and strength, and it touches something primitive in her. Still, she's got a practical head in charge of her romantic heart. She just loves them and wants to be near them. She's done the schooling and burned off a good share of her youth working toward her goal."

"You've known her for the same length of time I have. You don't know anything about her." Wyatt grabbed a sixth burger and worked on the stack of potatoes.

Wolf poured him another glass of tea. "But I'm a different story. I don't have the heart of a practical dreamer. I have the heart of a Sioux warrior. I see buff. I see food."

"Does *Leonard* know you're eating his herd?"

Wolf laughed again. "Leonard and I almost understand each other."

"Almost?"

"Leonard isn't what he seems."

"A spoiled, rich East Coast liberal who says the right thing in front of the television cameras then does exactly what he wants in private?"

Wolf seemed amused by that. "Okay, he's *exactly* what he seems. He's got the rest of the world fooled, but I should have known better than to underestimate you."

"So, what do you mean, almost? What doesn't Leonard understand?"

Wolf said thoughtfully, "He likes the idea of being an environmentalist because it's popular. It's his cause. He doesn't have a clue what it means, but he *hires* people to understand, and he hires the best, like Buffy, like me. So he's doing good, I think."

Wyatt thought of his ruined ranch and his herd, maybe ruined. He set the buffalo burger down. His appetite was gone.

Wolf was a smart guy. He had to notice Wyatt's change in attitude, but he kept on trying to explain. "The thing he doesn't understand is that the Buffalo Commons can't survive as a rich man's toy. He's raising a herd of buffalo so big that, if something happens to him, if his heirs don't share his ideas of how to spend the family money, or if the stock market crashes, he's got a huge herd of big, dangerous animals with nowhere to go. He spends a fortune on staff and fence. He flies in and tosses big checks around and sends us every specialist we need. But the Commons can't survive like that."

"And you think you know a way to make it survive?"

Wolf gave him a long look. "I'd say you got right to the heart of the matter."

"So what's your idea?"

"It's simple. You're eating my idea. Buff weren't put on this earth to be admired and cosseted like Buffy wants to do. They were put on the earth to be part of the food chain. If Leonard would give me a year to run this place like I want, I could make it pay. I'd start by making buff into a delicacy that people would buy for special occasions, and then I'd turn it into a staple as common as hamburger. If this place could support itself, we wouldn't need Leonard's money."

"Why buffalo, Wolf? This meat is good, but it's no better than beef. And beef cattle are nowhere near as dangerous to handle or as hard to fence in."

"Yeah, but buff naturally thrive out here. They don't need the babying."

Wyatt knew that for a fact. "They're hardy, but my Angus do okay."

"They need more water, better grass, and more doctoring than a buff ever would."

"But buff will never be safe. There's no taming them and nothing except a million dollars in fence that'll keep 'em in."

"I haven't figured out the fence yet. The fence is the thing that keeps stopping me."

"But it would be solved if you could really create a buffalo commons, right?" Wyatt asked coldly. "Forget the fence and let the buffalo have the whole Great Plains."

"If I had my way, I'd use the Missouri River for the east fence and the Rockies for the west fence. I'd turn 'em loose." Wolf held up his hand to stop Wyatt. "I know that's impossible."

"My great-grandfather—"

"I know. He homesteaded this land. It's in your blood. I've heard it all. Big deal."

"Big deal?" Wyatt had taken one more bite of burger, and it was his turn to choke. He had to chew for a moment, and while he did, he studied Wolf. He had known Wolf for a long time, and he'd never seen the almost mystical calm in the man waver. Until now. Suddenly he could see the Sioux warrior. He could imagine Wolf, riding wild across the prairie, ramming a spear into a charging buffalo.

"You heard me. Big deal. My great-great-grandfather is buried under these hills. This is sacred land to my people since before recorded history. All my ancestors lived and died in these mountains and valleys. Why is your four generations of family something I should respect when you don't respect the blood that calls out to me from these hills?"

"You know I respect you, Wolf. But it's a little late to be re-fighting the Battle of the Little Big Horn. I'm here. You're here. Why isn't that enough? Why does your plan have to include me moving east of the Missouri?"

"I'll tell you why, Wyatt. It's because I've never heard you say I have a right to be here. You've wanted these buff gone from the first day they unloaded the truck."

Wyatt took a deep breath. It burned him to admit Wolf was right. He couldn't bring himself to say it now. "Now's a bad time to try and convince me these buffalo are a good idea."

Wolf snorted. "When is there ever a good time with you?"

Wyatt had to give him that one, too. "You really think you can make it pay?"

Wolf hesitated.

Wyatt saw the blazing eyes of the warrior subside. He reached for another burger.

"Now that the fence is here, yes, I think it could pay. I've even made some contacts with specialty meat buyers. I could start supplying them with buffalo meat with a phone call. I've approached Leonard about it. He lets a few buff be sold off for meat when they're injured or older, but that's not the best meat. The best is young, tender. Like what you're eating right now. Leonard lets me buy one for my own use from time to time. I'd try and get Buffy to have a bite if she wasn't a vegetarian." Wolf shook his head. "I've never figured that one out. The whole animal world eats each other, but we're not supposed to join in. It don't make sense."

Wyatt drained his glass of tea and stood up. "You've finally said something we agree on. I think we'd better go to sleep while we're ahead."

Wolf laughed and turned back to his burger. He looked at it thoughtfully. "A million dollars' worth of fence. What am I supposed to do about that?"

—⁂—

Buffy rolled out of bed when the alarm rang at five thirty.

She almost dropped to her knees.

She groaned and would have lowered herself back into bed if she wasn't afraid she'd never get out again. Every muscle in her body was screaming at her for yesterday. She staggered to the shower, even though she'd showered last night before she went to bed. She let hot water blast down on her muscles, and it helped enough to keep her going. She swallowed more than her share of aspirin and pulled on her work clothes. She was outside at the buffalo pens long before light.

The sun peaked over the horizon just as Wolf emerged from his trailer. Wyatt and Seth came out of the bunkhouse at the same time.

She glanced at them and went back to counting buff. "Coffee in the thermos." She pointed to it and some coffee cups on the hood of her truck and went back to counting.

None of them spoke to her beyond "Morning." They just poured coffee and started their own count.

The buffalo stood or lay on the dewy grass. They weren't agitated like they'd been yesterday, which made counting easy. The day was already hot.

The heat and Buffy's movement eased the ache in her muscles more than the shower and the aspirin. They had ten sturdy yards close around the ranch yard, and they'd divided the herd up so the number was manageable.

Buffy marked the number in the tally book, counting each pen until she got the same number twice. She was done and adding up the totals on her pocket calculator when Wyatt joined her. They compared numbers.

Wolf walked over. "We just had a good count a few weeks ago, when all the spring calving was done. They're all here."

Buffy stretched her back, and a mild groan of pain escaped.

Wyatt ran his knuckles up and down Buffy's spine. She appreciated the gesture. Too bad it was coming from a man who wished her buffalo had all died.

One of the new hands Leonard had sent came tearing into the yard in a pickup and jumped out of his cab. He hit the ground running. "We've got trouble on the west fence."

Buffy stepped past Wyatt and Wolf. "What trouble?"

"We've been putting this down as an accident—the lightning spooked the herd, and they stampeded through the fence. I've just had a closer look, and that fence was cut."

Wyatt stepped up beside her. "Deliberately cut? Someone let these buffalo loose?"

"And stampeded them, I'm guessing. It looks like fireworks were set off, aimed right at them. We found shredded Roman candles and other trash. There are tire tracks all over out there, and I found this."

It was a mirror from the side of a car. The word SUBARU was painted on the base.

"Where'd you find it?" Wyatt took the mirror. He plucked some long hairs off. Buffalo hair.

"It was in the Commons, inside the yard. There were no other tracks."

"So someone driving this rig"—Wyatt waved the mirror—"did this? It doesn't make sense. No one's this stupid."

Buffy took the mirror and turned it over in her hands. "Someone is."

Wyatt leaned down until his nose almost touched her. He said through clenched teeth, "So now I have to deal with vandalism? Which means this could happen again?"

"The fireworks sound like the work of kids. We'll beef up security on the fence and worry about who did it when we've cleaned up the mess from the stampede. For now, just let it go." She turned away.

Wyatt caught her arm and turned her back.

"Please, Wyatt. Not now. We have the rest of our lives to argue."

Wyatt was suddenly not breathing fire. His eyes were still hot on her, but it was a different kind of heat.

Wolf said, "C'mon, Seth, we've got a fence to fix."

Buffy and Wyatt stared at each other.

Finally Wyatt said, "Do we?"

"Do we what?" She couldn't remember her name, let alone understand the question.

"Do we have the rest of our lives to argue?" His hand relaxed on her arm, but he didn't let her go.

She could have pulled free, but she didn't.

"Wyatt, I didn't know you were here."

Buffy's eyes fell closed at the sound of Jeanie's breathless pleasure. She wrenched her arm away from Wyatt. "Maybe she'll make you some breakfast. Oh, wait, she might break a nail."

Jeanie was hurrying toward them, coming out to the buffalo pens for the first time since they'd moved. "Why don't you come in and have coffee with me?"

Wyatt looked away from Buffy only after Jeanie stepped between them.

"Hi, Wyatt." Jeanie ran a finger down the snapped front of his blue denim shirt.

Buffy refused to give in to her urge to protect the big lummox.

Jeanie latched onto his arm with her well-polished claws.

Buffy pulled her work gloves from behind her belt buckle and began jerking them on. "Enjoy your visit. Some of us have work to do."

Chapter 10

Buffy wondered how long Wyatt had stayed having coffee...or whatever... with Jeanie.

Buffy knew what she was doing around buffalo. It was only with people that she was a complete moron. She walked into the kitchen to find Jeanie fiddling with rabbit ears on their little TV.

With a disgruntled glance over her shoulder, Jeanie said, "I can't get anything."

"What's that you're watching now?" The television seemed to be working fine to Buffy.

"It's just regular TV. There's no cable out here, and there's a satellite out back, but Wolf said the last guy here disconnected it because he never watched TV."

"Jeanie, you haven't been bothering Wolf, have you?" Buffy imagined Wolf dodging buffalo horns while trying to appease Jeanie.

Jeanie turned the set off with a discontented *snap*. "I just asked him a few questions. I can't ask you. You're never around."

"I'll be able to help you once we clear up this mess with the stampede." Buffy went to the refrigerator, hoping for a sandwich. She saw the rest of the egg salad she'd made yesterday had been eaten. There weren't any more eggs, so an omelet was out. There were cold cuts and several packages of hamburger. There was Coke and enough junk food to live on for a week, if she didn't mind dying young.

Buffy clenched her jaw. She knew she should just eat a ham sandwich and leave. She didn't really think it was a sin or anything. It was just so much healthier to eat her way, and she couldn't help picturing the pig. What really burned her was that Jeanie had done this deliberately. Just more hostility.

"There's nothing wrong with the food in there. Eat it or go without." Jeanie turned her back with a little *humph* of annoyance and went back to the TV.

Buffy saw red. "I earn the money you spent on that food!"

Jeanie rounded on her. "I get child support checks from Michael."

"You never chip any of it in to supporting us. You don't even buy things for Sally!" Buffy started looking in the cupboards for something to eat, a can of tomato soup or anything. She found cookies, snack cakes, potato chips, sugary cereal. Row after row of food that would give her a sugar high for the next hour then leave her feeling sick all afternoon.

"If you think you're so much better of a mother than I am, why don't you just say so!"

"Well, I couldn't be much worse! I'm working twenty-hour days, and I still spend more quality time with her than you do!"

"You didn't even see her yesterday!"

"I was gone in the middle of the night, and I didn't get to bed until almost midnight. And I did *so* see her. I came in for lunch, which Wyatt's niece made. And Anna kept Sally while you went to town. And you were gone for hours."

"I met someone and got to talking." Jeanie's eyes shifted in a way that worried Buffy.

"Met someone? Who?"

"None of your business. Just someone who's sick of living in the wilderness like me. I wasn't gone that long."

What was Jeanie up to? A boyfriend? Buffy hoped not, because Jeanie was still married and she'd taken no steps to divorce Michael. "If Anna hadn't been here, I'd have spent the whole day with her. And today I've been up since five thirty working, and you don't even have lunch ready! Did you feed Sally yet today?"

Jeanie ignored the question. "So you haven't seen her today. Who do you think takes care of her while you're out and about?"

Buffy had a sick feeling that Sally fended for herself. Buffy finally spotted a jar of peanut butter. "Did you at least get some bread?"

Jeanie ignored her.

Buffy opened a few drawers until she found a loaf of plain white bread. No fiber. No whole grain. With a poorly concealed growl, she made herself a peanut butter sandwich and drank a glass of milk. At least it didn't take her long.

She ate three sandwiches before the gnawing in her stomach subsided. Then she sat and nursed her second glass of milk. She pictured Jeanie clinging to Wyatt's arm and felt a pang of guilt because she was afraid her temper had at least a little—oh all right, a *lot*—to do with that. Jeanie had taken Michael's desertion hard, and it had changed her. She was still healing, and Buffy had agreed to give her time.

Buffy drained the glass of milk then tried one more time. "I do think you should be in here with Sally. And I know she's a handful."

Jeanie didn't turn, but she said quietly, "It's all meaningless without Mike. I can't seem to care about anything. I know I don't help like I should, but. . ." Jeanie shrugged and turned around. Her eyes were bleak, like a child who had become separated from her parent in a shopping mall. She was lost and too scared to think.

It broke Buffy's heart just as it had been breaking her heart for the last year, but she'd babied her sister long enough. "You have to go back to the grocery store and get something so I can eat a quick meal. I need you to do that for me."

Buffy tugged her tally book out of her breast pocket. She quickly wrote a short list of food she wanted on hand. Jeanie's face took on a mulish look, but Buffy ignored it. "I expect this list to be filled today. And I shouldn't have to write the list. You know what I like to eat. You deliberately bought things I didn't like. It's time to grow up. If I earn the money, you take care of the house and the meals and Sally. That means have a hot dinner waiting tonight."

Buffy held her sister's eyes until Jeanie looked away. Buffy knew Jeanie was no match for her when it came to being strong-willed. But Buffy hated to browbeat her. "And take Sally with you to the store. I can't watch her today."

"I might stop by Wyatt's house," Jeanie said. "If I found someone to marry me, I'd be out from under your feet."

Buffy suppressed a pang of jealousy. "You're already married. You can't start a relationship with a man until you've finished things with Michael."

Jeanie had twice her skill with men. She'd always been able to pick and choose when they were teenagers, while Buffy had been the studious, buffalo-loving geek who was two years younger than her classmates. And Jeanie liked strong men, which Buffy didn't. If Jeanie wanted Wyatt, she could probably have him.

"If you decide you want Wyatt, you'd better be prepared to live out here for the rest of your life. There are no malls, no movies, no dress shops. And he'll expect you to take care of Sally and both of his boys and have three hot meals a day waiting for him. Plus you'll have to garden, tend his chickens, and probably ride herd on his cattle. So don't set your sights on the man unless you want the whole package. That's not fair to him or you."

Jeanie studied her shrewdly. Buffy suspected Jeanie was using what she knew about her little sister to read between the lines.

"I think I'll just go ahead and stop by anyway, but thanks for the advice."

Buffy slapped the short list on the table. "Suit yourself." She almost ran out of the house to keep herself from saying, "Leave Wyatt alone. He's mine," or "I love him," or something equally ridiculous. Except as she thought it, she knew it was true. She didn't know him that well, and what she did know, she mostly didn't like. But there was no denying the feeling in her heart. And there was no way she could ever act on that love.

She went hunting for the peace she always felt with her buffalo, even though they were domineering and stubborn and dangerous. As she walked toward the pens, it occurred to her that Wyatt was domineering and stubborn and more than a little bit dangerous. Good grief, she'd fallen in love with a buffalo!

She would bet anything the man was incapable of feeling any soft emotions at all.

—⁊⁊—

Wyatt sat on the front porch of his house and looked at the ruin of his ranch and wanted to cry.

The boys came outside and climbed into his lap, strangely subdued even considering the circumstances.

"Are you sure Gumby's going to be all right, Dad?" Cody asked, resting his head on Wyatt's chest.

Wyatt ran his hand through Cody's unruly dark curls, so like his own. "Yes, Wolf said he's okay. He's got a badly hurt leg, and we won't be able to ride him for a while, but we'll baby him, and he'll heal."

Wyatt was getting the biggest machine shed Morton made. A work crew was cleaning up the yard. The local Ford dealer was bringing out a brand-new car for Anna and a new truck for Wyatt. A planeload of veterinarians had come out to check Wyatt's herd and decide how to handle the threat of disease and pregnancy. An assessor was wandering around the ranch, studying the premises with his sharpened pencil and Mr. Leonard's checkbook.

Wyatt wanted to punch the guy in the face and suggest he pass that along to Leonard.

"It's going to be okay, Uncle Wyatt."

Wyatt glanced sideways at Anna as she emerged from the house. Even with the new car on the way, she still had that same flash of rage in her eyes. He knew he'd been complaining about the buffalo too loud for too long. Now this happened, and maybe Anna really did need money for pain and suffering. Maybe she needed counseling to get past this.

He reached out an arm to where she stood in the doorway and pulled her close to him and the boys. "I guess I'm in shock or something. I can't seem to think of anything to do but sit."

Some of the anger faded from her eyes. "The cleaning crew is almost done, and the new carpet is in. They said the new window will arrive later today and they'll have it installed by quitting time."

Wyatt thought about the stampede and the danger of having his boys in a room with an outside door, not that the little imps weren't fully capable of climbing out an upstairs window and escaping if they took the notion. "I've decided I'm going to move downstairs and let the boys have my room."

"Why, Dad? The front room is bigger. We want the biggest because we're two and you're only one."

"I've just decided is all. You'll be closer to the bathroom up there. My room's not the biggest room, but it's big enough. It'll work okay."

The boys, who argued about everything, accepted his decision. Colt finally stood up and said, "Let's go do it. I don't want to look anymore."

Wyatt said, "Sounds good to me. I'll bet if I ask that cleaning crew to help, they'll jump right to it. All these people seem real worried about me being upset. We can get that room moved in a few minutes."

They had the whole thing done in half an hour, and Wyatt got in the swing of being a human being again. Then Buffy's truck pulled into his driveway. He saw it from his upstairs window, where his room was now filled with toy guns and Matchbox cars. All his lethargy evaporated, and he thought of a dozen things he could go argue about. He jogged down the stairs and stormed out on the porch, eager for another round.

Then he saw Jeanie's blond hair, and his spirits sank even further into his boots, where they'd been all day. Ever since he'd quit arguing with Buffy this morning.

Great. Just what he needed. Perky.

He went to the door and yelled up the stairs, "Anna, boys! Get out here!"

He hadn't thought of needing a buffer zone until he'd recognized the leech.

Chapter 11

A week later, Wyatt stared at the huge steel machine shed going up on top of the memory of his grandpa's barn. It was a beautiful building. It was going to be of far more use to him than his old red barn.

Then he looked down at the check in his hand. A quarter of a million dollars. He wanted to crush it. Rip it to pieces. Burn it. Tell Leonard what he could do with his hush money. Instead, with bitter self-derision, he climbed into the new Ford 350 monster pickup truck Leonard had delivered from a dealer in Hot Springs and drove to Cold Creek to put the check in the bank. Then he came home in his one-ton black monster truck, with a four-door crew cab—every toy a man ever dreamed of.

Leonard had even paid for five years' worth of insurance on the overpriced beast. It was easily the most expensive rig in the county, and Wyatt felt like a fool driving it.

There was a brand-new Mustang in the yard at home for Anna. Leonard had offered a Porsche, but Anna's parents had refused to let their daughter drive such a powerful car. They'd agreed to let her accept the Mustang with a state-of-the-art CD player and in the color of her choice—red. Then Leonard's assessor offered the rest of the value of a Porsche in cash. Anna had started yelling and crying, so the guy promised her a hefty check for her pain and suffering and said he was sending it to her parents with or without her approval.

Wyatt didn't know what would be the point in refusing the money. Still, he was a sellout, and all the horsepower in the world under his mammoth Ford hood wouldn't change that.

Then, in the midst of his self-contempt, a wild hair had him turning toward the Buffalo Commons. He hadn't seen Buffy in a week, and that gave him a strange itch he didn't understand. He only knew seeing Buffy would scratch it.

—⁓—

He pulled into the Commons, and the first thing he saw was Buffy perched precariously on top of the corral timbers.

The buffalo were being let out of the sturdy pens for the first time since the stampede. They were wandering in their lazy way out into the pasture. Wyatt's gut twisted as he thought of all those big animals loose again.

Buffy swung around as he neared her. She looked straight at him with those warm brown eyes, in a way that made Wyatt wonder if she didn't have some special radar where he was concerned. Or maybe he just clomped when he walked.

She looked past him to his truck and arched her eyebrows. "Those're some mean wheels, Wyatt. Compliments of Mr. Leonard?"

"He didn't even ask me what kind. He just had the biggest one on the planet driven out to my place with the license and registration already in my name. I'm embarrassed to be seen driving it."

Buffy laughed. It was a deep, throaty laugh, and it was the first time he'd heard it, although she'd laughed more mildly at the boys' antics that first day. He knew if he started yelling, she'd certainly quit laughing.

Still, a man had to say what was on his mind. "Would you mind coming down off that fence?"

"I think I'll stay here. If I get down there, you'll tower over me, and I don't like that."

"Buffy," Wyatt barked, "get down now!"

She smiled at him then shrugged her shoulders. "Why not."

She swung her legs to Wyatt's side of the fence and jumped to the ground, landing with the grace of an Olympic gymnast. She dusted the seat of her pants and yelled over her shoulder, "I'll take the first watch, Wolf. We need men on that fence all night. Break it down to four two-hour shifts."

"Already done. You want to take the truck or a horse?"

"I'll drive my truck." Buffy turned back to Wyatt. "Let's go have a look at that hot rod you're driving." She began walking toward the truck, and Wyatt followed along reluctantly.

"Okay, we're out of earshot; what did you want to yell at me about?" Buffy asked.

"I didn't come over here to yell at you."

"Oh sure you did. I've missed it anyway. I'd have probably come over there and insulted your political party or gun owners or something precious to you for sure, just to get a fix."

"I did *not* come over here to yell. I just wanted to know what's being done about the lunatics who cut your fence."

Buffy shoved her hands into the back pockets of her blue jeans. "It's out of my hands. Mr. Leonard's people are looking into it."

"Have you called the police?"

Buffy shook her head. "Not since that first night. I left that to Mr. Leonard's people at his specific instructions."

"So the county sheriff hasn't even been out?" Wyatt got to the truck and opened the driver's side door for Buffy to look in.

Buffy stared at the rig. "Good grief, the seat is as high as my nose."

"Has he been out?" Wyatt demanded.

Buffy turned from the truck to face Wyatt. "He called one day. I referred him to the phone number Mr. Leonard gave me. I've never heard back."

He reluctantly admired her guts as she stonewalled him about something that was life and death. "So nothing is being done," Wyatt said flatly.

"I can't answer that. I don't know what's being done."

Wyatt leaned close to her. She was filthy dirty again and dripping with sweat. He rested his hands on her waist and hoisted her onto his seat.

She squeaked with surprise and steadied herself by grabbing his forearms.

He jerked his head. "Scoot over. I'll take you for a ride."

"I don't have time to go for a ride. You heard me tell Wolf I'd take the first watch."

He shoved her across the seat. "This won't take long, but I'd like some privacy."

"What for?" Buffy slid, and Wyatt scaled the truck.

"Because you're right after all." Wyatt twisted the key, and the rig roared instantly to life.

"About what?" Buffy clung to her door which left about an acre of space between them.

"I do want to yell at you." Wyatt jammed the truck into gear and laid a path of dust a half mile long as he tore out of the driveway.

Buffy had her fingers clasped on the door handle as Wyatt did his best to give her whiplash. He wondered if he might have scared her, but a glance at her expression told him she was impatient and annoyed but a long way from scared. Drat it.

"As long as we're not headed anywhere specific, let's drive out to the spot where the fence was cut. I want another look."

"Have you investigated at all? The police could be tracking down that Subaru. How many can there be in that shade of green?"

"The truth is, Wyatt, I think Mr. Leonard is trying to make this whole thing go away. I have gotten a few calls from the press. A couple of radio stations in Rapid City called and one in Pierre. They said they'd gotten a tip. I said," Buffy's voice went all Southern-belle fake, and she fluttered her eyelashes, " 'Why, whatever do you mean? We don't have any buffalo out.' "

Wyatt smiled at the phoniness.

"It was the truth, since we had them all back in when the calls came. They accepted my answer like it was what they expected to hear. Even though everyone around here knows about it, there wasn't a word about it in the local paper. Even if someone does go to the press about it now, there's not much to tell. It's all cleaned up."

"Leonard is good." Wyatt quit driving like a maniac and steered along the fence line, passing the stretched-out line of ambling buffalo. "He never told me the money was on the condition I not talk. He knew I'd refuse. But he also made the settlement so generous that it's embarrassing. I mean, here I am, driving this dumb truck. How much is anyone going to listen if I claim I've been hurt?"

"Is the new machine shed going up?" Buffy relaxed her death grip on the door handle and turned to him.

"Yes, and it's beautiful. It's even going to have a heated office."

They drove in silence that was broken by the deep-throated roar of Wyatt's high-powered truck engine. Wyatt finally reached the far end of the pasture and slowed as he drove along the reinforced fence.

"Stop here!" Buffy said suddenly. "I can still see the tracks. I want to have a closer look."

Wyatt pulled his truck to a stop and climbed out.

Buffy had to get out of her seat like she was riding a slippery slide. Even with the running board, it was a long way down.

Buffy started toward the tracks, and Wyatt fell in beside her. She went down on one knee beside a particularly deep rut. "I don't know anything about tire marks, but these are clear enough. Someone should take a picture of it or a molding. It could be used to double-check that this is the same car that lost the side mirror. We don't know how many people were in on this."

Wyatt looked up from the tire marks and studied the landscape around them. He pointed toward a rise. "If anyone was scouting your property, they'd watch from up there. And there's an underground spring that makes that whole hillside soft. There might be more tracks."

Buffy rose. "Surely some of Leonard's people have looked into it."

"It doesn't matter if they have or not." Wyatt went back to his truck. "That hill doesn't belong to Mr. Leonard. It's on Shaw land. And if they're trespassing on my land to scout an attack on the Buffalo Commons, then they don't just have a problem with Leonard. They've got a problem with me."

Buffy looked away from the hill as she walked beside him to the truck. "And having a problem with a rancher is worse than having a problem with a multibillionaire?"

Wyatt narrowed his eyes as he looked at her. "What do you think?"

"I think I'm more interested in getting to the bottom of this than Leonard is. I think I'd like to see what's on top of that hill."

Wyatt jerked his head in a nod of approval. He swung up to the seat as she got in her side. He slammed the door. "The minute this is over, I'm trading this stupid thing in for two reasonable trucks."

"Sounds good."

Wyatt grinned. He'd been right to come and see Buffy. He hadn't felt this good in. . .six and a half days. He headed up the gentle slope of the highest hill around.

Buffy said, "Will you look at that?"

Wyatt stopped his truck.

Buffy jerked open her door and rushed over to the obvious campsite. It wasn't just a couple of tire tracks. The ground was torn up until there was hardly any grass. Buffy felt her temper explode. "Leonard's men didn't even look around! No one could miss this!"

Buffy crouched by the fire and reached for a scrap of paper that was burned around the edges. She pulled her hand back. "Wyatt!"

He was beside her instantly. "What?"

"These ashes are still hot!"

Wyatt crouched beside her and held his hand close to the campfire. "They didn't leave after the stampede. They're still around."

Buffy grabbed his arm. "They're not done. They're planning another attack!"

Wyatt studied the horizon in all directions.

"So where do you hide in these hills?" Buffy pulled the scrap of paper out of the fire. She stared at it, and her gut twisted. "My name?"

Wyatt took the paper. "It doesn't mean anything. They probably just know you run the place."

Buffy leaned closer and tried to figure out why her name had given her such a jolt. Then she got it. "My name. . .in Jeanie's handwriting."

Wyatt looked at Buffy, and she saw the compassion in his eyes. "She might not know what they're really up to. Maybe she just talked to someone, gave them information without realizing what they'd use it for."

But Buffy had seen Jeanie's anger. "I haven't told you all that's gone on at the Commons this week."

"Like what?" Wyatt asked, watching her closely.

Buffy ran one hand through her hair. "Jeanie's been going to town a lot. Leaving Sally with me and spending late afternoons and evenings in Cold Creek. Only I checked my truck, and she's piling up too many miles. I'd decided she had a boyfriend somewhere, but. . ."

Wyatt crumpled the scrap of paper in his fist. "She couldn't be involved. Not after she came to my place. She saw the burned-out shells of my truck and Anna's car. She saw the rubble where my barn used to be."

"Whether Jeanie's in it or not, someone is definitely planning something," Buffy snapped. "If they've got another attack planned and Jeanie knows about it, I'm going to find out. Let's go back to the Commons." She stood and turned to the truck.

"Wait," Wyatt said, looking down the hill away from the Commons. "I think I know where they might be."

Buffy caught his arm and pulled. "We've got to get back. I still have time to round the buffalo up and put them back in the pens. Whoever did this has obviously been watching the Commons. They might plan on striking as soon as the buff are loose. That's now!"

"There's a deserted house just off the edge of my property. It's not that far from here as the crow flies. These tracks even head in that direction."

"It's getting dark. If we miss them, we won't be in time to stop the attack."

"Then we'd better hurry." Wyatt strong-armed her into the truck.

Buffy let herself be manhandled. They disagreed on how to handle it, but they both wanted to act. "Do you have a CB in this carnival ride?"

Wyatt said grimly, "Nope. Everything else in the universe but."

Buffy said, "Let's get over to that house and find out if they're there. If they're not, I need to get back to the Commons and get those buffalo back in the pens."

Wyatt bounced his truck down the hill. It was getting dark, and he managed to hit every rut and rock. He glanced at Buffy. "What's the point in having a heavy-duty pickup if you don't abuse it?"

Buffy fastened her seat belt after her head hit the roof. "Slow down. I want to get there in one piece."

Wyatt kept pushing, and they rounded the last hillock to see the outline of a mansion in the encroaching dusk.

"Good grief, who built that?"

"We call it the Barrett Place. The old folks are dead and gone, and their kids moved to the city. My dad bought the land, but the Barrett family kept the house and a few acres around it for some reason. Sentimental, I guess. It's falling in."

"It's spectacular." The house was three stories, a Victorian dream house full of elaborate rooflines and gingerbread accents.

Wyatt drove around to a shed. Empty. "Look at the tracks. They're definitely using this place." He pulled up to the house, got out, and strode to the back door, which hung on one hinge. Wyatt swung the door open, and it fell flat on the floor.

"There's no one here." Buffy peeked over his shoulder. "Let's go. I've got to get back to the Commons. And this time, I'm going to handle this without calling Leonard."

They ran for the truck, and Wyatt drove like a madman.

Buffy rubbed a hand over her face and tried to deny the possibility that her sister had sold her out to a stranger who offered her a strong shoulder.

Chapter 12

Here he comes. The moron didn't even turn his headlights off until just a minute ago." Wolf wired the last pen shut on the secured buffalo. He sent the men up and down the length of the pens to stop the oncoming car.

"What if he doesn't stop?" Buffy sat in Wyatt's megatruck, facing the intruders.

"He'll stop." Wyatt nodded to Wolf and began driving forward slowly, his lights off, his motor running as slowly as possible so they could pick up any night sounds. "He's a coward, remember? As soon as he sees that there's someone around, he'll try to hightail it. But we're not letting him out of here."

Buffy clutched Wyatt's strong arm, surprised at how good it felt to have someone to depend on. "Thanks for getting Anna and the boys over here. I can't believe Jeanie left Sally asleep alone in the house."

Wyatt looked at her, his hazel eyes flashing in the dashboard lights. "Let's stop here and wait for them. There's no sense going out any farther. They might get past us in the dark." Wyatt stopped the truck. When he switched off the motor, the sound of an approaching vehicle was audible. "Tell me what she said in her note again."

"She said she's leaving for good and not to hunt for her. The note gives me the right to adopt Sally. I know it's not a legal document, but it still shows her state of mind, that she wants to be done with both of us. How can she abandon her own child? Wyatt, she wasn't always like this. It's just that Michael, her husband, told her every move to make, and when he left her, she just lost her anchor."

"Was he abusive?"

Buffy was startled by the question. "I've never considered that he was. If you ask Jeanie, she'll tell you they were blissfully happy."

"A lot of domineering men use their fists to enforce the rules. And a lot of women accept it."

"My dad was a tyrant, but he just yelled all the time and told every one of us how to act."

Wyatt laid his hand on her shoulder. "Let me guess. Military? An army drill sergeant?"

"Actually he was an accountant. I think he was obsessed with making things balance at work, and that need for control just got landed right on our heads."

"And your mom put up with it?"

Buffy couldn't help but enjoy the weight of Wyatt's hand on her shoulder. She shifted a little to get closer. "My mom always blamed herself if he yelled. Jeanie thought he was wonderful, too. I was the troublemaker. I was always defying him, and I always ended up being sent to my room. I've avoided men like him." She didn't add, "and you," but she thought it.

"So you have an accountant phobia?" Wyatt asked lightly.

That surprised a laugh out of her. "You gotta watch those CPAs."

Wyatt dragged her the last four feet across the expanse of truck seat. "Good thing I was a failure at algebra."

She didn't see his head lowering in the dark, but she felt it. She felt him. His warmth and strength. The earthy smell of hard work that was a part of him. His hands were strong and steady. His lips firm and yet gentle at the same time. She didn't feel in danger. She felt protected. And that was the greatest danger of all.

She tried to push him away and ended up with her arms around his neck. She needed to tell him to stop but instead let the kiss deepen.

Wyatt set her firmly away. "They're coming. Get ready."

Who was coming? Get ready for what? Then she heard the motor only a few yards ahead of them and remembered why they were out here.

Wyatt gunned his truck to life and switched on his headlights.

The car coming toward them stopped.

Wyatt swung his truck door open and slid to the ground.

Just as he landed, the oncoming car roared toward them. The door Wyatt had left open slammed closed brutally then tore away. The car scraped the whole driver's side of the truck. The ugly sound of metal on metal twisted Buffy's stomach. The monster truck shook but didn't move while the smaller vehicle bounced off and drove right over Wyatt.

As quickly as it had struck, the smaller car was gone, driving for the ranch yard and the herd.

"Wyatt!" Buffy scrambled to the driver's side of the rig, ready to leap out the gaping opening. She came nose to nose with Wyatt, who was rolling out from under the truck.

Wyatt shoved her across the seat. "Are you all right?"

"I'm fine."

He threw his truck into gear and spun it around in a sickening U-turn. Wind blew in from the missing door as he fumbled for the CB, which he'd scrounged from the Commons. "They're coming!"

Wolf's voice, metallic through the radio, shouted, "I heard the crash. Are you both all right?"

"Yes, but they've destroyed another truck! He slammed right into me. He's crazy. Did the sheriff ever get there?"

"He's here. He brought half the county with him. Plenty of people mad about this mess."

"I don't want any of my neighbors hurt," Wyatt said grimly. "The driver of that car is acting like this is a suicide mission. Get everybody out of the line of fire!"

"We're ready for 'em," Wolf said.

"I'm coming right behind. I'll try and slow them down. Don't let anyone get trigger happy while we're out here."

Then the Subaru's brake lights lit up. Wyatt was closing in fast. Wyatt's new truck was far better suited to the terrain than the battered Outback.

Wyatt said, "Buckle up." He buckled his own seat belt as Buffy quickly fastened hers. Wyatt hit the brakes to slow down then rammed the back end of the Subaru. It spun sideways, and the two vehicles hit broadside, driver's sides together.

With Wyatt's door ripped away, Buffy could see into the smaller rig. She saw rage in the eyes of a young man. His car slid up on two wheels, and as if it were in slow motion, it rolled onto its side, still sliding.

Wyatt leaped from his truck. Six pairs of headlights were coming toward them from the Commons but were still a ways off.

Buffy jumped down. "Be careful."

Wyatt ran around to the other side of the car and leaned over the windshield to look inside. A plume of smoke curled up from the engine.

"Wyatt, it's on fire!"

"Get back!" Wyatt shouted.

Buffy hoped he wasn't talking to her, because no way was she leaving him. She ran around to his side and heard the screams of fear and pain coming from inside the car. Wyatt kicked the windshield out; then he kicked again to make a bigger hole and slithered into the burning vehicle on his belly.

Wolf ran up beside Buffy just as she dropped on her knees to climb in after Wyatt. He caught her around the waist and pulled her away.

Fighting the grip, she screamed, "No, I'm going after Wyatt!"

"Keep out of his way." Wolf shook her. "There's not room for two of you inside there."

Wyatt came out backward, dragging a young man with short, dark hair. The man clung to a shotgun, but Wyatt disarmed him quickly.

"Jeanie, she's in there." Blood dripped from the man's forehead as he collapsed beside the burning car. "She got thrown into the back. There are bottles of gas in there. I was going to torch the fence and the barns. They're going to blow."

Buffy lunged for the shattered window.

Wyatt caught her around the waist, and for a second, their eyes met. In that look was everything—right down to Wyatt's soul—that made him the man he was. The man she loved. He spun her away from the car and thrust her into someone else's strong arms.

Wolf's.

Then Wyatt turned back to the car.

"Stop him!"

Wolf had his arm around her like a steel band. He turned and said, "You hold her back. I'm going to help Wyatt."

Buffy felt herself handed off again. She fought against the grip as she saw Wyatt's legs vanish into the car. He needed to climb all the way to the back. He couldn't get in and drag an injured passenger out before the car exploded. She wrenched against the man, who she now saw wore a sheriff's badge.

He shouted over the crackling of the flames, "You can't help him except to stay out of the way!"

Buffy rounded on him, still clamped against his body. He dragged her away from the car as the flames began to get too hot. She twisted her head around.

Wolf scrambled, shouted, ducking past the flames, peering into the interior of the car.

Buffy suddenly knew Wyatt was out of time. She heard the whine of something under pressure, getting ready to blow. She couldn't fight the man who restrained her any more than she could fight Wyatt or Wolf or her father. So she used her wiles. She relaxed, smiling sweetly at the big lummox who was holding her. "All right, Sheriff. I panicked there for a second, but I'm better now." She heard the shrill whine of that building pressure, but she remained calm.

The sheriff said in a patronizing voice, "I understand. Too much excitement can get a little lady all worked up."

"You're so right. But I'm okay now."

More cars pulled up.

The sheriff let her go.

She spun around and charged for the back of the Subaru. She got around to the rear of the car just as whatever was whining began screaming under the pressure.

Flames shot up higher than Wolf's head at the front of the car, and he staggered backward into the sheriff, who'd been coming after Buffy. The crackling flames drowned out their shouting.

She reached for the door latch on the back, but it burned her fingers. She dropped to the ground and kicked in the back window just as Wolf got to her side.

Wyatt was backed against the window, facing a wall of flames.

Buffy grabbed him by the back of his shirt and dragged him out of the fire. Wyatt's pant legs were on fire, and he had Jeanie in his arms.

Wolf grabbed Jeanie, whose jacket was ablaze.

Buffy and Wolf pulled them clear.

Buffy threw herself at Wyatt's feet. Beating at the flames with her bare hands, she screamed Wyatt's name.

Wyatt coughed, nearly choking.

Wolf rolled Jeanie, unconscious, away from the fire, ripped off her jacket, and scooped dirt onto her clothes.

Wyatt yelled, "It's gonna blow. That car is full of gas cans!"

Buffy caught Wyatt around the middle and hoisted him to his feet. Then the two of them staggered away as Wolf dragged Jeanie to safety.

The gas erupted. The force of the explosion knocked everyone to the ground. Fire rained down. Everyone fought a short, brutal battle against the flames.

The flames climbed into the starlit night, but the burning cinders quit falling.

Wyatt sagged backward onto the ground.

Wolf turned to check on Jeanie.

"How bad is it?" Buffy demanded. She grabbed the bottom hem of Wyatt's blackened denim jeans and ripped them up to his knees. Heavy boots had protected him.

"I'm fine. I'm not burned." Wyatt got wearily to his feet.

She turned and dropped to her knees beside Jeanie. "Is she badly burned?"

"No." Wolf had two fingers on Jeanie's throat, checking for a pulse. "Probably inhaled too much smoke. She's breathing. Her pulse is strong. We called the ambulance when Wyatt first said you'd been hit. They'll be here pretty soon."

Buffy felt the first tears burn her eyes. She stood and threw herself into Wyatt's arms.

He stumbled backward, but he steadied himself and caught on to what she was doing right away. He kissed her. Right there in front of the blazing Subaru, the brainless kid who had made this mess, and every man and buffalo in Custer County, South Dakota.

The county men weren't so busy watching the fire that they couldn't give them a round of applause.

Chapter 13

Jeanie was awake before the ambulance came. She refused to look at Buffy and told her to stay away from the hospital. The county sheriff took the young man into custody and told Jeanie she would be arrested when she left the hospital.

Wyatt distracted Buffy from her anger and fear for Jeanie by asking her to marry him. This Saturday.

He wanted a wedding smaller than small. The boys and Sally and maybe Wolf, if he wasn't busy with the buffalo. They had things settled before they pulled into the yard at the Commons.

Wolf came striding over to see them.

Buffy jumped down from the truck, eager to tell Wolf they'd set a date. Before she could speak, in the bright yard light, she saw Wolf's furious anger.

"What is it?" Wyatt said before she could.

Wyatt came up beside Buffy and put his arm around her, as if he knew whatever was coming might require his support.

"We're fired!"

"We're. . .you and me?" Buffy asked.

"I got the word before we went out to catch the vandals, but I couldn't tell you while we were dealing with that mess. All of us. Seth, the men riding the fence, all the staff. We've just gotten our two weeks' notice. Leonard didn't even have the class to call himself. He had one of his aides do it."

"Then maybe it isn't right. He can't just fire everybody. Someone's got to ride herd on—"

"The Buffalo Commons is history. The stock market did one of its dives, and Leonard is all of a sudden not such a rich man. This is one of the toys he's selling."

"But where will they go? No one wants a thousand head of buffalo. There's no one who can afford to keep them. The national parks are already fighting an overgrazing problem."

"He's already taken care of the problem. His aide told me all about it." Wolf turned to look at the buffalo pens. His fists were clenched, and Buffy thought he was imagining getting his hands on Leonard.

"How can he have? No one will buy them. He can't have solved the problem."

"Sure, someone will buy them, Buffy," Wolf said with vicious sarcasm. "Dog food companies. Leonard's gofer said he is calling them today. They'll buy them for less than the cost of trucking them to their plant. They'll start picking them up a semi load at a time in a couple of days, and that's it. Problem solved."

Buffy staggered backward. "That's not possible. He can't do that. These buffalo are—"

Wyatt caught her as her knees gave out.

"They're not an endangered species," Wolf cut in. "They're privately owned, and Leonard can do what he wants with them."

"But the press will eat him alive," Wyatt said.

Buffy said, "That's right! This would be a public relations nightmare."

"He's going broke, Buffy. He can't afford this place anymore. He's putting the land for sale and washing his hands of the whole thing. He doesn't care about the public relations when he's fighting for his financial life."

Wyatt asked, "Do you have his number?"

Wolf turned slowly back from the pens at the tone in Wyatt's voice. "Sure. There was a time, when we were just starting this, I thought of the man as a friend."

"You have Louis Leonard's private number?" Buffy asked incredulously.

Wolf rattled off the number, and Wyatt grabbed his tally book and jotted it down. Wolf asked, "What are you thinking? Have you got an idea that could save this place?"

"I'm thinking there's a huge piece of land for sale, and I'm all of a sudden a rich man. I think Mr. Leonard and I could do some business."

"You'd sell us out like that, Shaw?" Wolf said angrily. "I wouldn't have given you the number if I'd known that!"

"Wyatt," Buffy said, "you can't do this. You can't profit by this disaster."

"Buffy, I know how much you love these buffalo." Wyatt tried to sound kind, but Buffy heard a domineering, patronizing male running roughshod over her. "I understand you—"

"You don't understand anything!" She felt her temper ignite, and she knew she should walk away. She loved Wyatt, but right now, she might say something she'd regret.

Then he patted her on the shoulder like she was a fussy child.

Her temper blew. "You can't take away the thing I love most in the world and expect to have a future with me!"

Wyatt's expression hardened. "I thought I was the thing you loved most in the world."

"Wyatt, don't do this," Wolf said. "We've been friends, but—"

"You, too, Wolf?" Wyatt sounded almost hurt. With cold sarcasm, he said, "And here I thought you might be willing to work with me once the Commons was gone."

"As your hired man, Wyatt?" Wolf sneered. "I don't need a job so bad I'd work with a traitor."

Wyatt's jaw clenched until his mouth was one angry straight line. "I think you should know me a little better than that, Wolf. I think, after all these years, you should trust me."

Buffy tried to calm down. "Wyatt, if we can keep anyone from buying the ranch, maybe Leonard will at least wait to sell the buffalo until we can find a buyer. There are a lot of small animal parks who would buy them five or ten at a time. But if you step in with an offer, he'll grab it and send in the semis."

"And you, Buffy"—Wyatt turned on her—"you have told me a dozen times, a hundred times, that you love buffalo. I respect that, but I thought you loved me, too. I would have hoped to at least be in a tie with them. I would have hoped maybe Sally might rank above them, even if I didn't. I know how independent and strong you are, and those are things I love about you."

Buffy could hear Wyatt's temper building until it reached a flash point. "So now it comes down to this—the buffalo or trusting the man you said you loved. Why am I so surprised you picked the buffalo? How could I have ever fooled myself into believing you'd do it any other way?"

Wyatt tugged his Stetson down until it nearly covered his eyes and took a long, hard look at the phone number in his hand. "Enjoy Yellowstone. I've got a phone call to make." He turned and moved away with his usual fluid grace.

Buffy reached her hand out, knowing her only chance for love was walking away. She had seen his hurt, but as usual, he reacted with anger. He was going home to destroy her dreams.

Wolf fumed beside her, the buffalo snuffled in the darkness, and Wyatt drove out of the yard in his battered black truck without spinning a wheel or throwing up a single piece of gravel. Cold. Controlled. Domineering.

Everything she didn't want, wrapped up in the man of her dreams.

Chapter 14

Leonard called the next morning and woke Buffy up.

She was still trying to get the phone centered on her ear when Leonard said, "I can't get ahold of Wolf, so you pass the word on. I've sold the place to Wyatt Shaw."

"No!"

"He bought the buffalo, too," Leonard announced with his usual high energy.

Her confused heart mended a bit. "Mr. Leonard, you sold the buffalo to Wyatt? Why did he want—"

"I gave them to him. The dog food company wasn't going to pay much. By the time I paid for trucking, it was going to be a wash. As Wyatt pointed out, this way is better PR, and it's chump change considering my financial situation. Getting out from under the tax burden is worth it. He wants all of you to stay on and work at the Commons, but he's going to run it his way. He said you're headed to Yellowstone, so he'll hire someone new or just leave Wolf in charge. He doesn't care much about college degrees."

Buffy stammered, "Wyatt doesn't like buffalo. He'd never—"

"The sale is final. I've got a full morning. Take it up with your new boss." The phone clicked in her ear.

Buffy stared at the receiver for a few blank seconds as her sleep-fogged brain tried to make sense of the abrupt call. She hung up in a daze. Then it all added up. With a squeal of delight, she threw the covers back, jumped into her clothes, and ran outside.

Wolf was just coming out of his trailer. "Did you hear?"

Buffy ran up to him, smiling. "That Wyatt bought the ranch and wants to run the Commons? Yes, Leonard called me. He called you, too?"

"No." Wolf jerked his thumb at his trailer. "I just got off the phone with Wyatt. He hired me to manage the Commons. Although he said the Commons was a stupid name that insulted every rancher in the state and he was renaming it the S Bar B Ranch."

"What? He hired you?" Buffy's stomach sank as she remembered Leonard talking about her going to Yellowstone. Wyatt was already planning his life without her. "To do my job?"

"Yep, well, sort of. We're going to run things different. We're going to raise

112

buffalo for. . ." Wolf stopped. His face took on a look that almost seemed like pity. "For meat."

"Meat?" Buffy said, aghast.

Wolf squared his shoulders and looked her in the eye. "Wyatt and I talked about it awhile back. He thinks. . .well, I think. . .we can make this ranch pay. Make buffalo into a real product that people will pay well for. I know I can get the business into the black, especially since Leonard already made all the big investments—in fence and buildings. That's what I've always wanted, and Wyatt wants to do it my way."

"Your way?" Buffy began pulling herself together. The shocks of last night. Being fired by Leonard. Being dumped by Wyatt. The fate of her beautiful buffalo herd. After she'd gotten her temper under control, she'd cried herself to sleep. Then to wake up this morning and have it all fixed. The buffalo would live. Wyatt would hire her back, and if he wanted to hire her, then he wanted her to stay. But now he was going to turn her buffalo into a food crop. Buffy got a stranglehold on her feelings and packed them into a tight little box and shoved that box into the deepest corner of her heart to be dealt with later—or better yet, forgotten altogether.

"There will be a place for you here, Buffy. If you want it. But you know the only possible way for buffalo to ever really prosper in this world is if they pay. No one can afford to do what Leonard was doing for long. We can't rely on the whims of a rich landlord to tell us if we can exist. Buffalo can either sustain themselves, or they can't. Wyatt and I are going to find out."

"So capitalism is what it's all about?" Buffy said bitterly.

Wolf looked at her coolly as if taking her measure. She didn't like it that she seemed to be coming up short. "You need to talk to Wyatt about this. I think this is a better idea than anything Leonard ever did. You can get behind this. You can be a part of this. If it works and buffalo meat really catches on, we could create a real buffalo commons. Buffalo are better suited to this land than cattle, and I think ranchers might switch to buffalo if they could see a business in it."

"I don't see where I fit into this scheme. I won't be part of turning these majestic animals into food. I'd just as soon see them go to the dog food factory. I think I'll just follow the plan I settled on last night and head for Wyoming. I can vacation in Yellowstone until it's time for my job to start."

"What about your doctoral dissertation? Isn't it based on research you're doing here?"

"It's not a research project that works if the buffalo get eaten!"

"We won't start eating them for another couple of months," Wolf said sarcastically. "I thought that job in Yellowstone only went to someone with a doctorate. I thought the preliminary work on the dissertation is what got you the job. They might have understood if Leonard pulled the rug out from under you, but are you sure it will still be there if you walk out?"

Buffy held his gaze. Then she looked beyond him at her buffalo, and her heart turned over to think of them butchered for the dinner table.

Wolf must have read her mind. "I'm a full-blooded Sioux. I come from a line of people who survived eating buffalo. My people believed buffalo served a noble purpose by giving their lives for us. We respected and even revered them for that. But we still ate them. It was survival. It was life. And you need to get your head out of the clouds and figure that out."

Wolf held her gaze with his black eyes. He waited, but Buffy didn't know for what, unless it was for her to give up everything she believed.

"I'm disappointed in you, girl. You're going to give up on the thing that could really save buffalo in this country. *That* is your dream. You're going to give up on a man who loves you. *That* is your future. I think you'll figure that all out someday. But by then, it'll be too late. Instead of being part of something, you'll be a spectator, a stuffed shirt intellectual sniffing at capitalism from some tenured position on a college campus."

His words cut her all the way to her heart. "I—I thought you liked me. I thought you respected me."

"I do like you, girl. I like you just fine. But respect? Well, now that's another thing altogether."

"And in order to earn your respect, I have to give up on what I believe is right and wrong? That's something you would respect?"

"I'm not asking you to do anything wrong, Buffy. You're an idealist, and that's a wonderful thing. But idealism is something you need to save for God. For your faith. When it comes to ranching, being a realist is as simple as life and death. Most people get around to being one after awhile. It's called growing up, and it's high time you did it. Until you do," Wolf's tone softened to kindness, "your life is going to be an empty one."

Buffy almost caved. She almost asked him to tell her more about how he wanted to make a true buffalo commons. But stubbornness settled over her heart.

Wolf must have sensed it, because without another word, he headed for his truck and drove away.

—⁓—

Yellowstone didn't want her.

The doctorate was a crucial piece of the puzzle they were putting together to research their herd. They needed her credentials. They didn't say she couldn't come. They said, "Finish the research. Write the dissertation."

"Aunt Buffy, take me out to look at the buffalo." Sally ran to the window a hundred times a day, but Buffy wouldn't let her go out.

Jeanie had been released from the hospital. The county attorney recommended probation, and both agreed to it. Jarvis, new to the area, had a history of psychological problems, and hostile and friendless, he'd let the local anger at the buffalo goad him into his first act of vandalism, cutting the fence and throwing the firecrackers. He hadn't meant it as anything more than a vicious prank. Then he'd met Jeanie, and the two of them had found soul mates in their resentment and talked each other into making a bigger strike at the herd.

His parents promised the court they'd get their troubled son into counseling, and they'd left the area. Jeanie had signed adoption papers for Sally, and she'd left without saying good-bye to anyone. Only after she was gone did Buffy realize that Jeanie had cleaned out her bank account.

Sally missed her mother, and Buffy would have done almost anything to make Sally happy. But not visiting the buffalo. She couldn't bear to see her big friends fattened for the grill. She saw Wyatt's truck come in and out several times a day, and why not? It was his ranch. He came to the door once and knocked, but she didn't answer.

She admitted after only a few hours that she had to stay and finish her project, but doing it made her sick. Three days had gone by, and still she couldn't go crawling to Wyatt, begging him for a job.

Long after Sally was asleep on the third day since she'd heard about Wyatt buying the Buffalo Commons, Buffy stared out the window and saw in the starlight that the herd had wandered close to the house. She let the peace buffalo always brought to her lure her to the corral. She sat on the top rung of the fence and stared.

"They're beautiful, aren't they?"

Buffy turned and saw Wyatt. "Where's your truck?" A stupid question but the first thing that came out of her mouth.

"Leonard bought me a new one. Yellow. It looks like a five-ton canary. I drove over here on field roads, inspecting the fence line. I left it behind Wolf's trailer so no one would see me and laugh."

"I thought Leonard was broke." Buffy frowned.

"I don't think broke means the same thing to billionaires as it does to us." Wyatt climbed the fence beside her and swung his legs around so he faced the herd. He didn't talk, and the silence, at first awkward, grew more companionable as the tranquility of the buffalo soaked into her soul.

"What do they say to you, Buffalo Gal? What was it that drew you to them to begin with?"

It was a question she'd been asked before, but she'd never told anyone the truth. "They're strong."

"That's it? Strong? Lots of animals are strong. Elephants, rhinos, Angus bulls."

Buffy smiled. "I was twelve years old, and I was on a field trip with my school. I'd had a fight with my father the night before over nothing and everything. He wanted to tell me every breath I could take. I talked on the phone too much. I chewed gum. Half my skirts were too short, and half were too long. My shirts were all either too baggy or too tight. If I wore makeup, I was loose. If I left it off, I was ugly. It had nothing to do with me, and I know that now."

"How could it have nothing to do with you?"

"He was a man who liked to hurt people. Jeanie did everything he wanted as quickly as she could. I defied him every chance I got. Nothing either of us or our mother did made him stop yelling."

"I'm sorry he was unkind to you."

Buffy smiled. "Another apology."

"Just as useless as all the rest."

"Anyway, I was grounded for the thousandth time. He'd taken my lunch money away from me and made Mom send me a peanut butter sandwich for lunch, which to a twelve-year-old girl, at least to me, was humiliating. All the other kids had money, and the field trip included a stop at McDonald's. He'd banned me from talking on the phone for a month—no big deal as I didn't have any friends. But the man had a knack for cutting me to my heart. He made me feel ugly, but, well, he couldn't say I was stupid, not with my grades. He used that on Jeanie and Mom. He made me feel like a freak who was completely alone in the world."

Buffy heard Wyatt grinding his teeth and looked at his protective anger. "Stop that. You don't have to come charging to my rescue all the time."

Wyatt forced his shoulders to relax. Tears stung her eyes as she watched him try and respect her independence.

"Didn't you have any friends?" he asked.

Buffy turned from Wyatt to watch the buffalo. "Not really. I was two years younger than my classmates, in the same grade as Jeanie, which made her feel stupid, which she isn't. But because she was really popular, her hostility rubbed off on the other kids."

"So where does the buffalo come in?"

"We went to a natural history museum, and I wandered away from the group to bask in self-pity. I found an Animals of the Prairie Exhibit."

"And there was the buffalo," Wyatt said, nodding.

"A lot of the animals had little groups. You know. A doe, a buck, and a fawn. A wolf and his mate and their pups. There was even an opossum with its babies hanging from its tail. It was all so perfect, all these families. And there stood that buffalo. I guess the museum didn't have space or money for a family of them. There was just one. Alone, like me. I stared at that buffalo, into its black glass eyes, for what seemed like hours. It was an experience I really can't describe, Wyatt."

She looked at him. He was completely open to her, letting her talk, absorbing her words. Something her father was incapable of. She wished so much that he could understand.

"God was with me there in that museum. I looked at that strong animal standing alone." Tears burned her eyes, and her voice broke. "God told me I was going to have stand alone for a while."

Wyatt slid a little closer to her on that sturdy railing and took her hand.

"But He said it, so I could do it. He'd be with me, loving me. I will always believe in God without reservation because of that moment. It was absolute and true and undeniable. God has helped me through hard times, when my father seemed determined to break me. God has led me to the right people to encourage me. Did you know I graduated from high school when I was sixteen?"

"Wow."

"Yeah, and I already had two years of college behind me because of dual-credit courses the high school helped me find. I graduated from vet school when I was twenty."

"Man, our kids are gonna be smart, unless I drag down the average." Wyatt must not have been very worried about their kids, because he rooted his arm around her shoulders. "And now you're free of your family, but you don't know how to quit being alone."

"And the buffalo I love is going to be reduced to a commodity."

Wyatt pulled her closer. "Tell me what to do. I can't afford to keep these buffalo for you as a toy. If I could, I would. I know how horrified you were at the thought of them being turned into dog food. I thought I came up with a good plan that night. When I said I was going to buy the land, I meant for us and the buffalo. But you didn't even give me a chance to explain. And then I got so mad I didn't want to explain. You were so ready to believe I'd stab you in the back. What kind of love is that? What kind of marriage could we have if you did that all the time?"

"I guess I was ready to be betrayed. I think I was expecting it."

"Well, quit expecting it from me." He looked down at her and blocked out the whole world. "I'll never betray you. I love you. Tell me. I'm listening. Give me a way to save these guys. Tourism? I've thought of that. I don't know how many people will come all the way out here, but we can try. Mt. Rushmore's not that far away. We could draw a few people in. Supplying wild animal parks? We can do that for as many of them as we can sell. I'll let you take charge of all that. We'll save as many as we can, and maybe, once the herd is smaller, we can save them all. But for right now, we both know it's not going to be enough."

Buffy nodded and leaned her head against Wyatt's shoulder. So strong. So alone because she wasn't with him. "I've spent my whole life studying buffalo.

I've researched their history, their genetics, their health, and how money is made from them."

"You'd be the perfect person to run this business."

"And the ones I couldn't save would have to die."

"Yes," Wyatt said without flinching. "It's not a perfect solution, but you know Yellowstone sells off part of its herd for meat. Leonard would have had to start doing it. You have to cull the herd somehow, or they overgraze the range and ruin the prairie grass and die of starvation."

"I've thought about it for years." Tears stung Buffy's eyes. "I've thought about it until I've got brain fatigue from thinking about it."

"You can't turn South Dakota into a buffalo commons. There are nearly a million people in this state. There's no natural barrier between here and Denver. It's impossible to move Denver. You know that."

Buffy nodded. "I know that."

"So tell Yellowstone to get themselves another girl. Stay here and finish your dissertation and be the most overeducated woman to ever hitch herself to a country boy with a high school diploma."

"I feel like I'm betraying them, Wyatt. Just like I've been betrayed."

"You're not. You're saving them. You'll be the woman who turned a novelty into a thriving breed. Stay here with me." He lowered his head and kissed her gently. "Be my Buffalo Gal."

He kissed her again.

Buffy let herself sink into the kiss. . .and her future.

At last she turned and studied the herd. Her friends. She said a prayer under her breath, "God, there is no other way." She was asking for forgiveness, and as simply as that, she knew God didn't think she needed it.

She sat still and felt Wyatt's tension and hope. And his love. "You're my future, Wyatt. You and Sally and the boys."

"And buffalo. You were called to care for them. I won't ever make you give that up."

"What if we can't make it pay?"

Wyatt hesitated. "Wolf is as passionate about these buff as you. He's not just hoping. He's done a lot of research. He thinks it'll work."

"If we can't afford to keep them, can I at least have one as a pet?"

Wyatt smiled in the moonlight; then he laughed. "It's a deal. And not just one. We'll make sure it's at least a family."

They sat together in the dark, with the buffalo. It had always been the time they were best together.

She turned away from the herd. "We can make it work."

"Is that a yes?"

Buffy rested her hand on his cheek and felt his strength. "That's a yes."

"No more standing alone," Wyatt added. "From now on, you're not a buffalo. You're that mama possum with babies hanging from her tail."

"Just how many children do you want to have?" Buffy asked suspiciously.

"How's seven sound?" Wyatt gave her a quick kiss on the nose.

"Seven?" Buffy slapped his arm, but there wasn't any force behind it.

"Well, we've got three already."

Buffy nodded. "That's a good start."

"This weekend—five days from now—we're getting married."

"There you go, being domineering again."

Wyatt gave her an unrepentant grin. "Let's go tell Sally and the boys."

"No, Sally's asleep." Buffy pointed at the baby monitor sitting beside her on the fence. "And so are the boys and Anna. Let's sit here awhile longer. I want to think among my buffalo."

So they sat, and she thought, but not for long.

God had told her she'd have to stand alone for a while. She'd done it. It had been hard, but it had forged her into the woman she wanted to be.

But the time was past. Now she'd stand with Wyatt.

She wasn't alone anymore.

Epilogue

Buffy Lange became Ally Shaw, standing in front of a preacher, with a buffalo herd munching grass at her back.

Sally perched on Wyatt's shoulders throughout the ceremony. Cody and Colt only tried to shoot each other twice while the pastor was talking.

Wolf stood up with both of them, because although he refused to be a bridesmaid, he said it was disloyal to pick Wyatt over Buffy.

The S Bar B Ranch—Shaw Buffalo Ranch—was born.

THE CLUELESS
COWBOY

Dedication

This book is dedicated to my husband, Ivan; not because he's a clueless cowboy though—exactly the opposite. This is a book I wrote very early on in my writing life, and he was so kind about the time I spent writing and has been ever since. I would never have gotten a book published if he hadn't been such a good sport. It means so much when he says he's proud of me.

Chapter 1

Emily Johannson hadn't had a spare minute in a month.

Now, instead of a pleasant walk in the woods to unwind after spring planting, she was going to—she snagged a thick branch off the forest floor—run off some idiot.

A man tugged an ax from the bark of the magnificent tree in the Barretts' front yard. Muscles rippled under his sweat-soaked white T-shirt all the way to the narrow waistband of his blue jeans as he pulled the blade free. He hoisted the ax again.

Emily couldn't watch him hack away at that elm another second. She sprinted across the Barretts' lawn. Reaching him as his ax swung back, she grabbed the ax and jerked, throwing it wide.

The impact twisted him around, tipped him off balance, and dragged him over on top of her.

Emily's handy club flew as she fell. Her Stetson toppled off her head.

His roar would have knocked her down even if he hadn't fallen on her. His weight carried her flat onto her back and knocked a grunt out of her. The smell of a hard-working man and the ancient forest soaked into her head.

"Get off me." Her face, pressed against his chest, muffled the words.

He was already moving, but she gave him a good shove anyway. Sawdust scratched her fingers. His shirt was drenched and her hands slid up his arms and shoulders. For a split second she had her arms around his neck.

Furious brown eyes burned into her blue ones. . .then he rolled sideways and jumped to his feet.

Turning, he glared at her, his corded arms glistening with sweat in the dappled sunlight.

She swallowed hard and tried to forget how nice he smelled. Oh yeah, the ax, her tree. She knew what she was doing again. She shoved the heels of her hands against the ground and stood.

"What are you doing on my property?" he snapped.

She heard anger in his voice as she dusted her backside. But his eyes spoke more of heartache and exhaustion. "*Your* property? The Barrett place is mine." It wasn't hers exactly, but close enough. "Who are you? And why are you hacking away at that beautiful elm tree?"

"How did you find me? Did Sid send you? Well, tell him to forget it." The man slashed his hand in the air. "I'm done."

"I don't know any Sid." Emily tucked her hands in the back pockets of her Wranglers, studying the varmint who'd invaded her home.

"Then I'll bet that real estate agent in Denver put you up to this. She's the only one who knew where I was." He ran a hand over whisker stubble and groaned. "A woman. . .of course a woman. Why can't I ever learn?"

"What are you talking about?" She raised her hands in the universal sign of surrender. "I don't know who you are."

He stared at her like a prairie rattler had turned up on his doorstep. Reaching for the blue denim shirt he'd shed when his slaughtering of innocent trees had gotten him too hot, he wiped his face with it.

Giving sweet reason a shot, she said, "My name is Emily." She nodded up the path she'd followed. "I live over the hill."

Raising his face from the shirt, his cheeks turned an amazing shade of red under what looked like two weeks' worth of scruffy beard. "How far over the hill?"

"A few hundred yards." Rats, she was going to have to lock her doors at night; the new neighbor was nuts.

"A few hundred yards? That's impossible. I was told there were no homes for ten miles. There are no other houses around here." He jerked his shirt on over his T-shirt so roughly she thought he'd tear the fabric. He stepped right up to her face. "I want some honest answers and I want them right now. How did you track me here?"

She knew she ought to be afraid—a complete stranger, remote location, no way to call for help—but she just couldn't work up a single shiver of fear for the poor guy. He looked exhausted and sad, thin. . .almost gaunt. He didn't stink or have the dissipated look of a drunk. No prison pallor. Not even an orange jumpsuit that said STATE PENITENTIARY on it. He just wasn't scary.

She had no trouble holding her ground. "Listen, hotshot. You're the one who doesn't belong here. Who are you and what makes you think you live here? And what kind of locoweed chops down an American elm tree?"

He looked up to heaven, as if praying and lodging a complaint at the same time. "I don't have to answer to anyone about that tree." He jabbed one finger toward heaven. "I own this land, and I can live any way I want. No one can stop me. And no one had better try."

As prayers go, Emily thought it needed work.

He glared at her. "I checked the plat maps. I talked to the real estate agent. You do *not* live a few hundred yards away."

"Barry Linscott told you no one lived out here?" Now Emily was mad. "Barry pulled a fast one to unload this white elephant on you? He hadn't oughta done that. The house is a wreck."

"Barry nothing, there was no Barry."

"There had to be a Barry. He's the only real estate agent in Custer County. We don't call him a real estate agent though. Too snooty. We call him the Guy That Sells Houses."

"I had a real estate agent out of Denver."

"That's right." Emily snapped her fingers. "You mentioned some woman you can't ever learn about. You were talking about her, right?"

"Look, lady—"

"It's Johannson."

His eyes sharpened. "Johannson is your name? That's weird. That's my name."

"Your name is Johannson? We're getting close. Any minute now I'm going to know who you are."

"My name isn't Johannson. It's Joe Hanson."

Dead silence fell over the two of them. Emily squirmed with impatience. Finally, she snapped. "What was the deal, hotshot? Did you get a whack and then the tree got a whack? My name's not Joe Hanson, it's *Johannson.*"

"My name," he said through gritted teeth, "isn't Johannson. My name is *Joe* and my last name is *Hanson.* And my friends call me *Jake.* Please don't bother calling me *anything.*"

That startled a grin out of Emily. Maybe he wasn't as stupid as she thought. "Joe Hanson and Johannson. That's kinda cute."

"Don't start monogramming pillowcases for us, sweetheart."

Her grin faded. "Don't flatter yourself. The only thing I'd monogram for you is a straitjacket."

Her new neighbor finished buttoning his shirt in grim silence.

"Why don't we talk about that tree?" She tipped an index finger toward the elm. That was the point of this, right? That and welcoming him to the neighborhood. She fought back a grin.

"What about the tree?"

"That's an American elm tree. You can't cut it down."

"We are surrounded by thousands of acres of trees. Are they all special or are your initials carved in this one?"

"Don't you know anything about trees?"

"Well, let's see. . ." He looked at the sky like he was thinking, then turned eyes the color of a chocolate Easter bunny—with rabies—back on Emily. "They burn well."

"Firewood?" Emily stormed up until their noses almost touched, even though he was about six inches taller than she was. She stood on her tiptoes and he accommodated her efforts to intimidate him by leaning down, vulturelike, to meet her. "You are cutting down this tree for firewood? *Are you out of your mind?*"

Jake took a step backward. "Let's start monogramming those straitjackets right now. I have a broom closet I can lock you in until the jacket's done. Or maybe you can just grab a broom and fly home."

"There is nowhere you can lock me"—she poked him in the chest—"and nowhere you can hide if you cut down that tree for firewood."

"Look, lady—"

"It is Emily. Emily Johannson. Stop calling me lady."

His jawed was clamped until his lips barely moved. "I won't call you lady. I'm not under any illusions that you are one. First you roll around on the ground with a total stranger—"

Emily's indignant gasp stopped him. "It wasn't *my* idea. You're the one who. . ." His expression hardened until the incredibly impolite things she wanted to say stuck in her throat. She sucked in a long breath. "I'm going to try and say one coherent sentence—one calm, rational sentence—'cuz, believe it or not, I'm a calm, rational person. I don't normally meet a stranger and start right in arguing. So let me say one sentence—"

"Just say it."

His interruption was so brusque Emily lost her train of thought. "Say what?"

"This sentence you're promising me. You've had three. You haven't said anything yet."

"Oh, okay, hotshot, here goes. Have you ever heard of Dutch elm disease?"

"That's it?" Jake's arms swung wide. "You get one sentence and that's it?"

"May I finish?" she asked with exaggerated politeness.

One corner of Jake's mouth twitched in what Emily thought might be a smile. "At least you're learning who's boss. By the way, why don't you drop the 'hotshot' while you're pretending to behave yourself? Finish your sentence."

"Answer my question."

"Question? Was there a question?" Jake ran one hand into his brown hair, sending wood chips flying. "The straightest line between two points is an impossibility with you, isn't it?"

"Dutch elm disease. Have you heard of it?"

"Yeah, I've heard of it—sort of."

Emily groaned and walked over to the elm tree to inspect the wound. "I should've known better than to ask a city boy. Dutch elm disease has killed nearly every American elm tree in this country. This old tree was planted by the Barretts' parents when they homesteaded in the 1860s. These trees started dying fifty years ago. My place, the Barretts', and the whole Black Hills lost millions of elm trees. It was a disaster."

Emily shook her head. "My parents and grandparents talked about all the trees standing dead, their branches naked and raining down for years all through the Custer State Park and the whole Black Hills National Forest that backs our land. For some reason this one survived. It's the only American elm tree left in these parts. It deserves better than to be hacked down by some Paul Bunyan wannabe for *firewood*." She noticed her Stetson on the ground, grabbed it, smacked it on her leg to knock off the dirt, and jammed it on her head.

"Look around you." Jake made a broad arc with one arm. "This place is lousy with trees. And I'm *not* going to burn it for firewood. I'm cutting it down because I'm planning to landscape the yard, and it's in my way."

Emily, in the middle of adjusting her hat, grabbed the brim so hard she almost ripped it off. "You'd destroy a majestic old tree because it's *in your way?*" Emily grabbed her stick, just to let him know she had one.

Jake glanced at the stout branch.

"Well, I say *it* was here first and you're in *its* way. How d'ya like that? And as for landscaping, this house is falling down around your ears. If you were stupid enough to buy the place, landscaping isn't even in the five-year *plan*. The flooring is all rotten, especially on the porch. And for heaven's sake, don't lean on any railings. They're just waiting for an excuse to collapse. The roof is shot. The bathrooms are forty years old and never worked that well to begin with. There are broken windows everywhere—"

"Look again."

After a moment to figure out what he'd said, she turned to really look at the house she had loved for so long. The roof was reshingled. The broken windows were securely boarded. The front steps were reinforced. He'd obviously spent a lot of time and money on it.

She turned back, confused. "When did you do all this?"

"I spent the last two weeks, working eighteen-hour days. How is it you've never shown your face until now?"

"You've been here for two weeks?" She knew even before he nodded with a single jerk of his chin that this work had taken that long. "It's spring. I've been working in the field from sunrise to after dark."

"Doing what?"

"Ranching."

"Ranching? You're a rancher? Do you have a family over that hill? Let me guess. Your cousin married you when you were twelve. You've got eight kids."

Emily laughed. How long had she been standing here fighting with him? Once she started taking bites out of him, she couldn't stop. The man was a living, breathing Lay's potato chip.

"My cousin?" she gasped the words out, laughing. "Eight kids?" She leaned against her precious elm tree, then straightened when Jake chuckled, too. From the rusty sound, she wondered how long it had been since he'd last done it.

"No cousin-husband then? No kids?" He sounded almost neighborly.

"No husband, cousin, or otherwise. I do have a kid. . .sort of."

The smiled dried off his face so fast Emily figured they were squaring off for round two. Or were they up to round five?

"How can you have a kid 'sort of'?" His lips formed a stiff, straight line.

"My sister lives with me. I dropped out of college and moved home when my mother died, to take care of my father and little sister. We've been alone since Dad died two years ago. Stephie is eight and she's at school right now." She saw him relax and wondered what other hornets' nests were waiting to be stirred.

With a start she looked up at the sky. The sun was getting lower. "I've got to be going. School's about out. I didn't reckon on having to save this tree when I set out for my walk. You know, now that I think of it, I have heard some sounds from this direction. I've been chalking them up to long hours and short sleep."

"Can you tell the time from looking at the sun?"

"Greenhorn." She rubbed her hand against the scarred trunk she was leaning on, looking down at the palm-sized chunk he'd hacked out of it. "Before I go, we've got to settle things about this tree. Your life really isn't worth a plugged nickel if you swing that ax again. I'll do you in, and if you're the loner you seem to be, no one'll ever miss you."

"I'm not a loner."

"Secrecy about buying this place. No local purchases. You're a regular hermit, Jake."

All trace of humor vanished. "Where did you hear all that?"

She'd hit another hornet's nest. "It's not what I've heard. . .it's what I *haven't* heard. If you'd so much as stepped into a store in Cold Creek, or even driven through town in that thing"—she tilted her head at Jake's shining black Jeep Cherokee—"I'd have known about it. Cold Creek is tiny. We notice strangers.

"You don't seem like the hiding-from-the-law type. I'd guess this is a back-to-nature kick or escape from your life. So, you're a hermit no one knows about 'cept me and that man-hungry real estate agent in Denver."

"Stop acting like you know me. You don't." His jaw clamped shut.

Emily grinned. "Now about this tree. . ."

He glanced at her club.

"If you take that stick, it won't save you. I'm bristling with weapons over yonder."

"The tree or my life, huh?"

She nodded. "Those are your choices, stranger."

He shook his head, sighing. "Would you believe that's the nicest offer I've had from a woman in a long time?"

"You think it nice of me to threaten to kill you?" He *was* loco. She hoped he didn't call her bluff because she didn't have any guns.

"No, I've just had some really nasty offers."

Chapter 2

Emily didn't even want to think about that. "So the tree?"

"The tree lives." Jake offered her his hand.

She looked at it. "Is a handshake from a city boy playing lumberjack worth anything?"

His lips quirked into a smile.

She took his hand and looked at the sky again, anything but pay attention to his strong fingers surrounding hers. "I gotta go. Stephie'll be waiting."

She tried to pull away, but Jake held on until she looked at him. "Can you really tell the time from looking at the sun?"

Emily snorted and reclaimed her hand. "Straight up is noon. Dawn is at six and sunset is at eight. . .about. . .today. Add two minutes a day on each end till the first day of summer, then start subtracting. And don't forget daylight savings time." Emily was pretty much winging it. She'd checked the clock in her pickup truck before she'd come for this walk. But the sun told her time was passing. She turned toward the path. Just to be a brat, she held on to her stick.

She'd made it across the Barretts' yard when Jake caught up. "I agreed to spare the tree. You have to make me some promises."

She stopped. She didn't want this guy following her home. "Let's hear it."

"First, I want to see where you live. If you're lying and there's no house, I'm going to quit being so nice." He went on past her, toward the woods.

"You mean you can be less nice than this?"

Jake stopped suddenly at the foot of the trail. "This is so obvious it might as well have neon arrows. I can't believe I've never noticed it."

"Well, Daniel Boone is still king of the woodsmen." She jogged to catch up and politely tapped his arm with her stick. "About these promises, you aren't hiding from drug runners are you?"

Jake spared her a look of disgust. "Quit watching so much television."

Which wasn't really an answer. "Talk, hotshot. You asked for promises. Let's hear 'em."

He whirled around in front of her so suddenly she slammed against his chest. She looked into a pair of very annoyed eyes.

"I thought we agreed you'd quit calling me that."

"No-o-o." She shook her head. "Think back. We agreed you'd quit chopping down the tree. We never talked about *hotshot*."

"Keep it up, sweetheart. I could stand here and argue all day, and no one will be there to get your sister."

"No more hotshot?"

"No more."

"It really suits you."

He reached a jabbing finger toward her.

"Jake's fine. I can live with Jake."

"Good girl. Maybe you're trainable. I've been thinking of a collie, but you might do just as well."

He headed on toward her house.

"You know, Jake, ranching is a cold business. We bring baby calves into the world. We feed them, pet them, love them"—Emily's voice dropped low—"and then we eat them."

He shook his head and kept striding up the path.

She jogged even with him as they crested the hill.

He froze, staring at her old ranch house. "This is unbelievable. She'd said there were no houses for ten miles."

"Technically she's right. I do live ten miles from you."

Jake gave her a look that might have peeled her skin if she hadn't grown a thick hide since they'd met. "*You* may have escaped the cousin-husband thing, but they are thick like flies in your family tree, I'll bet."

"The road that leads to your driveway is a dead end. Everything west of you is in the Custer State Park. On the east is the Shaw ranch. He runs some cattle out here, but his fence line is at least a mile from you. He'd never come all the way into your place. Beyond that is the buffalo ranch he runs with his wife. So there are no houses forever that way. Plus he's got his cattle close up to his place right now because they're just done calving. You can walk to my place in two minutes, but on the road it's at least ten miles. To make it worse, they've got the old house site on the plat map on the south side of my land. I live in the new house."

"You have a new house?" He turned back to her obviously old house.

Emily laughed. "Sorry about that. No new house. My grandparents built this when my dad was three. They called it the new house, and I picked up the habit. Now about these promises?"

Jake rested his hands on his hips. "I don't want you to tell anyone I'm here."

"You *are* hiding from drug dealers." Emily lifted her stick. It felt like a solid oak security blanket.

He dropped his head back with a groan of impatience. "I'm not hiding from anything. I just want to be alone."

He tapped his index finger into her chest. "I don't want you to tell anyone

I'm here. Should I say it again? Is it the cousin thing? Are you deaf? You didn't have any trouble hearing me chop your precious tree."

"Do I dare ask why?"

Jake folded his arms stubbornly. "Does it matter?"

"Beyond the fact that I'm dying of curiosity. . .no."

"Is there a chance you might really die of curiosity?"

Emily shook her head and wrinkled her nose at him.

Jake looked disgusted. "I never have that kind of luck. You look healthy as a dog."

She didn't miss his quick glance up and down her body, appraising her health.

"Get your hayseed expressions right. It's healthy as a horse."

"No, it's eat like a horse. Or is it a pig? Eat like a pig? That sounds familiar." Jake relaxed his stance enough to rub one hand absently over his stomach.

After one look, she forced her eyes up. "They both eat a lot. So do dogs."

"While we're on the subject of food, I don't suppose you have any."

Emily's heart turned over. With one thumb, she tipped the brim of her hat back. "You don't have any food?"

"I've got food," he growled. "I was just kidding."

He wasn't kidding, Emily could tell. "Come for supper. Does keeping you a secret include from Stephie?"

His fists clenched and his face darkened. "This is so familiar. I know *exactly* how women keep secrets. They all tell each other one at a time, swearing each other to secrecy. Pretty soon everyone knows and is laughing at the poor schmuck who trusted the first woman."

Emily shook her head. "Wow, how did you find that out? It's true, but I thought women were the only ones who knew it." She added darkly. "Some woman didn't keep the secret."

"Asking you to keep quiet is a joke, isn't it? Do you have any intention of respecting my wishes?"

"All right." Emily raised one hand as if she were being sworn in to testify in court. "No one hears it from me. Not even Stephie. It's only a matter of time until she finds you herself. She spent most of the last two weekends at the neighbors' 'cuz I was busy, but the Barrett place has never been off limits."

"You let your little sister run wild in the woods? What kind of reckless behavior is that?"

Emily shrugged. "I did it when I was a kid. My dad did it before me. Until now, there's never been anything more dangerous here than a bumblebee."

"What do you mean, until now?"

"You're here."

"I'm not dangerous."

Emily couldn't explain it, but she knew without a doubt that was true.

"Just tell her to stay on her own property." Jake crossed his arms.

"Great, and how am I supposed to explain that without telling her about you?"

"See if you can't find the light switch for some of those unused rooms in your brain and figure it out. I bought ten miles of privacy." He looked skyward and jabbed his finger at the passing clouds. "That was the deal."

"You pray more strangely than anyone I've ever met."

"What difference does it make? He doesn't listen."

"Sure He does. Is that what you're out here for? To find God?"

"How about your sister?"

Emily gave up on evangelism. For now. "Stephie's going to find you. She'll be out of school for the summer soon, and I can't keep her away from your house."

Emily glanced at the sun again. "I've got to go, charming though this has been. I'll bring some food over later."

"Why would you feed me?"

She could see he couldn't comprehend her offer. "I always feed the new neighbors, and anyone within twenty-five miles counts. If you'd introduce yourself around, women would feed you." She could almost see the hair stand up on the back of his neck. "Nice, happily married women. People around here would be real good to you. Give them a chance. It might sweeten your disposition."

"What's wrong with my disposition?"

Emily couldn't help laughing. She turned away first for a change—that felt good.

"Why would you feed me?" he yelled after her.

Maybe no one had ever given him something with no strings attached. That idea made her want to be kind to him so badly she had to sass him to cover it up. "My intentions are honorable, hotshot. I'm fattening you up. You're way too skinny to interest any self-respecting carnivore."

She jumped in her old Dodge Ram, slamming the door. She looked back. Their eyes met and she couldn't look away.

With a little smirk, he touched one finger to his forehead and headed home.

—◦◦◦—

Sid Coltrain's search turned to destruction.

Jake had disappeared. He was running around loose. And if Jake started adding things up, Sid was in trouble. The company they'd started, Hanson and Coltrain, made a fortune. Jake led a team of engineers; Sid managed the money. Sid did his best to keep Jake too busy to get a close look at the books. He slammed both fists onto the desktop, then shoved the heavy piece of furniture. This remote log cabin was stark. The few pieces of furniture in the three-room cabin were as rustic as the building and heavy with dust—and a few footprints no doubt left by Jake.

Sid had finally tracked Jake here to Colorado. But Jake was long gone. Sid noticed the crumpled slip of paper under the desk. Smoothing it, he read *Cold Creek, South Dakota*, in Jake's bold, slashing handwriting. "Impossible," Sid muttered. "Jake hasn't stepped off a plane in the Midwest since the Tulsa tornado."

His voice in the empty mountain cabin mocked him. Reminding him there were no other leads. He pulled his cell phone out and punched 411. He hated talking to a computer, so he'd learned how to bypass them—no small trick. "Cold Creek, South Dakota," he snapped at the operator. "I don't know the area code. Look it up."

Sid seethed as he waited. "Operator, I'd like the number of. . .Jake Hanson."

No listing.

"Try J. Joe Hanson."

Nothing.

"Is there a Chamber of Commerce number in Cold Creek? Tourist information center?" Sid rapped his knuckles on the beveled corner of Jake's oak desk.

"A city office. . .a mayor's office? Well, what is there then?" Sid's only answer was a sharp *click* as the operator broke the connection. He snapped the phone shut. Jake wasn't in Chicago. Sid had people checking everywhere and this lodge in Aspen was the closest he'd come.

He looked again at the four words Jake had left behind. Everyone knew everyone in these small towns. Sid decided to put Tish on it. This whole mess was her fault. Jake would have never quit working if Tish hadn't messed up.

Sid knew he'd pushed his luck sending Jake to Honduras. He hadn't been home a week from the earthquake mess in Bolivia. But even an exhausted, burned-out engineer would have recognized the touchy financial situation at the office. Sid intended to put the money back soon, but for right now, he had some personal losses to cover. Sid couldn't let Jake hang around.

Whatever Tish had done sent Jake over the edge. No one had seen him for two months. Sid clenched his fist on the slender clue in his hand. Tish needed her boyfriend as much as Hanson and Coltrain needed its lead engineer. Jake was everyone's golden parachute.

Tish could take charge of this slender lead. He had to find Jake before Hanson and Coltrain collapsed around his ears.

Sid looked again at the note he'd found. South Dakota? Not in a million years! Jake employed a French chef and a chauffeur. Wherever Jake was, he lazed around in the lap of luxury.

— ∞ —

He was pretty much living on Spam.

Jake knew how to rough it. That's pretty much all he did when he was on the job. But he was too burned out and depressed to even arrange the basics for himself. He'd driven into Cold Creek, seen what he was up against, and had driven back to Rapid City, bought a trailer, filled it with building materials and canned goods, and come back to the ranch.

He'd gotten so sick of cold, canned meat he had to be starving before he could swallow it. He was close.

Soaked with sweat, filthy, every muscle in his body aching, Jake climbed down the ladder. He hadn't eaten since Spam at lunch. Under the grizzly stubble, his cheeks were sunken from the weight he'd lost.

He collapsed on the ground and leaned against the elm tree that had upset his neighbor so much. Truth was, it was a relief to let it live. Chopping down this huge tree was more work than he'd bargained for. He'd known after a couple of whacks he was going to forget the whole thing.

He thought about prickly, stick-toting Emily Johannson and grinned. Her hair—Jake closed his eyes and thought about that luscious, endless hair—her hair was like the forest, burnished oak, dark glowing walnut, and reddish chestnut glinting in the sun. And the blue of her eyes was as pure and honest as the wide South Dakota sky, while that soft cowgirl drawl eased into his bones.

None of that got to him like her sass, her courage, the warmth when she smiled, and the contagious way she laughed. She'd bring food. He instinctively knew she would.

Then he remembered Tish.

His instincts were garbage.

—⁂—

Should she impress Jake with supper or slingshot him a pack of frozen hot dogs?

Emily weighed her options as she followed the winding gravel road on the six-mile drive from the lush valley Emily lived in to the clearing her neighbors owned. Beyond this rich, loamy, wooded area, the land spread out into the vast South Dakota Sandhills, with its sparse prairie grass, perfect for grazing cattle. The way was so familiar she could daydream full-time.

She pulled into the Murrays' drive. Stephie, swinging in their backyard, spotted her and jumped off the swing on its forward arch. Yelling, Stephie dashed toward Emily's pickup. Lila, the youngest of the Murrays' three kids, flew off the swing and ran over, too.

Helen poked her head out the door. "Come in for coffee."

"I can't, Helen. I'm way behind today."

Stout, dependable Helen—twenty years older than Emily but still a good friend—began striding toward the truck. Helen was firmly settled into the salt-and-pepper gray hair stage.

Emily remembered Jake's desire to be a secret, to avoid women, and Emily bit back a grin as she pictured Helen chasing after Jake. With a rolling pin maybe.

"If you're way behind, maybe you'll let short stuff stay the night." Helen ran a gentle hand over Stephie's light brown hair. Helen seemed as content with a dozen kids as with three. Nothing fazed her.

It would solve so many problems to leave Stephie. "She's been over here too much. I'm taking advantage of you."

Helen laughed and waved away Emily's protest. "You know they're less work when they're together."

Stephie clutched her hands together and started jumping up and down, begging. Lila Murray, Stephie's classmate, chimed in. Lila was a straggler in the Murray family, and she loved having someone her own age around.

Helen's gentle laugh rang through the riot. "We'd keep her all weekend if you said okay."

Emily held up her hands in surrender. "I give up. Do you need a toothbrush or pajamas?"

"We've got everything she could need. Are you sure you won't come in? Without this wild one around you might have some spare time."

"If I have to do her chores, I'm more behind than ever."

Stephie froze in her celebration. Her eyes widened with regret. "I'll come if you need me."

Emily regretted her teasing. Stephie's chores were simple. Emily could do them in about five minutes, though they kept Stephie busy longer.

Emily stepped out of the truck and gave Stephie a big hug and kissed the top of her head. "I'll be fine, sweetie. I'll pick you up in the morning. And I'll leave time for coffee, okay, Helen?" She climbed back into the truck without looking Helen in the eye.

"I saw you going home around two thirty. Did something happen to keep you from unloading?"

Emily glanced at her groceries, still perched on the pickup seat. Emily kept her head turned to avoid the simple question. "I just got. . .uh. . .sidetracked." Emily waved without meeting Helen's eyes, called out, "Behave yourself, Stephanie!" and backed out of the lane.

Jake was safe for tonight. What would she make him for supper? She'd never thought of herself as lonely, but her reaction to Jake made her wonder.

She hit the gas.

Chapter 3

She raced through her chores as if wolves were chasing her.

Not that she was eager to see Jake again or anything.

Then she made a meat loaf, scalloped potatoes, and a corn casserole. It was simple because everything went in the oven. She dug out of the deep freeze some sliced apples and a pie crust, knowing this was solely to impress him. She put the meat loaf in to bake, then added everything else except the pie. After a quick shower, she reached for her prettiest sundress. "Get a grip, Emily. This isn't a date. You barely know the man. . .and what you do know isn't good."

Emily forgot the dress and pulled blue jeans and a short-sleeved sweater out of the drawer. She drew a brush through her damp hair, then went and checked the oven, its door squeaking as the fragrant steam of cooking food escaped. In the gush of heat, Emily rearranged the casserole dishes to make room for the pie and slid it into place.

Then she forced herself to walk, not run, up the path.

Jake hadn't had more than a momentary flash of guilt in three hours. Way under his usual quota.

He was too busy thinking about Emily. He had to get her away from him, but before he did, he wanted one more taste of all that feminine kindness.

Despite his rudeness, he knew she'd show up with food. He listened for the padding of her feet and, when he heard her, he went into action.

Jake yelled, shoved the ladder leaned against the side of the house away from Emily's path, and then lay on the ground. She dashed around the house like he knew she would. He moaned and put a hand to his head and started to sit up.

She was kneeling by him in a second. "Oh, Jake, let me see if you're all right. Lay still."

Jake relaxed back on the dirt. He groaned, trying not to overact. Her hands smoothed over his arms and down his legs, checking for injuries. Contentment leached into his fully intact bones. How could such tenderness and grace be part of this prickly stranger?

She leaned over, her endless brown hair, unbraided, slipped over her shoulder and rained down onto his chest. His fingers itched to bury themselves in the silken length. She smelled so good—no perfume, just sunlight and fresh air and herself.

He opened his eyes and saw her fear. For him. Tears burned his eyes.

The last time he'd cried he was eight years old, the day he'd realized his mother had left for good. He'd cried one last time, then never again. No tears when he buried his father, none when he pulled tiny broken bodies out of mudslides, and he certainly wasn't going to start now.

"Did you land on your back? Did you hit your head?" Her hands flowed over him like warm rain. She caressed his forehead, brushed back his hair.

Her concern was too genuine, her touch too gentle. It awakened a need as real as thirst or hunger. A need he didn't know he had until now. A need so profound it scared him into action. He pushed her hands away and sat up.

"No, be careful. I think you might have lost consciousness for a minute." She pushed his shoulders back on the ground.

He found safety in hostility. "I'm fine. Back off."

She held him down. His eyes ran over the whipcord muscles in her slender arms.

"Don't fool around. You need to see a doctor. Lie still while I call an ambulance." She jumped up.

He grabbed her wrist and pulled her right back down on top of him. "Knock it off, Florence Nightingale." She'd have the whole state down on him in a minute. He'd have to prove he was all right. Time for Plan B: Send her running.

He dragged her head down and kissed her.

Emily jerked back and knelt on his chest. There was nothing soft and feminine about her knees.

She dug her kneecap into a rib and he let her go. She stood as he rolled onto one elbow and grinned. "I told you I was fine. The only thing you could offer me was that sweet sympathy."

Her faced flushed with anger. His plan was working.

"Come back here." He patted the ground beside him. Now she'd go away and stay away from the barbarian over the hill.

"Dinner's ready, hotshot."

"You're really feeding me?" Delight wiped all his planning from his mind. Then he remembered. "Where's your kid sister? Have you managed to keep our little secret for three whole hours?"

"My sister is staying with friends overnight."

Jake realized Emily had no survival skills to admit something like that to a complete stranger. He needed to teach her to be more careful. "She's gone all night? You arranged some time alone with old Jake? Good girl."

The rage on her face convinced him to stand up for his own safety.

"Do you want to eat or not?"

"I want to eat."

"I left it baking. If you have chores, you've got a few minutes before it's done. But I need to get back and turn the heat down on the pie." She started around the house.

He was beside her like a shot. "Pie? You made pie? You know how to make pie and tell the time from the sun?"

"That's right." She looked sideways at him. "I'm the last of my kind. You've stumbled on to Jurassic Ranch, hotshot."

He was starting to like his nickname. "So you made me a pie? You must really be hoping to impress me."

"If I want to make an impression on you, I'll use a hammer on your skull."

"I think I can smell it." He stepped up their pace as they walked under the canopy of trees on the wooded path.

"I've always figured perfume was wasted on men. The way they like hanging around in bars, I thought essence of beer and cigarettes was the way to go." Emily nodded like she was planning to go into business immediately.

"Are you trying to pick a scent to attract me?"

"Dream on." She walked faster. "I'm making a scientific observation. You're going to eat your dinner with the dog if you don't mind your manners."

"You know I'm having a wild thought."

"Not another one." Emily looked sideways at him.

"I'm thinking I might behave. Not because I believe you'd feed me in the dog dish. I've decided you're mostly hot air with these threats."

"Welcome to the party, Einstein. Your brain must've been runnin' wild all afternoon to figure that out." They crested the hill and headed across Emily's sloping lawn. "I didn't have much time to get ready for company." Her chin rose. "You'll take it as it is and like it. Our house isn't a showplace like the Barretts'."

"I think your memories are about twenty years old, honey. I've been living a life a caveman would pity the last two weeks. The old Barrett 'showplace' is a dump and it doesn't interest me at all right now. If the food I smell is for real, I'll gladly fight over it with the dog." He felt confident making the offer because there was no sign of a dog anywhere.

He pulled open the wooden door of the screened porch and held it open for her. She stepped past him onto the creaking wood floorboards painted brick red. Heading quickly to the inner wooden door, she shifted around so her back was pressed to the entrance, obviously reluctant to let him in.

He'd pretty much insulted her nonstop from the moment they'd met, and she hadn't paid much attention. From her expression, he suspected offending her home might be a mistake. Jake reached around her for the doorknob and she dodged away from his arm. He swung the door open and held it as she rushed ahead of him.

Jake stepped inside and his heart skipped a beat. The appliances were ten or twenty years old. The floor was beige linoleum trying to look like ceramic tile, roughed up in spots and curling in one corner. The walls were papered with faded yellow checks. The cupboards were fifty-year-old scarred oak, with little round white knobs, a couple of them missing. A round table with a white Formica top and tubular steel chairs upholstered with gold vinyl were against one wall of the small room, with a doorway on each side—one leading to the bathroom, another to a living room.

It was home. A real home. He'd never seen anything like it, and he loved it to the point of being speechless.

She moved quickly to the oven.

To cover his reaction to the house, Jake crossed his arms and leaned against the counter nearest the door, fighting a strong desire to move in.

To further his efforts to appear cool and collected, he said, "You've really got that happy homemaker bustle down. Where's the housedress? You need something in calico, floor length, and an apron made from flour sacks."

Emily checked whatever was in the oven. "Thanks. I thought I was acting more like June Cleaver, but you've backed me up a hundred years."

"June Cleaver, huh? Speaking of the Beave, how'd you arrange the privacy? Drop the munchkin along the road because you were desperate to be alone with me?" He had to tease her to keep from begging to stay. He breathed in the delicious aromas.

"Stephanie was invited to stay overnight at the neighbors."

"You shouldn't admit that to me."

"Why not?" She shut the stove and grabbed silverware, letting it clatter onto the table with no regard for her namesake, Emily Post.

"I'm a stranger. You just told me you're completely alone. That's crazy." Jake had to focus to scold her. The aroma in the kitchen was enough to make him polite.

"Oh, sorry. Maybe if you wore a sign around your neck to remind me you're dangerous."

Jake shook his head. "You have no survival skills."

"Yeah, and which one of us is starving?"

She had him there.

"She's staying with Helen and Carl Murray. They are lovely people, and you should be so lucky as to someday have friends that nice." Emily set salt, pepper, and napkins on the table.

Maybe he'd been born suspicious. "You told her I'm here, didn't you?"

"Relax, I didn't say a word. I promised, remember? In South Dakota, that still means something. I agreed to it to protect you from Stephie for a little while longer."

"Can't you just tell her not to trespass? Don't you people know anything about private property?"

"Don't you know anything about living in the country? What are you planning to do, hide forever? Every little town around here will notice a newcomer. Will you drive to Rapid City every time you need milk?" Emily turned to the oven and jabbed a fork into something.

Jake wondered if she were pretending it was him.

Since Emily'd asked about his plans, however sarcastically, he decided to share his dream with her. "I'm going to live off the land." He couldn't control the pride and excitement. "I'm going to grow a garden and raise a cow and some chickens. I'm going to burn wood for fuel. I'll even make candles." His heart expanded with the longing to live close to nature. To experience health and clean air and simple food. He looked to her to share the beauty of it.

"Are you nuts?" She looked at him as if he'd grown a second head.

The woman had no vision. How far out in the wilderness did he have to go to find the true pioneer spirit?

"No electricity?" She pulled the meat loaf out and set it on a pot holder on the table.

Jake shook his head, waiting.

"No gas?"

"My mind's made up, and I'm hungry." He'd have been crankier if hot food hadn't been steaming in front of him.

"What have you been doing for food? No refrigerator? No stove? Are you cooking over an open fire? Eating canned stuff?"

He felt a flush climb his neck. "Well, I tried to build a fire. I did get one going. . .once. It takes an insane amount of time to collect firewood and light it and then, well, my cooking pan isn't right." He wanted to live off the land, not rough it by way of Cabela's and all their luxury camping equipment.

"Pan? One pan?"

There was that blasted compassion again. He wanted her to insult him so he could yell at her. Now that was fun. Instead she started that bustling thing again, all docile fifties' homemaker, putting hot casserole dishes on the table.

It smelled so good a wave of dizziness passed over him. He nearly collapsed into a chair. He wasn't starving, exactly, but he hadn't eaten anything good for two weeks. The food and her kindness drew him like a moth to a flame.

She slapped a plate in front of him so hard he looked up to see if she was angry. She spooned his food up without setting herself a place, like he was wasting away before her eyes.

Since she seemed worried, good manners demanded he put her mind at ease by eating. "What is all this? It smells fantastic."

"It's just plain food. Meat and potatoes and a vegetable. You must be starving if you think this is special." She piled corn beside the creamy slices of potato and a slab of steaming meat.

"It's fantastic food."

"You didn't eat this at home?" Emily scooped again for a bit, then sank onto the chair opposite him.

"Our housekeeper made. . .oh, I don't know. . .fancy stuff." Jake wished she'd stop shaking her head and staring at him like he was an extraterrestrial.

"Didn't your mother ever cook?"

"I didn't have a mother. And whatever housekeepers Dad hired were French chef types."

"No mother?"

He'd hoped he'd skimmed over that lightly enough, but she latched right on to it. "Look, I'm not going to discuss her. She's just another predatory female as far as I'm concerned."

He saw the questions in her eyes, but Emily was all mercy and restraint. She dropped the subject.

"Eat your supper. It was blazing hot from the oven, but it should be cool enough now." She injected a lighter tone. "If you've never had meat loaf before, you're going to die from pleasure, so say good-bye now."

Chapter 4

Emily watched Jake take a cautious bite of meat. It looked like he was afraid it would bite him back.

She covered her dismay over his denial of his mother by serving up her own food, then watched the blissful expression on his face as he chewed in silence, and felt a surge of pride that he was enjoying her cooking. As he wolfed down his meal, she tried to get their relationship back where it belonged by being rude.

She set her spoon down with a sharp *click*. "I've finally figured it out."

Jake swallowed but, instead of speaking, put another forkful of meat loaf in his mouth.

"I know how to keep that mouth of yours quiet. I'll feed you. It'll cost a fortune, but the silence will be worth every penny."

Jake gulped down the last bit of food on his plate. Emily dished him seconds. He held his fork determinedly away. She could tell what it cost him.

"This is delicious. I didn't know how starved I was. But there's more to it than that. I feel like I've been hungry for this food all my life."

"Now do you believe I didn't follow you here?" While she had him softened up, she'd clear the air.

"No woman who can cook like this would ever have to chase a man. You must have a husband around here somewhere." Jake peeked under the table.

Emily laughed. "All women cook like this."

"I don't think I've ever even *seen* a woman cook. Our chef didn't like me watching." He started eating again.

Emily had been so fascinated by Jake's ecstatic reaction she'd forgotten her own meal. She took a few bites of a perfectly tasty meal that was nowhere near as interesting as Jake. "How can you live in a house without seeing where your food comes from?"

Jake just kept eating, apparently willing to let her say anything to him if he could have food.

"Have you ever had home-baked bread?"

Jake said, "No," around his potatoes, then swallowed. "You can bake bread?"

"You make it sound like cold fusion. How about ice cream, churned by hand?"

Jake shook his head.

"We try to make it a couple of times a summer." Emily smiled. "Feeding you's going to be fun. I hope you're this easy to please all the time?"

"Is this food really easy? Honestly, Emily, no fooling around. You didn't work on this all afternoon."

"Sorry if it deflates your ego, hotshot. I spent. . .maybe half an hour throwing this together."

"The pie, too?"

"Yep, but I had a crust and sliced apples in the freezer."

"Do you think you could teach me?"

Emily's own ego deflated. If she taught him she lost a perfect chance to make him her slave. "How am I going to give cooking lessons while you're hiding out from Stephie?"

Jake set his fork down with a clatter. "We've come full circle. What are we going to do?"

Emily missed his gushing compliments. "There's no way we are going to be able to keep Stephie in the dark."

Jake sighed. "This wasn't how it was supposed to be. I came out here to escape my old life. I'm no hotshot. I'm just a guy trying to slow down. If my business associate finds me, I'll be right back working hundred-hour weeks."

When he mentioned hundred-hour weeks, she suppressed a smile. She had just endured calving and spring planting. She wondered what kind of easy life Jake pictured with no electricity and firewood to chop for heat. He was in for a rude awakening.

He picked up his fork and tapped it against his plate. "I'm going to die young if I don't make some changes."

All her amusement evaporated. "Is something wrong?"

He rubbed his hand across his mouth. Resting both forearms on the chipped Formica of her grandmother's table, he shook his head. "Nothing's wrong. I'm healthy. Surely you noticed I'm a nearly perfect male specimen."

Laughter surfaced from under her worry.

He chuckled, too.

Then she sobered as she thought of what he'd said. She looked into the rich chocolate brown of his eyes. "Seriously, what do you mean about dying young?"

His smile faded. "It's. . .well. . .my father died a year ago of a heart attack. He was fifty-six. We looked alike. We acted alike. He was a workaholic. I've spent the last year trying to slow down, but there seems to be only two speeds at Hanson and Coltrain—the speed of light or quit."

Hanson and Coltrain. She stored up this information about his identity. "So you're a workaholic, too?"

"If anything I'm worse than Dad. He at least took time to marry and have a son, though I'm sure I was an accident. . .or more likely a trap my mother set."

"Why a trap?"

Jake stared at his plate. "If she wanted me. . .why'd she leave me behind when she took off?"

Emily had no answer for the confusion and sorrow in his voice. She'd lost both her parents and knew that pain. But her folks had loved her and Stephie.

With a dismissive shake of his head, Jake went on. "I'm glad he managed to have a kid, even if he never spent a moment with me once I was here."

The derision twisted Emily's heart. "Well, life can't be so bad if you're glad you were born."

Jake glared. "What's that. . .cornpone wisdom?"

Now wasn't the time to get irritated just when he was talking about himself, but he sounded so superior. "I'd say it's just plain wisdom."

"I came out here to find a simple life. I wanted to get close to the soil. I didn't want anyone to know where I was because Sid will come charging in here from Chicago and wheedle me into going back. And I wasn't supposed to have to deal with neighbors." He looked furiously at her as if all his troubles could be blamed on her existence.

Sid. Chicago. Hanson and Coltrain. Jake Hanson and Sid Coltrain maybe? "The world is full of people, in case you haven't noticed. There is nowhere to really be alone. People aren't your enemy. Look in the mirror, hotshot. There's your enemy."

"I told you not to call me that." Jake stood with a fluid grace she tried not to admire.

Emily thought it was a shame his temper didn't scare her. Something needed to control her.

He rounded the table and she rose, backing away, retreating nearly to the living room before he caught her wrist.

"Let go of me."

Their eyes caught. The wounded man lured her. His hand tightened and he pulled her close. The timer went off.

His eyelashes fluttered. He released her and stepped away. Turning his back to her, he ran one hand through his hair, standing it wildly on end.

She hurried to the stove, snapped off the timer, and yanked open the oven door. She grabbed two potholders and pulled out her bubbling apple pie, sliding in onto the stove top. She clicked the heat off, braced her hands on the countertop on either side of the stove, and tried to gather her scattered wits.

She breathed a quick prayer for some common sense. With unsteady hands, she cut the pie and set a slice in front of a subdued Jake, who had sunk back into his chair.

"We have a problem."

He looked up. "What problem is that?"

"You. . .we. . .we have to keep our hands off each other. I don't believe in it."

"You don't believe in letting a man touch your wrist?" He pulled the pie toward him.

"Not a strange man."

"Am I a stranger, Emily? Haven't I known you forever?"

She settled into her chair. "It feels like it, doesn't it? It's been a very strange day." She covered her face with her hands, then slid them so she could see him and still keep her burning cheeks covered. "I don't really know what to do with the ideas I have in my head. It's all new to me."

"Believe it or not, it's new to me, too."

"I don't believe it."

Jake shrugged. "All I know is there seems to be something inevitable about holding you."

Emily was stunned. "Jake, you don't even like women."

"You're right about that."

"We're just going to have to stay away from each other."

Jake looked down at the pie in front of him. "I'd die."

"From missing me?" Emily's heart started pounding.

"I was thinking about starvation."

And then she was laughing. She reached across the table and pulled the pie plate away from him before he could sink his fork in. "I know. I'll start trying to change you. That'll cool you off. And it'll be easy, too, 'cuz you're gonna hafta change."

Jake groaned.

"There, you're already irritated. Now I'll list off the things wrong with you."

"All right, you might be on to something here. Let's have it. Count off my faults. This is good. It's working. I already don't like you anymore." He raised his eyes to lock on hers. For an instant they flicked down to her lips. "Much."

Emily swallowed hard. "I didn't say faults exactly, just stuff you have to change."

"Let's just hear it."

"You have to get hooked up to electricity."

"No."

"Good, this is going great. You're really bugging me. No one lives without electricity if they don't have to. You'll figure it out soon enough, but get your stubborn pride and your male ego in the way so it'll be harder to back down. That way you'll suffer longer and blame me. That ought to keep you away from me." She nodded in satisfaction.

"I don't have a problem with my ego. And I'm not getting electricity. That's final."

"This is going great. Next, you have to have a new furnace. The house has an old one, but you need to tear it out and start over from scratch. That'll mean a bunch of workmen, so everyone will know you're here."

"No."

"Your idea of heating that whole house with firewood is ridiculous. It's got three floors and eight fireplaces. Do you know how much wood that will take? And it still won't be warm because chimneys make the house drafty."

"Barretts built it. They survived the cold."

"Yeah, but that's all they did. . .survive."

"How cold can it get in South Dakota anyway?"

The laugh that escaped Emily was pure derision. "I know you're not stupid, Jake. So why does stupidity keep coming out of your mouth?"

"Good one." Jake seemed to approve. "This is getting better all the time. I've got a forest full of wood, even without your pet American elm. I can live in the downstairs room with the main fireplace when it's cold and shut off the upper floors. If I hook up the gas and electric, the whole world will know I'm here. That's what you really want, isn't it? It's killing you not to gossip. Or do Helen and Goober Walton know all about me?"

Shoot, no amount of criticism was going to make her dislike him if she couldn't stop laughing. "Their names are Helen and Carl Murray, and I did *not* tell them about you. You won't even survive the summer. That's the real reason you need to stay away from me. Because you are playing Little Dope in the Big Woods, and you'll be out of here as soon as the novelty wears off. Wouldn't that be a nasty joke on you if the thrill was gone and you woke from your rustic pipe dream and found yourself with the girl next door clinging to you? A girl who has no intention of letting some burned-out house builder become important to her, while he runs around the world playing What Do I Want to Be When I Grow Up?"

"I'm an architect, not a house builder. An architectural engineer to be exact. They're long words but try to remember. I'm good at it, too. I'm not burned out, I'm simplifying my life. I'm planning to go to work again but on a smaller scale."

"Right, and I'm not a rancher. I'm in agribusiness and I do domestic engineering as a sideline. You're worried about dying young, but I've got a news flash for you. You're going to die before the summer's out. You'll poison yourself with spoiled food, or you'll hurt yourself and not have a phone to call 911."

"I won't—"

"And quit interrupting me. I've got a whole bunch more changes you need to make. We haven't even scratched the surface."

"I think I've heard enough. It's having the desired effect."

"Too bad if it's enough. We've skirted around it all night, but the truth is I'm going to have to tell Stephie about you. She will find you by the end of the week. I might be able to keep her away until then. But school is out Thursday. After that she'll be around all day every day."

"I don't want her over there."

"You can stop saying that because she *will* be over there."

Jake clenched his fists until his knuckles went white. He breathed several quick shallow breaths and then forced his hands open. "Is there a chance she'd be able to keep it a secret?"

She knew the question was a major concession. "Look, I'll ask her. But she's eight. She's an open, honest little girl."

"A woman, of course."

Chapter 5

She should have been offended by the shot at women, but near as Emily could tell, Jake didn't like anyone, so it was hard to take it personally.

"She doesn't see other children too often in the summer. She goes to town with me for groceries and church, but I'll watch her. I can't make any promises. But I can promise you she's going to find out."

"I know I can't keep living here a secret. I thought I could, but I didn't understand the crowd situation."

This time she had to grin. There were forty people in twenty miles.

"Listen, I don't just want to hide on a whim. I really need to have some time before I deal with my old job. The last five years I've become a troubleshooter, working with natural and man-made disasters all over the world."

Emily decided to google Hanson and Coltrain later.

"My life is just crisis to crisis. My father's death was a wake-up call. I hadn't seen him for ages. He was a lawyer, lived right there in Chicago, but we had nothing to do with each other. I've been trying to cut back, but my partner won't let up. So I left. I disappeared. If they find me, they'll need me. Lives will be at stake. . .or homes, or the air, or water, or the whole blasted planet. I've never been able to figure out how to say no. If they show up here, I'll go with them."

"And you're afraid it will kill you?"

"I *know* it will kill me. But it's not so much that I'm afraid I'll die. It's that my father never did anything but work. I don't want to die without living."

She stopped herself from reaching for his hand.

"So I changed my life. I saw the picture of the Barrett place in a real estate office, and it touched a chord. The slopes on the roof and porches, the balconies on the upstairs windows. . . I love that house."

"The tower." She understood the appeal of the old house.

Jake smiled. "The picture seemed like a dream."

"Like a place where Rapunzel might be imprisoned."

Jake smiled. "You're really in love with the place. That's what you meant when you said, right at first, it was yours. I bought it for a song. How come you didn't buy it and fix it up?"

Emily shrugged. They were in accord again and that wasn't what they'd been going for. But she couldn't pretend she didn't adore that old house. "You know I've never given it a thought. My life just sort of happened to me. I didn't exactly choose it, although I'm sure things have worked out according to God's plan for me."

"God's plan?"

"Yes, I was full of my own ideas. You know. . .vet school, a career in the city."

"A veterinarian?"

"Yeah, that was the plan. I had two years of college when my mom's death pulled me home, and my dad's death held me. That's how God meant for it to be. Stephie and I love it here. After Dad died, I was more interested in stability for Stephie than fantasies about a romantic old heap."

"Romantic, huh?"

Emily shrugged at the impression that word, from Jake's mouth, made on her. "It's like a fairy-tale house."

"It's definitely unique."

"Great-grandma Barrett was rumored to be a German aristocrat. Somehow, during a time when this whole area was still barely settled, they built that house with all its elaborate flounces. I've hated to see it fall into disrepair. I suppose I could have saved it. Mom and Dad's life insurance left us pretty secure, but it would have been a waste for just Stephie and me. I can't believe you want the job now that you've seen it. I would have thought the floors would have rotted through."

"It's a mess in places, but the foundation is solid." His smile was self-deprecating. "I responded to the picture and the isolation. And here I am. I'm going to chop wood and eat food cooked over an open fire, breathe clean air, and sleep at night. You can't imagine how bad I've been sleeping for years. But since I've been here, doing manual labor instead of wrangling in my head about load-bearing walls, and state-of-the-art earthquake management, and miles of government regulations, and. . ." He fell silent. His eyes dropped to his pie plate. Then he rubbed his whiskery face with one hand.

She didn't think he'd go on.

"And body counts," he whispered.

Her breathing stuttered.

He rubbed his open palm over his eyes as if he would wipe away his thoughts. "I've been sleeping hard for eight hours a night. It's wonderful. I like it and I want to stay. If Sid finds me, he'll manipulate me into leaving. That means no public documents like electric bills. What are we going to do?"

Emily smiled. "I have an answer that's so simple you're going to bite my head off."

"All your answers have that effect on me."

"I've noticed." She shrugged. "Learn to say no."

Jake shook his head, scowling. "Great. Thanks, you've saved my life."

"I have. You're just too stubborn to know it. Learn to say no." Emily softened her words with a smile. "Learn to laugh. Learn to cry. Enjoy being glad you were born."

"You call that simple; I call it impossible."

"Well, you know what they say. . . ."

"Sure, they say big boys don't cry."

Emily laughed. "That's big girls don't cry and that's not what I meant. They say women cry, men have heart attacks. Isn't that what you're running from? A heart attack?"

"Who says that?" Jake's eyes widened in horror.

"I can get you started. I've got something that will make you cry your eyes out." Jake's eyes narrowed with suspicion.

She slid his pie back in front of him. "Hot apple pie. It's so delicious it will make you weep like a baby."

Jake started chuckling deep in his chest and reached for his fork.

"How much laughing do you do?"

"You've heard every note of the laughing I've done since my father died."

"Do you miss him? I know I miss my parents."

"I don't miss him. His death just gave me a wake-up call."

In a gesture she knew was pathetic, she tried to substitute food for a negligent father. "Would you like a second piece of pie? You didn't get much supper."

"Are you kidding? I was most of the way done with seconds when other. . . um. . .things got in the way." He looked chagrined. "Sorry, no more of that. We're doing pretty good, aren't we?"

"Yeah, pretty good." She cut him another piece of pie and got ice cream out of the refrigerator without asking if he wanted any. The man didn't seem to know anything about food anyway. She dropped a generous scoop of it on Jake's pie and set it in front of him.

"What about Stephie?" She hated to ask.

Jake shrugged. "Ask her to keep it secret. Maybe I can buy some practice time."

"Practice time?"

"Saying no." Jake sighed contentedly.

Emily didn't even bother to serve herself any pie. She was saving all of her strength for pushing her luck. "What about the electricity and gas?"

"No."

"There's plenty of roughing it you can do even with electricity."

"Sid will be on me in a minute. The man is a bulldog."

"Okay, how about I get the hookups in my name. I could tell them I'm running some cows on your pasture, and I need electricity and gas. I couldn't put a furnace in, but you can get by without that until winter."

"It's not how I want to do it, and if this pie wasn't so good I'd start fighting with you again."

"Just think about it. You can live like you are now if I feed you. The water works, doesn't it?"

"Yes, the windmill on the place keeps the supply tank full, and I've got lots of water and good pressure, but it's cold water, of course."

"You haven't had a hot shower in two weeks?"

"Well, the cold ones get you just as clean."

"But that well water is freezing cold."

Jake shivered. "Tell me about it." He went back to his pie.

Chapter 6

S he served herself a piece of pie just as the sound of a motor drew her attention.

"Someone's here." Jake shoved his chair back with a loud scrape and dashed into the other room. Emily ran after him.

He shoved open a window in the living room, unlatched the screen, swung one leg over the ledge, and ducked his head through the opening.

"No, Jake. Not that window. There's a. . ."

He dropped from sight. Snapping bush mixed with muffled cries of pain.

"Rosebush." She rushed to the window and saw him limp out of sight into the trees, hoping he remembered about the creek.

Her porch door slammed. "Emily, where are you?" Helen Murray's voice made her jump away from the window and hurry toward the kitchen. "Stephie got sick and wanted you."

With what she hoped was supreme calmness, Emily stepped into the kitchen and saw the table, obviously set for two.

"Did you have company for dinner?" Helen asked.

Emily glanced at the living room where Jake had escaped, realized how that would look to Helen, and turned back. She'd promised Jake.

"Uh. . ." Lying was a sin. "Uh. . ."

Helen might be a country woman born and bred, with no education past high school, but that didn't make her stupid. Her eyes followed the direction Emily's had a moment before, and Emily knew Helen was thinking something worse than the truth.

Stephie helped ease the situation. "I'm going to throw up."

Emily dashed after Stephie to the bathroom and began rubbing her little sister's back as she emptied the contents from her stomach.

"Nick Thompson went home from school sick on Wednesday. I suppose it'll spread to all the kids." Helen, who'd followed the girls into the bathroom, was minding her own business even though it had to be killing her.

"All your kids will get it now. I'm sorry." Emily tried to make the apology cover everything.

"I've seen the flu before. I know better than to worry about it. Do you need anything before I go? A hand with the dishes?"

Emily kept her eyes fixed on Stephie, ignoring the hint. "I'm fine. We'll manage. Thanks for bringing her home." She soaked a cloth with cool water and bathed Stephie's warm face.

"Are you going to be all right, honey?" Helen asked with maternal gentleness.

"I'm fine," Stephie said.

"I guess," Emily answered at the same moment. Emily then realized Helen had been speaking to Stephie.

Then Helen, with a furrow between her eyes, patted Emily's shoulder. "If you need anything, I'm here."

Emily nodded. "Thanks. I appreciate that. More than you know. Good night."

"Good night. Hope you're feeling better tomorrow, Stephie." Helen turned away with no answers.

Emily gave her full attention to Stephie. "Let's get you to bed, honey. Do you feel awful?"

"No, I'm better since I threw up."

"Did you throw up at the Murrays', too?" Emily gritted her teeth, dreading the response. She started Stephie toward the bedroom.

"Just once."

"Did you make it to the bathroom?"

"Sort of."

Poor Helen.

Emily helped Stephie undress. "Climb into bed."

"I'm hot."

Emily slid a nightgown over her little sister's tangled hair. The fever wasn't dangerous, but it was enough to make a little girl miserable.

"I hurt."

"Do you think you can take some medicine?"

"I had some at Lila's. Please don't give me any more." Stephie started to cry and rolled close to Emily kneeling by the bed. "Stay with me."

Emily sighed and brushed the soft brown hair back from Stephie's flushed, tear-soaked face.

Emily spent the next two hours tending to Stephie. When her little sister finally dozed, Emily cleaned up the kitchen.

As Emily wiped the last surface, she came to the pile of mail she'd tossed there this afternoon. She picked it up in town once a week. There seemed to be an awful lot of it. She reached for the first envelope and tore it open.

Dear J.J.,

Darling, I love you. What you saw between me and the pool man was a moment of madness. You know there's never been anyone but you. Please

give me another chance. I ache with an emptiness that only you can fill.
You're the one I want to warm my. . .

Emily jerked her head sideways and slapped the letter against her chest in a desperate effort to stop reading. This wasn't hers! She ignored the clamoring curiosity that urged her to read further and grabbed the envelope.

J. Joe Hanson
Cold Creek, SD

It was so close she just assumed. . . Stu Fielding, the postman, had just assumed. . . She snatched another letter.

J. Joe Hanson. Again. Not J. Johannson for John Johannson, her father. J. Joe Hanson. Jake!

She started a pile. There must be ten letters for him. Someone knew where Jake was. It meant she was coming. Emily had to warn him. Unless maybe the woman who had written this letter had broken his heart. Maybe he had turned his back on the world because she had rejected him. Maybe he'd forgive her when he saw this letter and leave without a backward glance. Maybe he'd been imagining her when he'd pulled Emily close.

She closed her eyes, surprised by the hurt. There was no rational reason to care what Jake thought.

She flipped a second envelope over and saw the return address.

Hanson and Coltrain
Chicago, IL

Stephie was the least of Jake's problems.

Emily shook her head. It was past midnight. Her day had started at five. A loud groan from Stephie and a cry for water interrupted her thoughts. She helped Stephie sip some water, then sank into a rocking chair near Stephie's bed and watched her sister settle into sleep.

Emily tiptoed to her room. She finally collapsed into bed in time to hear Stephie moaning. One last check on her sister, restless and vulnerable in her bed, and Emily slept.

Emily awakened at five like she did every morning. If she didn't get up, the cows would probably come into her bedroom and get her. She had done a half-day's work before Stephie stirred at nine. Stephie's flu was pure luck. Emily's guilt at the horrible thought didn't stop her from being relieved that she could keep her little sister indoors all day, maybe all weekend.

The only trouble was Stephie was feeling much better. She didn't want to stay indoors, and normally Emily wouldn't have made her. This time she stuck to it like a burr. She had to have more time before she tried to deal with Jake meeting Stephie. If they could just get through this weekend. . .

Emily thought of the mail and knew her mental gymnastics were a waste of time. Jake's secret was out. She had to warn him.

Stephie fell asleep after a light meal at noon. It was the perfect time to run the mail over to Jake and watch that explosion. She waffled for a minute, fighting the desire to take him some dinner. It would be easy. She could make up a plate of leftovers from last night.

Why bother? He wouldn't eat once he saw the mail anyway. He'd be busy packing.

She reached the edge of the woods and couldn't stop herself from slipping behind the same tree that had concealed her yesterday. She needed to gather her wits. How could she possibly have reacted to him as strongly as she had?

To clear her head, she paused for a moment to look at the old Barrett place. Jake's work was already paying dividends, but there was a long way to go before the house regained its old majesty.

Three stories were covered with ornamental details in the best tradition of high Victorian architecture. A wide veranda wrapped around the entire house until it was cut off by a tower that anchored the front corner. Balustrades, anchored by posts every six feet, trimmed the veranda. A smaller copy of the balustrades surrounded balconies around each window on the upper floors. On the third floor, gables grew out of the central window on each side of the house.

She loved every ridiculous flourish on this house, but her favorite part was the circular tower. It was four stories at its highest point and topped by a cupola. The Barretts had treated her like their own grandchild and let her explore every inch of this old place. She touched two fingers to her forehead to pay homage to her very much invaded realm and stepped from behind the tree.

He wasn't outside. She'd have to knock on the door. It would be interesting to see what he had done with the place inside.

She glanced down at her clothes. For a moment she regretted her decision not to change out of her work clothes. The faded blue jeans and flannel work shirt with the sleeves rolled up were tacky. She had been determined not to make a single effort to look good.

She had succeeded.

The mail tucked under one arm, she squared her shoulders and marched up to the front door and knocked. She waited a minute and knocked again. No answer. She looked at his Jeep, parked right where it had been last night. She scanned the area around the house for any sign of him working on an outdoor project. Where could he be?

She wanted to drop the mail and run. But she couldn't leave it on the ground.

She didn't have the nerve to do what she'd have done for the Murrays—step inside and leave it on the first clear surface. She pounded a third time.

The door flew open. She nearly stumbled into Jake. His face was red and his shoulders were heaving. At first she thought he'd run from somewhere to answer the door, then she saw he was furious.

"Get in here." He grabbed her arm and yanked her over the threshold. "What do you think you're doing?"

The mail scattered all over his floor as he towed her into the kitchen. He dragged her around to face him. "I was planning to die alone before I asked *you* for help. But you're here now. Make yourself useful."

"What are you talking about? Let me go." She jerked her arm against his grip and he let go. Of course she was where he wanted her already. "Is this what passes for good manners in the big city?"

"No, this is about my back." He pointed a thumb over his shoulder. "You throwing me out a window into a rosebush last night."

"Me throwing you out? You jumped."

"And had my first rotten night's sleep since I moved to this God-forsaken place."

"God hasn't forsaken any place, pal. So quit complaining and speak English. I had a rotten night's sleep myself. Stephie got sick at the Murrays' last night. That's why Helen came over."

She whirled away to grab his mail, shove it down his throat, and make a grand exit.

Chapter 7

She didn't even get her back turned before he grabbed her wrist.

"Get your hands off me." Emily tugged hard against Jake's iron grip, and when that did no good, she shoved against his shoulder. He staggered backward with a groan of pain.

Emily froze. "I didn't mean to hit you so hard."

"Don't flatter yourself." He released her and turned around and lowered his blue denim shirt a few inches off his shoulders.

Emily gasped in horror. His back was covered with slivers and thorns. There were terrible scratches and one large raw gouge on the back of his shoulder, right where Emily had shoved him. "This happened last night?"

Jake tried to straighten his back and Emily could see how much each move cost him. "Brilliant deduction, Sherlock."

"Sit down. Let me help you. Your poor back. I'm so sorry." Emily pulled him toward a chair.

"Just fix it, will you?" His teeth were clenched and the words growled out.

"Sit still. This will take awhile." Emily's stomach sank. "Do you have a first aid kit?"

"I don't have a bunch of fancy stuff around here. Just get the thorns out."

"How about a needle?"

"Why would I have a needle? My back-to-nature kick didn't include embroidery. Are you going to help me or not?"

Emily braced herself. "You're going to have to come to my house."

"Stephie's there."

"I can't get these stickers out without tweezers, and I can't leave Stephie alone much longer."

"No." Jake ground the word out.

Convincing him was hopeless, so she blackmailed him instead. "Then I'm going to call an ambulance. You have to have them removed and you know it. Now will it be Stephie or the whole world?"

The silence was deafening. It stretched until she thought choosing was beyond him.

Through gritted teeth, he said, "Let's go."

Emily couldn't imagine how much pain he must be in to agree.

He stood, raising his shirt up gingerly. Stooped, he headed out the door.

Emily noticed the mail strewn across the floor. She picked it up and tucked it discreetly under her arm, deciding to delay the bad news.

Jake entered her house without waiting for her, turned a chair so he straddled it, and eased himself down.

Without speaking, Emily placed his mail on the kitchen counter and then rushed to the bathroom for her first aid kit, taking a second to check on Stephie. Then she faced the enormity of the task. She heaved a long sigh to settle her fluttering nerves and, tweezers in hand, started.

Jake flinched at the first touch of the cold metal, but he didn't speak. She worked on him in silence, systematically removing the slivers. The occasional hiss of indrawn breath was her only clue when she hurt him.

"There, that's the last of the slivers." She flexed her cramped fingers and prepared to start on the dozens of thorns.

"You're done?" Jake's voice was awash in relief.

"Oh no. I've done the slivers, but the thorns will take a long time. Maybe hours."

Jake's back stiffened. "Hours?"

"You can't see how awful it is. I'll work as fast as I can. I'm sorry I'm hurting you." Emily's voice broke.

"You're not crying are you?" His voice softened a little.

"No, of course not." She rubbed the back of one hand over her eyes. "I should have warned you about that window. I tried but I was too late. You don't really believe I wanted this to happen to you?"

"I suppose not." Jake's shoulders slumped. "I had a lot of time to work up a solid case against you. It's amazing all you can get mad about when you have hours to fume."

"I heard you hit the bush. I should have known you might need help. With Stephie sick I just never thought. I'm so sorry."

"Look, quit apologizing, okay? It's not your fault. It was an accident."

She worked in a more relaxed silence for a few minutes. "I can't reach your lower back. The kitchen table is sturdy." She moved the salt and pepper shakers to the stove.

He stood and looked at the table uncertainly.

"It's okay." She pulled it away from the wall and motioned for him to climb on. "Lie down."

He glanced at her once, then slid onto the table without a word.

Her hands trembled as she began. Her tweezers slipped sharply, and Jake couldn't control his gasp of pain. "I'm sorry."

"That's all right." Jake's voice was hoarse but calm and encouraging. "You're doing great."

She wished he'd yell at her. His gentle tone made her fingers tingle where they rested on his narrow waist, and the tingling spread to her hands and up her arms. She gripped the tweezers more firmly and tried to control her wayward emotions. She had to finish so she could get him out of here before—

"Hi, Jake."

They both gasped and turned their heads hard toward the sound of that little voice. Their reaction startled Stephie into backing up a step.

"J–Jake? You know Jake?" Emily couldn't believe her ears.

"So, you couldn't keep a secret for a whole day." Jake's voice was low and angry.

She looked down at him.

He had raised himself onto his right elbow and turned halfway around. His eyes bored into hers.

"I didn't tell her. Stephie, how did you know about Jake?" Emily turned back to her little sister and Jake did, too. A long silence settled over the room.

"Come here, Stephie. It's nice to meet you." Jake stretched a hand out to her and Stephie shyly stepped toward him. She reached out her own hand.

"Stephie, I asked you how you knew Jake?" Emily repeated sternly.

Stephie dropped her hand and looked wide-eyed at Emily.

Jake glared over his shoulder. "Don't be mean to her."

Mean to her?

"I'm not!"

Stephie took a step backward again.

Jake turned to the little girl. "I'm sorry Emily scared you. She isn't mad, just surprised."

Where on this earth had that sweet voice come from? He hadn't bothered to use it on her.

Stephie stepped toward Jake again, and this time, she gave him a confident smile, reached out her hand, and took his. She didn't shake. Instead, she held on and looked at him.

"How do you know who I am, Stephie?"

"You live at the Barrett place."

Jake and Emily exchanged another glance, and Emily shrugged her shoulders. "You mean you've known he was over there and didn't tell me, honey?"

Jake shot her another warning look, like he was ready to jump to Stephie's defense at any time.

"He's been there two weeks. I didn't tell you because he wanted to be a secret."

"What?" Emily and Jake echoed their amazement.

Stephie pulled back but Jake held on to her. Tugging on Jake's hand, she asked, "Didn't you?"

Jake's voice, barely louder than a breath, just reached Emily's ears. "Finally, a woman who can keep a secret."

Then in a more normal volume, he answered, "Yes, I did. But how could you tell? And how did you know my name?"

Stephie shrugged. "It was on something in your car."

Emily raised her eyes to heaven. "You've been snooping around his car? You shouldn't have—"

"It's only natural she'd be curious," Jake interrupted.

Emily resisted the urge to stab him with the tweezers. At least the tingling had stopped in her fingers. Having Stephie in the room was going to make it possible for her to finish Jake's back. Then she could throw him into the rosebush again.

"It's okay to be curious?" Stephie could ask more questions than a prosecuting attorney.

"Sure it is, sweetheart," Jake said.

Sweetheart? Who was this guy and what had he done with the grouch who had come home with her?

"How'd you get the stickers in your back?"

Emily fumbled with some version of the truth. Would Jake want to admit he was here last night? Did he want Stephie—

"I fell."

Stephie nodded in complete and trusting sympathy.

Emily wanted to hear more about her little sister's sneaking. It had never occurred to Emily that Stephie shouldn't roam freely in the woods. The Barrett place was locked up and there wasn't much in the woods that could hurt her. And there were certainly no people around way out here. Or so Emily had thought.

"Tell us about how you found Jake."

Stephie would have impressed the CIA. She'd spied and sneaked around the Barrett house, inside and out.

"You can't go in that old house. It's not safe." Emily knew Stephie had always considered the woods her personal playground, but she had long been forbidden to go inside the rickety old house, locked or not. Emily had a pang of failure as a mother. She wasn't old enough herself to know what rules to make or how strict to be. And Stephie was so well behaved and she'd been through so much. Emily had the sudden realization that her little sister needed some discipline, and Emily had no practice at it.

Stephie pulled a chair away from the table just enough to plant herself inches from Jake.

Emily forced her attention back to her doctoring.

Chapter 8

Jake hadn't been around children much. Mainly in airplanes, where he firmly believed they should be kept in cages in the belly of the plane with the pets.

But this one was special. He rested his eyes on the miniature of Emily. Her hair was a tangle of brown waves, finer than Emily's but just as long. Her sleepy eyes were pure blue innocence.

If Emily scolded her one more time he'd—

"Are you going to stay here forever?" Stephie sounded hopeful. She wanted him to stay.

He wanted to tell her yes, but he remembered the pain of broken promises from his own childhood. "Right now I'm planning to. That's why I'm fixing the house."

"It looks great. I love the bathroom."

"You like it?" So what if she'd been inside his house without permission. She was just a child for heaven's sake.

"I haven't seen it since you went to town last Monday."

"Well, come over anytime. I still want to be a secret from everybody else, but you can visit."

Stephie grinned. "Why did you leave Chicago?"

Emily choked.

Jake wondered what all this little imp knew. He looked at Emily. He'd forgotten she was there. Hard considering she stabbed him in the back a dozen times a minute.

"You okay, Emily?" Stephie asked.

Jake arched an eyebrow and watched Emily bite back a grin.

"I'm okay."

Jake turned back to Stephie and started talking about his father's heart attack.

Stephie held his hand and talked about her own daddy.

Then Jake picked up the trail of his own story. "I just spent three months in Central America in the aftermath of a hurricane. Climbing around in those buildings we found. . ." Jake ran a hand over his face, remembering the injuries with so little hope of healing in that primitive area.

Emily kneaded his neck. He was talking to Stephie but Emily was the one who could imagine the details. As her hands worked on his knotted muscles he began, without changing his tone, to talk to her.

"The need was so great. I didn't bother with buildings. I just helped carry people. . .children. . ." He couldn't go on about what he'd seen. He didn't want anyone burdened with those horrors.

"It's so selfish to worry about my own exhaustion after all they'd suffered. But. . .I can't do it anymore."

Emily ran soothing hands across the nape of his neck and between his shoulder blades.

He reveled in the touch until he remembered. "I finally got home. The long-lost engineer. The conquering hero returns. And found my girlfriend in my apartment with—" He stopped, remembering Stephie.

Tish had been a companion. If Jake needed a date for some event while he was in town, he took Tish. They were friendly acquaintances, that was all. He knew Tish liked to brag to her friends that it was more, but Jake had no real interest in her, nor she in him. But to find her there, using his condo, the disrespect of it when he was ready to quit anyway, so burned out—

He clenched a fist and rested his chin on it. "So here I am ranching. What do you think, Stephie? Would a real country boy fall into a sticker patch?" Jake made a face at Stephie and she grinned.

"I've done all I can do." Emily patted his shoulder. "There will be some I've missed. I'll check again in a few days. I'm so sorry you got hurt last ni—"

"I'll stay away from those stickers," Jake said, cutting her off. No one had said anything about last night. "Thanks for taking care of me. I'd better get home."

"Do you want some cookies? Emily makes the best homemade chocolate chip cookies in the whole world."

He needed to get out of here. Emily's groan told him she was dismayed at the invitation. To be contrary, he accepted. Well, not just to be contrary. He hadn't eaten anything since last night. He climbed off the table, pulled his shirt on, and took the chair Stephie slid toward him. He straddled it to protect his back.

"Does he need Band-Aids, Emily?"

Jake smiled. "Band-Aids, the most prized of all medical treatments to an eight-year-old."

"No, the best thing for him—"

"I'd like a Band-Aid." Jake knew better than to grin when Emily's eyes narrowed at him, but he did it anyway.

Stephie pawed through the first aid kit.

Emily leaned two inches from his face. "It would take five hundred Band-Aids to cover those battered shoulders, hotshot."

Jake grinned as Emily's face flushed with anger. He couldn't remember ever being so entertained by a woman. He watched her steal a glance at Stephie and wondered what ego-bruising crack she wanted to make. He really wasn't in the mood for that. What he was in the mood for was a kiss from Em—

"Here they are. Do you want me to put them on?" Stephie wanted to help, not to mention play with the Band-Aids.

Jake couldn't say no.

The story of his life.

"Just put two on the big scratch on his neck, okay? The rest will heal better uncovered." Emily glared at him.

Stephie ducked behind his back to start fussing.

Jake was surrounded by the Johannson women's care even if the one in front did hiss from time to time. Nothing had ever felt so good.

He couldn't remember why he didn't like women.

—⁕—

Emily turned away and grabbed the cookie jar. She fished cookies out and grabbed a plastic sandwich bag out of a drawer and threw the cookies in. "Jake told me he has to go home now." She looked at him.

"No, not yet. Please stay." Stephie jumped up and down.

Emily saw the anger in Jake's eyes. "How about if you come home with me, Stephie?"

A tigress awoke in Emily. "No."

"Oh, please, Emily. Please, please, please. I won't stay long. I'll do all my chores and help—"

The litany of promises was lost on Emily. She knew exactly what Jake was doing. He was proving that there was no way Emily could keep Stephie away from him. And the more Emily stood in Stephie's way the more she'd drive them together. And the more completely shattered Stephie's heart would be when he left.

Emily dropped to one knee in front of Stephie. "Honey, Jake seems like a really nice guy. I'm sure he is." When he wasn't torturing her. "But he's a stranger. You learned about strangers in school. And we had a lesson about it in Sunday school, too."

"Jake's not a stranger."

Emily thought of how much Stephie had snooped around the poor man's house. Stephie probably knew the man better than anyone. "Jake—"

"I wouldn't hurt her."

Emily looked away from Stephie, and the hurt in Jake's eyes brought her to her feet. "But this isn't about you, is it? It's about rules and being safe." Emily did her best to beg with her eyes. "Back me up."

Proving beyond Emily's ability to doubt that Jake *wasn't* dangerous, he turned to Stephie. "She's right about strangers. I know you feel like you know me, but you need to practice all the rules you've learned, so practice on me, okay? You stay here and I'll come and see you later, with your big sister here. I'll come for supper. That'd be great. I'm starving."

Stephie grudgingly agreed.

"You're always starving," Emily muttered. Wonderful. She felt like she'd adopted a stray dog. Wrong. Jake was going to be way more trouble.

"And later you and Emily can come over and have a tour." Jake smirked at her, then headed toward the door.

Which cornered Emily pretty neatly into having to spend even more time with him. Which reminded her of her tingling fingers and the fact that Jake had a life he couldn't say no to, that was bound to catch up with him at any time and he'd leave—breaking Stephie's heart in the process. So how did she keep him away from her?

She knew. "Don't forget your mail, Jake."

Jake looked over his shoulder, no doubt to toss a smart remark at her. Nothing came out.

Emily passed him and grabbed the letters off the kitchen counter.

He was right behind her. "What is this?"

Emily glanced at Stephie and enjoyed watching Jake keep the explosion inside. He rifled through the letters, muttering words Emily was glad neither she nor her little sister could hear.

Chapter 9

"Where did you get these?" Jake's strangled question made Stephie twist her fingers together nervously.

He saw a pang of remorse cross Emily's face. She was being ten different kinds of coward to dump this on him with Stephie as a witness.

Emily squared her shoulders. "Stephie, you know how Jake wanted to be a secret?"

Stephie nodded, looking between them.

"Well, these letters may mean someone knows he's here, and he's upset. Why don't you go outside while we decide what to do?"

Jake couldn't believe it. Here was Emily's chance to turn Stephie against him. About five well-chosen words from her and his temper would erupt, and Stephie would never trust him again. And Emily obviously didn't want Stephie trusting him. But she hadn't goaded him. She was too fair, too honest, too decent, too kind. Resentfully, he knew that made him the biggest jerk in the room. The better he knew Emily the more he couldn't stand her.

"Does this mean you have to leave?" Stephie whispered, catching hold of his fingertips.

Stephie Johannson was probably already the best friend he'd ever had. He dropped to one knee in front of Stephie. "I'm not going anywhere, sweetheart. Let me talk to Emily alone, okay?"

Stephie laid a butterfly-soft kiss on his cheek.

Tears stung his eyes. He rested a big hand, callused from touching destruction, against her baby soft hair. Considering the bad news he'd just been handed, he was remarkably at peace.

"I want you to stay." She threw her arms around his neck.

He gently wrapped his arms around her and drew strength from her. Jake let her go and stood up with a calm that surprised him. "Go on out now, please?"

Stephie nodded and ran outside.

"Where did you get these?" He shuffled through them.

"The mailman gave them to me when I was in town. My father's name was John. I still get things addressed to J. Johannson. These are to J. Joe Hanson. You know how addresses get messed up on junk mail. It seemed likely they were mine."

He flipped to the open one, fingered it as he read Tish's return address.

"Did you read all of them?" It was obvious the rest were untouched. But Emily had read Tish's drivel. Since Tish wasn't here to blame, Emily seemed the natural choice.

"No, I didn't read them. I opened that one from someone named Tish. Is she—"

"She's none of your business." He pulled the letter out and compressed his lips. "You read this. You must have. No woman could resist."

"I said I didn't read it, and I didn't. Well, at least not all of it. As soon as I realized it wasn't for me, I stopped."

He kept reading, glancing up to try to catch Emily's reaction, embarrassed to think Emily had been subjected to this. None of this implied-romance garbage was true. All he was looking for was a reason she'd sent the letter to Cold Creek.

Tish had precious little to do with why he'd taken off. But she'd definitely been the last straw. He'd been away three months and barely thought of her. He'd come home overwhelmed, knowing he had to get out of Hanson and Coltrain. He'd walked into his own apartment and seen the woman who had his keys so she could water his plants, entwined with his pool man.

Jake had left his apartment with the clothes on his back. There wasn't even anything in his home he wanted to keep. No pictures, no scrapbooks, not even an old football trophy. He'd sent a note to Sid, saying he was through.

Taking every bit of cash he could scrape together out of several bank accounts—a considerable amount—he hit the road. He'd stopped at his cabin in the Rockies, and in the window of a Realtor's office in the nearest town, he'd seen the picture of the Barrett house, huge, impractical, isolated, and so cheap he should have known better. But he'd recognized home.

Home had turned out to be a white elephant in Cold Creek, South Dakota, that was trying to kill him. Isolation was a snoopy, argumentative woman who cooked like a dream and an angelic little girl who didn't want him to leave.

Emily broke into his whirling thoughts. "These letters are sent to the town. There is no box or route number. Somehow they got the name Cold Creek and they're taking a shot in the dark. I'll return them with a note in the open one, explaining about my name."

Jake couldn't gather his thoughts enough to respond.

"Look, if you want to call her up and beg for forgiveness, feel free to use my phone."

The thought of talking with Tish made him shudder. "Send them back. Sid'll be here sooner or later. I make him too much money. But maybe they'll learn they can get along without me in the meantime." Jake shoved the letters into Emily's hands. "What a mess. I'm tempted to pull up stakes and hide somewhere else."

He looked out the window in the kitchen door and saw Stephie running across the lawn.

"I'll try to make it sound good, Jake. And I'll tell the post office to return any new mail."

"No, I'd better see it."

"But why? Surely it would be better to—"

"Just bring it home and let me look through it before you return it."

"Listen, hotshot. I'm not your secretary. Don't—"

"You're the one who offered to help," Jake said, cutting her off. "Then the minute I want something, you start meddling." She was a woman. She had manipulated him from the moment they met. About the tree. About the way he was living.

Emily's straight-forward differences of opinion and Tish's deviousness were just different sides of the same coin.

He glared at Emily. "Just do as I ask for once."

Emily sighed. "Fine."

Jake wanted to storm off, but of course he had to say one last thing. "What time's supper?"

—❦—

"Have you found him?" Tish stormed into Sid's office.

Her yellow spandex dress started low on top and ended high on the bottom. Her mass of blond curls swayed and bounced right along with the rest of her.

"No, I haven't found him," Sid snarled. At least she spared him that vapid help-me-big-strong-man voice. "Any response from those letters?"

"Yeah, look at this." Tish snapped a piece of paper out flat and dropped it on his desk. "What do you think?"

Sid scanned it.

"Should we send the PI?" Tish jiggled her wrist while he studied the letter.

The sound of her bracelets set Sid's teeth on edge. The polite Miss Johannson told him nothing. But that scrap of paper from Jake's lodge in Aspen had said Cold Creek. "Yeah, I'll get the agency on it."

Tish kept jingling until Sid grabbed her arm. "That racket is driving me crazy."

Tish narrowed her eyes, and he let her go. She wasn't someone he wanted mad. She knew too much about how short Hanson and Coltrain was on cash. Without Jake, half the engineers had quit. Sid hadn't slowed his spending, neither had Tish, who had been on the payroll since Sid had introduced her to Jake.

"We're in trouble if we don't find him soon. Sorry I grabbed you." Then, because apologizing made him choke, he added, "You never did tell me why Jake took off."

"Yeah, I did." Tish jingled her arm a couple of times, caught herself, and clenched her hands.

"No, you didn't."

"Sending him to another job was what did it." Tish slid a hand up to rest on one hip.

Sid knew she was probably right. But he hadn't had much choice. "I'll call the PI." Sid grabbed the phone.

—⁕—

Jake had managed to stay underfoot at most meals. He'd been so kind to Stephie that Emily was very close to lifting the "stranger" label from the man.

Not that he wasn't dangerous. Watching him enjoy his food and dote on Stephie put Emily's heart in terrible danger.

After picking up the mail, Emily stopped in the feedstore for mineral blocks on her way to fetch Stephie and Lila Murray from their last day of school.

Men sat around a table, drinking coffee, and they called greetings to her. She noticed Wyatt Shaw among them. "How's the buffalo business?"

The whole room erupted into laughter. Wyatt's former hostility to buffalo and his now being the proud owner of a herd of them was the source of a lot of good-natured teasing.

"Fine."

"Tell Buffy I'll see her in church on Sunday."

"She'll be there if the baby doesn't come first." Wyatt's love for his wife was enough to handle all of the teasing in the world.

Emily did her best not to envy her childhood friend his happiness. The men went back to their gossiping while she paid for her mineral.

Just as she stepped out of the building, someone said, "A guy came around my shop askin' for someone named Jake Hanson. Told him about Lizzie and Edgar Hanson, but he said this Jake is a young guy." The low-pitched voice slipped out the rapidly closing door.

Wyatt Shaw asked, "Fella driving a maroon Taurus? All rusted out?"

"Yeah, that's him. Hung around town all day. Said he. . ."

The door snapped shut. Emily reached to yank it back open. She stopped herself. How could she go back in? She'd draw attention to herself if she asked about the stranger. She forced herself to go to the truck. She had to warn Jake.

Emily whirled to jump in her truck and race home and almost ran over Buffy Shaw.

"Whoa, girl." Buffy, hugely pregnant and smiling, raised her hands to catch Emily before she plowed right over her friend.

"Hey, Buffy. I'm sorry. I didn't see you."

Laughing, Buffy gave her an awkward hug. "That is the nicest thing anyone's said to me in months. I'm so big satellites can see me."

"Hey, you're due pretty soon, aren't you?" Buffy had on a lightweight black tank top with a picture of a buffalo on the front and the words SHAW BUFFALO RANCH in a curve about the buffalo. Emily had seen plenty of the shirts around— the Shaws sold them out at the ranch and in the mini-mart in Cold Springs—but Emily had never seen a maternity version of the shirt before.

Groaning, Buffy shook her head. "I've got two months to go."

"Well, that's not long."

Buffy's eyes narrowed. "Only someone who isn't pregnant would say such an obscene thing."

"Sorry." Emily laughed. Then, because Jake was always in the forefront of her mind, Emily added, "I just heard Wyatt say something about a guy snooping around."

"Yeah, it was weird. He said he was a private detective. I don't think I've ever met one for real before, but he had ID. Wyatt checked. At first we thought he might be asking about your dad. He said Joe Hanson, and Wyatt misunderstood and thought he meant Johannson, you know."

"Yeah, I can imagine doing that."

All too well.

"Wyatt wasn't about to send some strange man out to your place, so once he was sure the guy wasn't looking for you, he didn't tell him any more. Did he show up at your place?"

"No. We're so far out we don't get any traffic, so I'd have noticed if he even drove by the place. When was this?"

"Maybe four days ago. I'm not sure. Don't you ever get lonely, living out that far?"

Not wanting to ask more and maybe raise Buffy's suspicions about why Emily was so interested, she let Buffy change the subject. "I'm used to it. Stephie's great company."

They talked about the buffalo for a few minutes. "Well, I've got to pick up Stephie and Lila, so I need to head out."

"It was great to see you. Come over for dinner after church sometime."

"I'd like that. I've been so busy with spring work I haven't been anywhere. Bye." Emily fretted about the private detective all the way to school.

Emily picked up Stephie and Lila. The two girls screamed and giggled, thrilled that summer vacation had begun. Emily dropped Lila off at home and backed out of the driveway before Helen could catch her. She still hadn't come up with a good explanation about Friday night.

Stephie hadn't told a soul about Jake. She loved having a secret.

"It's okay if you run over to Jake's and give him his mail, but you come right home."

"Em-i-ly," Stephie drew her name out into about six syllables. "Jake isn't a stranger anymore."

Emily nodded. She didn't know when to take the "stranger" label off the man. Emily didn't know the rules.

Stephie ran off to Jake's.

Emily headed to the barn to feed her steers.

Chapter 10

E mi-leeeee!" Stephie came tearing over the hill only minutes after she'd left.

Emily dropped her scoop and ran. "Stephie, what?"

"Jake's hurt." Stephie skidded, wheeled around, and took off.

Emily sprinted to catch her. Stephie veered off the path and Emily followed, ducking branches Stephie sent slapping back.

Stephie dashed down a slope.

Emily lost her footing, sat down hard, and began sliding down the hill. Her jeans ripped. She clawed at the ground to stop, then scrambled to her feet and raced on after Stephie.

Stephie ran around a huge, felled cottonwood and dropped out of sight as if she'd fallen into a hole.

Emily rounded the tree and her heart twisted in terror. Jake was pinned under the massive trunk.

"You found her. Thanks, sweetheart." He was talking. His eyes were open. His face was sickly white. What kind of internal injuries might he have? "Emily, thank God you're here."

Frantically praying as she tried to figure out what to do, she knew an ambulance could never get back in here, but the EMTs could carry a stretcher. But the tree? How could they move it? She looked up the hill. She could get her tractor in there but she didn't have enough chain.

"I don't think I'm badly hurt. Just stuck." Jake spoke with a scratchy whisper.

"What happened?" She could see where he had attempted to dig with his left hand. He hadn't made much progress, but it was a good idea. If he really wasn't hurt, maybe she could dig him loose. She slid down beside him.

"The tree rolled while I was chopping it. I found a dead one. To spare the American elm." He attempted a weak laugh, but it ended in a moan of pain.

The tree clung to the side of the hill, the top farther down than the roots. It had already moved once. If it started rolling, they'd be crushed.

Stephie. She had to get Stephie out of here. Stephie held Jake's left hand. Emily would have a fight on her hands if she tried to send Stephie away. She didn't have time for a fight.

Jake's right arm was pinned between the tree and his stomach. He lay in a

171

little crevasse washed out by spring runoff. That was the only reason he was still alive.

"Jake, hang on. I'll see if I can. . ." She shut up and started digging. She needed just a bit larger depression. With her hands it would take a long time. Stephie saw Emily and imitated her. The tree quivered.

"Stop." Emily used a voice that gained absolute and immediate obedience. She didn't know where it came from.

Stephie looked up, terrified. Emily had to get Stephie out of here. Maybe she could stabilize the tree somehow.

"Stephie, I want you to go back to our house and get something for me."

Eager to help, Stephie jumped to her feet.

"I need a. . .get. . .do you know where I keep the shovel? You know, the one with the blue handle in the toolshed?"

Stephie nodded. "I know where it is."

"Good girl. And a rope. There's one in the barn, but you'll have to—" The only one she could think of was knotted to an overhead door. Stephie couldn't get it. She'd have to go herself.

"How about the swing rope we took down and put in the basement last fall?"

Perfect. "That's exactly right. Get that and the shovel and bring them to me."

Stephie bent, gave Jake's hand a last squeeze, and ran.

Emily turned back to find Jake's eyes on her. Something cracked in her heart to see him so vulnerable.

"Tell me what happened." She put all her fear into digging.

"I was chopping firewood, planning to build a fire and cook some real food." Jake took a ragged breath. He twisted his head to watch her. "I stood on the trunk, hacking at a limb. It slid. I lost my footing and fell, and it pinned me. I tried to dig."

Emily's stomach turned when she pictured Jake falling in front of this massive tree. If he had landed just inches up or down the hill or if the tree had buried him under the gnarled roots hovering by their heads, he would be dead. "How long have you been here?"

"I've probably been here since two o'clock."

Two hours. She worked doggedly, ignoring the rocky soil scraping her hands, praying as she worked.

"I don't think anything is hurt. I can feel my legs. My toes wiggle."

"What happened to your voice?" She wiped a filthy hand across her brow as sweat stung her eyes.

"I yelled for help for a long time, hoping you'd hear me." Jake's head sank back onto the ground and his eyes fell shut.

Emily stopped pawing in the dirt and leaned over him. "Are you all right?"

She rested a muddy hand on his forehead.

His eyes flickered open under her cool touch. "I'm all right. It's just. . . I'm resting."

Emily leaned close. "We're going to get you out of here. Now don't go fainting on me. I may need some help."

"What can I do?" He sounded hopeless.

Emily couldn't stand it. "You'll do whatever I tell you to do, hotshot. Just because you're useless as a lumberjack doesn't mean you can't help me haul your ragged backside out from under this tree."

Jake grabbed her wrist and pulled it off his forehead. "Ragged backside? Where'd a nice girl like you learn that kind of rough talk?" The little flash of spirit was encouraging.

Emily smiled, pulled her wrist free, and turned back to digging.

Stephie came dashing through the woods, yelling, "I found the shovel and rope!" Sticks hung from Stephie's tousled hair. She had nearly as much dirt on her face as Jake.

"Great, honey." Emily jumped up, took the rope, wrapped it around the tree, and knotted it. She tied it to the nearest live tree. The rope couldn't hold the weight of this tree for long, but it might give them the seconds they'd need.

Stephie knelt by Jake, holding his hand. Emily wanted Stephie away, but her little sister needed to help.

With the shovel, Emily moved dirt in earnest. Her arms ached from the hard work and tension.

At last she threw down the shovel. Reaching under the tree, she scraped out a Jake-sized trench. She ran around the tree and dug until she met the opening she'd made. "Okay, Stephie. I'm ready to work where you are now. Can you let me in there?"

Stephie backed away but hovered nearby.

"I want you up the hill. Do you see that wild plum tree up there? The one with the white flowers?"

"Yeah, but can't I help? I want to—"

Emily faced her little sister. "You can help Jake by doing as you're told. I'm ready to pull him out now and I need space. Now go." Emily didn't issue many orders.

Stephie went.

Emily called after her, "You know how to call 911, right?"

"Yeah, do you want me to go call?"

"No, not now. But if—" Emily's throat closed, she swallowed and finished, "If you need to, you call, and call the Murrays, too. They'll come running."

"How will I know if I need to?" Stephie sounded so scared.

Emily hated putting her though this. If this went badly, Stephie would see awful things. Emily quit thinking about it. "You'll know. Just go on up the hill, darlin'." Emily turned back to Jake.

Jake grabbed her ankle. "We both know this thing is barely clinging to the hill. I don't want you in the way if it rolls."

Emily glanced up to make sure Stephie couldn't hear. "We try my way, or I call for help."

"I'm not saying I know a better way. I'm looking at that trunk hanging over our heads and I'm telling you, if the moment comes and you have to make a choice, I want your word you'll get out of the way."

"What do you want me to say? I won't die for you?" She tried for sarcasm, but her voice trembled.

"That's right. It's real noble, but what about Stephie? She's had enough people die. If this tree starts to slide, get out. That rope will give you the time you need and no more."

"What are you guys doing?" Stephie took two steps toward them.

"Stay by the tree." Emily tried to keep the fear out of her voice. If she was killed, Stephie's closest family was a retired uncle in Phoenix.

She looked down at Jake. "We're going to do this. It's going to work. So stop talking about people dying."

Jake gripped her ankle with surprising strength. "Promise me. I won't let go until you do."

Something warm turned over in her. She *would* die for him.

He must have read her expression. "Say it, Emily. Promise."

Instead, she said, " 'Greater love has no one than this, that he lay down his life for his friends.' "

"That sounds perfect. So let me give up my life for you."

"I didn't mean that."

"Why does your saying apply to you but not me?"

"It's not a saying. It's in the Bible."

"I've seen so many people die." His painful grip on her ankle eased. "I've seen the pain it leaves behind. If something happened to me, it wouldn't even create a ripple in this world, but Stephie needs you."

"I'm not going to argue about whose life is more valuable."

"Promise. Please. If I came out of this alive and you didn't, it would kill me anyway."

She had to put his mind at ease. "I promise. I won't die for you, and you won't die. For me."

She held his gaze until he released her leg. "Let's do it."

Emily turned to the uphill side of the tree. "If I can get your arm loose. . ." She concentrated on pulling dirt from under Jake's back.

"It's pretty numb. It won't be much use to us."

She quit digging and braced both hands on his chest. "This might hurt."

"It's been that kind of day."

She pushed down. His arm slipped free. The tree inched sideways.

"Get out of here." Jake's voice was a barely human growl.

"Get out yourself, hotshot." She jumped over him and tugged him into the hollow she'd dug. The tree quivered and slid another inch.

Emily grabbed his shoulders and pulled. The moist forest soil helped Jake slide. The tree pivoted on the rope. Jake's knees came out. He got his feet loose.

Jake's prison vanished under the roots. The roots swung toward them. The tree paused, straining against the rope.

Then with a loud *snap*, the rope broke and the log rolled straight at them.

Chapter 11

Emily grabbed Jake and dragged him to his feet.

The thick, uprooted tree trunk bore down on them.

She shouted, "Jump!"

Jake found the strength to obey.

Emily dived after him. Something slapped her face.

Jake and Emily landed in the dirt, side by side, and turned to watch the tree crush everything in its path. Then Jake pulled Emily close with his left arm. A small tornado hit.

Stephie.

"You did it," Stephie squealed.

Jake grabbed Stephie, pulled her onto his lap, and tickled her.

Emily sat up. Things started to go black, and she dropped back on the cool dirt so she wouldn't pass out.

She rolled her head sideways at Stephie's giggles, studying Jake. He favored his right arm, but it seemed to be working. Stephie jumped away from Jake, yelling in excitement, and Jake got to his feet slowly, but he made it.

When the black receded and Emily's vision cleared, she stood, leaned against a less malevolent tree, and watched as Jake and Stephie celebrated.

"Jake, I want to look at your arm. You may need a doctor."

"Boy, you start crying doctor every time there's the least little trouble."

Emily looked up sharply.

"Gotcha." Jake laughed, came over, and touched her neck. The humor faded from his eyes. "You're bleeding."

"I am?" She looked into the warmest expression she'd ever seen on his face. And that included the first time she'd fed him meat loaf.

"You saved my life, pure and simple. I am your slave for life. Thank you. And I'm so, so very sorry you are hurt." He pulled his hand away from her neck and there was blood on his muddy fingertips. With a shudder, he pulled her into his arms.

Stephie threw her arms around both of them, nearly knocking them down the hill.

Emily's panicky reaction eased in Jake's strong arms. When she felt steady, she pulled away. "Let's get on down to the house."

She pushed out of their little circle and stood for a minute to make sure her wobbly legs would support her before she headed down the hill.

Stephie's childish chatter and Jake's smooth, deep voice followed her. They walked past the dead tree, rolled halfway to the house, and she couldn't stop the tears that spilled down her face. She kept ahead of them so Stephie wouldn't see. Emily wiped the tears with her muddy hands as she shooed Jake toward the kitchen chair.

The old Barrett place, despite its new roof, looked the same inside as she remembered. She'd been in and out too fast the day she'd found Jake hurt to notice much. Dark oak cupboards, half of them with doors missing, lined the kitchen walls over a row of floor cabinets. A cracked porcelain sink, stained with rust, was the only fixture. No stove, no refrigerator. The floor was covered with ancient linoleum, swirled light tan under a coating of dirt.

There were a few cans and boxes in the cupboard, a loaf of bread lying on the countertop, and a half-empty case of Spam on the kitchen floor. She shuddered. "I suppose you don't have any first aid stuff yet?"

Jake studied her face, then shook his head.

Emily was too upset to scold. "You're going to have to shed that shirt, hotshot."

"Since you saved my life, I'll let you get away with that name. I'm starting to kind of like it." He tried to pull off his battered T-shirt, but his right hand wasn't cooperating. Finally he reached behind his neck with the left and pulled the whole thing over his head. He looked at the decimated piece of clothing, then tossed it at a cardboard box full of trash. "Country life is hard on clothes."

"Oh, Jake." A scrape dark with dried blood covered his right arm from shoulder to elbow, the skin raw. His chest was covered in abrasions. She struggled to control her tears.

"It looks worse than it is." Jake cradled his right arm.

Emily started scrubbing her hands in the ice-cold water from the kitchen tap. "Steph, I'm going to need some things from our house. Run and get. . .get. . ." Emily stopped. There was so much. "Jake, can you make it over to our place?"

"I think I can." He didn't sound all that sure.

"Do you have any way to heat water?"

Jake tightened his lips and shook his head.

Determined not to nag, Emily said, "Stephie, fetch the thermos from under the sink, fill it with the hottest water. . ." As the mental list lengthened, she paused. "You know what? Why don't you stay here and mind Jake?"

Emily hoped it was all right to leave him. She flashed on him lying under that tree, afraid that image was going to haunt her for a long time. "While I'm gone, you get him a drink of water."

"Uh, maybe Stephie should go with you." Jake was trying too hard to support Emily.

"I think stranger-danger time is over. The only person you're dangerous to is yourself, Jake. When's the last time you ate?"

"I had a little breakfast."

"Nothing at dinner?" Emily clamped her mouth shut on the scolding.

"The tree fell about the time I'd have quit for lunch."

"I'll scrabble something together."

He smiled apologetically and shrugged his shoulders.

She saw him wince, then she headed home at a run. She came back, packed like a mule. A cooler full of food and ice in one hand, in her other she pulled Stephie's old little red wagon bearing a thermos of hot water, a first aid kit, a tiny camping stove, and the kerosene lantern they kept around in case of power outages.

She cleaned and bandaged his arm, then quickly put together a hamburger and bean concoction and set it on the stove her parents had used for camping trips. While supper bubbled on the little stove setting just outside the back door, she and Stephie cleaned the kitchen. Then she spooned up food for Jake and Stephie. Her own churning stomach wouldn't settle enough for her to eat.

"I'm feeling almost human again." Jake finished wolfing down his supper. "That was delicious."

"I think you'd better go to bed now."

"What kind of host goes to bed while he still has company?"

Emily was relieved at his flash of spirit. "We're going now. I have chores to do at home." She thought of the two hours of hard work awaiting her just to do the bare minimum. "We'll clear up the supper dishes. But you look done in. You need help getting upstairs?"

"I sleep downstairs. I tossed a mattress on the floor."

"No sheets?"

Jake snorted. "Women invented sheets. What are they for except to get dirty and feel guilty about because they aren't washed?"

If he had been at full strength she might have braced Jake about his rude attitude toward women. His exhaustion saved him. "So instead, your mattress gets dirty and it can't be washed."

"When it gets too dirty, maybe I'll put a sheet on it."

"Yuck. Fine, get into your grubby bed. You look done in, except for your mouth. That's still at full strength."

"Don't you like Jake?" Stephie twisted her hands together.

Emily regretted her shots at Jake even if he had them coming. "Of course I like him. If he wants to live like this, it's his call, but I like to give him a hard time."

"You sound mad." Stephie's brow crinkled with worry.

"He's ruining a perfectly good mattress, but I'm not really mad." She shot

Jake a warning glance to back her up.

Jake made a comical face at Stephie. "You mean she can be worse than this?"

Stephie giggled.

Emily managed a smile. "Go to bed, Jake."

"I'd like to take a shower."

"You shouldn't. You should keep your shoulder dry."

"What about my poor mattress? I'll get it dirty." Jake grinned wickedly.

For a second their eyes locked and her heart seemed to slow as she looked into the tempting warmth of his hot fudge eyes. She forced herself to look away. "Let me remove the bandages. I'll replace them before you go to sleep. Don't slip in the shower."

"Aren't you afraid I'll faint?" His teasing brought her gaze back.

"I'll listen for a thud."

Jake laughed.

As he disappeared down the hallway, Emily turned to Stephie. "You want to surprise Jake?"

By the time Jake emerged from a long shower, Emily and Stephie had worked wonders. He walked into the room, wearing sweatpants and a blue robe. His right arm was out of its sleeve, cradled against his stomach. His hair was still dripping wet, like he hadn't been capable of drying it. He had dark circles under his eyes and his face was drawn with fatigue and pain.

"Get into bed, Jake. I want to make sure you're settled before we leave." She knew she sounded gruff.

Jake's eyes narrowed, his jaw clenched, and he glanced at Stephie. "You don't have to send me to bed like a child."

The urge to protect him was so strong she had to be rude to stop herself from holding him. "Just hurry up. I've still got hours of chores at home." Emily squeezed every possible drop of poor-overworked-me into her remark.

Jake repaid her with a long silence before he turned to his room. He stepped in the doorway, and Emily waited for his words of thanks for all her effort.

"Where'd that come from?"

"That old bed frame has been in the Barretts' upstairs bedroom for years." She was pretty proud of herself.

"I ran home for the sheets. And that's an old bedspread we don't use anymore." Stephie, vibrating with happiness, dashed between them as they stood at opposite ends of the short hallway.

"Thanks." His eyes flashed anger at Emily as he forced the word past his lips.

Stephie danced up and took hold of Jake's good arm. She pulled Jake down low enough to plant a kiss on his cheek. "I gave you my favorite sheets."

He turned to Stephie, and all his anger faded. "It looks wonderful. Thanks, honey."

How dare he be so gruff with her, then so kind to Stephie. "We're going. Do you need anything else?"

Stephie gave Jake a final grin and danced out the door, leaving them alone.

Chapter 12

He stepped close and bent near, the words for Emily only. "You'd better be planning to come over and make my bed every day and do my laundry. I told you I didn't want any of this, and I'm tired of you nagging me every—"

"Listen, you ungrateful—"

The slap of a door reminded her they weren't the only ones here. She glared at him as she spoke to Stephie. "What happened to Jake's mail this afternoon?"

Stephie came running, looking worried. "I dropped it out by the tree."

"Can you go and get it, honey?" She saw Jake's expression and knew he had a few choice comments to make. Well, so did she.

"Sure, be right back."

Emily followed Stephie to the front door. Then when she was out of hearing distance, she turned on Jake, who had followed her, glowering. "How dare you ask me to do your laundry after what you put me through today?"

"What I put *you* through? I was the one under the tree. And don't change the subject. This isn't about the accident. It's about your meddling."

"Of course it's about the accident. What you call meddling is me trying to keep you from getting yourself *killed*. Any moron could see that tree wasn't safe. It was barely hanging on the side of that hill."

"That tree looked like it had been there for years. How was I supposed to know it was so unstable?"

Emily fought down her temper because she could see Jake was out on his feet. "We'll sort it out tomorrow. I'll take everything away I brought over. But for tonight, just get some rest."

Stephie came skipping into the house with a fistful of letters addressed to Jake. "Here's your mail, Jake." Her voice was so full of hope and sweetness, if that big ox yelled at her—

"That's great, Stephie. I'll see you."

How could he be so nice to Stephie when he'd just been snarling at her? "Let's go home, Stephie. Let Jake get some rest."

"Okay, good night."

"Good night. Thanks for everything." He sounded like Mr. Perky.

She glanced at the sun. It was after eight. She'd wasted a whole day keeping Jake Hanson in one piece. And she'd probably have to do it all over again tomorrow if he insisted on chopping wood.

Of course he'd try again. He had to have wood. She thought of all the trouble he could get into and made a decision.

— ‑ ∿ —

The crash almost knocked Jake out of bed.

The house shook. Earthquake safety measures flashed through his sleep-soaked brain. He was on his feet, dragging on his pants despite his agonized muscles. The crash was followed by a roar. He thought of dams breaking as he raced around the side of the house. It was the worst natural disaster he could imagine.

Emily.

Driving a tractor taller than the first story of his house. Dumping wood out of a huge shovel mounted on the front of the bellowing machine. She backed away from the side of the house, leaving behind a small mountain of wood. She stopped the rolling monster and, leaving its motor roaring, jumped down from the cab and marched over to him.

She jerked leather gloves off of her hands and tucked them behind her belt buckle. "I figured that would wake you up, Sleeping Beauty."

She yelled to be heard over the clamor of the diesel engine. "Now you've got enough wood to last until Christmas, supposing you live that long."

Emily had risked her life to save him. By way of thanks, he'd insulted her, yelled at her, and then thrown her out of his house. He'd given up trying to understand himself, deciding to apologize first thing this morning. He remembered that for about two seconds. "Take the wood yourself. I don't need your help."

"What's the matter, hotshot? Afraid you'll be contaminated by wood cut with a chain saw and a log splitter and hauled with one o' them new-fangled tractors?" She exaggerated her soft South Dakota drawl. Coated with sawdust and sweat, her shirt was soaking wet even though the morning was cool. She had to have been working for hours to do all of this. And she'd had chores left last night.

He tried to imagine how incensed she must be to have worked this hard just to put him in his place. "Did you work all morning so you'd have an excuse to insult me?"

"Leave the ranch work to people who know what they're doing. You want exercise, stack the wood. You oughta be able to handle that." She sounded so smug and superior.

"I'm not taking that wood. I'm not taking anything from you."

"And I'm not going to let Stephie find you like that again."

"You did this for Stephie, huh? I don't think so."

"Go back to sleep for a few more hours. I've been up since 5:00 a.m. Those are rancher hours."

"I stayed awake most of the night because my arm hurt. You've probably had more sleep than I have."

Her eyes lost their fire. She'd been spoiling for a fight, and he hadn't disappointed her. But there was her dratted compassion when he talked about pain.

"Is it bad?"

He loved that tone—the caretaker, the nurturer. No, he hated it when she went all soft and sweet. It was all manipulation. So why had he played on her sympathy? His irritation faded. Her gentle words drew his eyes to her lips.

"Jake, I. . ." The words seemed to catch in her throat.

"What, sweetheart? Tell me what you want."

She looked like she wanted to melt into him. "Have we ever been alone for ten seconds without fighting?"

"I don't think so." Looking at Emily, he knew she didn't just want his money and his status. She wanted the deepest part of him. And she wanted him to give with his eyes wide open. He hardened his heart.

It must have shown on his face because trust faded from her innocent gaze. He was responsible for that and it struck him as the worst sin he'd ever committed. He clenched his fists to keep from reaching for her.

She took two faltering steps backward, then turned and stumbled toward the tractor. She climbed on and drove away.

He watched her disappear around the grove of trees that separated their homes. And he was left safely alone.

Chapter 13

A week without a crisis.

Stephie was at Jake's all the time now. Emily had given up pretending he was dangerous to her little sister. He came over to eat at least once a day, and he and Emily were polite to each other for Stephie's sake.

He'd kept the camping stove. Stephie said he was eating better. Emily had never run her ranch and home so efficiently. She did her chores and started inventing new ones. Working hard kept her mind off her neighbor. Or at least it kept her *away* from her neighbor.

She'd never told him about the conversation she'd overheard in town and she wasn't going to. Jake knew his past was going to catch up to him sometime. What difference would it make when?

He was healing and he'd started planting a garden. How could that be dangerous?

Stephie finished her chores after lunch, then headed over to Jake's. Emily wiped pouring sweat off her forehead and took a long drink from her battered gallon water jug, taking a break from scooping that last few bushels of corn out of an otherwise empty bin. She was sweltering but grateful for the work out of the direct sun. It had been blistering hot all day, unseasonable for early June.

"Emily, come quick!" Stephie came flying over the hill from Jake's.

Emily's stomach lurched.

"Something's wrong with Jake."

Emily grabbed the top of the small round door in the side of the bin and swung herself through the opening, nearly knocking her head off in her haste. She landed and started running.

Jake was on his hands and knees in the middle of his garden.

Emily knelt beside him. She noticed he was badly sunburned. From the look of the spaded ground, he'd dug up a huge garden bed.

Jake groaned and raised his head as if it weighed a hundred pounds.

"Stephie, run into Jake's house and get me a big glass of water." Emily helped steady him as she tried to stand. "We need to get you inside."

He nodded. Emily dragged him to his feet. His legs showed all the strength of cooked spaghetti. With Jake leaning heavily on Emily, they made it to the house just as Stephie came out with a dripping tumbler full of water.

Stephie pulled the screen door wide.

"Thanks," Emily said.

She glanced up at Jake and saw his throat work silently. Too dry to speak even the simplest words.

Stephie held out the glass of water, and Jake reached for it with shaking hands.

Emily helped guide it to his lips.

He sipped twice, took a deep breath, and then finished the water in one long drink. He managed a ragged, "Thanks."

"Let's get you into a cool bath."

He stumbled forward toward the bathroom. As they walked, Emily noticed the improvement in the house. Once the work necessary for survival was done, like the roof, Jake had turned his attention to the inside. Old carpet had been torn up, uncovering solid oak floors.

As they passed the open bedroom door, she saw Jake had kept the bed. He had brought furniture down from the attic that matched it—two chests of drawers and an end table. He had cleaned the whole set and polished it. They gave the room a lived-in look, and for the first time Emily wondered if he might stay.

Emily ran her hand across his brow. Hot and dry. Not good. Heat exhaustion. "Jake, when you're working in the sun and you stop sweating, it's a danger signal."

Jake reacted with such a small nod of his head Emily couldn't bear to lecture him further.

Emily guided him into the bathroom and twisted the cold water knob on the tub. She switched the shower head on. She wished it wasn't so cold, afraid it might be too much of a shock, but Jake didn't have any hot water to add to the cold. She helped him take his boots off, then steadied him as he stepped over the rim and under the stream of ice-cold water.

Jake yelped at the icy blast, then sank into the tub under the running water. Emily left the water on so he'd get good and soaked.

What if Stephie hadn't run over when she did? Emily looked up at her little sister. Her eyes were wide with fear. Her face was flushed red from her long run in the intense heat. As Stephie panted, trying to catch her breath, Emily worried she'd hyperventilate.

"Stephie, would you go to the kitchen and get Jake more water?" Emily felt stupid for asking, considering the gushing water soaking her as she bent over Jake, but she hoped Stephie's wild fear would ease if she could help.

Stephie grabbed at the glass on the sink.

"No hurry, Steph. Jake's fine."

Jake's head came up and worry creased his brow. "Stephie, I'm sorry I scared you. I promise I won't work in the heat like that again. I know better, but. . . but. . .it's June in South Dakota. I never considered it could be dangerous."

Stephie listened but didn't lose the frantic look.

He shrugged his crimson shoulders, and although he didn't let it show on his face, Emily knew each gesture tugged at his damaged skin. "I'm sorry I scared you. How about if I let Emily teach me all about ranching so I won't ever scare you again?"

Some of the panic faded from Stephie's eyes. "I'll get you some water if you want me to."

"I'd like that. Thanks."

Stephie hurried away.

Emily turned to Jake. He held her gaze for a split second before he let his whole body sag against the back of the tub. "I did it again. She's been my only friend. I hate that I scared her. I deserve anything you say, and I'm too weak to run. So I'll just sit quietly while you tear me apart."

Scolding him wasn't any use when he was all docile like this. She decided to give him a few minutes to regain his strength. She glanced around the bathroom for a washcloth. Of course there were none. The bathroom was remodeled though—new fixtures, new plumbing, new walls and flooring, the works. It was beautiful. Jake must have slipped out with his trailer and resupplied his building material.

Emily knelt on the bathroom floor by the tub. "Jake, you may be a rotten pioneer, but you're a great plumber and a talented carpenter. There's no chance you might forget about getting back to nature and just go with your strengths is there?"

His eyes widened with surprise. "Come on, don't compliment me. I want you to treat me like the worm I am. Let's have it, the whole sermon. Get it over with while I'm sitting down."

She hunted through a cabinet, found a towel, and brought it back to his side. The water was getting deep and she shut it off. She dunked the towel in and bathed Jake's neck and face. "Just relax and cool down for a while. And don't worry. I'm planning to yell long and hard as soon as I'm sure you're going to live." She smiled and he dug up a wobbly grin of his own from somewhere.

Stephie came back with the water glass.

Jake reached a dripping arm over Emily's head. The water trickled down her neck. The shocking cold startled a squeak out of her, and he grinned. He swallowed the water in three gulps and handed the glass back to Stephie.

She quickly offered to get more.

"I'm really starting to feel better, thank you."

"I'm glad." Stephie grinned.

Emily wondered how this love had sprung up between the two of them. Stephie's face was still beet red and dripping. Her flying braid straggled, sticking to her sweat-soaked cheeks and neck.

186

"Come here, Steph." Emily wrung the towel out and wiped it over Stephie's face. Stephie sighed. Emily wiped her own face with the chilly cloth. "That does feel nice."

Stephie nodded, her panic forgotten.

Emily's own stomach was still twisting over "almosts" and "what ifs." "Now, I want you to go into the living room and leave Jake and me alone for a while. Is that okay?"

"Sure. Are you going to start teaching him about ranching right now?"

Ah, the innocence of youth. "That's right. Jake and I are going to have a long talk." Emily wanted Stephie to be well clear of the "talk." No sense having any witnesses.

Stephie skipped away, her fears forgotten. Emily knew, as always, Stephie believed her big sister could fix anything.

One look at Jake told her he hadn't missed the tone. She admired his bravery as he braced himself.

—⁂—

Jake wasn't going to win any fights with her as long as she had him dunked in a bathtub. It made him feel about two years old.

He took a deep breath and started before she could. "I blew it. I hate myself for scaring Stephie. I'm the lowest slug on earth and I know better than to let myself get so dehydrated and burnt, but I've spent so much time working in the tropics that I didn't think about a South Dakota afternoon in early June being dangerous. So, I'm an idiot who thinks he's a hotshot. There, I beat you to it."

Emily sighed. "All I have to do is look at this house and see you are a talented, intelligent, hardworking man. You just don't know the first thing about living off the land. I'm sure I would be just as lost trying to read a blueprint or"—Emily looked around her and gestured with a wide swing of one dripping hand—"fixing up a bathroom like this. How can I tell you what to do when I have to stay away from you?" She looked back at Jake.

He knew this was the bottom line. They had to find a way to work together for Stephie's sake, if nothing else.

"Tell me what to do?" Her voice broke. "You know I told you to learn to cry, but truth be told, I don't do much of it myself, not since Dad died. Life is usually so easy. I can't stand finding you hurt again. What can I do to help you?"

Jake could have shriveled up and died from the hurt in her voice. He was prepared for a temper tantrum. That he could handle. "Aren't you going to yell at me? Come on. It will make you feel better."

She tried to smile. "Give me some time. I'll get around to it."

"I'm sure you will." They lapsed into silence.

As soon as he regained his first drop of energy, his awareness of Emily began to build. He didn't know how to stop it. He'd been attracted to her from the first moment he'd landed on top of her. Whatever was between them had some chemical element. They reacted when they got together. But maybe, just maybe, for the first time, he'd try to control himself. "You know what I think?" Jake removed the towel from her hand.

Emily let it go without a struggle. "Nope, but I'd like to."

Jake had the distinct impression she was starting to be bothered by their proximity, too. She sat back on the bathroom floor with her knees pulled up to her chest and her arms wrapped firmly around them.

"I think you should give me ranching lessons."

"The trouble with us working together is we end up—"

"I'm going to grow up. How does that sound? There's enough electricity between us to power this house with no help from wires, but I'm going to behave myself. I have realized by now that I don't have a clue about ranching. That's one of the reasons the house is improving so fast. I'm not doing anything else. I forced myself to go out and start spading up a spot for a garden this morning. I don't have any seeds, but I thought I could just get the dirt turned over and then maybe buy a book. Stephie made some suggestions about what to plant, but aside from corn and pumpkins, she's not really that much help."

Jake rinsed the towel over his face and around his neck and down each arm. His right arm was still scabbed over but it wasn't tender anymore. Only a few of the deepest scrapes remained on his chest. The sound of the cold trickling water helped restore his strength. And he recovered enough to feel like a dope sitting in the tub, wearing his jeans.

Emily filled his glass from the bathroom faucet and he gulped it down.

He lowered the glass and admitted, "I don't know how to get any food out of this land. I'm supposed to live off the land, but how? Where's the food?" He looked sideways at Emily, feeling as dumb as she kept telling him he was.

She remained silent, watching him.

"So say something. What am I supposed to eat, huh?"

She opened her mouth, then closed it again.

"What? Say it." Jake started to goad her, then thought the better of it in the new spirit of behaving like an adult.

"Okay, ummm, I'm trying to make myself offer to help you live off the land, but living off the land is hard work. And I'm going to have to do most of it at first."

Chapter 14

No." Jake laid the soggy towel over his heart. "I promise I'll help. And how about if I help with your chores. . .at 5:00 a.m.? Then you won't be doing that much extra."

Emily's snort made him want to sink under the water.

Instead he sat up straighter and wrung out the entire towel over his head. As soon as the water stopped flowing and his annoyance faded, he got back to the subject at hand. "What exactly am I supposed to do that's so much work? Explain it."

Emily sighed deeply. "Well, you need to grow your own vegetables and meat. You need a milk cow. You'll need chickens for meat and eggs. It's too late to plant most of the quick-growing garden food. Peas and onions and potatoes go in early. We're already eating those at our place."

"Yeah, I know. They're delicious."

"We'll keep sharing our spring garden with you and let you plant pumpkins and tomatoes and sweet corn over here for us."

"Chickens and a cow? Where do I get those? I don't want anyone to know—"

"Yeah, yeah, no one can know you're here. Big deal." Emily waved her hand at him. "I had a cow that lost her calf this spring. You could have milked her by hand."

"What?" Jake sat up a little straighter in the tub, forgetting his weakness and pain in this new horror.

"I'll show you, although I'm not too good at it myself. I could wean one of my calves early and bottle-feed it. The cows don't have enough milk for both." She considered it for a moment, then shook her head emphatically. "No, that won't work. My cows are just too wild."

"I've seen your cows come crowding into the yard at feeding time. They don't seem wild to me."

"Well, you haven't tried to grab one by the—"

"I'm not much of a milk drinker really," Jake interjected.

"You've got to have a cow to live off the land. It's a renewable source of food that stays fresh as long—" Emily snickered. "As long as it stays inside the cow."

"What's so funny?"

"I'm imagining you milking a cow, that's all. It's not funny because I'll

189

probably get my head kicked off trying to train the cow to put up with it. Then you'll get to drink all the milk."

"They kick?"

Emily groaned and let her forehead drop onto her knees. She rested for a minute, then seemed to rally.

Jake silently scolded himself for asking so many questions. And determined that from this moment on he'd just say things like, "Yes, Emily," and, "Whatever you say, Emily."

"You'll need chickens, and for them you just have to have electricity."

"No, absolutely not. Out of the question. I'm not going to get electricity hooked up, I told you—"

"Okay, okay, let me think." She looked up at him fiercely.

He remembered his vow of obedience. Okay, starting now.

"I know Laura Ingalls Wilder's pa didn't have electricity. Let me think." She glared at him. "I don't know how to live off the land myself, you know. The natural way would be to have a mother hen hatch some chicks, and you can do that. But what this boils down to is which comes first, the chicken or the egg. I think it has to be the chicken. I'll buy baby chicks and you can let them grow up and you can raise your own generation of them from those chickens. But the first generation has no mother, so you have to have a heat lamp."

"Can't I just buy a pregnant chicken?"

Emily started to laugh so hard she let go of her knees and flopped over backward onto the floor. She rested her hands over her stomach and laughed, and as much as Jake wanted to toss the soggy towel on her face, he was beginning to get the swing of this mature-adult-in-control-of-himself thing.

"Would you mind telling me what's so funny?" He thought his voice was the very model of respect, however totally she was failing on her side.

"Pregnant chickens?" She barely uttered the words before she was lost again.

It was hard to tell, his being so hot from a sunburn, but he thought he might be blushing. "Look, I know chickens hatch from eggs, okay? I meant a chicken ready to lay eggs that would hatch." He sounded a bit testy, but he still had control.

"It just sounded so funny." Emily still couldn't coordinate herself well enough to sit up.

Jake was severely tempted to get out of the tub and grab her and— He'd counted to ten for the fifth time when she suddenly quit laughing.

"What did you do to the ceiling?" From her position flat on her back she had noticed his pride and joy.

He grabbed desperately at the change of subject. "It's pressed tin. I'm going to put it in the kitchen, too. I'm trying to blend the true Victorian style with modern amenities all through the house."

Emily sat up, wiping tears from her eyes, and looked around some more. She ran her hand over the tiled floor. "This is real tile. You didn't use linoleum."

"I chose the pattern and laid it."

"It's beautiful. You designed it yourself? It's so intricate it must have taken days." Her eyes shone with pleasure.

He thought he saw the first inkling of respect he'd ever gotten from her and it helped dispel the immature desire to get her to quit laughing at him by kissing her. "It's how a Victorian home should look. The ceiling was something I ordered from a specialty catalogue at the Home Depot in Rapid City. I've been to town for supplies a couple of times."

"What do you do, sneak out before sunrise so no one sees you?"

"Yes, with the trailer. I can load a lot of stuff in it. I'm in town before the doors open at seven. Then I get home as fast as I can."

"Someone's going to notice you. This can't last."

Jake shrugged. "I've found a route that's out of the way, and it doesn't go past any houses until I get to a bigger highway. I think I am going to make my own ceiling for the kitchen. I've looked at this one and I think I know how to do it. I made the heavy cornices." He pointed to the ceiling again.

"You mean the molding along the ceiling and the wall? You carved all that wood?" Emily sat with her legs crossed at the ankles, looking at all the details.

He loved it that she was impressed. "It's not carved, though that's the effect I wanted. I added quarter round and a small molding to the largest molding I could find, and nailed it together. The leaf pattern is plaster stenciled to match the leaves in the tin ceiling. I painted the whole thing white. That's how a lot of Victorian houses were, so I didn't cheat on the ceiling, but I did on the fixtures."

Emily ran her hand across the odd wrought iron legs that held up the cream and white marble sink. "It looks ancient. It wasn't in here before."

"No, and it's not an antique. It's got all the strength of porcelain, it looks and feels like marble, and it's really plastic. Since I got it, I found some catalogues I might use to buy antique pieces, but I wanted the bathroom to be functional. I did save the commode though. I tore out all the insides and put in new, but I couldn't part with that cast iron lion."

"I always loved that lion. I never missed a chance to come in here and talk to him." Emily ran her hand over the ridiculous white lion sitting proudly, creating the base for a toilet. "It was just another way this house made me feel like a princess when I played over here." Her eyes drifted back up to the ceiling. "The Barretts were so nice to me. When I think of how they let me have the run of this place. . ." Emily dropped her eyes from the ceiling and touched again the mosaic of earth-toned floor tiles. "I know what this reminds me of. My grandma made a quilt that looks just like this."

He saw the sentiment in her gaze, and he was glad she had been in time to save her tree. He suspected she'd like the source of his floor motif, too. When he picked it, he had just done it to suit his own taste, but now it seemed like he'd done it to pay his respects to one of Emily's ancestors. "I saw the quilt. That's where I got the idea."

Emily looked up, confused. "When did you see it?"

"The day you took out my stickers. It's thrown over your couch in the living room. It looked just like something I'd been playing around with in my head, the squares and triangles combined in these shades." He continued to bathe himself, feeling almost normal. He looked at the red skin of his arms and knew he'd pay for this act of idiocy for days.

She looked up to catch him studying his burn. "How are we ever going to keep you alive?"

"You're going to help me. Starting with getting me a pregnant chicken." He scowled at her, daring her to laugh.

She didn't let his scowl slow down her giggling at all. "So, you know where chickens come from? That's good. You'll still need chicks and a heat lamp. The Barretts' old brooder house will take some repairs to keep the rats and weasels out."

"Rats and weasels?" The horror at having to fight off rats must have been noticeable because he saw she wasn't impressed. In fact, if he wasn't mistaken, she was trying valiantly not to start laughing again. "What kind of place is this?"

"And snakes. Don't forget snakes. Life is hard on something as defenseless as baby chicks. The truth is you probably need a dog and a couple of cats. They keep the pests away as well as anything. Of course they like to eat chicks, too, but you can usually fence them out."

"Dogs and cats and cows and chickens." And suddenly through all the annoying details, Jake's dream came back to him. He really wanted all of this. He wanted huge orange pumpkins, a friendly dog, and a cat that would curl itself around his leg while he read by the fireplace at night.

The humor that had been lurking under the surface warmed in Emily's eyes and, for just a minute, he thought she almost shared his dream.

Then she went and spoiled everything by talking. "You'll have to have electricity."

"No. I told you—"

"The chicks have to have a heat lamp. It's a substitute for their mother sitting on top of them. They won't survive even on warm days without it." She was trying so hard to be reasonable.

He had no intention of letting her get away with being reasonable. "No power. No way. That's final."

"The chicks will die."

"We'll skip the chickens. We'll just do the rest."

"But chickens are the only quick source of protein I can think of. The eggs and the meat. You can't butcher a cow or pig without a freezer to store the meat. But you can kill a chicken and eat it all in one day, so the meat never spoils."

"Kill it? I thought I was going to eat eggs."

"The girls lay eggs and the boys you eat."

Jake's fist hit the water. "Who invented that sick system?"

"What other use are the boys? That is their purpose in life. It's been years, but I think I remember how to chop off their heads with an ax."

Jake surged to his feet. He was self-aware enough to know a fight-or-flight reflex had kicked in. "I'm not going to chop something's head off with an ax." Water swished over the sides of the tub when he stood. "What is *wrong* with you?"

Emily rose, dodging most of the water. "I thought you wanted to live off the land? Do you really think the chickens in the store are from noble chickens who, after a full life and a death from natural causes, donated their bodies to grocery stores?" She stepped way too close to him and about did him in when she poked him in the chest. "Just because you're going to be intimately involved in their deaths doesn't make them any more dead than the ones hermetically sealed on Styrofoam trays. It's where meat comes from, hotshot."

Hotshot really set him off, and for one tense moment he forgot his pledge to treat Emily better. His hands clenched as he stopped himself from grabbing that irritating finger.

Something blazed between them. Emily dropped her hand without his making her. She wavered a minute and he wasn't sure if she was going to step away or lean into him.

For once he wanted to go first. He sat back down in the icy water. It was the best place for him.

When he finally glanced up, she looked relieved and surprised and maybe just one tiny speck disappointed. He went back to cooling himself off, deeply proud of his self-control.

Letting her teach him just might work. But he didn't think he could kill a chicken. He'd wait and give her the bad news later.

She cleared her throat. "About electricity. . ."

"No." He loved that word. He was going to be saying it to himself pretty regularly in the coming days. He might as well bury her with it, too. For an instant he remembered his "Yes, Emily. Whatever you say, Emily," pledge but dismissed it. A man had to have some fun. He'd start being obedient as soon as they settled the electricity question.

"How about an extension cord? I could buy a few hundred yards of heavy duty extension cords and run them from my place."

"No."

"A generator. I have one of those, gas powered. We'd just run it overnight for a week or two, for the chicks. Or I could raise the chicks until they're past the age of needing heat and send them over to you."

"No, I'll raise them here. I'll find a heat source."

"Chicks don't respond well to a wood fire," she informed him sarcastically. "All you'll get for your trouble is a barbecue. Let me start them. I'll let you come over and do everything, I promise. In fact, I insist."

He really wanted to say no again, but he was starting to bore himself. "We'll figure something out. I'll give you the money and you buy the cow and chicks and—"

"We'll worry about the money later. That's enough at first. No more gardening today. Why don't you rest for the afternoon and come for supper tonight?"

"Can we have apple pie again?"

"I've got a busy afternoon." She smiled and the words had no bite.

"But you said they were easy, remember?" And he couldn't believe how pathetic he sounded. He couldn't ever remember caring much about food before.

"Not a chance, bud. I have a roast in the Crock-Pot. It's been slow-cooking since noon. It's no-dessert tonight, but you'll like what I make well enough, I suppose."

"I'm sure of it." Jake lifted the towel to his face and breathed cool air through the soaking cloth. It was probably time to get out of the tub. His skin didn't hurt so badly, and he had a permanent case of goose bumps.

He lowered the towel. "You've saved me again. This time, I promise, is the last. From now on I'll consult with you before I start anything."

"It's not all your fault you didn't consult me. I haven't made it easy."

Those eyes were so deep with all of her feminine power and softness that he wanted to get lost in them. Instead, he slapped himself a little bit too hard with the dripping towel. He wasn't going to get lost. Not anymore. Not now that maybe he was finally finding himself. He was a changed man. "You've done the right thing all along. Now I'm going to help you instead of working against you. I'm going to listen and learn."

She leaned over to rest one callused hand on his forehead, testing his skin temperature. He wondered if she was checking for a fever because his being so decent to her came off as delirium.

And after just a bit more fussing and advice, she went. All the while she was smiling so sweetly he knew he could get another pie without any trouble at all.

Chapter 15

The morning after Jake's brush with heatstroke, an insistent rapping on the door woke him at 8:00 a.m.

Every muscle in his body ached as he thrust himself out of bed and into his jeans and blue chambray shirt.

Stumbling to his front door barefoot, he reminded himself he was going to be friendly.

He had made a steadfast civility oath and he was going to keep it or die trying. Right now, with her irritating habit of waking him up, seemed like a good time to start. He breathed in a long patient breath and opened the door. "Good morning." There was no need to fake sincerity, he was too sincerely delighted. "You brought me a cow?"

Emily held a lead rope connected to a small black and white cow and carried a large box under her arm that emitted ominous squeaking sounds. "A cow and some baby chicks."

"Are you okay this morning?" Stephie stood behind her with a little red wagon overflowing with two big paper bags and a small cooler.

"I'm sorry if we woke you. You had a hard day yesterday." Emily didn't seem to have any real remorse.

But Jake didn't complain as they fussed pleasantly over his sunburn and his general health until he was thoroughly ashamed of his irritation. He silently vowed they'd never catch him sleeping again. Jake started down the veranda steps.

Emily tied the cow to the corner railing. "Go get your boots on, cowboy, while the womenfolk make breakfast."

Jake tipped an imaginary Stetson, noting Emily's real one. He needed a cowboy hat, too, now that he had a cow. "Much obliged, ma'am." He hurried back inside, eager to start this day.

Using only Emily's little camping stove and ingredients they brought along, they made him a huge breakfast of bacon and eggs and pancakes in the time it took him to brush his teeth and pull on his boots. Emily insisted he sit long enough to drink a second cup of coffee out of her thermos before they took him outside to display their purchases.

The cow chewed her cud placidly as Emily stroked her back. "This is the gentlest cow I could find. I know the boy who raised her. She was his 4-H project and he took her to the fair last year, so she's been handled a lot. Never milked by hand though."

Fear chilled Jake's overcooked skin. How gentle was gentle? "Do we milk her right now?"

Stephie grinned as she tipped the sacks out of her wagon. "She's gonna have a baby. You can't milk her till it's born."

"A baby. . .really? Don't cows have their babies in the spring? You said yours did." Jake, reprieved from climbing under the cow, looked forward to the calf.

Emily nodded as she set the noisy box on the grass, well away from the heifer's hooves. "Beef cattle do, but not Holsteins. A dairy farmer calves year round. This will be her first calf. Holsteins give enough milk for a baby with plenty to share with you. She's been handled a lot, so we ought to be able to milk her." Emily managed to look doubtful and determined at the same time.

Jake loved the way Emily said "we."

Stephie set off back into the trees with the wagon. Jake wanted to ask her what she needed to get and maybe help her. The feed had been a pretty heavy load, but the conspiratorial look that passed between Stephie and Emily kept him still. Stephie obviously wanted to surprise him, so he'd let her.

"See that weird little roof over there?" Emily pointed to something he'd dismissed as a collapsed shed. Weeds were grown up around it. "It's a brooder house. We need to drag it out of the tall grass and patch it."

It was about two feet tall, including a foot of gradually sloping roof. She helped him pull it across the ground to a grassy spot. With a tact that delighted him, she plunked down a sack full of small boards, a hammer, and nails, then gave him the respect of offering no direction. Instead she carried the feed sacks to the barn.

She stayed a long time in the barn, and when she returned, she opened the top of the squeaking box.

Suddenly the air was full of the tiny high-pitched cheeps. He laid his tools aside and looked in at dozens of baby chicks. They looked like bright yellow cotton balls with legs. Legs and vocal cords. He reached into the box and jumped back when all of them tried to peck him at once.

Emily laughed and picked one up.

To restore his manly pride, he boldly took a chick of his own and soon realized that the pecking and scratching tickled more than it hurt. Up close he could see the yellow fuzz was thinning in spots and little white feathers were growing in place of the fluff.

Emily took out a little flat tray, opened a section of the brooder house roof that was hinged, set the tray in, and then knelt by the brooder house to pour a jar full of water into the tray.

"They're white leghorns. They'll be good egg layers. Here, watch. We need to give each of them a drink before we let them go." She picked up a chick and dipped its beak in the water, then tipped the chick upward as if the water could only get down its throat using gravity.

"Why?"

Emily straightened away from the water, still holding the chick. "I don't know. I just remember my mom and grandma doing it." She grinned, then set the chick in the brooder house, caught another one, and dipped its beak.

Before she set the second chick down, the first had escaped through a hole. "Now you know where to patch." She smiled again.

He had to scramble to get the building patched. Some escape routes were so tiny he'd have never considered them.

When the chicks were all settled and drinking and safely trapped inside, Emily led the cow to a fenced-in yard around another old building that was almost swallowed up by the trees. He'd been so busy with the house, he hadn't spared any thought to the half dozen little shacks scattered around his place. He'd explored the hulking old barn a bit, but Emily seemed delighted with the existence of every building.

Stephie came back down the forest path.

Jake was startled to see a wriggling brown creature in her wagon that he couldn't identify. It looked like a fifty-pound worm.

When she got closer, he couldn't look at the wagon because he was so overwhelmed by the angelic smile on Stephie's face. She pulled the wagon with tender care, and he could tell she was dying to show him her cargo, so her caution was all the more impressive. She stopped next to him. "Are the chicks safe? Can they get out anymore?" She asked the question with terrible seriousness.

He forced down his curiosity and checked the little building again. "I have it sealed up now."

Stephie closed the door that swung up out of the brooder house roof, then she quickly opened what Jake now recognized as a gunny sack, and produced two half-grown kittens. "Aren't they cute?" She hugged each of them close, then handed them to Jake.

He took only one because he could tell she couldn't bear to give up both. He heard the loud purring coming from the yellow-and-white-striped kitten in Stephie's arms and was honored that his little gray one started in with the same contented rumbling against his chest.

Emily came up behind Stephie and watched the whole proceeding with a big smile. "Always feed them in the barn. Then they'll live out there. Feed them one time, just one single time," she warned ominously, "outside your back door, and you've got house cats. And then you have to get more cats for the outside and they'll all want to be house cats, too."

"Where can we put them, Em?" Stephie's question told Jake there was more to come.

"There's going to be fireworks no matter what we do, so I guess just put them down on the ground. We might as well get it over with." Emily gave the brooder house a quick once-over as Stephie set her kitten on the rough grass like it was a china figurine and turned to untie another sack on the wagon. "You'd better put yours down, too, Jake. You might get scratched."

He obeyed her because he had promised himself he would let her be boss. He was glad he'd turned it loose when Stephie withdrew her hands from the bag holding a squirming puppy.

He greeted freedom with sharp little yips that pierced the air and sent the kittens flying across the lawn in a frenzy to get away from the noisy little pup. Eventually the gray one ended up in the branches of Emily's American elm tree and the tiger kitten disappeared into the shed with his cow. His cow. His chickens. His cats. His puppy. Jake couldn't stop smiling.

Stephie struggled with the hyperactive little creature, and Jake laughed out loud at the antics as the brown-and-white fur ball alternately licked Stephie's giggling mouth and tried desperately to get away.

"Puppies are trouble, Jake. I almost regret getting you one. But they're so cute you forgive them, and he'll keep the varmints away. Don't leave anything outside you don't want chewed up and buried. Especially boots." Emily, despite her hard words, couldn't keep the smile off her face.

Stephie sat down on the grass and let the puppy jump all over her.

Jake was surprised at his pleasure over the puppy. He'd never had a dog. Until this moment he'd never wanted one. "He's great. I want to hear all about everything. I can't believe you got so much done so quickly."

"Well, puppies and kittens come easily, although I think I got you good ones. The kittens come from a great mouser on the farm where I got the cow. The puppy was advertised in the Hot Springs paper. He's the result of an unfortunate encounter between a purebred bloodhound and an Airedale. So he'll either be the world's calmest rodent-hating dog, which would be fantastic, or he'll be a bundle of nerves who bays at the moon all night and sleeps all day—that could get old. One thing's for sure, he's going to be big, and even if it's just the noise he'll make, he ought to keep raccoons and possums away from the chicks."

"I thought it was rats and weasels," Jake interjected.

Emily smiled and shrugged. "Them, too. The trouble is the puppy may want to eat the chicks himself at first, and if we ever let him get one, it'll be really hard to break him of the habit. So it's important to keep the chicks locked up in the brooder house. The kittens will be happy to snack on them, too. Six weeks from now the chicks will be full grown, but the pup and kittens will still be babies, and the chickens will be able to push them around. Until then we have to be on guard.

"The chicks were in a farm supply store in Hot Springs. Stephie always wants to play with them when we're there, so today was a thrill."

"You've done all this before I ever got out of bed." Jake had thought he was a slacker when they caught him sleeping. Now he knew it.

"You had a tough day yesterday. You needed to rest." Emily went on talking with no sign of the censure he knew he deserved. "The family that raised your heifer lives close to Hot Springs. That's why I went there. I took a field road that doesn't pass any homes to get back to my place, so none of the neighbors saw me drive by with the heifer in my truck. Chances are the word won't get around that I bought her. You should still be a secret."

Jake wondered how difficult it had been for her to pick a route home so she wouldn't be seen. He was asking too much of her. And what about money? "This must have cost a fortune."

"Don't worry. I'm planning to let you repay me. Although if you have more eggs than you need in a few months, we'll help you eat them, so I don't mind splitting the cost of the chickens. The cow cost the most. That kid really valued his cow." Emily raised her eyebrows in mock fear. "She can never give enough milk to pay for herself."

"That's okay. I'm not going to try to squeeze a bargain out of a little boy." Jake noticed that Emily was concerned over spending too much of his money without his approval. That was a totally unique experience for him with a woman.

"We have cat food and dog food and I'll bring the mash over for the chicks in a minute." Emily ticked purchases off on her fingers.

Stephie jumped up from her frolicking and thrust the puppy into Jake's hands. "I'll get the next load."

He had been dying to pet the little fellow, but he hadn't wanted to ask Stephie to part with him. Now he was thrilled as his hands sank into the soft fur while the puppy panted and yipped, and in the background, fifty tiny peeps amounted to a roar.

Stephie walked off pulling the rattling little wagon.

Over the din was Emily's steady instruction. He looked at her and saw intelligence and grace as she shared with him the life she loved.

He had to lift the puppy in front of his face. His behavior was going to be exemplary, but Emily the helpful teacher was even more compelling than Emily the crabby neighbor. And he'd been dangerously attracted to the crabby version, so he was in trouble.

He held the pup under its rotund tummy and hooked his thumbs around its front legs. Then he looked eye to eye with his new companion, its tongue hanging out. Jake even let the little wiggler lick his cheek just to get his mind on something besides how lovely Emily looked in her work boots and braid. And how, with no makeup or expensive clothing, she enhanced the natural beauty he found all around him and became the center of it.

Her fingers brushed against his hands and he wondered if she could possibly be experiencing all that he was. Her hands seemed to slip over his, and as she touched him he gave serious thought to forgetting all his noble promises, especially if she wasn't interested in behaving.

"Quit hogging the puppy." She slid her hands past his and around the dog.

Jake was as jealous as he'd ever been in his life. But he released his hold on the squirming little hound.

"The chicks will eat the grass from under the brooder house. You'll need to move it every day so they're always on clean ground. Stephie's bringing a waterer. The store even sold them to me for a bargain because people usually want the younger chicks. Since they're a little older and the forecast sounds warm, they'll probably be okay without a heat lamp."

Jake watched Emily let the puppy win his struggle to be free. It scampered away and immediately began happily terrorizing the chicks by jumping against the side of the brooder house, barking in pure frenzy.

Emily grabbed him by the scruff of the neck and deflected his attention by kneeling beside him and rolling him over to tickle his tummy. "I'm sorry about all this. I don't know how you'll manage. I shouldn't have brought everything at once."

Jake wanted to roll her over and tickle her tummy. He wanted to laugh and touch the softness of the chicks and wrestle with his pup. He wanted to find out what was involved in delivering a baby calf. "I don't know how I'm going to do it either, but I can't wait to try. I'm really living off the land now."

Jake was used to menacing cracks sagging over his head and buckling under his feet as he assessed damage from some natural disaster or, in a few terrible cases, bombs. He was used to people—pleading people, suffering people, dying people. He was used to his heart pounding with the pressure and peril and despair.

The country life was solitary and quiet. Progress was as slow as watching a seed come up or an animal grow. He noticed the absence of the pounding heart and rubbed his hand over his chest as he thought about the price his father had paid for making work the center of his life. He hoped he'd finally made a break from the trail his father had blazed.

"Yes, I think maybe you're a pioneer now, hotshot."

Their eyes met and, for Jake, it was a perfect moment. The young life all around him. The sweetness of Stephie's little voice as she made her way back to them, singing. And the beautiful, teasing woman who couldn't keep from caressing a puppy even as she listed off the dire trouble the little sprout would cause.

His eyes rose to the branches of the American elm tree that swayed over his head, and he thanked God that Emily had stopped him before he could chop it down.

He thanked God.

In that perfect moment, a thousand random twists and turns that had led him to this place all locked together. What had once seemed like a life lived randomly was in fact just pieces of a jigsaw puzzle that now came together. He hadn't just been wandering aimlessly all this time. He'd been traveling to here and now. The sum of his experience had prepared him to appreciate where he was with a full heart. A full, healthy heart.

"You know something?" With all the easy camaraderie that had typified this morning, he could tell when she looked up at him that she knew it was important.

"What?"

"God led me here. God put me right here."

"And that surprises you?"

Jake almost laughed. He expected her to be awed. Instead, she accepted it easily. Of course God put him here. It was just another thing to love about this life—the "of course" about God.

"I hadn't thought of it in years, but I remember now, after my mom left and I realized how alone I was, I used to pray. I'd lie in bed at night and know my father wouldn't be home before I went to sleep. And he'd be gone when I woke up. I'd pray for someone to come in and care about me."

Emily started to stand from where she sat cross-legged on the grass, but he raised a hand to stop her. He wanted to finish and he knew if he let her, she'd hold him, and he was too vulnerable to keep his resolutions if she was in his arms.

She stopped when he signaled, but she was there. And knowing it made all the difference. It gave him the courage to remember.

"I must have prayed that same prayer for a year before I finally gave up. It was how I put myself to sleep at night. I'd talk to God about my mom. Our housekeeper told me she had a new husband. I'd ask God to make her come for me. Or I'd pray for my father to come in, just once, and tuck me in bed. We had live-in help that took care of me. The one that was there when Mom left was really kind. She'd come in and read me stories and help me say my prayers. But Dad changed hired help constantly, and before I knew it she was gone, and the new housekeeper didn't like bothering with me. I kept saying my prayers though. Not just for my parents but even for the housekeeper to come. Anything to break up that aloneness."

"Jake, I'm so sorry." Her compassion washed away the pain of his reflection.

Jake looked at her and smiled. "Don't be. I'm not feeling sorry for myself.

I just realized I wasn't alone all those long, dark nights. God was with me. He was always there. I knew it then." He knelt next to her in the grass, just as Stephie came into the clearing. He reached for the puppy to keep himself from reaching for Emily. "Hope hurt too much after awhile. So I quit asking, quit praying. But by doing that, I see now I shut out the only One who was there."

Emily smiled up at him, but he saw a sheen of tears in her eyes. Whatever she saw in his expression, helped to keep her tears from spilling.

"I've found Him again, Emily. I want to say He's here, here on this ranch. But the truth is He's been with me everywhere. I'm the one who quit talking. I'm the one who made my loneliness come true. But I'm never going to be alone again. This time I'm keeping Him close."

"When you're done being a secret, you can come to our church. It's a country church with lovely people in it. I think you'd like them. They'd welcome you. You'd make friends, Christian friends who'd be interested in you for yourself, not your money. You never have to be alone again."

Their eyes met.

Jake knew then, with God in his heart and Emily in his arms and little Stephie at his side, he had already left his lonely life behind. His eyes locked with hers and too much passed between them to ignore.

Stephie arrived with her latest load. Jake rose, the puppy in one hand, and reached down with the other to assist his lovely neighbor to her feet. "Get up and teach me what to do with all these animals. Then I'll come over and help you with your chores. You must be hours behind."

Emily hesitated, but she looked from his outstretched hand to his smiling eyes and, with the generosity he'd come to expect from her, she reached out to him. He pulled her to her feet, and just for a second she was too close.

"Can I hold the puppy?" Stephie begged.

Jake dropped Emily's hand. He turned to Stephie and, needing to find an acceptable way to express his joy, he gave her the little dog, then swished Stephie off her feet and swung her and the puppy around in the air until they were helpless with laughter.

Chapter 16

Anew neighbor had moved in next door.

There was no other way to describe it. Whoever lived there wasn't Jake. No one could change like he had.

Or maybe it was fairer to say this was Jake, and whoever had lived there before was gone. She had to admit she'd seen flashes of this relaxed, kind gentleman over the weeks, especially around Stephie. But now there seemed to be nothing left of the old. Like a butterfly emerging from its cocoon, Jake had transformed into something wonderful.

He was at her house constantly. He ate all his meals there, including breakfast. He prayed fervently before he ate each meal, taking over the prayers as if he were head of the household.

He did so many of her chores she felt guilty, and he had more patience with Stephie than Emily did. Stephie and she were at his house every day, fussing over the chicks and trying in vain to train the puppy.

The chicks grew with startling speed. By the end of June, they'd changed from precious, fragile babies into clucking scavengers. Emily was relieved that they got by without the heat because she knew Jake would feel terrible if they died.

Emily decided to force Jake to accept one tiny modern convenience. She showed up at his house one morning with a portable bottle of propane. The dog barked like crazy when she came over, but Jake didn't wake up. What was the point of having a guard dog if you slept through his alarm?

She sneaked into his basement through the sloped cellar door, then hooked the little bottle of gas into the hot water heater in the belly of Jake's castle. She lit the heater without his seeing her.

Later in the morning, she turned on the tap. "Welcome to the twenty-first century, Jake."

Jake looked up from the kitchen table where he and Stephie were taking a milk and cookie break. "What do you mean?"

The faucet began to steam.

"Hot water."

Jake rose slowly from the table.

Emily waited for the explosion. To head it off, she said, "A hot shower will feel great."

He caved with only a token fight and Emily knew he was a goner. He'd taken the first step down the slippery slope of convenience.

Later, as Emily plotted what to force on him next—a gas stove maybe— she realized she pictured herself cooking at his stove. With a sinking heart, she admitted to herself she cared about him. It wasn't friendship anymore.

And he was leaving.

Chapter 17

He was staying forever!

Jake grinned as he tossed a bale of hay high in the air, clearing the wooden fence by several feet. The cows shoved their way close to the feeder set on the other side of the fence as he grabbed the next bale. They chomped and snorted as they shoved their way to the feed. He could throw bales so much faster than Emily she didn't even help anymore.

He loved it. In this one tiny area of his life he was better at ranching than Emily. Enjoying the pressure on his muscles as he heaved another bale, he knew it was silly to gloat, but he wanted to be in Emily's league. He wanted to know everything there was to know. Not just memorize the chores to be done but understand all the whys.

He wanted to sing out loud and shout praises to God. His reawakened faith was the best part of this lifestyle change. Yes, even better than Emily and Stephie, because he could care about them more with God in charge of his life. And the more he learned about Emily, the more he cared.

He tried to conjure up indignation when she sneaked over and started up his hot water heater. How could she believe he hadn't heard her with Lucky's yipping? He'd almost called a halt to the gambit when she crept into his basement. She was breaking and entering, trespassing, plumbing without a license. Some of those were felonies. But before he generated the gumption to get out of bed and get dressed and go scold her, he thought of how great a hot shower would feel, and he decided they weren't really *important* felonies. He'd bent his arms behind his head and nestled deeper into his pillow to listen contentedly to her clanking around in his basement.

The last bale delivered to the greedy cattle, he tugged his leather work gloves off his hands and watched the big, placid animals crowd around the feed bunk. He heard the soft munching of their teeth against the bristling hay. He looked across the feedlot and watched Emily's three-month-old calves frolic on the hillside. Beyond the rolling pastures of Emily's land, the majestic peaks of the Black Hills stretched for miles. All around this clearing, tree branches rustled in the late afternoon July breeze.

A beautiful place, a beautiful life. He wondered what amazing, fresh-vegetable-rich feast Emily was making for supper. The peas and radishes and leaf lettuce were gone now, but there were new potatoes and green beans, and the tomatoes hung heavy on the vine, a few showing the first tantalizing blush as they promised to turn from green to red.

He tucked his gloves behind his belt buckle the way Emily did it, and enjoyed the sights, the sounds, the smells. The warmth of the afternoon sun on his denim-covered back felt great. His skin had finished peeling and he used caution now. He was learning.

He ran one hand over his chest and let the strong beat of his heart reassure him that this was the life for him, not the burning, dying, high-stakes existence he had abandoned.

Scampering footsteps warned him of the approach of Stephie and Lucky. "Did Cowlick have her baby?" Stephie skidded to a halt in front of him. She'd been asking him that same question a half-dozen times a day. Jake couldn't help but be amused by her fascination, considering the dozens of calves right in front of her.

"Not last time I looked. I was heading home now. Want to go with me to check?"

"Sure. I'll tell Emily." Stephie ran off as fast as she'd come, and Jake started for home, knowing Emily would say yes. Lucky nipped at Stephie's heels, and Jake admitted who the dog belonged to. Jake didn't mind. He was over here as often as the dog.

By the time Jake crested the hill toward his house, Stephie caught up and slid her hand into his with her usual breezy friendliness.

Preoccupied with his enjoyment of the day, he didn't notice anything different as he stepped in the barn. By the time his eyes adjusted to the slightly darker interior of the old building, Stephie had run back outside to check the pen.

She dashed inside, grabbed his hand, and hauled him into the sunlight. "She's gone. Cowlick's gone!"

Rustlers!

A frantic look around the little yard where his heifer lazed her life away, awaiting the blessed event, revealed no cow. Someone had come onto his place in broad daylight, because he'd checked Cowlick just a couple of hours ago. Rustlers had driven away his entire herd. No one would get away with this bold assault on his property. He'd hunt for tracks. He'd form a posse. Hanging was too good for—

"She's having her baby."

Jake looked up from hunting for tracks. "How do you know that?"

Stephie pointed to the ten-foot gap in his fence. "Look, she's knocked that big wooden gate down over there. I know 'cuz cows run off to be by themselves when they're gonna have babies. They do it at our place all the time."

He'd have noticed in a minute. He couldn't read all the signs at once.

"Come on. Let's get Emily and go look for her."

It irritated him to go running to Emily for help. Maybe because he had appeared a teensy bit stupid to not spot the missing gate. "Why do we need to get Emily? She says the cow doesn't need any help. She's told me that a hundred times." A couple hundred, because he'd been worrying and he'd asked and asked and asked.

"Well, we should find Cowlick and bring her back, or at least make sure she hasn't wandered too far. I guess we could go alone." Stephie looked at him with such doubt in her eyes that Jake waged a war with his wounded manhood.

Stephie adored him. She thought he could do no wrong. If she thought they needed Emily, they probably did. And he had taken a solemn oath to never scare Stephie or almost get himself killed again. Now might be his first chance to prove he possessed a learning curve. "Okay, let's go get Emily."

Five minutes later, Emily crawled out from under her hay baler and deserted whatever adjustments she was making. "There's no fence for miles to the north so she could be anywhere, but my guess is she didn't go far."

Cowlick was over the crest of the first hill south of his house, standing so close to the fence she could touch noses with Emily's cows if they wandered to that side of the pasture. For now, Cowlick was completely apart. Jake wondered if cows got lonely.

"Yep, she's calving for sure." Emily absently dusted grime from her hands without taking her eyes off the mother-to-be.

"She's just standing there. How do you know she's in labor?"

Emily laughed at him for no reason he could understand. "Because she's just standing there, that's how I know."

Her amusement pinched more than it should. "That doesn't tell me anything. You're supposed to be teaching me." He should be used to being the dumb one.

She quit laughing. "Sorry, you're right. I don't mean to go laughing at your question. What she's doing isn't normal. So, I'm sure she's calving. What made me laugh is *labor*. I'm not used to thinking of cattle that way. They're a long way from humans when it comes to babies. The mama stands there and the baby is born. No birthing classes, no doctor in a white coat. Right now I'd like to shoo her on back to your barn. Being out here is just an old instinct. It doesn't do her any good. I'd rather have her close up to the place."

Jake shook his head in disbelief at Emily's insensitivity. "We can't make her walk all that way. It's cruel."

"What's cruel is letting her have the baby out here and then making you carry the slippery little thing back to the barn on those big broad shoulders of yours, hotshot. I say let her tote the little tyke in before it's born. Besides, if she has any difficulties, my doctoring stuff is back there. Let's go."

"Doctoring stuff? Wait. . .what difficulties? I thought you said—" He was talking to himself.

Stephie headed up the hill, and Emily followed. Jake went along but he thought the whole idea of making a lady in the throes of calf-birth take a long walk was barbaric. They headed Cowlick toward the barn. She strolled along like she didn't have a care in the world. By the time they had her locked up, Jake had decided they were wrong about the baby being delivered any time soon.

"Let's grab an early supper, then come back and check her. I'm guessing you want to see the whole thing, right Jake?" Emily hefted the ten-foot panel back into place without asking for help. She found some baling wire and was half done securing it before Jake could lend a hand.

"Weeellll. . ." Jake shrugged his shoulders sheepishly, suddenly feeling like a voyeur. "Yeah."

"Okay, it'll be awhile, so let's eat, feed the chickens, and tie Lucky up. He might make the new mama nervous if he comes in at the wrong time." With a final tug at the fence, Emily glanced at him for agreement, and they headed back to the Johannson ranch.

Chapter 18

Jake barely tasted the new potatoes, steaming and tender, boiled with their skins on, that he and Stephie had dug. He nearly swallowed the crunchy, perfectly undercooked green beans whole even though he'd helped snap them. He had seconds of everything and a third grilled hamburger, just so it wouldn't go to waste.

He did slow down to savor the cherry cobbler Emily had made with the last of the cherries from her own tree. He'd helped freeze a couple of dozen quarts of cherries and Emily had taught him how to make jelly, then given him half of the jars. She put food like this on the table for every meal. Whatever was ripe in the garden.

He was trying to cut back on his lavish compliments because she would look at him like he was some lab specimen when he marveled at her cooking. But on the rare occasion he held the gushing flattery, he could tell she missed it.

Today, since Cowlick was probably in desperate need of him, he kept it to a minimum.

―⁂―

Hay hung from the corners of Cowlick's mouth when they reentered. She gave them a bored look and kept chewing.

Jake and Stephie began petting the cow's head while Emily turned her attention immediately to the business end of birth.

"Uh oh. Those aren't front feet."

"Do you have to pull it, Emily?" Stephie was an old pro.

It was Jake Emily was worried about. She didn't have time to hold his hand.

"Is there something wrong?" Jake came around to Emily's side, then staggered backward, gasping.

Two legs protruding from the back end of a cow could be a shock for a greenhorn. "Stephie, toss a scoop of corn in Cowlick's feeder. Let's get her in the head gate." She slapped the heifer on her back, urging her forward.

"Don't hit her!" Jake grabbed her wrist.

Emily smiled. "Cows have a tough hide. I'm not hurting her."

Jake held tight. "Can't we get her to move without that?"

Emily's temper flared. "This calf is coming backward, and the longer it stays inside of her, the greater the chance of losing it. Let go." She held his gaze until he reluctantly dropped her arm.

Out of respect for Jake, she clapped the cow gently on her back, then a little harder. Cowlick didn't budge. Stephie poured corn into the feeder, and the heifer stuck her head through the open head gate. Emily leaned forward to slide the stanchion shut around Cowlick's neck. The cow ignored them and ate her grain.

Emily dragged a heavy apparatus across the barn, along with a toolbox she had converted to a veterinary kit.

Jake looked anxiously at the six-foot-long, Y-shaped metal brace with its dangling chain. "Where did that stuff come from?"

"I moved it over here awhile ago." She upended a plastic bucket, then set it down, disconnected the chain from the brace, and dropped the chain in the bucket.

"You mean you knew there was going to be a problem?"

Rummaging in the vet kit she'd also moved over here earlier, she produced a pint bottle of iodine and poured most of the dark yellow liquid over the chain. "No, I was just being a Boy Scout. You know, be prepared?"

Jake prodded the Y-brace with his toe. "It looks like a medieval torture device."

Emily spared him a quick smile. "It may look like that, but pulling a breech calf without it is backbreaking." She reached into her first aid kit and grabbed a sealed package containing one sterile, shoulder-length, clear plastic glove. She tore it open and pulled the loose-fitting glove onto her right hand and up to cover her sleeve. She spilled the last of the iodine over her protected fingers. Sliding a loop of the sanitized chain over the baby's legs, she tightened them and turned to the brace.

Jake came around the other side of the placid animal. "Tell me where you want it."

Emily instructed Jake to hold the brace against Cowlick's back legs. She connected the chain to the lever on the brace. Emily pumped the lever up and down to take up the slack in the chain until it was taut. She stopped levering and turned to Jake. "Once I start, I've got to get it out of there fast. As its chest passes through the birth canal, its lungs are crushed. When the pressure comes off its lungs, the baby takes its first breath. Trouble is, when the chest delivers first, before its head, that breath is taken inside the mother. That means this little baby will be drowning."

"Let me pull the lever. I'm stronger."

Emily hesitated. "Your strength will help, but you've got to keep going even if it seems to be hurting Cowlick. I've heard cows make very distressed sounds. I've even seen a few fall down. When the going gets hardest, that's the exact moment you *can't* quit."

Jake met her eyes. "I won't quit."

She held his gaze, judging him. "Let's say a prayer before we start."

Jake nodded. "I'll say it."

Emily felt better after Jake's sincere request for help from God. "Okay, let's go."

Jake started hiking the lever. His muscles bulged under his T-shirt.

Emily knew a prayerful moment of gratitude. She would have been in trouble doing this alone. She watched the calf's hind legs emerge fully.

"Now's when it gets hard. Once its little rump is delivered it should be easy."

Jake worked the lever steadily, winding up one chain link at a time with the click of metal on metal.

Emily saw his lips moving and knew he'd kept up his prayers. She added her own. "Just a few more inches."

The lever stalled.

"It's not moving." Jake spoke through gritted teeth, leaning on the lever with all of his strength. His feet slipped a bit on the crackling straw.

Emily grabbed the calf's legs above the chain and pulled.

For a second, then two, nothing happened. Cowlick mooed in distress and twisted her head around, fighting the stanchion, to look over her shoulder.

Emily glanced up at Jake and saw regret over the pain he was causing. Then, with a sudden burst, the calf's little tail emerged and its hips, then it slid and landed on Emily like a wet sack of cement.

Rolling the soggy calf aside, Emily pulled the baby away from Cowlick's heels and knelt beside it. The calf wheezed. Emily grabbed a handful of clean straw and tickled its broad pink nose. "It's a little bull." Emily automatically checked. She glanced at Jake. "Grab his front leg. Like this." Emily bent one front leg double, pressing it against the calf's chest.

Jake was beside her instantly.

"Work his front leg up and down this way. It works like CPR. Maybe we can get the water out of him. Stephie, can you get the chains off his legs?"

They all three worked in silence. Emily got a few satisfactory sneezes out of the little bull, then he started fighting Jake.

Emily sat back on her heels. "Hold up."

Jake eased the leg out straight and sat back on his heels. "He doesn't seem too good."

"I think he's going to be okay." A soft crooning hum drew Emily's attention to Cowlick. Those gentle lowing noises were as natural to the little cow as giving milk. "Steph, let Cowlick out to meet her son." She pulled Jake away as the stanchion clicked open.

"You're a mommy now," Stephie sang.

Cowlick went immediately to her baby's side and started licking the white stripe down the center of its black face. The calf lifted its nose until he touched his mother's rough tongue with his own. Then, with a burst of energy, the baby shook his head vigorously and flailed his legs. Cowlick knocked him flat on his side with her tongue.

"She's hurting him." Jake rose from where he knelt on the barn floor.

Emily put a staying hand on his forearm. "Watch him liven up when she pushes him around. He pushes back. See." Emily pointed to the little one's uncoordinated efforts. "He's starting to use his muscles."

The baby sat up and resisted the seemingly careless ministrations of his mama. He leaned in to her licking, supporting himself against it.

Jake sank back on the floor, and Stephie's arms came around Emily's neck. The messy part of her work was done, so Emily stripped the plastic sleeve off her arm and tossed it into the iodine bucket. In silence, they watched the mother and calf.

Cowlick kept up a steady vibration from deep in her throat. The calf returned a juvenile imitation of the soothing song. The crooning settled into something spiritual.

Emily would have been content to sit there all night. She glanced at Jake to see if he was enjoying this as much as she was. A single tear rolled down his cheek.

Jake Hanson had learned to cry.

She smiled, then hoisted herself to her feet. "We need to get him up. He should have colostrum."

With a quick dash of his wrist across his eyes, Jake stood beside her ready to help. "What's colostrum?"

Emily's heart couldn't help but beat a little faster. He'd made all the difference tonight. "Colostrum is the first milk the mother gives. It has a high concentration of protein and contains a natural antibiotic. The quicker we get some inside him the better. Especially since the fluid in his lungs can cause pneumonia."

"What do we do?"

"First let me get him on his feet." She could see that Jake thought it was too soon, but he nodded.

Emily pressed on the calf's hind quarters. The baby reacted by pulling its front legs more fully underneath it. Next it leaned forward on its knees, lurched on its back legs, and raised its hindquarters into the air. Emily waited for the little bull to get his balance, then, when she thought it was time, she wrapped her arms around his slimy belly and hoisted him onto all fours. He wavered on those long stilts for a precarious count of three before he dropped back to the floor.

Emily laughed. "Not bad for the first time, little guy. Let's go again."

The second time he didn't try at all. He just looked over his shoulder at Emily's prodding.

The third time, Jake helped lift and they had him on his feet for a split second before Cowlick knocked him over with her curious nose.

The fourth time he got up and stayed. He was so wobbly, standing upright looked like nothing short of a miracle. When he took his first staggered steps they all cheered, and the noise almost sent him back to the floor. Jake caught him. Emily then pushed him toward Cowlick's udder. Cowlick turned to follow the calf, which had the effect of moving her udder away from her hungry baby.

Emily shook her head in disgust. "Beef cattle are better at this. A lot of natural instincts have been bred out of Holsteins in an effort to get more milk."

"Why would getting more milk ruin a cow's instincts?"

Emily kept urging the calf toward the circling cow. "It's not that they tried to wreck the instincts, it's just that a dairy cow can live without them. A beef cow has her calf outside, with no people to help. The cow gives birth without trouble or she dies. The calf gets up without help and starts in eating or it dies. Survival of the fittest." Emily started urging the calf and Cowlick into a corner. "Although, I do check my cattle and I end up helping a few babies into the world every year. That's why I've got all this equipment. You know that buffalo herd near here?"

Jake looked away from Cowlick's baby. "You've mentioned it before."

"I was over there once when a buffalo cow gave birth. Compared to them even beef cattle are wimpy."

"How's that?"

"When I was there the herd was walking along, grazing, and Buffy pointed to one of them and said, 'Look, she's going to have a baby right now.' "

"The buffalo didn't head for some lonely spot?"

"Nope, they stay together. They know the herd is protection for them. The buffalo cow never stopped moving. The calf was born while she was walking and fell to the ground."

"Was it hurt?" Jake looked like he was ready to go have a stern talk with Buffy about protecting her herd better.

Emily smiled. "Not only was it not hurt, it bounced right onto its feet and chased after the mother."

Jake looked doubtful as he glanced at the wobbly Holstein calf.

"Buffy told me the mothers never look back. The calf catches up and eats on its own or it dies. She said with almost every birth she'd ever seen, the calf was on its feet and walking after its mother within sixty seconds."

"Wow, I'd like to see that." Jake almost looked like he'd come out of hiding.

It gave Emily hope. "Compare that to dairy farmers. They keep constant watch, especially on high-producing cows because the calves are worth sometimes thousands of dollars. Dairy farmers intervene in troubled births, like we just did. Cows that don't calf easily and don't have natural maternal instinct, *like standing still to let her calf eat,*"—Emily aimed the last words at Cowlick and jammed her fists onto her hips as Cowlick nuzzled her baby, keeping her milk end far from her baby's mouth, and the calf standing there wobbling without a thought of eating—"still have babies that survive and grow up to reproduce, *no matter how dumb they are.*"

Emily pushed the baby again and Cowlick moved in the wrong direction. "Jake, stand on that side of her and keep her back end from moving away from me. Stephie, stay by her head and talk to her, distract her from licking the calf. If we can get the calf to eat once, they ought to get the idea."

Jake almost got shoved over for his trouble and Stephie wasn't as interesting to Cowlick as the calf, but finally the little bull latched on to supper.

His mama turned her head to watch him eat, now careful not to move her udder. Cowlick resumed her gentle lowing and licked along the baby's spine. With every drink, the calf gained strength and muscle control. His tiny tail began to twitch in time to his nursing.

Emily silently offered a prayer of thanks. She hadn't wanted Jake's first brush with the death of an animal to come so soon. It was a fact of life on the ranch, but he didn't have to learn that yet. With a satisfied sigh, she began picking up her equipment.

Jake took the heavy brace for her. "Let me carry it home for you."

"Leave it over by that wall for tonight. I don't have the energy to pack everything back home."

"Fine." Jake put the brace away. "What else do you need done?"

"Well, we need to treat his navel." Emily stooped and got her aerosol can of iodine out of the toolbox. She crouched beside the calf and sprayed under his stomach, careful to reach both sides. The sharp smell of iodine filled the barn as the bull's raw umbilical cord, hanging down under his belly, got painted bright purple from the spray.

"Then he needs a shot." She replaced the iodine can and extracted her hypodermic needle and the bottle of broad-spectrum antibiotic. She poked the needle into the rubber cover on the bottle, pulled back the plunger on the syringe, and, giving Jake an apologetic grin, stabbed the poor little bull right in front of his tail, a few inches off to the side of his backbone.

"I know that must be necessary," Jake said through clenched teeth.

Emily patted him on the arm. "It is. New calves are so prone to infection, especially with such a difficult birth. I don't do it for my calves, but between the complicated birth and being a wimpy Holstein, I'm doing it as a precaution. I have to give him this one and a vitamin shot." She concentrated on the calf, not wanting to see Jake flinch when the needle stabbed in.

"If this was one of my calves, I'd tag his ear to identify him. Yours is going to be spared the piercing. Since you only have one calf, I think we'll be able to keep track of him." She grinned at Jake. "Let's move the two of them into the bigger stall at that end of the barn. Then we can go. I'd like to check him once more before bedtime, to make sure his lungs are clear, and maybe once around two."

In deference to Jake, Emily lured Cowlick into the stall with a bucket of grain without a single slap on her broad back. The calf trailed along unsteadily, chasing his escaping supper.

Emily and Stephie walked Jake back to his house, enjoying the pleasant evening and the chirping of grasshoppers. An owl hooted in the trees, and a warm breeze rustled the leaves and grass.

"Right now I'm really glad I didn't come out and stop you when you brought that tank of propane to the house." Jake looked down at his grubby clothes, then looked sideways at her with a naughty glint in his eye.

It took Emily a second to get it. "You saw me? You knew I was working on your water heater?"

He grinned. "Why should you be mad?"

"That bottle of gas was heavy. If you knew I was doing it you could have helped." She gave his filthy shoulder just the littlest shove with her equally filthy hand.

Jake laughed. "I'm the one who was getting modernized against my will." He bent and gave her the briefest possible kiss on the cheek. "See you later, in the maternity ward."

He went into the house, and she turned to her own home, still tingling from the drama and joy of the night and Jake's teasing, and maybe, just slightly, from that purely platonic kiss.

Chapter 19

I f the calf had gotten sick, Jake knew he'd come out of hiding to find a cow emergency ward—if there was such a thing.

And Emily wouldn't respect spending thousands of dollars to save a calf worth a couple of hundred. It wasn't good business. To Jake's relief the calf was fine.

It was a good thing he was rich to begin with, because he couldn't make tough business choices about his animals' lives. He didn't mind. He could ranch for a long time before he used up all his money. Still, he was glad Emily didn't have to know.

He let the calf have all the milk it wanted and still got a gallon from Cowlick every morning and night. It was more than Jake, the Johannsons, and the kittens could drink, so they were throwing the extra away.

Stephie surprised him by loving to milk. As soon as Emily was satisfied that Cowlick wouldn't kick, she agreed to turn the chore over to her little sister.

Jake helped with the haying and couldn't believe the hard work involved. "You throw bales by yourself?"

Emily shrugged and gave him an evil grin. "Normally I'd hire a couple of high school boys to help. But I can't because they'd find out about you. So you get to take up the slack."

Jake looked at her as she climbed down from the hayrack. She stopped the tractor every dozen or so bales and pretended to help him straighten the load, but the load was perfectly straight. She was just giving him a break. Good thing, hoisting seventy-five-pound bales continuously for four hours almost killed him.

He ached for a week. The heavy lifting wakened a white-knight reflex and made him fiercely glad he could help. Her gratitude rang in his ears until he cherished every one of his stiff muscles.

Around the end of July, Emily announced the chickens were old enough to eat. It sent Jake into a tailspin. He endured several days of Emily's abuse before he noticed she wasn't chasing any of them down either.

At lunch one day—fried chicken from the grocery store—Jake braced her about it. "You don't want to eat those chickens any more than I do."

Emily got really busy dishing up slices of the first tomatoes of the summer and didn't look him in the eye. "It's not that I mind eating them. . .much." She looked up, her eyes wide. "I just don't want to get them ready to eat."

Stephie made a gagging noise, then went back to gobbling down the coleslaw they'd made from the cabbage in the garden.

Jake scowled at Emily. "You mean you can't look into their trusting little eyes and chop their heads off?" Jake would never go after one of his very own chickens with an ax.

Near as he could tell, Emily was suddenly fascinated by the task of buttering her corn on the cob. "It's not like I *couldn't* do it. I could. If I had to."

"You've been torturing me for days."

She flung her arms wide. "It's not like we're starving."

So the chickens were spared.

About that time, Jake discovered chickens were stupid. They would not stay in their pen. Despite constant patching, they always found a way out. He found droppings all over, in extremely unpleasant ways.

Then they began to vanish. Jake knew because Emily had ordered him to count his chickens every morning.

He had about forty left. "What is going on? There were fifty chickens when you brought them home."

"Hawks or owls probably. It's just a hazard that goes along with raising chickens."

Jake planted his fists on his hips. "Well if they're going to be eaten anyway, it seems like we ought to get to eat them."

"Ain't that the truth." Emily didn't go for the ax, and Jake couldn't, so the hawks were living large.

Next the dumb clucks all started picking on one chicken. To save it, Jake built it a separate yard. Then the birds simply chose another of their kind to harass.

When he had seven separate pens scattered around his yard, he could have killed a few leghorns, fried them up, and savored every bite. When the blasted birds discovered his fledgling garden and cleared out every speck of green, he entered a martyr zone.

The end came when they started on Emily's garden. The rancher in her rediscovered itself and Jake didn't even bat an eye when she announced the high-tech compromise of taking the roosters, about half the dwindling flock, to the local meat locker to be butchered. It wasn't what a pioneer would have done, but having Emily's freezer stuffed with chicken was one modern compromise Jake decided he liked.

Emily had to drive miles out of her way to get to his place, but she showed up with a stack of wooden crates in her truck late one night while the chickens were roosting for the night in the chicken house. She quietly entered the small building, then caught the unsuspecting roosters by the legs. They squawked and flapped, but the other chickens stayed put as their brethren got hauled away.

Emily tucked them in the crates and it took a few trips before Jake waded in and started helping.

As they took away the last of the roosters, Jake remembered his poor pumpkin plants. "The hens are eating the garden, too. Let's throw them in." Jake felt like he'd just imposed the death penalty on his friends. Of course he was royally sick of his friends, so he found he could live with it.

"Good call." Emily started snagging the rest of them. "Eggs are cheap."

—∽∿∽—

Jake had rediscovered his love of farming when Stephie came running into his house one Sunday evening, shortly after Jake had come home from supper and settled in to study the Bible Emily had given him. Emily brought him the bulletin from church every week and gave him a few notes about the sermon. He spent time daily in prayer and Bible study, but on Sunday nights he made it a point to worship.

"I can't find Cowlick."

"I checked her just before I came over to your place to eat." Jake grabbed a jacket and followed Stephie outside in the drizzle. His yard was soaked from a weekend of heavy rains. Emily had been smiling ever since the downpour started Friday night, saying a heavy rain in July made all the difference in her third-cutting hay crop. Jake saw Cowlick's tracks leaving the cow yard through that stupid, knocked-down gate. Why hadn't he gotten it wired up more solidly?

"I'll go after her. You go get Emily, okay?"

Stephie nodded and ran for her big sister. The two of them caught up with him coming back from the spot where Cowlick had gone to have her baby. "I went all the way to the edge of the pasture. She's not there."

Emily looked grim. "I'd better get my pickup. No sense ruining your Jeep on this rutted field."

Emily was awhile driving over because of the circuitous route she had to take around the creek, but she finally arrived. Jake and Stephie came out of the barn where they'd gone to avoid the rain, and climbed in. The rain had slowed to a sprinkle, but the pasture was soft.

They swung around a five-mile stretch of land between Jake's place and the nearest highway.

"We're running out of places to look." Emily wrestled the truck over the muddy, rutted pastureland.

Stephie screamed. "I see the calf." She pointed to a spot right beside the wooded creek. The calf stood inches from the bank.

Emily pulled to a stop. They jumped out and went to the calf, expecting to see Cowlick in the woods, but when Jake stepped past the first tree, the ground, mushy from rain, broke off under his feet.

Emily grabbed him as he stumbled backward from the edge or he'd have fallen into the creek. "Why isn't that fenced?"

"Because cows are instinctively smart enough to stay away from the edge," Emily answered.

Jake's throat went dry. "Didn't you say dairy cattle had the instincts bred out of them?"

Chapter 20

That calf isn't standing here for his health." Emily looked at the muddy bank. The calf bawled at the creek.

Jake shook his head as he ran one hand into his damp hair.

"I'm going to have to go down there." Emily stood in the drizzling rain, glaring at that cold muddy bank. She thought of the hot supper she'd just slid off the stove and her clean, comfortable kitchen. But ranchers learn about hard work at a young age.

"All right, you guys hold on to the calf. Don't let it loose or it might fall in next." Emily took two steps.

Jake grabbed her arm. "I'll do it."

Emily smiled. "You're not wearing overshoes."

He glanced at his feet sheepishly.

"There's still enough light if we hurry. Let go." She jerked her arm.

His jaw worked, then he released her.

Dusk gathered in the gloomy sky as Emily, clinging to passing branches, slipped and slid and ran and mostly fell to the bottom of the bank. The leaves overhead dripped with misting rain. Bending under branches, Emily slogged through the deep mud that bordered the meandering rivulet of creek water. She was ready to turn and scout the other direction when she saw an unusually smooth stretch of mud.

Then the mud blinked.

Emily's stomach twisted as she realized Cowlick was lying on her side, coated with mud and sunk in until she hardly made a bump on the muddy surface. Her head was coated and her nose. She couldn't be alive.

Then that eye blinked again.

Emily waded in. Mud flowed over the tops of her boots. She got to Cowlick's head and, with a sucking sound, lifted. Emily sank to her knees as she wiped out Cowlick's nose with the sleeve of her denim jacket. Then she tore the jacket off and used every inch of it to clear Cowlick's air passages.

Emily twisted herself around until she sat in the mud under Cowlick's head. "Jake, can you hear me?" The top of the creek bank seemed a million miles away.

"Yeah, I'm here. You want me to come down?" His voice, clearly audible, had to be twenty feet straight above her head. How were they ever going to get Cowlick up that hill?

"No, I found her but I can't get her out. We're going to. . ." Emily didn't know if Jake could do everything, but she couldn't leave Cowlick. "This is gonna get complicated."

"Tell me." His voice was like a weight lifting off Emily. She had appreciated all he did to make her life easier through this summer, but until this minute she didn't realize how alone she'd been. "Go to my place. The tractor we bale with—"

"The Thirty-Twenty International?"

He really did know what to do. "Yeah, you have to take the baler off and hook up the blade."

"The yellow one in your machine shed?"

"That's right. You know how to attach it, right?"

"Does it have those quick attaching clamps like the baler?"

"Yes, it's the same. Bring it." The mud oozed higher on Emily's body. "And bring all the log chain you can find. There's some in all four tractors, one in the toolbox in my truck, and two lengths in the barn. We're going to need enough to stretch from up there to Cowlick, and we can't get the tractor too close to the edge."

There was an extended moment of silence.

"I'll come down. You go do all this." He sounded like he hated to leave her.

She appreciated that. "Hurry up, hotshot. I'm taking a mud bath down here and it's not the thrill you might expect."

"Be right back. Let's go, Stephie."

The truck's engine started up and quickly faded into the distance. The calf bawled and Emily wished she'd thought to tell them to take the calf. The way this night was going, the calf would fall over the edge next, although the little guy had shown more sense than his mother so far.

It was fully dark now. At first she just sat and absorbed how alone she and Cowlick were. Except for the mud and the cold rain that dripped through the tree and down her neck, it wasn't a bad feeling.

The night closed in around Emily. Crickets chirping and frogs croaking began to take on a menacing edge. Hours seemed to pass as she sat surrounded by the night. She spent a nice chunk of it in prayer. For strength to get this cow out of the creek. And thanking God that they'd found her alive.

When she heard the roar of her tractor, Emily breathed a sigh of relief.

The motor cut back to a lower growl and the cab door slammed. "What now?" Jake's voice gave her a boost of energy.

"Link the chains and lower them. We'll use them to get Cowlick unstuck first. We have to get her out of this mudhole. There's a more gradual slope down a few feet that if we cut it down with the blade, once she's unstuck and we get her up, she might be able to climb out."

Emily heard the clinking of the heavy chain and watched for the black chain on the black ground in the black night. When she finally spotted it, Emily pulled out from under Cowlick with some difficulty. Cowlick, exhausted, dropped her head in the mud.

Emily grabbed the chain, then scrambled around to Cowlick's belly. Burrowing her arms under the little cow, Emily shoved the chain under her belly right behind the cow's front legs.

"Let me lift her." Jake's deep voice sounded inches behind her.

Emily squeaked with fright. Then his strong hands joined hers as he knelt beside her in the muck, sliding the chain further. Cowlick lurched, struggling to free herself. Emily's hands skidded. She landed face first on Cowlick's belly. She knocked into Jake, who lost his footing and tipped sideways into the mud up to his shoulder on the left side.

Emily pulled herself up as Jake scrambled back to his knees. Swiping the sludge off her face, Emily shook her hands, then looked grimly at her mud-soaked neighbor. Her eyes had adjusted to the dark enough to see the left half of his face was coated with mud.

"You know, Jake, animals get in trouble more often than you'd think. You sacrifice meals and sleep and your body to take care of them. A rancher does that because that's what a rancher does."

Jake angled his body toward her, but his knees were so deep in the mud they didn't move. "Are you saying a rancher's gotta do what a rancher's gotta do?" Jake asked sardonically.

Emily smiled, but the mud on her face had started to harden so she doubted if her lips actually curved up. "The point is, this moment, right here, right now, this is what ranching is really like."

Jake gave an unintelligible grunt that matched Emily's mood pretty well. "This moment, right here, right now, I'm glad I came to ranching later in life. I'll always be happy to know I missed thirty years of it." He went back to work on the log chain.

Finally, they got it fastened.

"You go up and drive," Jake offered. "I'll push."

Emily nodded, not sure she had the energy to climb the steep bank but sure she didn't match Jake in brute strength. His muscle would ease the strain on Cowlick when the tractor pulled on her. "Hold her head out of the mud. She's drowning."

Jake was already doing it.

Emily dragged herself out of the mudhole and headed up. She crawled up the bank on her hands and knees.

"Emily, you're muddy." Stephie stood hugging the baby calf.

Emily thought that summed it up nicely. "You listen to Jake. I won't be able to hear him over the tractor."

"Okay." Stephie let go of the little bull.

"You get that, Jake?" Emily yelled.

"Got it."

Emily kept yelling at the disembodied voice in the darkness. "We'll pull her free, then figure out how to get her up! Yell when she's loose!"

"Stephie"—Emily turned to her little sister—"when Jake yells, run in front of the tractor and wave your arms and yell your head off. But be careful. Stay away from the tractor and get out front where my headlights can find you. I'll be going really slow. Make a big motion like this." Emily raised both hands over her head and crossed them at the wrist, then lowered them straight out at her sides. "Got it?"

Stephie imitated the motion.

"Don't get close to the tractor." Emily picked up the chain, attached it to the back of the tractor, and scaled the high steps. She put the big machine in gear, increased the torque to a roar, and eased the tractor forward. Seconds after she started, Stephie dashed forward, shouting and waving frantically. Emily locked the brake and jumped back to the ground. She slipped and slid and ran and mostly fell down the bank and slogged to Jake's side.

Cowlick refused to stand.

"I'm going to use the blade to knock out a slope. Right over there." Emily pointed to the place she'd just come down. "Stay with her."

"You've already been up and down that bank four times. I'll climb out."

Emily, already halfway up the slope, yelled, "I'm not strong enough to stop her if she starts sliding back into the mud!"

Emily gave up ten seconds after she started. The creek bank was too unstable to risk getting her tractor that close. "Jake, has she stood up yet?"

"No, she won't even try." His deep voice seemed disembodied, like the creek was speaking to her.

"Okay, we're going to have to pull her up with the chain."

"It's too hard on her!" Jake yelled. "You'll kill her!"

"I don't know how else to do it." Grimly worried about the cow, Emily didn't wait for an answer. She backed the tractor up to the chain and reattached it.

"Stephie, signal just like before if Jake wanted the tractor stopped." Her jaw clenched, Emily pulled slowly away from the bank.

At last, Stephie charged in front of the tractor, waving.

Emily jumped to the ground.

"We got her up, Emily!" Stephie yelled.

Emily hurried to Cowlick's side. Jake was just getting to the top of the bank. Cowlick, lying out flat on the ground, didn't even react as they unhooked the chain. The baby calf bawled and bunted at his mother. Cowlick's legs jerked and she lifted her head, but she didn't try to get up.

"We're just going to have to let her rest." Emily patted the cow's muddy side. "Let's get some feed and water for her. If we can get her to eat, she may be okay in the morning."

They rode back in the overcrowded tractor cab. Emily got a small bucket of corn and some water. The mud was dry and flaking off in big chunks. She drove out to the spot where they had left Cowlick, her truck's windshield wipers swiping at the drizzling rain.

Jake, on the passenger's side, reached across Stephie to grip Emily's arm. "She's gone."

"That means she got up." Emily smiled, and the mud on her face cracked. "She'll live."

Jake sagged against the seat. He hadn't worried out loud about Cowlick, but Emily knew he loved the little cow.

"Let's see where she's gotten to." Emily drove along the creek. When she was sure Cowlick couldn't have come this far, she swung her truck around. Her headlights fell broadside on Cowlick, calmly grazing right beside the creek. The headlights startled her and she jumped.

Emily watched in horror as Cowlick disappeared over the edge of the creek bank. The three of them sat in stunned silence for what seemed like an eternity.

At last, Emily turned to Jake. "Go get the tractor and the log chains. I'll make sure she isn't drowning." She stepped out of the truck. "And this time, take the calf back and lock it in the barn." Without a backward glance, she dropped over the edge of the bank and they repeated everything.

When they got Cowlick up, Emily refused to believe her injured act and insisted the cow get to her feet.

Emily walked behind Cowlick and herded her all the way back to the barn. Jake drove in on the tractor with Stephie, half asleep, squashed beside him.

It was eleven thirty when Emily finished triple-wiring the faulty gate panel. Jake, Stephie, and Emily stood in the sullen rain and stared at the mud-caked cow eating placidly out of her feed bunk while her baby nursed.

Emily tugged her gloves off. "Jake?" she said quietly.

"Hmmm?" Jake looked away from Cowlick.

"I've been ranching, really all my life. Twenty-four years." Half a pound of mud broke off her gloves and fell to the ground. Stephie, still mostly clean but drenched, took a step away from her big sister.

Jake nodded. "That's a long time."

"It's a quarter of a century." She started to tuck her gloves behind her belt, then stopped. "I've seen a lot. Handled thousands of cows. In all circumstances. In all weather."

Jake looked up at the drizzle that had soaked them all to the bone. "Your point?"

"I have one," Emily said.

Jake stood silently.

"In all those years. . ." Emily pounded her ruined leather work gloves—expensive suckers, fifteen dollars a pair—against her leg. "In all those years," she repeated ominously, "that"—she jabbed her gloves at Cowlick—"is the stupidest cow I have ever seen."

Jake just nodded his head.

Emily and Stephie headed for home.

Chapter 21

The mud bath was the clincher for Jake.

He quit feeling like he had anything to prove. He was a rancher now, or maybe a farmer. He might need more cows and a lot more land to qualify for a ranch. Still, this was the Black Hills. Out here everyone ranched. So why not him?

He gave up his desire to be a pioneer. He agreed to let Emily use her name to get his electricity turned on, and he agreed to get new kitchen appliances. Intimidated by the unfamiliar job of buying a stove and refrigerator, he begged Emily and Stephie to go with him.

"You can't buy appliances in Cold Creek. Hot Springs has a hardware store that sells some, but we'll see someone we know there and I'll have to explain who you are."

He waved away her concern. For some reason it seemed awfully important to take Emily along. "What's the big deal? Hi, I'm Emily's cousin." He put tons of sincerity in his voice.

"That's excellent. You're a wonderful liar. You must be very proud," Emily said dryly. "The trouble is everyone knows I don't have any cousins around here. They'd immediately ask"—Emily raised the pitch of her voice to imitate a nosy old lady—"'Are you a cousin on Emily's mother's side or her father's side?'" Her voice returned to normal. "Then they'd want to know whose boy you are."

"Boy?"

"Sorry, but if you're my cousin, then you're somebody's child. Anyone who knows me knows my dad has two older brothers and my mom has one sister. They'd want to know about—"

"Okay, I get it." He hesitated, torn between wanting her help and wanting to keep his secret. He snapped his fingers. "We'll just go farther."

"I guess we could go to Rapid City. But it's a long ways. Just go alone to Hot Springs. Being with me is the problem."

"I really think I need some help with the stove and refrigerator." He was disgusted with himself for deliberately trying to sound pathetic, especially when it worked. He supposed that meant he wasn't faking. He really *was* pathetic.

"Okay, we'll do Rapid City. It will have everything we need, a two-hour drive."

"I'm up for that. Maybe we can take Stephie to a movie or something, go

226

to a nice restaurant for lunch. Let's go in the morning, after milking. We can be home for evening chores."

Emily nodded her head. "All right. But it's probably a mistake. We might see people I know in Rapid City, too. I'm just trying to protect your secret."

"I appreciate that." Jake smiled at her. "You haven't ever told anyone, have you? I can't believe that."

"I gave you my word." Emily crossed her arms.

"Yes, you did. I'm learning that really means something. I'm learning a lot of things out here."

"How about no?"

"No? What are you talking about? Don't you want to help me buy the appliances?"

"Have you learned to say no? Are you ready to face your old life?"

She'd told him to learn to laugh, and to cry, and to say no. Well, he'd never laughed so much in his life. And he'd shed a few tears of joy over the survival of his baby calf. But Emily didn't really understand what he had to contend with at Hanson and Coltrain. How could he turn his back on people in such dreadful need?

He tried not to think about it, but that night the anticipation over the trip kept him awake. He, who had jetted to his ski lodge in Aspen and owned a condo in Chicago, places he'd inherited from his wealthy father, was excited over a cookstove.

His thoughts chased in circles. People were dying somewhere in the world, right now, and he could help save them. What about those heavy hay bales? He was needed here.

He wanted to stay. He wanted his animals and his garden. He wanted Stephie holding his hand, her eyes full of trust. He wanted to work alongside Emily for the rest of his life.

He wanted Emily.

Jake's hands started shaking. Being part of a family was like stepping into pure darkness and hoping the black didn't hide a bottomless pit. Only now, as he lay in bed, did he realize how terrified he was of taking this risk. He prayed for the courage to choose love; he prayed for God to lead him. But how could God want Jake to turn his back on people suffering, bleeding, dying?

When he'd walked in on Tish with another man, well, he'd been disgusted, but he'd known what kind of woman she was. That was one of the reasons he'd kept company with her, and there'd never been a chance he'd love Tish.

Emily was different. She had the power to hurt him. No one, not his mother or father, no girlfriend, had ever cared enough about him to stay. He had no control over his parents, except the confused feeling that if he'd been more lovable somehow maybe they'd have loved him. But the girlfriends—he'd had very few because his job made him leave town suddenly and for extended periods of time.

It came to him in a rush. He wanted to stand next to Emily, holding her hand, as she gave birth to their child. Then, over the joyous image, washed visions of lives lost because he was too late evacuating a building.

He sank back onto his mattress. For all his doubts he was sure of two things: He had to deal with Hanson and Coltrain, and he had no peace about abandoning his work. If he left here to face Sid Coltrain and sever his ties to his old life, he might never be back. He knew he still hadn't learned to say no.

Until he did, he and Emily could never be together.

Chapter 22

I've got him." Sid slammed the phone down.

"You're sure?" Tish came out looking artfully disheveled.

"I've got a flight out of O'Hare in two hours and a helicopter on standby in Rapid City. Wear that red dress." *It took her two hours to get that casual look,* Sid thought with a sneer.

"But how will you get him to come back?" Tish's crimson nails fluffed her blond curls, looking like blood dripping through her hair.

"Let me call the office. There have to be orphans dying somewhere." He listened a few minutes, then rapped some orders into the phone and slammed down the receiver.

"Move it, Tish. There's a limo waiting out front to take us to the airport."

Emily might as well have ridden to town with Cowlick in the seat beside her. The little cow would have had more to say. An occasional moo. . .something.

Yesterday he had begged her to go along, as if buying a stove was so difficult. Now he barely looked at them.

Stephie kept patting him on the knee and trying to talk to him. The ride to Rapid City would have been accomplished in total silence if it hadn't been for Stephie. She was probably in seventh heaven, talking to her heart's content.

Emily's stomach twisted because the only thing that could be bothering Jake this much was leaving.

Maybe he was fighting it now, but he would leave. He had too much honor to hide for long. When he'd healed, he'd return to his old life. She'd known it from the first. But knowing hadn't protected Emily's heart.

Once the city finally came into sight, they drove straight to the mall and she led the way inside. She snagged the first employee she found and said, "Give me the cheapest stove and refrigerator you've got."

The heavyset man arched his eyebrows. "Gas or electric?"

"Doesn't matter." Emily thought she must have looked determined because he didn't try to talk her up to something better.

Jake paid with a wad of hundreds.

Their big day out was over by eleven o'clock. Emily drove straight to Jake's house. She didn't bother with the field roads, and even when they passed someone she knew, she never warned him to keep his head down. She helped him unload the stove and refrigerator, and hook them up. The gas flame jumped to life with a quiet *whoosh*, then Stephie ran out to see the calf.

"You want to tell me what's going on?" Emily switched off the flame with a sharp *click*, then faced Jake. Crossing her arms, she leaned against the stove.

Jake sank onto a kitchen chair and looked up. It was the first time he'd made eye contact all morning. "I did a lot of thinking last night."

"Come to any decisions?"

"I don't want to go." Suddenly his eyes, so dull all morning, blazed with a fire that seemed to come straight from his soul. "I don't want to leave you."

He erupted out of the chair, sending it sliding backward until it crashed against a wall and toppled over with a *bang*. He pulled her into his arms.

Emily wrapped her arms around him, wanting to cling, knowing it would do no good. Her face pressed against his chest, she said, "You don't want to go. But you have to. I understand."

Jake's hand slid into her hair, left loose for the trip to the city. "How can you understand when I don't?" He tilted her face up so she had to look at him.

"It's not so hard to understand. You don't have anything to offer me as long as you're running."

"It's because of you I've found the courage to go back. I want to promise I'll return, but. . ." His voice faltered.

Just when she was sure she couldn't love him any more than she already did, she loved him for not making a promise he couldn't keep. "When will you go?"

"Soon, but I'm not leaving without telling you what you mean to me. Emily, I—"

The house shook. Dirt hit the kitchen window and the glass rattled against the sill. Stephie must not have pulled the back door all the way shut because it flew open and banged against the wall.

Emily looked out the window. A helicopter landed on Jake's pumpkin patch.

Chapter 23

Jake stepped to the back door. Dirt blew in with stinging force.

Emily saw the door of the helicopter open and a dark-suited man stepped out, followed by a woman dressed in red.

"Sid." Jake sounded as if he were uttering profanity.

Emily waited to hear the woman's name, but Jake stormed out, slamming the door behind him. Emily watched Jake's arms flail. The other man appeared to be completely calm.

She didn't take her eyes off the confrontation until the door opened, admitting the lady in red Emily had seen emerge along with Sid. Emily looked at the silky dress, tight enough to have been spray painted on, short enough to wade through the worst mudhole without damage, low-cut enough to nurse a baby while barely stretching the neckline. She glanced down at her own attire—her best T-shirt and blue jeans. She noticed a greasy smear on her shirt that must have rubbed off the stove as they'd hauled it in.

The woman's blond hair was a perfect mass of curls, miraculously undisturbed by the rotor wind. Her makeup was flawless, her lips the same shade of red as her dress, shoes, and nails. Long claws reached for Emily.

It took Emily too long to realize she was being offered a handshake. By the time she figured it out, she felt like a bumpkin.

"I'm Tish. I'm Jake's fiancée. And you are. . . ?"

The announcement hit Emily like a blow. She managed an awkward shake. "I'm Emily Johannson."

"It's always nice to meet the woman keeping Jake. . .happy."

The comment was so loaded it left Emily speechless.

"He has to get away once in a while. Sid and I understand."

"He. . .he's done this before?" Something wasn't right. Emily looked into golden brown eyes that gleamed like a predator's.

"He works in a terribly high-pressure job. We indulge him if we can, but eventually he has to come home." The bombshell smiled kindly, but the kindness didn't reach those eyes.

Emily remained silent. There seemed to be no point. Whatever game these three were playing, she was sitting in the stands.

"I hope you understand that you have to let him go. He was honest with you I hope." Pity oozed through Tish's scarlet lips.

Emily couldn't stand another syllable. "Jake's always been honest with me."

"It's not the first time he's taken a break from our relationship." A glint of pity in Tish's eyes humiliated Emily. "But in the end he's mine." Tish raised her hand again and, as she was meant to, Emily noticed a huge diamond on Tish's hand.

All she knew about Jake told Emily this was a lie.

Stephie came in crying, her hair flying loose from her braids. "I've got dirt in my eyes."

Emily guided Stephie to the bathroom, glad to escape. She was done rinsing Stephie's eyes with cool water when Jake came in. He opened the door to the little refuge Emily had found.

"I've got to go."

Emily knew no amount of crying or begging would sway him, not that she would ever demean herself by doing that. She didn't know what to say, so she said nothing.

Stephie didn't fling herself into his arms. Instead she backed against Emily. "I'll miss you."

Emily rested her hand on Stephie's head and her little sister turned her face into Emily's stomach.

"Something's happened, hasn't it?" Whatever she meant to him, it wasn't enough to make him stay.

"There's been a typhoon in the Philippines. Tens of thousands of people are homeless. There's no water." Jake ran a hand into his hair and Emily realized he'd never gotten a haircut since he arrived. The bleak look that had faded from his eyes was back and the lines around his mouth were deep, pulling his lips downward. It was like he'd lost all the peace of mind he'd found after one quick meeting with his business partner.

Emily's heart ached for him.

"They're calling in every man in the country who can help with the job."

"Jake, I want you to know I—"

Tish soundlessly stepped into the doorway behind Jake.

"You what?" Hope glowed in Jake's eyes. But Emily couldn't say what was in her heart in front of Tish.

"I. . .understand."

He leaned forward, and for a moment she thought she saw promises in his eyes. She thought he would take her in his arms and kiss her and say he'd be back.

But instead he reached one hand out and rested it in Stephie's hair. "Take care of Lucky for me, okay?"

Stephie nodded. "We'll take care of everything."

Jake left his hand on Stephie's head like a benediction. Then he shared a final look of longing with Emily. He turned and swept past Tish. Tish gave Emily a single triumphant smirk and flounced away.

Emily didn't come out of the bathroom until she heard the roar of the helicopter die in the distance.

"Is Jake coming back, Emily?"

Emily struggled to be brave for Stephie. "I don't know."

She wondered if it would be okay to talk to Helen Murray now. She'd wait until Jake gave her permission. If that meant waiting forever, then so be it.

Stephie squeezed Emily's hand. "You liked him a lot, didn't you?"

"Yeah." She didn't know what else to say. "He was fun to have around."

Stephie, with the resignation in her voice of someone who had lived a great many years, said, "When you weren't saving his life."

They walked home, holding hands, Lucky dancing at their heels.

Chapter 24

A month and no word.

No phone calls, nothing. No disaster took this long to clean up. He had to be home. But he wasn't here, so that meant that this wasn't home. He had returned to Chicago and his old life.

Emily tried to figure out how she could have found him so irresistible. The reason, when it finally came to her, was so simple it was a miracle she hadn't thought of it sooner.

She loved him.

She loved him in a way that she had never known existed. She loved him like he was the other half of herself, just as her father had loved her mother, and her father had died from a broken heart. Emily knew she was too young and strong, and too desperately needed by Stephie, to let herself curl up and die. So she just died inside.

She went to church but she couldn't stand to visit, not even with Buffy, who had always been so friendly. Stephie rode to Sunday school with the Murrays, Emily slipped in late and hurried away. Stephie seemed to understand and cooperated. Or maybe Stephie was just heartbroken, too.

Emily's only consolation was that Jake didn't know how she felt. He and Tish probably laughed over the little country hick that adored him. It made her sick to think about Jake with that beautiful woman. How many times had she worn her ratty work boots and old jeans? She remembered Tish's sleek perfection and compared it to herself, tossing bales, soaked with sweat.

It was Saturday, so Stephie was around somewhere, running in the woods probably. School had started up, so most of Emily's days stretched long and silent. Emily did her best during the day to work and nurture her anger, but the nights were torture.

She dreamed of him. She stayed up late working, trying to avoid the memory. When she did sleep, she woke often with his name on her lips, and more sleep was impossible. Instead of lying in bed, torturing herself, she'd get up and start her day before sunrise.

She'd never said the words, but she'd loved him, maybe from the first day.

She wondered if he could even remember her name.

She was in her second week of building a rock garden on the side of the hill between her house and the woods that led to Jake's. They had an old rock pile overgrown with weeds. For years her father had tossed stones he dug up in the fields in the same spot. It was about a hundred yards down the hill from her new landscaping project. She was well on her way toward using up the whole collection. The backbreaking labor and the brutally aching muscles fit Emily's mood perfectly.

Today, with a blazing sun she would have ridiculed Jake for working under, she rolled a huge slab of limestone up the last few feet of the slope. On her knees, throwing every ounce of her strength into each inch of progress she gained, she counted off the days Jake had been gone. She'd gotten up to thirty-four days and started counting again. . .twice.

Someone touched her on the shoulder. With a startled twist, Emily jumped to her feet and almost fell over.

Helen Murray stood behind her, smiling. "Emily, I love what you're doing here. It's going to be beautiful."

Emily steadied herself, her heart slamming in her chest.

Helen gasped as she got a good look at Emily. "What's wrong? Are you sick?" Helen's eyes moved up and down Emily's body, pausing for a long time on her face.

"No, you just startled me." With one look at Helen's expression, Emily knew her neighbor wasn't asking about her jumpiness.

"You don't look well. You've lost weight. How hard have you been working on this?" Suddenly Helen started looking around the whole place.

There wasn't a weed anywhere. The fence and buildings had been painted. The vegetable garden and flower beds were picture perfect.

"Emily, are you getting ready for something? The place looks wonderful." Helen's wise eyes went back to Emily's face.

"I can't talk about it." Then Emily started crying. She covered her mouth with the back of one grubby hand to hold back the sobs.

Helen held Emily's eyes, then, with a sad smile, she brushed several sweat-soaked hairs off Emily's forehead, tucking them gently behind one ear. "Then it must be a man."

Emily shrugged her shaking shoulders and wearily nodded.

"It might help to tell me." Helen's work-roughened hand rested on Emily's shoulder and urged her down onto the rock Emily had been pushing.

"It might," she murmured through her tears.

"Where's Stephie, honey?"

"She's playing in the woods."

"You want me to call Carl and have him come and get her? We could talk in private then. For as long as you need to."

Emily shrugged again. She just didn't know what to do anymore. She sat for a long time, shedding all of her long overdue tears as Helen patted her back and made all the perfect sounds of comfort mothers know so well. When Emily's tears finally ended, Helen took her arm and guided her toward the house.

"I haven't heard from you all summer. I've tried to call a dozen times." Helen looked around the groomed yard. "Guess you've been outside, huh?"

Emily nodded.

They entered the house and Helen paused. The kitchen gleamed like it had been scrubbed by Mr. Clean on steroids. "You've been working inside some, too."

Emily swiped a few straggling tears away.

"When's the last time you ate?"

She'd been expecting some demand for a confession. The mention of food caught her off guard. "Breakfast."

"What time?"

"Five, I guess." Emily wished she'd answered differently when Helen's lips formed a grim line.

"It's past three. Did you feed Stephie dinner?"

"I fed her." For the first time Emily found a little spirit. "She had a good meal. I'm taking care of her."

"Just not yourself," Helen said.

Emily's weak show of self-defense evaporated.

"Wash your hands, young lady. Then sit. You can talk while I fix you something, and then you can eat while I fix your problems." Helen sounded stern but she had a generous smile.

Helen's confidence made Emily wonder if maybe her problems could be fixed. So Emily talked while Helen cooked.

"He lived up there all that time and no one knew? That's amazing."

"He lived there two weeks before I discovered him. Pretty weird, huh?"

"If it makes you feel better, you can call him weird," Helen said with mock seriousness.

"To be honest, it does a little." Emily felt a trace of waspishness.

Helen laughed. "Are you sure he's gone for good?"

"I don't know." Emily must have used up all of her tears, because the question broke her heart but her eyes remained dry. "I guess. Wouldn't he have called if he was coming back?"

"You've had no calls, no letters?"

Emily shook her head.

"Have you tried to call him?"

"No! And I'm not going to!" Emily shouted. "What would I say? 'Please come back anytime you're bored'?" It felt good to shout.

Helen put an omelet in front of her.

The anger gave Emily an appetite and made her think of her stomach instead of her heart. And not thinking of her heart gave her spare brain space to think of her little sister. "Stephie's been gone too long. I should go check on her."

"Eat first. Stephie's fine."

Emily started on the omelet and it tasted like sawdust, like everything else she'd eaten for a month. Sawdust. She couldn't think about sawdust without thinking about her first meeting with Jake. His chest had been sprinkled with. . .

"Stop daydreaming. Forget about him until you finish your food."

Emily had heard that voice before. It was the one Helen used to get her children to eat. It worked; she took another bite.

"I think you should try to find him." Helen gave her head a firm jerk and set her spare chins to wobbling.

Emily had just swallowed or she would have choked. She dropped her fork onto her plate with a clatter. "How could a phone call be anything but pathetic?"

"I'll call him right now if you don't finish your eggs."

Helen was a master at getting kids to eat, but Emily had a feeling broken hearts were outside her experience. Emily picked up her fork and forced another bite. "I don't have a phone number. I couldn't call him anyway."

"You just told me he works for Hanson and Coltrain in Chicago. You could find him with two phone calls. And you don't have to be pathetic. In fact, I'll stand beside you and thunk you on the head if you start sounding the least bit pitiful. What harm is there in an acquaintance calling to say hi? Or you could say you thought he'd like to know how his calf was doing. If you mean nothing to him, he won't think that's so strange. You know, he may have even tried to call. I've been phoning all month."

"I can't do it. He'll know how much I miss him. It's too humiliating."

"Honestly, Emily, can you feel any worse?" Helen waited for an answer.

Emily silently took another bite of food under Helen's watchful gaze. The thought of feeling even more miserable was unbearable.

"You know what I think? I think you'd feel better. If he is nasty to you, it will help you realize what a rat he is. Right now all you have are good memories and the big hero flying off into the sunset. You left too much unsettled. At least if he brushes you off, you'll get mad. Doesn't that make sense?"

Emily reached for more omelet and was surprised to find it gone. The food and Helen's solid support gave her a little stiffness in her spaghetti spine. "Some sense, I guess."

"So what do you say? Let's get the big dumb creep on the phone and see what he has to say for himself. I've never seen a situation get worse by facing it and talking about it. I'll call information and get his number."

"No, wait." Emily stood up from the table, desperate to stop Helen. "I'm not ready."

"I'll just get his number, not dial it." She marched to the phone, called information, and came up with a number for Hanson and Coltrain, but nothing for Jake Hanson or, at Emily's suggestion, J. Joe Hanson.

"His private phone is probably unlisted. I'll call the company and see if they'll give it to me."

Emily sank back into her chair. She shouldn't let Helen do this. But to hear Jake's voice again would be so wonderful. She bit her lip and grabbed the edge of the table to keep from stopping her friend.

"Yes, Jake Hanson's office please. Hmmmm, are you sure about that?" A long pause. "Do you have a number where I could reach him? He has? Thank you." Helen hung up the phone and turned around, a thoughtful expression on her face.

Emily couldn't imagine what Helen had heard. "C'mon, the suspense is killing me."

"Jake Hanson is no longer with the company. It seems he sold his shares and retired."

"Retired?" Emily echoed. "What does that mean?"

"It means I'm back, Emily."

Chapter 25

The masculine voice dropped into the room like a bomb.

Emily rose and whirled around. Her knees buckled, and Jake caught her.

Jake took in her pallor and the weight she'd lost as he settled her back into her chair and knelt beside her.

Stephie came up beside him, her brow furrowed with worry as she looked at her big sister.

"Are you all right?" He cradled Emily's face in his palms. "Emily, honey, Stephie told me you didn't get any of my letters. I'm so sorry. Sid was supposed to be forwarding them."

"Jake," Emily whispered his name and shook her head as if she was trying to clear it.

"I spent the last month in the Philippines. They sent me to an island off the coast of Mindanao where the closest thing to a phone was a two-way radio. I could send a message, but I couldn't talk to anyone except the home base in Zamboanga."

Jake took one hand away from Emily to clench his fist. "Sid manufactured the whole thing."

Emily looked dazed and so pale he was afraid she'd faint. Jake wanted to carry her off where they could be alone forever, except he wanted Stephie to come. . .and Lucky, and Cowlick.

"He. . .he manufactured a. . .a typhoon?" She wasn't getting it, but he didn't care. She was here. He could touch her.

"No, he just manufactured my isolation. He picked the most primitive, remote spot in the whole disastrous place. It was awful. The destruction, the death." Jake let his fist rest on Emily's knee and lowered his forehead to rest on his hand. He knew he had to take care of her, but the tragedy haunted him. He'd been desperate to get back here. Desperate to escape all that misery. Desperate to stop the hammering of his heart.

Emily—he had to think of her now, not himself. He had to find some remaining strength.

A hand rested on the top of his head and slid into his hair. A hand that could only be Emily's. Another, smaller hand, Stephie's, patted the corded knots on his shoulders.

He was home. They'd already begun taking care of him. He wanted to cry and he might have, except he was too happy. He raised his head with renewed strength. "You told me I had to learn to say no, but so many lives were at stake I couldn't. Sid had me convinced all the manpower possible was needed, but what he really wanted was me, back in harness and out of the loop."

"And Tish? Could you say no to her? Are you still engaged?" The voice was so weak, so hurt, not like his Emily's at all.

Jake hadn't thought about Tish in all this mess. The trouble had always been between him and Sid, but Emily hadn't known that.

"Engaged? I've never been engaged to her. I've only dated her when I've been in the country, and for the last few years that's only been a few weeks total. There's nothing between us. There never was. I—" Jake was suddenly aware that he had an audience. A strange woman.

He looked back into Emily's exhausted, shining eyes. "Are you all right, sweetheart?"

"I'm glad to see you, Jake. Are you here for a visit?"

Jake wasn't getting through to her. How could he say all he wanted with other people around? Emily had a hint of color in her face now. He let go of her and stood, wrapping an arm around Stephie.

"No, I'm not here for a visit."

He saw Emily's face fall and he wanted to hold her and comfort her and cry and laugh and maybe do a few dance steps, because he was so happy to be alive and in this place with the women he loved.

"I'm here to stay. I'm finished with Hanson and Coltrain." He saw her eyes narrow with doubt. Well, time would fix that. But he didn't have much time, since he was planning on marrying her this afternoon. He shouldn't have stopped to pet Lucky.

Jake looked at the woman standing with her arm resting protectively on Emily's shoulders. Not a stranger, for sure, so maybe she could babysit for a while. He extended his free hand, never letting go of Stephie. "I'm Jake. Jake Hanson. I live over the hill at the Barrett place."

"You don't say." Helen's hand came up but Jake didn't miss the sarcasm. "I'm Helen Murray. I'm Emily's nearest neighbor and best friend."

Jake got the implied threat. He took a deep breath and pressed onward. "Glad to meet you, Helen. Emily has told me a lot of good things about you."

"Emily has told me a lot about you, too." Unlike Jake's little greeting, Helen's wasn't a compliment.

Jake tried again. "I need to talk to Emily for a while. I don't suppose Stephie could go to your house for a while?"

"Not on your life." Helen crossed her arms.

Jake's eyes really met Helen's for the first time. He saw a formidable woman, one who wasn't budging.

"I'd be glad to wait outside for a few minutes though." Helen gave him a warmer smile than he deserved, considering Emily's thin shoulders and pale cheeks.

Jake squared his shoulders. It didn't matter. He'd been planning to be the perfect gentleman anyway.

"Helen, it's all right. I'll be fine with Jake."

"We'll see about that. So far things haven't been all that fine."

Jake saw humor alongside the wisdom in Helen.

Helen took Stephie's hand and led her outside. Just before the door swung shut, she turned. "Ten minutes."

The door clicked shut and Jake dragged Emily out of the chair and kissed her senseless. When he had to breathe, he said, "I love you, Emily. I've missed you every minute, every second. I thought I'd made arrangements for you to be contacted regularly."

He kissed her again, drawing strength just from touching her. "Before I left for the Philippines, I told Sid I was selling out and staying here with you. He must have hoped he could keep me in line if he ruined things between us."

Jake looked at Emily's thin face. "He hasn't, has he? Ruined things?"

Emily reached a trembling hand to Jake's face, as if to convince herself he was real. "You love me? Do you mean it? Are you really back to stay?"

"I'm really back to stay."

Emily shook her head.

Jake nodded. "You'll start to believe me after we've been married about ten years." He pulled her into his arms again and did his best to be entirely, thoroughly, exhaustively convincing. When he came up for air, they were sitting on her couch in the living room. She was on his lap and her long hair was loose from its braid and flowing around them like living water.

"Honey, this whole mess helped me to see that I'm not indispensable. I've wanted out of my old life, but for the first time I knew where else I wanted to be. Any competent engineer can do what I do. I'm not going to have any trouble saying no from now on. Listen, I've been practicing."

Jake lowered his voice nearly an octave. "I'm sorry. You'll have to get someone else." He spoke normally. "How's that? Or this one." The tone deepened again. "I can't leave my wife. She's eight months pregnant with our tenth child." Jake pulled back so he could see her eyes. "Or is that ten months pregnant with our eighth child?"

Emily laughed, and Jake knew they were going to get through this. He'd known anyway because he planned to marry Emily if it took twenty years to convince her to say yes. But he desperately did *not* want it to take twenty years. He pulled her close.

She pushed him away. Her blue eyes met the dark brown of his. "Was that a proposal? Because if it was, it was the worst one I've ever heard."

"Oh, how many have you heard?" His mock jealousy took the last of the misery out of her eyes.

She leaned until her forehead pressed against his, closed her eyes, and whispered, "Just one."

"You will marry me, won't you?" He rested both hands on her face and lifted her chin until he could see her eyes. "You deserve so much better than me. It took me so long to realize how wonderful you are. I was so awful at first. Remember the time I—"

Emily pressed two fingers softly against his lips and silenced him. "I remember every word you've ever spoken to me, Jake. I've been thinking of nothing else for a month."

He lifted her hand from his mouth and kissed each fingertip. "Oh, sweetheart, I'm sorry, so terribly sorry you've been so unhappy."

"Now that you're back"—her neat little speech faltered—"there's nothing left to be sorry for."

"You've never said you'll marry me, but you don't have to. We're already married in our hearts. I know that because I was only half alive without you, and I only have to look at you to see you feel the same. We share one heart, one soul. We're already married in the best sense of the word."

Emily blinked. "I've thought the same thing. But I thought I was feeling it alone."

"It took some doing for me to get past my job, my mother's desertion, and my father's neglect. But I was in love and committed to you for life from the moment"—he smiled—"I fell on top of you. You can say anything you want, it's only words. We are married. When do you want to do the paperwork?"

Emily laughed again.

"So, do you want a big ceremony, the white dress and the flowers? We can do anything you want."

"No big ceremony. I just want you. I love you, Jake."

Jake raised his eyes to hers as she spoke the words he longed to hear. "How could I have been such a fool to leave before we'd said all the important things to each other?"

"When you left, you weren't sure you cared about me."

"I loved you," Jake said sternly.

"You had doubts. So did I. We needed this time. Now we're both ready, we're both sure. That's so easy to say now that you're here." She added, "I want to do the paperwork just as soon as possible."

He chuckled. "Good. I know a few people and I pulled a few strings and managed to get this marriage license." Jake pulled it out of his pocket.

Her eyes widened. "Don't I need to be there to get this?"

"Sign it. I'm a notary public. I brought my stamp." He produced a stamp from the same pocket.

Emily laughed. "So, you're saying if I sign this we're married? I've never heard of this before. It sounds like a great system."

"Well, someone should speak some vows, I suppose. But the paperwork is what makes it legal. We're married enough for me."

Jake kissed her.

"Well, you're not married enough for me. So knock it off."

Emily jumped out of Jake's lap and Jake sagged back against the couch. He looked at the neighborhood guard dog. "The fair Helen has returned."

"I gave you twenty minutes instead of ten. So you should be thanking me."

"Yeah, thanks a lot." There wasn't a single teeny-tiny iota of thankfulness in him.

Helen took the paper out of Emily's hand. "This isn't legal."

Emily had the grace to blush. Jake had the grace not to kill Helen. "Yes, Helen, it is."

Helen fastened such a stern look on him it was all he could do to not sit up straight and revert to a schoolboy. "You can't get a marriage license without both of you going to the courthouse."

"I've been on the phone since I got back into a place my cell would work." He glared at Emily. "Including I tried to call you a thousand times from airports on my way back from the Philippines. You're getting an answering machine and cell phone that you will keep turned on at all times."

"B–But those are modern conveniences."

"So?"

"Pioneers didn't have them."

Jake narrowed his eyes.

"And besides, cell phones don't work out here."

"I found that out. But they worked fine in Tokyo and LA and Chicago and Rapid City."

"Is that how you get home from the Philippines?"

"Yes. Why didn't you answer the phone?"

"I was busy."

Jake sighed and turned back to Helen. "I had the marriage license faxed to me in my Chicago office."

"Emily has to be there."

"Not if the county judge comes to the wedding and verifies everything."

"You know the county judge?" Helen arched one brow doubtfully.

"No, but I know a guy who knows a guy who does." Jake glanced at his watch. "But he's just a backup. I want a pastor to bless our marriage. If not now, then soon. But we're getting married today and that's that."

Helen glared. "Emily never had a chance resisting you, did she?"

Jake wanted to be insulted, but a spark in Helen's eye made him realize it might be the very first compliment the old harpy had given him. "I never had a chance with her either."

Helen looked at Emily. Jake knew Helen could see the torment gone from Emily's expression and the color back in her cheeks. Helen wouldn't try to stop Emily from marrying him, not that he'd let her.

"Do you want to marry him, honey?"

Emily nodded. "Oh yes."

Jake smiled and she took a step toward him.

Helen's voice stopped her. "I suppose you want to marry him right now?"

Emily's eyes flashed, and Jake remembered the woman who had fought for her elm tree and chopped a load of wood before he was awake in the morning and spent hours up to her neck in the mud to save a cow. Despite the pain he'd caused her, she still had spirit.

"Well, Helen, either I can marry him right now or you can sign this license where it says 'witness' and take Stephie and leave us alone. Show her your stamp, Jake."

Helen laughed. "No, the stamp won't be necessary. How about if we do all three? Marriage first, signature second, taking Stephie third."

Emily blushed.

Helen said, "I think I can track down Pastor Lewis, and your dirty T-shirt isn't quite a wedding dress."

"Well, Jake, say something." Emily looked at him as if daring him to back out.

Like there was a chance in the world he'd let her escape.

He fired off a few orders of his own. "Emily, go get a dress on. Helen, call the pastor." He tugged on the lapel of his chambray shirt. "I'm going home to put a suit on. I'll be ready in ten minutes."

He went to Emily under Helen's watchful eye, and leaned close to her ear. "In our wedding, I had you pictured wearing blue jeans and work boots."

With shining eyes, she closed one fist over the collar of his blue work shirt. "I never pictured a wedding for us."

"I'll pick out a dress and get the shower started." Helen headed down the hall. Gone but not forgotten.

Emily called after her. "I want to wear my white sundress!"

Helen nodded.

"The sundress won't take ten minutes to put on, hotshot."

Jake grabbed her wrist for old time's sake. It was completely different than in the early days.

Emily laughed. "I had your electricity disconnected. Let's call and get it turned back on while we're at the church."

Jake nodded. "It's Saturday, so they won't get to it until Monday. We can stay here until they get it done."

"So, you're going to do it? Go all modern?"

"Yes, you win. . .again. . .like always."

"When have I ever won with you? I've been taking orders since we met." Emily shook him by the lapels.

"Are you kidding? I can't remember your being the least bit obedient."

Emily laughed. "You know I haven't laughed once since you left. I'm so glad you're back. I want you to know. . ." She hesitated.

"What? You can tell me anything."

"I want you to know I'm yours, Jake. This last month I found out where I am doesn't matter. I just have to be with you. So if things don't work out for you here, I'll follow you anywhere."

Jake hugged her until her feet lifted off the floor. "I've found out a lot, too. I found out Sid was embezzling. I found out my distrust of people came about because I was hanging around with the wrong ones. I'd trust you with my life. After ten minutes with Helen, ten lo-o-ng minutes"—Emily laughed again as Jake set her on her feet—"I'd trust her, too. I've lived my whole life either working myself to death in horrible conditions or with limo drivers and four-star restaurants. I didn't even know how real people lived. I wanted so badly to escape that life and get back to nature that I thought I had to give up everything— electricity, phones, mall, people."

"All you ever had to do was stop and look around. There are real people everywhere, including among the rich. How rich are you anyway?"

"Well, I was rich before I sold Hanson and Coltrain."

"Did that hurt you financially to do that?"

For a moment her interest almost resurrected his old, distrustful self. "Would it matter if it did?"

Emily's eyes narrowed. "I just hated to think of your giving up a fortune for me. It seems like the kind of thing you might regret later. I really ought to pound you for asking if it mattered, hotshot."

He let go of distrust for the last time. "Anyway, I was rich then, but now I'm *really* rich."

"Really rich?"

"Oh man."

"We don't have to spend it, do we, honey? I think too much wealth kind of wrecks people."

"No, we don't. And I like 'honey' better than 'hotshot.' "

"Oh, you do not!"

Jake laughed and swung her around in his arms. Her long hair flew out and his heart nearly exploded when he thought of all of this strength and beauty being his. "We can fix the Barrett place up all you want. Or would you rather live here? This would make a wonderful home." He held her with her feet dangling off the floor.

"I've always loved the Barrett. . .excuse me, I mean the Hanson place."

Jake nodded his approval. "I like the sound of that."

Emily looked into his eyes. "When I woke up this morning, my life stretched in front of me like a thousand miles of uninhabited Black Hills. I never expected to be happy again. I've always believed happiness came from inside. But you took it with you when you left. I'm almost scared to love you so much."

Jake saw the tears swimming in her blue eyes and knew the sting of his own. Yes, with Emily he was definitely going to live forever. Laughing and crying. Saying no and saying yes, yes, yes. Leaving his stress behind just by holding her in his arms.

"I didn't believe love existed until I met you. I don't think I've ever been given true love before. Not from my mother or father. Not from the women I dated. But one single day with you and my whole world turned around. And Stephie. She's so precious. I fell in love with her the minute she came into your kitchen and said, 'Hi, Jake,' after all our worrying about her finding out about me.

"And God. You helped me find enough peace so I could open myself to Him again. You're a gift to me, straight from a loving God. I only hope I can be worthy of that gift and make you and Stephie as happy as you've made me."

Emily had been holding him tight as he talked. He looked into her eyes and saw his love reflected back. "You want to make me happy?"

Jake nodded.

She kissed his lips as softly as a breath of air. "Then go away."

His eyebrows arched with surprise.

"And get a suit on and get back here."

Jake kissed her hard, then turned and ran.

For the very first time in his life he was running toward something—a family, love, faith.

At last, he was running toward home.

Epilogue

The judge showed up and had to produce some ID to convince Helen he was the real thing. It helped that Pastor Lewis was his fishing buddy.

Emily was embarrassed, but all things considered, it was probably best that Helen was in charge of this slapdash ceremony.

The word got out about the wedding even before they got to the church. Ladies with casserole dishes were at work in the church kitchen. The pastor's wife had driven into Hot Springs and grabbed an armload of roses in every color they had at the local discount store. She'd even come up with a wedding cake of sorts. It wasn't tiered with a bride and groom on top, but it was a sheet cake, pretty, dotted with flowers.

Helen played the organ as she did every week. Her music was as perfect as if she'd talked for hours with Emily about which songs would be best.

The vows were spoken. They sang a hymn together and ate a feast and were still home in time for chores and a honeymoon in Emily's dream house, which was nearly perfectly restored by Jake, a top-notch carpenter who was no longer a clueless cowboy.

THE BOSSY
BRIDEGROOM

Dedication

I didn't know who to dedicate this book to because I was afraid they'd either think I was calling them bossy like Michael or wimpy like Jeanie. I finally decided to dedicate this to my Seeker buddies, because they're perfect and will completely understand my intentions: Janet Dean, Debby Giusti, Audra Harder, Ruthy Logan Herne, Pam Hillman, Myra Johnson, Glynna Kaye, Sandra Leesmith, Julie Lessman, Tina Russo, Cara Slaughter, Camy Tang, Missy Tippens, and Cheryl Wyatt. Check out www.seekerville.blogspot.com.

Chapter 1

Jeanie Davidson believed in miracles because she believed God loved her.

And only a miracle could make anyone love her.

Exhausted after her long day, she slipped into her favorite faded blue jeans and her pink T-shirt with the buffalo on the front. The shirt made her feel close to her daughter.

She curled up in a ball on her dilapidated couch and prayed to become a person worthy of self-respect.

"Jeanie!" A fist slammed on her door.

She jumped.

"You get out here!"

Her heart thudded. She knew that voice. It had been over two years, but she still reacted the same way—fear.

The rickety wood shuddered as Michael kept pounding.

Jeanie stumbled forward, obeying by reflex. He'd had her trained to obey without question. Tripping over her own feet, she hurried to throw open the barrier and face her worst nightmare.

Michael's battering fist almost caught her in the face. He stormed in and grabbed her by both shoulders. Tall and dark, his handsome face was an unnatural shade of red. A shade she had, unfortunately, seen many times. Michael and his temper were inseparable.

"You gave our baby away?" he roared at her, lifting her onto her tiptoes. "You threw Sally out like a piece of trash?"

Jeanie had tried to be good since she found God. Tried so hard. But her old life wouldn't stop punishing her. Then she remembered that God loved her, which reminded her of all the promises she'd made to herself. "Get your hands off of me."

Michael jerked in surprise.

It surprised Jeanie, too. She'd never heard quite that tone come out of her mouth before. She hadn't known it existed.

She yanked her shoulders, and he let her go.

His surprise didn't last long. He stepped inside, swung the door to her second-floor apartment shut, and pulled an envelope out of the back pocket of his wrinkled black slacks. He had a white button-down shirt on, sleeves rolled up to his elbows. His hair was a mess, the curls he loathed sprung free. He looked as if he'd slept in his clothes and avoided a mirror—his best friend back in the day. "What is this?"

Jeanie didn't want to be shut inside with him. She wasn't afraid he'd hit her. Michael had always done his worst with words.

She glanced at the return address: Custer County Court, South Dakota. It was his final notice, sent months ago, and his time to protest was nearly past.

"I gave Sally up for adoption." She forced her voice to remain steady when her heart was breaking. "The court made a good faith effort to contact you. It's been over two years since they first sent notification. Your parental rights were terminated six months ago. You had a long time to complain."

"I never got a letter."

"I gave them your last known address as well as your parents' address."

"My parents are dead."

"Oh, well, I'm sorry to hear that." They hadn't been subtle letting her know their precious Michael had married well beneath him. "But surely the post office forwards things. . ."

"This isn't about the *mail*. This is about a mother abandoning her child."

"And a father."

Michael opened his mouth to keep up the verbal assault, but no words came out. Maybe even he had some shame.

"Haven't you noticed your child support checks, when you got around to sending them, haven't been cashed for a long, long time?"

Michael's mouth actually shut.

Jeanie had to keep a tight grip on her inner evil child, because it gave her great satisfaction to stand up to her tyrannical husband, and she wanted to keep at it. And she shouldn't. Meeting evil with evil wasn't God's solution.

Instead, she found the courage to step toward him calmly, neither raging nor cowering. "You abandoned both of us." She jabbed him in the chest with her index finger. Okay, a little rage there. "Even when the *money* came, *you* were never with it. Don't come in here now acting like you love our little girl or care what happens to her."

Michael's hands went to his chest as if her finger was a bullet to his heart.

"You blew it. Sally's gone. We're over. I don't have to put up with you yelling at me anymore. So get out!"

"Jeanie, I—I—"

His stutter shocked her, but it was probably due to her completely unexpected backbone.

His eyes settled. Determination.

Jeanie knew he was getting over the shock.

"You're right."

What?

Michael's head dropped until his chin rested on his chest.

"I just got this letter today. At my parents' house."

"In Chicago?" That wasn't an important question, but none of this was important. Jeanie was past caring about her jerk of a husband. Too big of a jerk to even bother filing divorce papers. And she hadn't filed. She'd married him for better or for worse and proceeded to live a life of unbelievable "worse" for six years. Since she'd become a Christian, she was even more certain that her vows were eternal. If he wanted out, he'd have to initiate it.

It didn't matter anyway. She had no intention of ever being married again, to anyone, least of all Michael "The Tyrant" Davidson. So being divorced meant being free to do. . .nothing.

"I went back to close up my parents' house, and I found this letter. It made me furious." He didn't sound furious, not like two minutes ago when he'd forced his way into her home.

"Your address here in Cold Creek is on the letter, too. I got on a plane and came straight here, in a rage."

"When are you ever not in a rage?" Jeanie shook her head in disgust.

"I'm not in a rage most of the time these days. I went back to close up Mom and Dad's house. Then I was going to find you and try to salvage our family."

Jeanie reared back, far more surprised by this than by his anger. "*You were not*. I haven't even seen you for years."

"Twenty-eight months, two weeks, and three days."

"You say that like you were counting the days of our separation, as if I *matter* to you."

"It didn't matter when I did it. But now it matters." Michael ran the fingers of both hands deep into his hair. "I had to stop at my folks' house. It's been sitting empty since Mom's funeral three months ago. I hoped she had some information in the house about where you lived. Then I saw this letter, and I saw red, and I've been running on rage ever since."

"When are you ever not running on rage?"

"I'm sorry. Before I saw the letter, I had planned to find you and beg your forgiveness. Instead, I used this letter as an excuse to be angry. You're right about Sally. It's my fault, all of it. Please say you'll give me another chance."

Seconds stretched to a minute.

Michael stared at the floor.

Jeanie stared at his dark curls.

Finally, Jeanie couldn't stand the wait anymore. "Who are you, and what have you done to my husband?"

Chapter 2

Michael would have beaten himself for raging at Jeanie like this—if he wasn't a newly confirmed pacifist.

He'd had this vision of coming to Jeanie a new man, a changed man, getting down on his knees and begging for forgiveness. Instead, he'd shown himself in the worst light imaginable. But who could have dreamed she'd give up Sally for adoption?

He brushed past her, still not looking her in the eye.

Jeanie. His wife. He'd loved her since they were kids. And he'd done a poor job of showing it.

"Come here, please." He sank onto her couch. It was awful, with rips in the arms and seat. Some greenish fabric with scratchy upholstery, worn and faded until it was nearly colorless. Jeanie never would have dared let his home look so shabby. He ran a hand over the tufts of escaped batting in the rounded sofa arm.

He felt, more than saw, Jeanie sink into the overstuffed chair across from him. He'd hoped she'd sit beside him, but he was a moron even to imagine it. A spindly coffee table separated them, as well as time and his miserable behavior.

"Where is Sally?" He clamped his mouth shut. He hadn't meant to start talking there.

"Buffy adopted her."

Michael looked up. Then he pulled the papers back out. "It says Wyatt and Allison Shaw."

"Buffy's name is Allison. You know that. She's married now to Wyatt Shaw. They were in a better position to make a home for Sally. After you abandoned us, Buffy took me in. She ended up being more of a mother to Sally than I ever was. I doubt Sally even noticed when I left."

Jeanie's head dropped back against the ratty chair.

"Buffy has her?" A huge wave of relief almost made him dizzy. Buffy had always been a better person than he or Jeanie. Buffy would take good care of Sally until Michael could get her back.

Michael saw a tear trickle down Jeanie's face. It cut a trail down her cheek and cut into his heart at the same time. He'd done it, convinced his wife she was worthless. Not fit to be a mother. It was all on his shoulders.

He stared at her and remembered that girl he'd claimed when she was far too young. So pretty, so sweet, so eager to please. He'd wanted her for her looks. He'd thrived on her sweetness. He'd married her for her compliant nature. Then he'd criticized constantly the things he loved most about her.

When the baby came and he was no longer the center of her universe, he left and blamed even that on her.

And then, through the shock of his father's death and the realization of how completely lost his mother was without a tyrant to tell her when to breathe and what to think, he'd found God and understood what love was and how badly he'd failed.

He scrubbed his face with both hands, praying silently. Strength—he needed true strength not to be the tyrant he'd been raised to be. "One thing at a time, Jeanie."

Jeanie lifted her head. A streak of tears cut down from her other eye. She stared, not even bothering to wipe her cheeks. "One thing at a time?" Her vulnerable expression hardened. "Okay, here's one thing: Get out." She stood.

Michael raised one hand. "Please sit. I'm not leaving. We've got to talk."

Jeanie gave a short, bitter laugh, but she sank back down. "Why? We never *talked*, not once the whole time we were married. Maybe not the whole time we *dated*. We were together what? Four years of dating and six years of marriage? Ten years in all? And we *never once talked*."

"I know. I remember. I talked, and you agreed with me. If you ever disagreed with me, I yelled until you agreed with me. It's one of a thousand things I'm trying to face and take responsibility for. I ruined our marriage, Jeanie. Now I want to fix it."

Jeanie snorted. It wasn't a sound Michael had heard from his wife in the past. She'd grown a backbone in the years he'd been gone. Good, he needed her to be tough, to hold him accountable.

"I'm not interested in fixing our marriage. You can go now."

She grabbed the arms of her chair to stand again, and Michael erupted from the couch, rounded the coffee table, and dropped to his knees in front of her before she got to her feet.

She jerked back as if a rattlesnake had landed on her lap.

"I'm not leaving. I'm here and I'm going to stay. I've changed, Jeanie. I'm a new man. I've become a Christian, and one of the things I've learned is that I *never* loved you like I should have. I was a terrible husband, a worse father, a sinner, a complete waste of human flesh. But I've changed." And he could prove it. "I sold my business."

Jeanie gasped.

He'd finally gotten her attention. That contracting business had been the only altar he worshipped at. He'd started it right after college graduation, and he'd been gone more than home for the six years of their marriage. Well, the marriage was over six years old, but they hadn't seen each other since Sally was just past her first birthday.

"You didn't!"

"I'm here to stay. If it takes the rest of my life, I'm going to convince you to love me again."

"Go get your company back. I'm making a life for myself here." Jeanie grabbed a handful of his hair and tipped his head back. "I'm never going to live like I did when we were together. I spent my life begging for crumbs of affection from you. I learned to say, 'I'm sorry,' like a trained poodle. I'm surprised you didn't toss me doggy biscuits when I said it. I'm done with that, Mike. I'm a Christian, too, and I've read enough of the Bible to know a husband doesn't come to his wife screaming, beating her door, scaring her to death, and then pretend he's changed. I have no intention of divorcing you. If you want that, it'll have to be your choice, but I will *never* live with you as your wife again. *Never!*"

She released his hair. Michael saw her rub her fingers together unconsciously. He remembered that she'd loved to touch his hair. She'd always been a sucker for his looks. It made him sad to realize what a shallow reason that was to love someone.

She stood, and Michael grabbed her knees, but she shook him off. "You cost me *everything*." Her voice broke, but she squared her shoulders and went on. "I gave up my daughter, my home, my heart, and—most of all—my *soul* to you. God has forgiven me for that, but I'll never forgive myself."

He heard her voice break again, but she didn't crumble. "I've lost my daughter, but I have found a home. My heart is my own. And my soul belongs to God. And to live under your thumb, I'd have to give all of that up. *I won't do it!*" She reached for the door.

Michael was upright before she could get out. He turned her around, pushed her back against the door, and leaned over her, knowing the thrill he'd always gotten from dominating her. She'd gotten a thrill from it, too. Such a messed-up excuse for a marriage.

It was sick. He was sick. A sinner.

God, God, God. Forgive me.

He released her, raised his hands, and stepped back. He looked at her, expecting that same familiar twisted pleasure at his bullying. He saw only contempt.

Shocked, he backed off another step.

Good for you, Jeanie.

She swung the door open and walked out. Once outside, she turned toward him on the landing of the outside stairway that led to the alley below. The only other way up to her apartment was through Farrens' Pharmacy on the ground floor, but she never used that.

"Are you leaving?" She crossed her arms and glared. "I won't let you drive me out of my home for long. People in this town will protect me. I've been here long enough and worked hard enough that they won't believe your lies when you tell them I'm lazy and a liar and not worthy of your *greatness*. So leave, or I'll get the sheriff and have him throw you out."

He'd blown it. He hadn't lost his temper in three months, ever since he'd made his commitment to the Lord. The peace that had washed over him had overcome all of the old demons that goaded him, and he'd thought he was healed.

You don't have to put up with that.

Satan had whispered lies justifying his anger.

Your employees are stupid.

He'd believed he was superior to everyone.

She'll shape up or she'll lose me.

But those lies had faded, and God had sent comfort like warm rain, hydrating the cracked soil of his heart, drenching the raging fire of his arrogance.

He'd been fine. . .until today.

God had deeply convicted him of the sin of his marriage. The way he'd treated sweet, malleable, beautiful little Jeanie. The way he'd abandoned his baby girl. His rage had been healed in the instant he'd been born again, replaced with conviction of his sins and the desperate need to make things right. He'd set out to find his family with a humble heart.

And now, after a few minutes with Jeanie, that sinful nature awoke like a hungry beast. He felt controlled by his need to vent his temper and always, always blame her.

He prayed as he stepped out on the landing. "You're right again. Is there a pastor in this town that you like?"

"You won't be able to turn him against me, Mike. I've done a lot of counseling with him, and he knows me well enough not to believe your insults."

"Good, then he'll know it's all my fault and we can save a lot of time. What's his name?"

Jeanie hesitated, but there was a depth to her expression that had never been there before. Yes, she'd changed. She was stronger, more confident, and if possible, sweeter than ever. She wouldn't deny him a chance to talk with her pastor.

"He's Pastor Albert Lewis. He's in the phone book." She gave him a level stare as she slipped past him and stood inside her wretched apartment. "We're not saving this marriage, Michael. I've fought too hard to stand on my own two feet and live a life God might—just might—respect. I'm not letting you denigrate me until you pull me back down to the level you need in a wife."

Michael returned that level look. The moment stretched. So sweet, so submissive, so pretty. He realized with a start that she was nearly thirty but she looked like a kid. She wasn't wearing a bit of makeup, and he saw freckles scattered across her nose. He'd always harassed her about covering them with makeup.

Her hair was pulled back in a no-nonsense ponytail. It was straight and honey blond, not the flashy, permed platinum he'd goaded her into. He'd called her hair mousy brown or dishwater blond. She had lost all of her curves, as if she'd starved away her womanhood. He'd goaded her about being fat once she'd gained an hourglass figure from giving birth. He'd been a nonstop bully, and he deserved her contempt. Deserved to be alone for the rest of his life.

God, please forgive me. Help me to make Jeanie forgive me.

She looked like the girl he'd fallen in love with. His Jeanie. Before he started "fixing" her.

Tears burned his eyes, and he blinked, not wanting her to give an inch. He knew the kindness of her heart. She might give him another chance just because he cried, and he didn't want that.

Not when he'd just discovered it was within his power to destroy God's miraculous healing of his temper.

"I'll go talk to him. But I'm not leaving town. I'm here to stay. I love you, sweetheart, and we are going to heal this marriage. I promise you that before God."

He turned and trotted down the squeaking, protesting iron steps.

At the bottom, he looked up and saw her leaning over the railing, staring down at him as if she were looking right into the eye of the devil himself.

He turned and jogged away from her, knowing he had only the slimmest control over his need to go back and convince her, by force if necessary, that they could be together again.

Chapter 3

Her mind had chased itself around and around until she thought she'd go mad.

Jeanie rolled out of bed the next morning, grateful for the first blush of sunrise that put an end to this farce of sleeping.

She should have gone down to the Cold Creek Manor to see if the night shift needed any help. As it was, she'd be three hours early for the senior center. She didn't usually show up until eight.

Showering in the tiny bathroom, she tried to get the cobwebs to clear from her aching head.

Michael was back.

Mike.

God, what can I do?

She stood in front of her miniscule bathroom mirror and stared at the scripture she'd claimed for a life verse. It was taped there as a reminder to start her day with God. Taped there to remind her that strength had never come easy. Quitting, depending, and blaming were more her style—along with living with shame.

"We want you to be very strong, in keeping with his glorious power. We want you to be patient. Never give up. Be joyful" (Colossians 1:11).

Pulling on khaki slacks, white sneakers, and a light blue cotton sweater because the kitchen at the Golden Days Senior Center was always cold, she spent a quiet time with her Bible, searching for new verses about being strong in the Lord. She studied ones she knew and made notes when she found another one. She'd been doing that since she accepted the Lord.

She prayed and claimed that strength. When she felt in control of her roiling emotions—something that would probably last only until she saw Mike again—she left her apartment. As she descended the stairs, she continued to reach with her soul for communion with God.

"We want you to be strong."

God, please make me strong.

"Never give up."

That's what Michael makes me want to do. Give up.

"Be joyful."

That one she could never manage. Oh, she was happy enough. She enjoyed her work and the friendly people in Cold Creek. And she felt joy in the Lord. But she never felt joy deep inside where she knew she'd failed at her most fundamental calling—motherhood.

She could feel her will slipping. She had it in her to be a doormat. She wanted it. Letting a man be in charge meant she had no responsibility. In exchange, she had to allow herself to be demeaned night and day for her whole life. And that was easy. She'd learned it at her father's knee.

Jeanie's father and Michael's father were matching tyrants. Their mothers— perpetual victims. Jeanie and Michael had created a home exactly like the ones they'd been raised in.

Jeanie quickened her pace, trying to escape her thoughts, until she was running the two blocks to the Golden Days Senior Center. But she couldn't outrun her mind.

Once inside, she fought to regain her calm. She was so early she could bake bread in plenty of time for lunch. There were twenty-five people who came to eat, a wonderful group of elderly who treated her as if she were their own daughter. That meant they meddled and nagged and gave her endless advice. But it was all done with love. And she'd never felt such love before.

Except from Buffy. Her little sister had tried to love her.

And Sally. Her daughter had endless, unconditional love to give, but Jeanie had thrown away what Sally so innocently offered.

Neglecting Sally, rejecting her daughter's love, then giving her up was a sin for which Jeanie couldn't forgive herself. No matter how fully God had forgiven her.

She began her busy day by slipping a roast into a slow cooker and adding seasoning. She usually baked the meat in the oven, but it wasn't yet 5:00 a.m. There would be plenty of time for it to cook. Her seniors would enjoy the especially tender meat.

This was Monday. She usually got here close to 8:00, got dinner started, then ducked out just before 9:00 to help with Peaceful Mountain's church service at the Cold Creek nursing home. Then she came back to the senior center and worked until 1:00. Next she went to her second part-time job as a nurse's aid at the nursing home. She was training to be an LPN through a program at the nursing home, and she was enjoying that.

Well, she didn't enjoy the textbooks. She'd never been good at her studies. Her grades were good, but she had to work hard to keep them up. Nevertheless, the hands-on work was an easy fit, and she felt a wonderful sense of accomplishment.

Jeanie spent her supper hour as a hospice volunteer. She currently had two patients at the manor whom she was helping escort into the next life with dignity, offering support to distraught families. Working with these families instead of eating had shaved twenty pounds off her overly round frame.

She had Bible study on Tuesdays and choir practice on Wednesdays. On Thursday evenings she worked her third part-time job, four hours at the Cold Creek library. She led a 4-H Club on one Saturday morning a month, helped with Girl Scouts the next week, and filled in at the local mini-mart the third and fourth Saturdays, for her fourth part-time job.

Saturday afternoons Pastor Bert gave her a ride out to the Peaceful Mountain Church she attended. She practiced the piano for Sunday services. It had taken hard work to remember those rusty lessons from childhood, but she was good enough now to play for church. After she practiced, she cleaned the little clapboard country church, mowed the lawn, and tended the flower beds when needed.

She still didn't do enough to make up for abandoning her daughter.

Kneading bread in the empty kitchen at the run-down senior center, she prayed, trying to get her mind to settle down so she could think.

"Hi, Jeanie."

A scream ripped out of her throat. She jumped and knocked the huge circle of dough sideways.

Mike snagged it in midair. He'd always been good in an emergency. Quickly, he set the dough back in front of her.

Heart hammering, she waited for the cutting remark.

Clumsy, jumpy, nervous, daydreamer, stupid, stupid, stupid.

"I'm sorry I scared you. I went by your apartment and you were gone. Pastor Lewis said you work here mornings."

Jeanie snapped, "What were you coming by for? I told you to stay away from me." Suddenly, kneading the bread was a perfect excuse to take out her frustrations. She turned all of her anger loose on the defenseless loaf.

Mike turned and leaned his back against the counter. He crossed his arms and ankles and looked at her.

She glanced up and saw his eyes shift to the pummeled dough. It was possible he got the message.

"I know you, Jeanie. Even if I never gave you any respect, I had to know you really well or I wouldn't have been able to hurt you like I did."

Jeanie's hands stopped in mid-punch. "What?"

Their eyes locked.

"I knew you doubted that you were smart, because Buffy was such a genius. I knew how your dad went for your intelligence when he wanted to hurt you. I knew that drew blood and you'd never defend yourself."

She couldn't look away. She'd never demanded respect. Never figured she deserved it. Now here he was admitting it. In effect handing her his best weapon.

"I knew you based every bit of your shaky self-esteem on your personality and looks. You were so popular and pretty and you worked so hard at both. I wanted it for myself. And once I had it—had you—I set out to take that bit of confidence away from you."

"Go away, please." Jeanie tore the huge, smooth circle of dough into three equal pieces and began forming loaves. Her hands worked automatically. She'd done this a hundred times in the six months she'd worked at the center. Twenty-five people for lunch, each loaf fed about twelve. Crust pieces were hard to chew, so that took away six.

Michael's right hand settled on her shoulder, and she couldn't ignore him anymore.

She narrowed her eyes at him, doing her best imitation of a woman with courage. "Oh, are you still here?" She held his gaze.

"I talked to Pastor Lewis last night for about two hours."

Jeanie gasped. "It was already late when you left my place."

"I was too desperate to wait."

"Too impatient, you mean."

Mike shook his head. "I was awful to you last night. I had all these plans about proving to you that I'd changed, and then I just fell right back into the same old habits. But that was one night. I went straight to talk to the pastor. I was clear about our breakup being all my fault. He agreed to be a marriage counselor for us." Michael grabbed the receiver of the black wall phone and punched in numbers while Jeanie tried to process what he'd said.

"Marriage counseling? No, we're not doing that. We're through."

"Hello, Pastor Bert? It's Michael. I'm at the senior center with Jeanie right now."

"Michael, hang up that phone!"

Michael obeyed her, which threw Jeanie for a loop.

"He was on his way to town for coffee anyway. He'll be here in about five minutes."

Jeanie resisted the urge to smash one of her lovely loaves right in his face.

Michael seemed to sense the direction of her thoughts. That didn't make him a genius. It wasn't as if she was trying to hide her rage, after all.

"So, do you work all morning to get the noon meal ready, or do you have a break?"

The nerve of the man almost choked her. "Are you serious about trying to breathe life back into our marriage?"

"Yes, absolutely." Michael came up to face her.

She turned and nestled each spongy dough ball in the greased loaf pans. "Then you're doing it just exactly wrong by forcing your way into my life and dictating that we'll go to marriage counseling. How am I supposed to think anything but that you're the same tyrant you always were?"

"So, if I'm doing it the wrong way, then there must be a right way. So you're saying we can fix this marriage."

"I'm saying get out. I've said that any number of times, but as usual you're calling the shots." Relentless jerk. That's how he'd convinced her to marry him right out of high school. He'd been a senior when he'd asked her out at the end of her freshman year. All through college he'd pressured her—in every way.

He'd pursued her, loved her, flattered her. She'd been thrilled and honored, and when he criticized, she'd twisted herself into a pretzel to make him proud.

"I'm not interested in healing this relationship. I'm finally learning to respect myself." Well, she intended to learn. . .someday. No luck yet.

"You told me you don't want a divorce." Michael-the-Deaf-Man settled on a chair at the rectangular kitchen table and scooted another chair out a bit. For her. She considered using it on his head.

She set the loaves in a sunny window, covering them with a dish towel to rise. It chafed that Michael was exactly right about one thing. She had nothing to do for about two hours.

She perhaps should speak a little louder. "Get out, Michael. We've got nothing to discuss. Unless you want to start divorce proceedings. I'm not going to do it, but I will go along with it if you wish. I made my vows before God, and I intend to keep them."

"I agree. We took vows, and they're eternal. Our marriage is for life. Sit down."

More orders. He was trying to be nice, and he still couldn't stop.

"That's wonderful." Hands clapped together in glee.

Jeanie jumped. The hardy voice turned her around.

"If you've got a good grasp of God's plan for marriage, you can make this work." Pastor Lewis was here. And he'd gotten just exactly the wrong message.

Michael stood and extended a hand to Jeanie's pastor. The two greeted each other like old friends. They back-slapped and smiled, and Jeanie felt it happening. Already she was being pushed aside, the submissive wife, the troublemaker who didn't want to fix her marriage. She washed her hands, trying to figure a way out of this trap.

"Pastor, we talked about this last night, but I want to repeat it in front of Jeanie, with you as a witness. I abandoned her and our daughter. I take full responsibility for the mess we're in. The reason I want you here is because I'm a tyrant, unkind, unloving. I've found Jesus since we broke up, and I'm here to try to make up for all I've done."

Jeanie felt like she was hearing words that she'd only imagined in her wildest dreams. Hanging up a hand towel, she shook her head a bit, trying to make sense of what he'd said.

"I thought I could come here and make things right." Michael shoved his fingers into his hair just as he had last night. Acting agitated, unsure—it was a completely foreign gesture. "But the first words out of my mouth were said in anger. Then later I started bullying her and, worse yet, enjoying it. I don't think we can handle it without professional help."

Michael turned to her. "I'm sorry about last night. When I was born again, I felt the anger lift off of my heart and I thought I was healed. But yesterday I found out it's still there, dormant for a while but still close at hand. I've got a long way to go, and even if you promised to be strong and keep me accountable, I'm afraid we'd slip right back into the same patterns. That's why I want the pastor involved."

He said it like their marriage was fixed. Like they were only working out details.

Tears burned at her eyes.

Pastor Lewis, a rotund man, tall and full of gruff kindness, rested one of his huge, gentle hands on her arm. "Sit down, Jeanie. I told Michael that you and I have talked about your fears many times and the pain of your marriage and giving Sally up. I understand how hard you've struggled. I just want us to talk together for a while and see if we can find a starting place. I don't expect a few minutes of talk to settle years of strife."

Jeanie looked from the pastor's red-cheeked face to Mike's chiseled, tanned profile. Both of them were strong men. She knew Pastor Lewis was her friend and a wise counselor. But he was trying to bend her to his will just like Michael did.

Or maybe he just thought this was the right thing to do.

She sank into the chair Pastor Bert pulled out. Michael, straight across the small table while the pastor sat on the end between them, reached out to clasp her hands as if she'd just declared her undying love and agreed to forgive him everything.

She moved to shake his grip away when the pastor said, "Let's join hands and pray."

With an exhausted, tearful sigh of defeat, Jeanie let Michael hang on even as she knew his grip would pull her under and destroy her.

Chapter 4

Michael fought down the triumphant sense of victory as he held Jeanie's hand.

"Jesus said we are to forgive seventy times seven," the pastor began.

Seventy times seven equaled four hundred and ninety, and Michael knew he was already way over. He'd probably needed forgiving four hundred and ninety times before their one-month anniversary.

When the prayer ended, Pastor Lewis focused on Jeanie. "You'll notice my prayer was one of forgiveness, from God and for each other. It's not just Michael who has sinned here, Jeanie. When one partner is the more dominant personality, the problem isn't just that he's calling the shots; it's that you're letting him. He gets in the habit of not listening to you, and you get in the habit of not even telling him what you want."

Pastor Bert reached in the breast pocket of his suit coat and pulled out. . .an inflatable baseball bat. "I want you to hit Michael with this every time he tries to bully you."

Jeanie lifted her head. Her shoulders squared. She jerked her hand loose from Michael's and reached for the bat. She ripped its cellophane wrapper open and began blowing it up with a vengeance.

"Uh, Pastor Bert, I've never heard of this before." Did he carry one with him at all times? How often did he recommend this technique?

The pastor ignored him and kept talking to Jeanie. "And this is just for him overruling you, being a bully, demeaning you, insisting on having his way without consulting you or respecting your opinion, hurting your feelings in any way. If you ever feel like Michael is *angry* at you—we've talked in counseling about the fear you lived with. If you feel that, call me anytime, day or night. I will personally come to your place and throw him out."

"H–her place?" Michael's heart started pounding. Was the pastor going to recommend they live together? Michael wanted that so badly he was afraid to hope.

"Yes, you need time together to fix this, and I believe you can do that best together, platonically for now." Pastor Lewis's eyes narrowed, and Michael wished the man would go back to talking to Jeanie. "But if your wife calls me, even *once*, I will personally come and throw you out, at which point you will do your counseling from separate addresses. And we will begin counseling immediately. Together for now, the three of us, at least once a week. I may decide you need individual counseling as we go along. I can come here early in the morning or whenever is most convenient. I'm not leaving Jeanie to contend with you on her own."

Knowing these were rules he needed, Michael agreed quickly.

Jeanie was too busy blowing up the bat to voice what Mike was sure would be a protest.

Maybe she was looking so forward to whacking him and throwing him out, she'd actually let him move in. Then all he had to do was be perfect, and he could stay. Praying silently for God to renew the miraculous healing of his temper, Mike knew it wouldn't be easy.

God, You know I need supernatural control. Help me to be a better person. Help me to find joy in kindness. I need You to be with me every second of every day.

"And now, Michael, we're going to talk about your sinful treatment of your wife, one of the smartest, sweetest, hardest-working women I've ever known. She has a beautiful heart for the Lord, and her gift is to serve others, one of Jesus' highest callings, and you've taken advantage of that."

The pastor was off, and by the time he was done telling some hard truths, all based on Michael's own confessions of last night, Michael felt like a worm—which he was.

"True strength doesn't come from anger and domination. True strength comes from self-sacrifice and patience. Jeanie is much closer to true strength than you. You think it proves you're strong when you bully her, but it doesn't. You're a weakling."

Michael was squirming in his chair, humiliated in front of his wife.

Then the pastor turned his fire and brimstone eyes on Jeanie. "And you think he's strong and you're weak. But there's nothing weak about the woman I know. You're a child of God, a precious creation. God calls us to be humble, but true humility doesn't mean you allow denigration and abuse. It means you stand strong enough against Michael to not *allow* him to sin."

He included them both as he finished. "The point of the bat is to *remind* Michael he's off track. It's Jeanie trying to help you. She could do that as well by holding up her hand or leaving the room."

"But that wouldn't be as much fun." Jeanie clutched the bat and looked at Michael until Michael was almost afraid to move. She was just looking for an excuse to whack him.

"And it doesn't matter if you think she's wrong, if you think she's being too harsh. The whole point of this is to *hear* her, to *listen*, to respect her feelings. Right or wrong, she's entitled to voice an opinion. If she's feeling controlled, then you need to figure that out and stop whatever you're doing and apologize and shape up."

"Now, I'm going to give you an assignment to work on tonight. Write down all the things you love about each other and share those lists while you're alone."

"That won't take long."

Michael didn't remember Jeanie having such a sarcastic sense of humor.

"Now, let's pray."

When the pastor finished, he said, "Michael, you're going to spend the day with Jeanie. I know Monday is a busy day for her, and you've admitted you're unemployed."

Michael flinched. Pastor Bert made it sound as if Michael were a homeless vagrant. He'd made a fortune selling his company. With building contracts stretching out two years, there'd been a bidding war to buy it. Plus he'd inherited more from his well-to-do parents. If he was smart, he could live comfortably for the rest of his life. And Michael knew he was, indeed, very smart.

Pastor Bert glared at Michael in a way that made him feel stupid. He had to fight to keep from sliding lower in his chair. "I want you to spend the day being a witness to your wife's beautiful servant's heart. So, whatever she does today, wherever she goes, you go along."

Then the pastor turned to Jeanie. "Bring the bat."

Chapter 5

S he hadn't whacked him yet, but neither had she spoken to him. Pastor Bert accompanied them to the Cold Creek nursing home and stayed through the first half of the Monday morning worship service. The social room of the nursing home was a brightly lit place filled with people who were, for the most part, sleeping.

"Good morning, Mrs. Tippens. How are you?" Jeanie crouched so her face was at a level Mrs. Tippens could see. The woman was so bent over in her wheelchair she had her chin resting nearly on her lap.

Michael was stunned as he watched Jeanie work the crowd. She knew all of the residents by name, had personal words for them, asked about their children and their health—even though half of them didn't react. When she'd touched nearly every shoulder, she took her place behind the piano, laying her bat on the low top of the spinet.

Michael hadn't known she could play. Maybe she couldn't when they'd been together.

He stood at the back of the sitting area with no idea what he should do. Pastor Bert stood in front of a semicircle of occupied wheelchairs and couches. He led a few hymns while Jeanie played the out-of-tune piano. Then the pastor told Jeanie and the three other women helping with the service to carry on.

On his way out of the door, the pastor stopped and patted Michael on the back. "I'll see you tomorrow at the Golden Days Senior Center at 6:00 a.m. to go over your lists."

He must be afraid to let them go two days without being observed. Smart man.

As Jeanie and her friends worked their way through the service, Michael wondered what he'd write on his list. What did he love about Jeanie? Why had he seen her and wanted her immediately?

He knew the truth was brutal. She was pretty. And she gave in to peer pressure out of a desperate hunger for approval. The second had been her most attractive trait. He prayed for God to let him take his batting like a man when he told her that.

Then it dawned on him that there was a lot more to Jeanie now than there had been then. Mainly because, without his telling her every move to make, she'd found herself and become a far more interesting person than the one he'd created.

He'd created? Michael flinched. Talk about playing God.

Michael was glad he didn't have to make a list of the things he loved about himself. Right now he wasn't sure he could come up with a single one.

After the service was wrapped up and Jeanie had taken time to tell each listener good-bye, one of the other church women—Pastor Bert had introduced her as Mrs. Herne, the mayor's wife—gave Jeanie a hug. "It's so nice to meet your husband."

Jeanie shrugged. "We've been separated. Michael wants to reconcile." She looked at him, her hand clutching the neck of her bat balloon, not even pretending they weren't talking about him. He walked over as Jeanie went on. "It's a bad idea, though. We had a terrible marriage. We're both new Christians now, but we married for all the wrong reasons, and we brought out the worst in each other."

Michael came to her side. "Hello, Mrs. Herne." He offered a hand.

The woman, about twenty years older than Jeanie, gave him a kind smile. "It's Carolyn. I hope you two can figure things out. Remember that with God all things are possible."

Jeanie spared one testy glare at Michael. "Meaning it will take a miracle to ever make me want to be married to you again."

Michael kept a smile on his face by sheer willpower.

"We've got a funeral at church tomorrow," Mrs. Herne said.

"Yes, I heard Myra passed away."

"Would you be able to bring something? Bars or sandwiches?"

Michael opened his mouth to tell the woman Jeanie was already too busy and any spare time she had needed to be spent with him.

The bat settled on Jeanie's shoulder, and Michael didn't voice his opinion. "I'll bring bars. I'll be down to help, too, as soon as we're done with lunch at the center. Pastor Bert seems to want Michael to stay nearby for a while, so he can come along."

"Thank you." The redheaded woman split her smile between Jeanie and Michael. "We really appreciate it." She left.

A second woman came up. "I heard you talking about Myra. I knew she was failing, but I hadn't heard she'd died."

Jeanie nodded. "Late yesterday."

"We're having a planning meeting for the Memorial Day celebration tonight. We'd love to have you there."

"I'll be there. Michael, too."

Michael turned to Jeanie. "I had hoped we could spend some time together tonight."

Jeanie narrowed her eyes. "Hope all you want."

The last church woman gave Jeanie a quick hug and invited her to tea when she had a free minute. They both laughed as if they knew that would never happen.

Jeanie said a final good-bye to her sleeping congregation.

Michael had to admit several of the elder folks had sung along with the old standard hymns, and he'd been moved by that. Jeanie was doing something worthwhile.

She left the building without looking back.

Michael felt a spurt of irritation as he scrambled to keep up with her.

As Jeanie strode across the paved parking lot, swinging her bat in time to some military march music, Michael had to jog to catch up to her. They reached the street, and Jeanie turned left. There were no sidewalks in this residential section of Cold Creek, but no traffic either, so walking in the street seemed safe enough.

"Where are we going?"

Jeanie glared. "How did you end up getting Pastor Bert to let you stay with me? It's a terrible idea. The only reason I didn't fuss about it is you won't last a single night. If you have to leave as soon as you lose your temper, we won't even get through one meal." She looked forward and picked up her pace.

Michael hesitated to ask where they were going again. It didn't matter anyway. He'd just follow her wherever. "So, what's the schedule for today?"

She whacked him with the bat.

Chapter 6

It had to be a sin. It felt too good.

Forgive me, God. I'll wait until he's got it coming.

That shouldn't take long.

"Jeanie, while we walk, talk to me about Sally. Please."

She turned on him, and he flinched, lifting his arms to cover his face. Oops, the tingle of joy told her she was sinning again.

"Please, I'm not going to say a word about your choices. I just want to know how she's doing."

Jeanie walked on, lengthening her stride. Of course that long-legged jerk Michael kept up easily. Sally was his daughter, even though he'd been as rotten a father as a child had ever been saddled with.

Fine.

"She's five, almost done with kindergarten. She lives out on Wyatt Shaw's ranch. *He's* her father, and he's a good man. A fifth-generation rancher. Buffy's really happy with him. They've got cattle and buffalo on the ranch, and Buffy's made a really nice tourist destination out of the buffalo. Plus they've started supplying a string of really top-flight restaurants all across the country."

Michael shoved his hands in his pockets. She could tell by his clenched jaw that he wasn't happy with her, probably because she was talking about Buffy, not Sally.

"She started half-day kindergarten last fall. She goes to Peaceful Mountain Church, and I see her every Sunday. She calls me Aunt Jeanie, and I know her really well. I babysit sometimes. Wyatt has twin sons older than Sally, and Wyatt and Buffy have a baby of their own."

"Four kids, huh?"

"Yes. Sally is really happy. She's got a great life. She doesn't know she's adopted."

"How can she not?"

"I moved in with Buffy right after you left. Sally was eighteen months old. She bonded with Buffy immediately, and I let it happen. I didn't even care that I was losing my daughter. I thought I deserved it. Sally knows I'm"—Jeanie shrugged, not sure how to put it into words—"special. We've developed a truly loving relationship. Buffy wants to tell her the truth when the time is right."

Michael nodded and didn't comment. Jeanie hated that. She really could have used an excuse to swing away. "She's blond like I was. Short for her age, but not overly. She's just beautiful, Michael. Happy, bright, she already reads a little. And she can count to one hundred with only a few numbers missing and write her name. She got your brains, praise the Lord."

"My IQ is probably high, but if they measure brains by the way you use them, then I'm an idiot, and we both know it."

Jeanie's heart twisted at Michael's words. How she'd have loved those words years ago. Now it seemed as if her heart was dead. She could fear him, she could despise him, but she just couldn't love him. Her love for him had cost her too much.

She turned up a side street lined with tall oaks. The sun was warm for spring. Rugged mountains hugged the little town. Sluggish Cold Creek, which gave the town its name, was visible between the trees on the south side of town as Jeanie led the way toward Main Street. It was a picture postcard of a town, tucked into the majestic Black Hills of South Dakota. Jeanie felt as if her peace, although it came from God, was nurtured by the beauty that surrounded her.

And with that peace came a trickle of courage. "One of the things I'd put on that list of why I loved you was *because* you were a tyrant. I needed that. It was part of being emotionally sick. I'm healthier now, but I don't feel strong enough to stand up to you."

"Jeanie, you're not going to need to do that."

She slammed the bat into his hip just on principle. She never broke her stride. "I believe you intend to be a partner in this marriage. You're sincere when you talk about your faith, but that means you're no longer the man I married. God has changed your heart and mine. He's created new people out of the ashes of the unhealthy marriage we had. Now you're like a stranger to me. A stranger who is living in my house. I hate that."

Jeanie stopped in the middle of the street. She saw a car coming two blocks away, the first that she'd seen in the middle of a work day at Cold Creek. It turned off before she needed to move to the side.

She crossed her arms to face Michael. "If you're not the tyrant I loved, then who are you? I might as well just pick a guy out at random and have *him* move in. I don't want you so close to me. I don't want any man, but most of all I don't want you." Jeanie stared at his handsome face. She'd fallen for him the first time he'd smiled at her. She'd been forbidden to date before she turned sixteen, but they'd started sneaking around together long before.

"I'm still the same man, Jeanie. My heart has changed. I'm a hard worker. I'm faithful. I've never cheated on you. I'm honest. Those are all part of me. Maybe, if we can get past that strange codependent thing we had where we found an almost sick pleasure in fighting and making up, we can rediscover the best of ourselves."

"I like being alone. I don't want to have a man or another child, ever. I blew my chance with Sally and you. I don't deserve another one."

Michael reached out and rested one hand on her arm. He didn't try to hang on or pull her close. Her bat was handy if he did. "Of course you deserve another chance. God forgives us. Everything about being a Christian is second chances."

Jeanie couldn't stand him touching her, so she turned and started moving again. Faster than ever.

Michael kept up. "You look fantastic. More beautiful than ever."

She swung the bat at his head and hoped it stung.

Michael smoothed his hair. "Why'd you do that?"

"Don't try to sweet-talk me. It makes my skin crawl." The truth was it made her skin shiver. Not at all like crawling.

How long had it been since a man had spoken flattering words to her? There'd been a few men in the last year, since she'd quit running and settled back in Cold Creek, who'd shown some interest. But she had mastered freezing men out. How galling to think she might have made herself vulnerable to Michael by her self-enforced loneliness. But what else could she have done? She was a married woman. She couldn't exactly date even if she'd wanted to—which she didn't.

She needed a bigger bat. Maybe oak. Better still—aluminum.

Main Street was coming up. The walk from the senior center was just under a mile. Jeanie didn't own a car, so she made the trek twice a day on foot. The Golden Days Senior Center was just around the corner ahead. She felt like that was her goal, that she'd be safe when she arrived. But she was kidding herself. All of her trouble came right along with her. And it—*he*—had longer legs than she did. She had no more chance of escape than a cupcake at fat camp.

She met a couple of neighbors as she rounded the corner to Main Street. The post office was there, and it was more likely to have traffic than any other place in town.

She greeted her neighbors, and they had time to get her to agree to head the craft committee and the talent show for the Memorial Day celebration. She promised again to come to the planning committee meeting tonight.

She felt Michael biting his tongue. Only the presence of witnesses kept her bat in check. But that wouldn't have saved him if he'd spoken. She didn't give a hoot if she embarrassed him.

They moved on toward the center, and Michael hustled a bit to grab the door and hold it for her. Nice manners. "You always were a gentleman, except when it came to treating me like a badly behaved child. Just that one little thing, endless emotional battering. Otherwise, Mr. Charm."

"Jeanie, I'm sorry."

Stepping into the center, she didn't reply. "Ten thirty. I'm right on time to put the final touches on dinner. So, you know how to peel potatoes?"

"Yes."

Jeanie sniffed. "I don't remember you ever helping with that at home. Did becoming a Christian make you start doing *women's work*?"

"Show me the potatoes and tell me how many to peel. You've got a lot of anger stored up, and I'm going to prove to you that I can take it. I deserve it, and you deserve a chance to vent."

Jeanie dumped a ten-pound bag of potatoes in the sink and snapped a peeler on the counter with a metallic click. She whacked him with the bat as he picked up the peeler.

"What's that for?"

"That's for giving me *permission* to be angry with the husband who deserted me and my child."

Michael started skinning the potatoes in silence.

She set the bat on the countertop so she could bake a couple of pans of brownies, but she kept it within grabbing distance.

Chapter 7

Michael was out of breath just keeping up with her.

They'd finished at the senior center, walked back to the nursing home—she'd worked a shift there—and visited her hospice patients who were residents of the manor. And the day wasn't over yet. They headed for the nursing home exit to—Michael presumed— walk another mile.

"Now you've got a town meeting? We've been up since 5:00 a.m., and I slept in my car last night." He jumped back, and the bat missed him.

Jeanie stopped and crossed her arms over Old Hickory. He knew that look. After one day he knew that look. "I'm sorry. It was instinct. Go ahead and let me have it."

He stepped closer but noticed she didn't bother to swing again. Was it possible her arm was tired? He was pretty sure that, even though it was latex and air, she'd left some bruises. The woman had a *lot* of suppressed anger.

"Well, I didn't sleep much at all. Having my husband show up and start screaming at me was pretty upsetting."

"I'm sorry." She didn't bother swinging. She was tired. Maybe now was a good time to try to make some headway in this mess of a marriage.

"I've studied the meaning of marriage. God's meaning. God called men to love their wives as Christ loved the church. Christ *died* for the church. He cried over it. He healed and performed miracles and pleaded and preached and walked all over the nation of Israel trying to spread His message of love. I'm going to do that for you, Jeanie. I promise before you and God. I've been convicted of the depth of my sin, and I only want a chance to make it up to you. I owe you so much. I've hurt you so much. I've—"

"Enough!" Jeanie left the nursing home and set out for Main Street. Michael trailed along one leash short of heeling like a dog.

He had followed her like this all day. He'd tried to help in any way he could while Jeanie put in a four-hour shift. The nursing home administrator put him to work. They had a list a mile long ready for unsuspecting volunteers. He'd mowed and weeded flower beds and moved furniture. Then he'd folded laundry, dragging a basket of it with him while he visited with patients. Jeanie had directed him to two different rooms with people lying immobile in their beds, asleep or unconscious.

"Talk to them," she'd said. "They're my hospice patients."

Not eager to be turned into a line drive, he'd obeyed. At a loss, he'd told the patients about his bungled marriage. He hoped the sound of his own voice would give him some bright ideas. The folks he visited slept.

Now here they were off to a committee meeting. Michael sighed, but even that he did quietly. Maybe there was something to that bat. He was definitely beginning to think before he spoke.

People stood in line to hug his wife, and it chafed him. Michael waited patiently, but his jaw was tense until the warm greetings ended. He knew this reaction. He'd called it love when they were married, but it was jealousy—or more accurately, self-centeredness. He wanted Jeanie to stand slightly behind him while people made a fuss over him.

God, please make me a better man. Forgive me for my sins. Take away that old nature.

He noticed Carolyn Herne from the nursing home church service and saw the man who must be her husband, Mayor Bucky. His wife was a slim redhead, full of motion and energy. Mayor Herne was grayer, rounder, and slower. But he had a great smile and a hearty manner that everyone responded to. The mayor took the center seat at a table at the front of the room. Two other men and one woman sat beside him.

The mayor rapped a gavel. They dispensed quickly with a roll call, minutes, and a treasurer's report. Then the mayor asked about new business and started talking. "All right, let's get the plans in motion for the Memorial Day celebration."

Jeanie and Michael sat at the back of the few short rows of chairs in the large auditorium. Michael quit listening. He prayed silently as he tried to look clearly at all the ins and outs of his selfishness. He was so focused on his prayers and asking for forgiveness and healing from what seemed like reactions imbedded on an instinctive level, terribly hard to overcome, he didn't notice the room had fallen silent for a while. He looked up.

Everyone stared at him.

"What?" He glanced at Jeanie for an explanation.

"I just told them you'd be involved with the Memorial Day celebration, too."

Michael only knew Jeanie was involved, and anything she did, he'd do. "That's right." He smiled at the gathered group of about twenty. "I want to help. You know Jeanie told me that the Shaw Ranch's buffalo are a pretty good tourist attraction. Maybe if you used—" Michael quit because Jeanie's fingernails had started digging into his forearm. If he kept talking, it might end up with him scarred for life. Some men got their wife's name tattooed on their arm. He'd have a slightly different permanent keepsake—claw marks.

"We thought this year we'd try to focus on the veterans more. We always do a ceremony at the city hall and end it at the cemetery, but we thought this time. . ."

Michael had felt a glimmer of excitement when he imagined the quiet little town bustling with tourists, tram rides out to the ranch, games and shows focusing on the former history of the area when buffalo roamed free, Wild West costumes, and maybe a small rodeo. Wild Bill Hickok was from South Dakota, wasn't he? Or Buffalo Bill Cody maybe? Deadwood. Mount Rushmore. Lots of possible ideas. And with Cold Creek flowing through town, wide enough for some water sports—at least canoeing or rafting or fishing tournaments—the town was full of possibilities. If they planned to play it safe instead of doing something exciting, he wasn't all that interested.

He mostly ignored the meeting, concentrating instead on praying for self-control and a miracle. He figured he needed both to win Jeanie back.

What little he caught was very routine. Standard Memorial Day fare. Blah, blah, blah, flags. Blah, blah, blah, trumpets. Blah, blah, blah, twenty-one-gun salute. Nothing much earthshaking there. Sure he'd help. Maybe they'd let him mow the grass at the cemetery or something. Jeanie, who kept raising her hand and saying, "I'll help," like some kind of jack-in-the-box, was probably already doing it, so he'd pitch in.

The meeting broke up, and the same round of hugs wore on his nerves.

Jeanie seemed to be quite the local celebrity. More likely the local doormat. Michael knew only too well she'd be good at that.

Pastor Bert had said she had a servant's heart. Well, the whole town had tapped into it. But not him. Oh no. The husband gets left out in the cold.

Everyone else left. He helped Jeanie fold up the chairs and return them to the rolling racks. When they were finished, she produced a key for the building.

How'd she get that?

They left through the back door of the aging Main Street structure that opened to the same alley containing Jeanie's staircase. She locked up, pocketed the key, and whacked him with the bat.

On about the fifth whack, when she showed no sign of stopping, he grabbed the stupid thing. "What did I do?"

She jerked it loose from his grip, but she stopped with the puffy beating. "I've known you a long time, Michael. I could read your mind. Well, what I do in this town is *my* choice. It's *my* life! You think I need to give up that life for you. I *won't*. Every time you grind your teeth or clench your jaw to keep from saying the bossy things you're thinking, I'm hitting you for that, too."

"That's not fair. I deserve some credit for controlling myself."

"You deserve *nothing*." With a guttural scream of frustration, she turned and marched toward her apartment, which meant she walked ten feet. "I can't believe I'm stuck with you tonight."

In all honesty, Michael couldn't believe it either.

"It won't last long. I've never seen you go a full day without losing your temper." She stomped up the old steps, making so much noise Michael was afraid the staircase might collapse. "I'll have you pitched out on your ear before the evening is over."

Michael jogged to catch up. "Let me take you out to supper. It's nine o'clock, I know, but you've barely eaten all day." He'd barely eaten either.

"Don't you mean *you've* barely eaten all day?"

"No, I'm just—I want to take care of you in some little way. Please, Jeanie? It's not about the food. It's about me trying to start, some little way, proving to you that I'm a changed man."

Jeanie snorted as she dug out her key for this ridiculous excuse for an apartment. If he rented a better place, she'd never agree to move into it with him, so he didn't say a word as he hurried inside, afraid she'd lock him out if she had the least chance.

"I told Mrs. Tippens you'd clean out her gutters tomorrow. She's living at the nursing home, but she still owns a house, and she worries about it."

"Mrs. Tippens? I remember her. She slept through the church service."

Jeanie's glare nearly caught his hair on fire. "She woke up once for a few minutes, and she frets. This will put her mind at ease. You clean gutters while I'm getting dinner at Golden Days."

"Okay, I'd be glad to."

Jeanie went into what might be laughingly described as the kitchen.

The whole main room of the apartment was about fifteen-by-fifteen feet. Three doors in the wall opposite where they'd come in were opened. One was Jeanie's bedroom, complete with a single bed. One was a tiny bathroom. The other seemed empty. He'd be sleeping there no doubt. He wondered if anyone in town sold inflatable mattresses.

The kitchen took up one corner. She opened a refrigerator circa 1950 and dragged out a loaf of bread and a couple of other things. "If you're hungry, I've got some sliced turkey." She set things on her countertop—which was two feet of cracked and curled black linoleum. She was so obviously making just one sandwich that Michael didn't hesitate. Good excuse to stand next to her anyway.

He built a nice turkey sandwich with mayo, dill pickles, cheese, and lettuce. He noticed she ate hers without mayo and with a meager serving of turkey. No wonder she was so thin. "After I'm done with Mrs. Tippens's gutters, I'll stop for groceries. I can help with the bills."

Jeanie turned on him. "You're not going to be here long enough to pay for anything."

Michael couldn't stop a smile when he heard the tone of her voice and saw the fire in her eyes.

"You think this is funny?"

"No, I think you're wonderful." He reached out, a little afraid he'd draw back a stump, but he couldn't resist resting his hand against her cheek. "I think I was a fool to try to mold you into some perfect, submissive wife, because I had no idea what perfect was. I love what you've become since you got away from me. I made it harder for you to get here, but you made it. I'm proud of you. Let's go sit on your couch and exchange our lists, like the pastor told us."

Jeanie's eyes wavered. She still loved him—he had to believe it. But she didn't trust him, and he had to respect that. She watched as he centered his sandwich on his plate, cut into two perfect triangles.

Jeanie had left hers whole, and it was far less tidy than Michael's. He knew, when they'd been together, he'd have said just a few mocking words about slapping a sandwich together. He'd have made sure she felt that little pinch of criticism. She hadn't been able to breathe to suit him during their entire marriage and most of their years of dating.

"You should have had a bat right from the first."

Jeanie looked at the bat she'd leaned against the refrigerator while she made her meal.

"I can't think of a single thing I love about you, Michael."

His stomach twisted as he internally rejected her words. "Well, I've got a lot I love about you, and I hope after we've been together for a while, you'll discover some things to love about me. I don't want it to be about before, because nothing we loved about each other was healthy. Let's go sit down."

He led the way, and when he sat down, he saw she'd brought along her trusty Louisville Slugger

Michael had jotted a few things down. He pulled the list out of his jeans pocket.

Chapter 8

Jeanie saw that piece of paper and felt as if Michael were going to read her death certificate.

He'd always had a rare gift of charming her out of a bad mood—in the early days—when he'd tried. Later he'd just browbeaten her. She fought to keep cool, keep distant.

Michael sat on the couch, and Jeanie headed for the one overstuffed chair.

"Please sit beside me."

"Fine, let's hear this list." She sank onto her bristly, thread-bare couch, made sure there was three feet between them, and took a hefty bite out of her sandwich, barely resisting the urge to do something gross like chew with her mouth open or dribble crumbs on her lap. That'd make him crazy.

She braced herself to slap down every superficial thing he said. She expected to hear him claim to love all the things he'd tried to change.

"I love that you've become a woman of faith."

Well, rats. How was she supposed to slap that down? She took another bite to keep from telling him she was proud of his new faith, too.

"I love that you're caring for people in need. Your kindness was always the most alluring thing about you."

Jeanie rolled her eyes, wanting him to know she wasn't affected by his words—even though she was. She kept eating, and her sandwich was shrinking fast. What excuse was she supposed to have for silence once the food was gone?

"It's true, Jeanie. I took advantage of your sweetness and your low opinion of yourself. I grabbed you and started right in making sure you thought you were lucky to have me. You were funny and popular. You could have had any guy you wanted."

"I don't want a guy."

"I want you to know that I've been faithful to you these years we've been apart. I'm not going to claim it was because I'm so honorable. No man who abandons his family can kid himself about honor. But the truth is I threw myself into working after I left. I was so cocky." He clenched his fists and shook them. "So sure I could rule the world, be rich, show you, show *everyone* how great I was. I just focused only on that."

"Whatever." She did her best to act like it didn't matter—but it did. It mattered so terribly. She'd always pictured him leaving her for another woman. The

280

thoughts had tormented her, deepened her sense of failure.

She set her empty plate aside and stared at her hands, folded in her lap like a good girl. The pastor had asked something of them, and Michael had delivered. Her husband-the-rat was sincere about his new faith. Three months ago he'd made a commitment to Christ. If she was too hard on him, could she possibly undermine a new baby Christian? She didn't want to mend their marriage. What could she do but be honest? God asked for nothing less.

"Michael, I'll tell you what I love about you." She met his eyes. His were a darker blue than hers. Right now they were locked on her, gazing, giving her a chance in a way he never had before.

"I'm a Christian. I became a Christian after I abandoned Sally. I ran off and left her, giving Buffy the papers she needed to begin adoption proceedings. When I left, I was as low as a person can sink. I hated myself, and I guess I'm not the suicidal type, because I never considered it, but I didn't feel like I deserved to live."

"Jeanie, I—"

"Stop." Jeanie held up her hand. She could see it cost him, but he quit talking. "I need to finish this."

Nodding, Michael subsided against the couch cushions, his lips clamped shut.

"I'm a believer. Jesus said plainly we're to love God and love our neighbors. Those are His greatest commandments. So I love you, I am happy for you that you've found Christ, and I can see the change in you. I can see you trying to be kind, and that's something you never wasted a second on before."

Michael rubbed his hand over his mouth, clearly trying to hold back words. His blatant regret weakened her resolve. If she gave him another chance, he really would try. She believed that. She also believed he'd fail.

"But as far as a romantic love, I just don't feel it. The only emotion you stir that isn't negative—and there are plenty of those—the only twinges of love I've had for you are sick. They seem like traces of that old dependence. I'm *afraid* of loving you. Honestly, Michael, loving you and mending our relationship might destroy me, and it might destroy you, too. Can you honestly say you're not afraid of slipping back into that awful excuse we had for a marriage?"

After so obviously wanting to interrupt her before, now he didn't speak. His shoulders slumped, and he set his own sandwich plate aside and reached out tentatively to take her hands. She almost pulled away, but his demeanor, so defeated and humble, was such a surprise that she hesitated and he had her. She decided not to dispute the touch—for now.

"I *am* afraid. I am. But I also believe God calls us to one marriage and the vows are for life. If we can't make our marriage work, then we both have to be alone forever. I don't want a life like that."

"I do."

Tightening his grip, he shook his head. "You only want to be alone because I made it so bad for us. Maybe it's true that we can't be together. But I think we dishonor God by not at least trying."

Jeanie shook her head.

"We owe God that much." He threaded his fingers through hers. "We owe our faith that much—to try. Just walking away from each other isn't honoring our vows any more than divorcing would be. God asks more of us than that. We need to get to know each other. Really start over. Nothing that we had before is a foundation for a marriage, so we throw that out and get to know each other as if we were strangers. Because we are strangers. We're new people. New in Christ. Let's just start over." He eased his hands free and reached one out to shake. "It's the right thing to do, isn't it?"

"Why is 'the right thing to do' always what I *don't* want?"

"You're not the one who has the struggle ahead of you. Or if it is a struggle, it will be to keep me accountable. I'm the one who has to change. I'm the one who has anger and control issues knotted up inside. Give me a chance, please, Jeanie? Please?" His eyes pleaded. His words begged. His hand waited.

She couldn't tell him no. And hadn't that always been her fundamental problem? But this time, galling though it was, she felt the truth of it. They weren't honoring their marriage vows by living separately and alone for the rest of their lives.

Heart sinking, tears threatening, she reached out. Their hands met and held. "All right. I'll try." Tears spilled over as they shook.

He pulled her forward and held her, hugging her. She didn't realize how long it had been since someone had really held her. Not a brief hello hug, but real contact. The loneliness of her life made her cling to him—in joy for the human touch and in despair because she sensed she'd just taken her first step toward self-destruction.

Chapter 9

Michael took his cue from Jeanie and began simply to say yes when something was asked of him.

It took less than a week before he'd gained a reputation as someone who'd lend a hand, and besides what he did for free, he made a few dollars. He was the Cold Creek handyman—a big change from a shark hustling building contracts.

He mowed lawns, did minor household repairs, fixed leaky faucets. He charged next to nothing and often didn't ask for money at all.

It was a way to make a living. The business and marketing strategy of his corporation consisted of hand-printed signs taped up at the senior center, grocery store, bank, and mini-mart.

He joined the volunteer fire department, chipped in on all the Memorial Day committees that were shorthanded, and agreed to help with the Monday morning church service at the nursing home.

He did as much with Jeanie as he could, but when their lives pulled them in separate directions, he went where he was needed, because he sensed Jeanie respected his willingness to serve others and he wanted her respect.

He returned his rented car to Rapid City and came home with a small pickup, careful not to buy anything too flashy, even though he could well afford it.

They'd been together five days when he came home one evening and announced fearfully, "Jeanie, I bought a house."

"What?"

He lifted both hands as if he were warding off a pit bull. "Listen, I didn't do it to control you or to judge where you live. I was repairing a drainpipe on Myra Dean's house, and her son showed up. He lives out of town, and we got to talking. He told me he really needed to get some money out of the house."

"You bought Myra's house?"

Michael had run himself ragged serving coffee at her funeral.

"Her family has a lot of bills to pay for the nursing home and the funeral, and they had no prospects. I promise I paid an honest price." A steal is what it was. If that huge old house had been sitting in Chicago somewhere, it would have cost a half million dollars. He'd bought it for fifty thousand, and Lance had practically wept with gratitude.

"It's a white elephant. It's practically falling down. It's been sitting empty for three years since Myra moved into the nursing home."

Michael shook his head. "It's been neglected, but it's got great bones, a solid foundation. And I love that American foursquare architecture. I'll enjoy refurbishing it. I had to do it for Myra's son, didn't I?"

Jeanie shook her head. "Yes, you're right." She whacked him with the bat. "But you should have talked to me first."

"It was a spur of the moment thing. I'm sorry."

"I'm busy. I'm not helping you pack and move."

"I'll close on it tomorrow and move everything by the weekend. You'll live with me in it, won't you? If not, we'll just stay here."

Jeanie knew Myra, and she knew the years in the nursing home had cost her family a lot. The Dean family did need the cash. "Yes, I'll live there."

"Thanks. I promise you won't have to lift a finger."

Jeanie rolled her eyes at him and turned to the kitchen to pull a pizza out of the oven. Frozen.

Michael felt lucky that she hadn't bought a personal pan size. She was cooking dinner for both of them. He was tempted to jump up and down and yell, but he was afraid the bat would come out.

Working on so many aspects of the Memorial Day celebration got him involved. Maybe too involved. The weekend events bothered him for their complete lack of flare, and he convinced the town fathers to let him put a couple of ads in the Rapid City paper, at his expense, to lure in tourists interested in the buffalo. He enlisted a couple of area seniors to be available to drive a minivan out to the herd if anyone showed up wanting to pay for the privilege.

And he met his daughter.

"She's huge." Michael caught Jeanie's hand, his eyes riveted on Sally. He took a step toward the little blond beauty, and someone blocked his path. He was so diverted by Sally he ran headlong into Buffy—his sister-in-law with the temperament of a buffalo.

"I heard you'd shown up in town." Buffy jammed her fists onto her hips and looked as if she'd tear into him with the least provocation. Michael sincerely hoped no one gave *her* a bat.

Buffy was two years younger than Jeanie, but they'd been in the same grade because of Buffy's genius IQ. While Jeanie played, Buffy studied. While Jeanie flirted, Buffy worked nights and weekends at a nearby wildlife park just outside Chicago. Buffy was lean and had dark, straight hair. He remembered she'd always worn it in a braid, but today it hung in loose, gentle curls. Then, as now, she'd ignored makeup. She'd been very solemn and quiet. The complete opposite of his blond, blue-eyed, flirty, flashy Jeanie.

She was six years younger than Michael, and back in high school, even from that disadvantaged level, she'd told him to his face he was scum for hanging around a girl as young as her sister. At the time he'd hated the little brat. Plain, no flare, no humor, no personality. But even then he'd recognized her as a better person than either Jeanie or him. Her words had echoed in his head like a sleeping conscience. And that only made him hate her more.

Maybe it was because he'd finally grown up, but he noticed immediately that she'd become a beautiful woman. Grouchy but beautiful.

"This is that no-account coyote who abandoned Sally?" A gruff voice pulled Michael's eyes up and up until they met Wyatt Shaw's. He stood behind Buffy. Jeanie had said Buffy's new husband was a rancher, but Michael would have known it at a glance. The weathered skin, dark hair hanging a bit long below a gray Stetson, and an attitude as cold as a South Dakota winter. Wyatt held his little girl, Audra, in his huge, work-scarred hands. Patting the toddler's back while the baby giggled until her dark curls bounced muted Wyatt's arctic demeanor.

Michael knew he deserved this scorn, and he was determined to stand here and take it like a man.

"This is him." Buffy turned her eyes on Jeanie, and Michael braced himself to protect his wife.

"Aunt Jeanie!" A small blond tornado hit Jeanie in the legs. Michael saw Sally up close at last.

Aunt Jeanie. The words registered and cut like a knife.

Then two more balls of energy came onto the scene. Wyatt had twin sons. Michael couldn't take his eyes off of Sally, the image of Jeanie.

Then Buffy caught his arm.

Reluctantly, he turned.

"We need to talk. You've got"—Buffy glanced at Sally, who was talking nonstop to Jeanie, along with the twins who were as identical as mirror images—"papers we need signed."

Michael clenched his jaw. Now wasn't the time or place to tell Buffy that he intended to get back together with Jeanie and reclaim his daughter. He nodded. "We do need to talk."

"After church. We can send the kids to a friend's house for lunch and have this out."

Michael wasn't quite ready to have anything out. He suspected that, as things stood, for him to start a fight over Sally might be the last straw with Jeanie. She'd kick him out and there'd be no further chance of reconciliation. But he had until the end of summer to protest the termination of his parental rights. He didn't need to tell anyone anything right now. He'd let things bump along as they were until he'd renewed his marriage.

"Fine, after church." He had one hour to figure out just what he was going to say. For now, he decided to change the subject to the one thing that might possibly distract his cranky sister-in-law. "Has the mayor contacted you about the buffalo excursions for Memorial Day?"

Buffy scowled. "We agreed to move a small group to the holding pens closer to town so the ride won't be so long and the buffalo will be close to the road."

"Good. That's settled then. You draw some tourists, right?"

Buffy nodded. "We do."

"Do you have any pamphlets we could spread around to advertise the buffalo?"

"We've got something." Wyatt caught Buffy's arm and added, "Come on, kids. The parson's getting read to start."

The twins and Sally whined and said a lot of good-byes to Jeanie without so much as looking Michael's way. His own daughter had walked right past him and had no idea who he was. It was like taking a knife to the heart. And it was a knife thrust by his own hand. His choices, his selfishness had led him to this pain.

He felt a hand on his elbow and looked up. Jeanie's sympathy was plain to see. She knew how he felt. Their eyes held.

What was it she'd said? "God has forgiven me for that, but I'll never forgive myself." The difference was he'd brought her to the point where she'd abandoned Sally. Whatever forgiveness she needed, he needed a hundred times more.

She tugged on his arm and led him into a pew near the back of the hundred-year-old church. Then she went up front to the piano and accompanied the organist.

Michael felt abandoned though he was fiercely proud of how well Jeanie played.

The Shaws were sitting about five rows ahead. Michael could watch Sally whisper to her father—Wyatt Shaw, not Michael—with adoring eyes. That was what he'd thrown away.

His eyes burned, but he refused to let the tears fall. Instead, they stayed inside, cutting his heart like acid rain.

Chapter 10

Michael deserved whatever he got.

Even so, Jeanie felt an almost compulsive need to protect Michael from Buffy, which was stupid, but she couldn't help herself. She prayed for this "talk" as she played the hymns.

Buffy had such a decent heart, she couldn't be truly cruel to anyone. She'd allowed Jeanie back into the family as an aunt. And they were closer now than they'd ever been, real friends. They worshiped together because Jeanie had returned to Cold Creek and started attending here about a year after she'd abandoned Sally.

Buffy had included Jeanie in get-togethers with her friend, Emily Hanson, another woman about their age, and Emily had become an even better friend than Buffy.

But Buffy had no use for Michael. Never had.

When church broke up, Jeanie left her place at the piano, fighting the urge to grab Michael and run.

But why? Let Buffy have at him. Wanting to protect her jerk of a husband was just a leftover reflex from long ago.

Jeanie emerged from church, aware Michael had a firm hold on her arm. Normally she'd have shaken him off. No bat at church, but if she would have had it, she would have whacked him, except she felt sorry for the big goon.

Jeanie saw Buffy waving good-bye to the kids as they drove away with Emily and her husband, Jake. Emily was far along in a pregnancy, but she didn't hesitate for a second to let the three rambunctious Shaw kids into her car.

Buffy turned to Michael, Audra in her arms. Wyatt relieved her of the baby, as if to get the child to shelter.

Michael headed straight for Buffy. No running and hiding for Michael Davidson; he seemed determined to take his tongue-lashing like a man. Though his steps were firm, his voice was gentle. "Buffy, before we start, I want you to know I've become a Christian since I left Jeanie and Sally. I'm back to make things right." Michael settled himself, his feet slightly spread, as if he expected Buffy to start swinging and he was going to take the whole thing standing.

"I want those papers signed before one more day goes by. You've—"

"I'm glad you're all together." Bucky Herne approached the group, not aware he'd stepped into a kill zone. He directed his words to Wyatt. "I've got to get things squared away about the buffalo for Memorial Day."

Buffy's eyes narrowed at the mayor. Jeanie could read Buffy's mind. She took care of the buffalo herd. For that matter, this whole thing was Michael's idea, and Jeanie volunteered to do almost all the work. And yet the mayor talked to Wyatt. Wyatt's family had been here five generations. Roots bought respect in South Dakota.

Michael turned to the mayor and cocked his head and focused. How well Jeanie remembered that focus. The man could make you feel like the center of the universe. That's how he'd made her feel at first. Later she'd been more like a bug under a microscope.

"Bucky, I've written up some detailed notes about Memorial Day. The Shaws are willing to bring about twenty head of buffalo to the holding pens near town."

Jeanie saw Bucky switch his attention from Wyatt, who wasn't interested at any rate, to Michael. The older man practically preened under Michael's respectful forcefulness.

"And about rides out there—," the mayor said.

"At first we planned on having a few Cold Creek residents lend their minivans. But I've gotten such a good response from the ads—it included a phone number to book the bus tour in advance—that I rented a bus from Rapid City. It's comfortable and seats about forty people. This will be at my expense, because I'm the one proposing it, and I don't want the city to take any financial risks. I'll make sure any profits go into the city coffers, too. And I've already arranged some publicity. *The Rapid City Journal* and the *Hot Springs Star* will run a story, and two of the local television stations have asked for interviews. Area radio stations have. . ."

Michael just took off talking and left them all in his dust. Jeanie had heard about the rented buses, but TV and the biggest newspaper in the area? She'd never heard a peep. How like Michael to just start handling things.

The mayor looked dazed. Wyatt looked intrigued as he bounced his little girl in his arms. Buffy looked irritated. She hadn't forgotten those adoption papers. And then the car with her—Jeanie flinched—*Buffy's* three kids came driving back into the church parking lot at top speed.

The three Shaw children jumped out of the car. Jake swung his door open with a wild expression on his face. "Hey, I'm sorry about this, but Emily's water just broke. We need to get to the hospital. We can't take the kids after all."

"That's fine." Wyatt waved. "You want us to take Stephie?"

"Nope, she wants to go along. Thanks, though." He swung the door shut and tore off.

Their little group grew, with the children adding to the chaos.

Two more parishioners and the pastor came up, and the Memorial Day committee began an impromptu meeting.

Buffy gave Michael a look that would have left a lesser man writhing in pain on the ground. Michael was too busy holding court to notice.

Jeanie went to Buffy's side. "We'll get it signed. Michael is determined to fix our marriage, and he has convinced me to at least try. I've been—" Jeanie realized Michael was inches away, and the man could multitask like nobody's business. He'd hear this, plus the children were swarming around everyone.

Jeanie pulled Buffy aside.

"I'll talk to him. He's only got about three months left until the deadline, so even if he does nothing, it'll be over soon." Tears suddenly cut across Jeanie's eyes, and she dashed a hand across them quickly, glad she didn't wear mascara anymore.

Buffy's hand rested on Jeanie's arm. "You know this is for the best."

Jeanie nodded. "It is. Even if Michael and I fix things, she"—Jeanie's gaze darted toward Sally—"is your daughter. We won't do anything to harm her."

Buffy looked skeptical. "Your husband has a knack for twisting the world to suit himself. I won't rest easy until he's signed those papers."

Jeanie had a moment of doubt. Michael hadn't said loud and clear that Sally's adoption was all right with him. At first he'd been furious. Then, when he found out Sally was in good hands, he'd accepted it. Or had he? Jeanie hadn't trusted Michael for a long time.

"We don't have a motel or any overnight accommodations." Mayor Herne tugged on his tie to loosen the knot, then pulled it all the way off, wrapped it around his hand, and slipped the tie in his suit coat pocket. The day was warm for early May.

"Nothing for overnight?" Michael rubbed his chin with one thumb. "Memorial Day is a three-day weekend. To really make some money with tourism, we need somewhere for folks to stay."

"Do you have the papers, Jeanie?" Buffy drew Jeanie back to the most important matter at hand. "I've got copies if you need them."

"Mike has the ones he's supposed to sign. And I promise I'll talk to him. This isn't the time or place."

"I'm starving, Dad." Cody or Colt, Jeanie could never tell them apart, tugged on Wyatt's arm.

"So if we could get a few people to maybe open up their homes, like a bed and breakfast, just for the weekend—"

"Well, I don't know about that." The mayor shrugged off his suit coat. "I mean, strangers in your house? Not too many folks will want that."

"Jeanie and I just bought a house. We've moved in, and we've only got a few pieces of furniture. But it's a neat old place. We could furnish a few more bedrooms, even move back to her apartment for the weekend."

"We've got to go, Buff. The kids are starving." Wyatt came over, Audra in one arm, both twins nagging that they were starving.

Buffy shook her head in defeat. "Okay." She glared at Michael, who glanced up and caught the look. The mayor was talking to Pastor Bert.

"We'll talk later, Buffy. I promise." Michael jerked his head at Sally as if that was what prevented him from saying more.

Buffy's eyes narrowed. It wasn't lost on Jeanie, nor Buffy, that Michael could easily promise to sign Buffy's papers without Sally understanding.

"I promise right back." Buffy made it a threat as she laid her hand on Sally's shoulder. "Let's go, honey. Mommy's got dinner in the oven, and the boys are starving."

"I've been thinking I might put up some A-frame buildings. Something really simple. A row of ten maybe. I could build them myself. There's a nice spot along Cold Creek right on the edge of town. I think it's part of the city's right-of-way, so the town council would have to approve it or sell it to me or whatever. And we could rent them out. I might be able to get a couple up by Memorial Day."

Jeanie stood watching Sally be driven away in a cloud of dust.

Watching Michael wheel and deal.

Watching her life slip completely out of her control.

And the worst part of Michael being back was Jeanie didn't *want* to be in control. She wanted to take orders and be obedient. It was easy and wrong. God didn't want her to give the reins of her life over to anyone but Him.

She stared at the group of movers and shakers, the biggest one of all in the very center of the action. Yes, the Peaceful Mountain Church was in the country. Yes, it was a five-mile walk home up and down a mountain pass and along a narrow country highway. Yes, she'd ridden here in Michael's new pickup. None of that mattered.

She needed to get out of here. He'd come for her before she got home. A new home she'd been moved into with precious little consultation. He'd pick her up whenever he came. It would be all too soon.

She wondered if Pastor Bert would allow her to bring her bat to church.

Chapter 11

The Memorial Day celebration got way out of hand for a normal human being.

Jeanie had never accused Michael of being normal.

Shaking her head, she watched her husband plot and plan with the city fathers about making it a real tourist event.

The media was involved.

Cold Creek was buzzing.

Michael was in his element. He bought what looked to everyone else in the world like wasteland along the steep banks of Cold Creek. Michael's sharp eyes saw a gold mine. He was single-handedly building a motel. A row of simple, rustic A-frames with roofs slanting all the way to the ground. He did the planning, the buying, the bulldozing, the sawing, and the nailing himself.

Except Jeanie knew him too well. He *didn't* do it himself. He just *started* it alone. Before the end of the first day, everyone in town was helping.

Jeanie remembered the story "Stone Soup." Michael started out with a stone and a dream, and everyone else threw in.

Two retired plumbers offered to help. The proud owner of a bulldozer had been bulldozed into volunteering his time and machine. The women were sewing curtains, the businesses were donating material, and the excitement only grew as Michael announced, one by one, that the little cabins were rented out. . .before they were built.

"You want me to what?" Jeanie had taken two weeks off from the nursing home and her other part-time jobs to help with the project. Some of the other nurse's aides put in longer hours to cover for her.

"Open a restaurant. The old gas station would make a great café and gift shop. I bought it this morning for just a few hundred dollars."

The decrepit stone building so close at hand had been abandoned for years. But as Michael did that magical thing with words and the force of his will, Jeanie completely saw his vision.

"We could clean it out in a few days. We can't bring it up to specs for a restaurant in time, but we could have food catered in. I've already mentioned it to Glynna Harder. You know what a great cook she is. We could offer sandwiches and soup and a few other things. All we need is a clean building and tables. I've already asked around town and found a few people who have tables in their garages and basements that they'd like to get rid of. And the used junk store has several they'll sell us cheap."

Jeanie went to work and found herself with a lot of help. The women of Cold Creek had been itching to get more involved, and the heavy work of the construction was beyond most of them.

The week ticked away, and Jeanie found herself too busy during the day and too tired at night to spend any time on her marriage or to pin Michael down about Sally's adoption papers. She didn't even have the energy to bat him.

They dragged home hours after dark and were up before the sun. Michael had ordered two sets of bedroom furniture and had it delivered. Jeanie slept in one corner of the huge upstairs, and Michael slept three rooms down and across the hall. He hadn't even tried to weasel his way into Jeanie's room.

He'd turned one downstairs room into an office with phone lines, a computer, Internet access, and a desk and filing cabinet. Another phone call. The man had no time to browse; he just phoned, ordered top of the line, and had it delivered and installed.

Jeanie still worked at Golden Days Senior Center through the morning, and Pastor Bert came into the center early, as he had that first day, and met with them weekly. A lot of Jeanie's volunteer work was suspended because so many of the people were working with Michael.

As Memorial Day crept closer, a party atmosphere grew in town until the community of Cold Creek became as close as family.

Michael had set out to build ten cabins, hoping to have three or four done in two weeks. He finished all ten. They were livable, and they'd all been rented. Michael had plans for ten more by the Fourth of July.

The gas station had become Jeanie's Café and was clean and shining inside. The mismatched tables and chairs were charming. The dinnerware was foraged from several auctions and junk stores in the area, and it lent the place a homey atmosphere. There was a lot more she could do with it, but it was useable for this one weekend.

When they finished for the night on the Thursday before the big weekend, Michael slung his arm around Jeanie, and they walked home, exhausted as usual. When they pushed their way through the sticking door of their new house, Michael smiled at her. "I've got all those buildings up, and I haven't done a thing to make this house more livable. 'The cobbler's children have no shoes.' Isn't that the saying?"

Jeanie smiled back. "It's okay. I love the work we're doing."

"I'm so proud of all you've accomplished with that gas station." Michael hugged her neck closer as he turned to close the door behind them. He dragged her just a bit, and she giggled and jabbed him in the ribs.

Flinching and laughing, he turned to her. "I didn't dare to hope it would look that good this fast."

"It's wonderful, isn't it? And I've got a lot of women lined up to bring in some crafts for the weekend. And there are more who want to be involved by Independence Day. And we've got fresh jelly, and there's a man bringing in honey to sell. It's your energy that's made it all happened, Mike."

"Maybe I started it, but it's a team effort. What's been accomplished is about everyone pulling together."

Jeanie wrapped her arms around his middle, since he wasn't letting go of her anyway. "I'm glad you came. I've loved having you back. I love—" Jeanie found herself caught by Michael's warm eyes.

Michael's smile faded as they stood. "We're together aren't we? Together in this marriage for the first time and forever."

"Yes." Jeanie's answer was a whisper.

Pulling back, Michael asked, "Were you going to say it?"

Jeanie knew what he meant. She still had doubts. Not doubts their marriage would work—she believed that was possible now—but doubts that they were ready for what she saw, right now, in Michael's eyes. But he was wonderful, and his arms felt so good.

"I was going to say, I love you." Jeanie hugged him. "And in the middle of all this, I remembered why I fell in love with you to begin with. I remembered the good things."

"Were there any good things?"

Jeanie sobered. "I fell so hard for you so fast. I was so proud of you. You're a leader, but you're generous, too. The way you've helped this town is just your nature. You have great vision and enthusiasm. I saw that in you when you were nineteen years old, and it's still there. . .that charm, the work ethic, the joy for life."

Brow furrowed, Michael said, "Our life together wasn't joyful. I don't want you to forget that. I'm almost afraid to let you love me. I want it so desperately." He hugged her again, lifting her to her toes. Then he set her down. "But I'm afraid I'll forget what a jerk I can be, and it'll happen all over again."

"I won't let you forget."

"Good girl." Michael lowered his head. "I love you, Jeanie. And this time I really know what that means."

Jeanie set aside her doubts and stretched up to meet her husband's lips.

Moments passed, long wonderful moments.

Then, his heart in his eyes, Michael asked, "We're together again, aren't we?" He ran one finger down her cheek, outlining her lips, tracing her jaw.

"Yes." Jeanie turned her head and kissed his palm, but a niggling of fear wouldn't let her give in to what Michael was obviously asking. "Yes, we're really together. And this time it's forever. But I don't think we're ready—at least I'm not."

Jeanie could see Michael fight the urge to push his wants on her, pressure her into accepting their marriage in all its fullness. But he won that fight. "I'll wait as long as you need. Hearing you say you love me is enough for now. It's what I've been praying for."

Relieved, Jeanie kissed him again.

Then they separated for their private rooms.

—⁓—

Michael sang while he worked the next day.

Only finishing touches to ten proud little triangles of unfinished wood along the creek. Inside, each cabin was one main room with bare stud walls, no insulation or drywall, twenty-four by twenty-four feet square at the base, rising to a peaked roof. A cement floor covered with cheap linoleum. A tiny bathroom—each cabin's only amenity besides a bed and electric lights—was partitioned out of each main room.

He'd rented these out so fast he knew he could build fifty more and keep them full. Line the whole creek bank on both sides. Maybe build a swinging footbridge and create some hiking trails. It was a beautiful, rustic spot. He had plans to polish the cabins up a bit, make them tight for winter and add heating and a tiny kitchen area. Rent them to tourists in the summer, ice fishermen in the winter, and hunters in the spring and fall. The smell of fresh wood and the outdoors was like the finest perfume. He was sure the customers would love them.

And speaking of love. . .

He pressed his hand flat to massage his heart. He'd glanced behind him a hundred times all through the morning, waiting for Jeanie to finish at the senior center and come to him. He could barely breathe when he thought of how madly in love he was.

God, forgive me for that awful excuse for love we shared before. Thank You, thank You, thank You for blessing me with my wife back. I didn't deserve it.

His eyes welled with tears as he remembered and cherished the new beginning.

God, thank You, thank You, thank You.

He couldn't say it enough times. He couldn't say it humbly enough. He couldn't ever begin to be worthy of this blessing.

He felt her and turned. Of course he'd turned around a hundred times before, thinking that he'd felt her those times, too.

She walked toward him, her hair pulled back in its no-nonsense ponytail, dressed in the jeans and T-shirt she wore to work. He dropped the broom he'd been using to sweep wood chips away from the front doors of his cabins and ran toward her. She was already nearly jogging, but when he ran, she raced to meet him.

Michael swept her into his arms in front of the refurbished gas station.

When the kiss ended, Michael swung her in a circle. "I've been watching for you all morning."

They were alone. The rest of the town was sprucing up their homes and streets to welcome the holiday crowds.

Jeanie laughed. "I set a new record cleaning up after dinner."

Michael set her feet back on the ground, and they just held each other. Michael cherished every breath, every moment, every touch.

Thank You, God. Thank You. Thank You.

"Are we going to stand here holding each other all day?" Jeanie asked.

"How about until we die of old age?" Michael kissed the top of her head, her temple, her eyes.

"I want to hold on to you for that long, Michael."

He kissed her soundly. "Good. Then we're in total agreement." He squeezed until her feet lifted off the ground and she squeaked. He set her down, laughing. "Now, what have we got left to do before the first renter arrives?"

They worked companionably together for several hours, having fun making the cabins perfect.

Then their first guest arrived. The day got hectic as Jeanie took the vacationers into the café to register and Michael helped with the luggage.

Glynna arrived with her neat foil containers of hot savory roast beef and side dishes. The guests ate as fast as Glynna and Jeanie spooned the food, and the rustic cash register they had found abandoned in the building rang up sale after sale.

It was early evening by the time there was a letup. The Buffalo Bus was ready, and rides had been scheduled for the morning. The cabins were full, Jeanie's café-in-training was cleaned and set up for breakfast, and Jeanie and Michael made their way home, tired but overjoyed with the success of the day.

They were a couple, Michael knew, in a way they'd never been before. Married in their hearts and souls and minds.

Married in the way God intended.

—∞—

Jeanie ran nonstop the whole weekend.

The activity was laced with joy as she watched Michael shine. He had a knack for bringing everyone along with him when he was enthusiastic.

Glynna's food sold out every meal. The Buffalo Bus was a huge hit, with people driving in for the day to ride it along with the people staying in the cabins.

The senior citizens had a fund-raising dinner Saturday at noon that had Jeanie running back and forth between that building and her café. But with all the extra hands helping in both places, she kept up and had fun.

On Sunday they had a community worship service in the park, and Monday morning featured the traditional Memorial Day program at the city auditorium. When the veterans marched in with the American flag, an army band Michael had arranged struck up "The Star-Spangled Banner." Pride nearly vibrated the building.

By the time everyone checked out of the cabins on Monday and the Buffalo Bus had made its last run, Jeanie was ready to collapse; but it was a good kind of exhaustion.

Michael helped her lock up the café. "You're a fantastic cook, Jeanie. Glynna did a great job, but I'd love some of your homemade bread on the menu. Do you think Glynna would maybe partner with you when we get the building up to specs? You'll need waitresses and at least one more cook. By Independence Day I'd like to. . ."

Jeanie listened with tired amusement as they walked through the darkened streets, trees sighing overhead in the cool May breeze. Nightingales setting their walk to music. The homes were mostly darkened, though an occasional window glowed with light.

Michael drew energy from people and plans, and she remembered, years ago, that she'd been a social butterfly, too.

"You keep planning and arranging, but tomorrow I go back to my normal life. I've got to work morning and afternoon. They let me off at the nursing home for the last two weeks, and I took time off from my other jobs, too. But people have been taking extra shifts to fill in."

Michael stopped so suddenly that Jeanie stumbled. He turned. "What other jobs?"

"I help out at the library on Thursday nights and at the mini-mart two Saturdays a month."

"You haven't done that since I've been back, not even those first two weeks."

"You knew I went to the library on Thursdays."

"That was a job? I thought you were volunteering."

"No, I get paid. And I only work two Saturdays a month at the mini-mart, and you came on an off week. Then I asked for a break because of all this activity, but—"

Michael pulled her so tight against him that she couldn't finish making her point. But she suspected he got the gist.

"What do you think about quitting the extra jobs? Maybe the senior center, too? I've got five of the cabins rented out for next week. Not just a couple of weekend nights—the whole week. We're going to want to keep Jeanie's Café open. It's not like the little bit of money you bring in from these part-time jobs is important. I can support us."

Jeanie worried her bottom lip as she considered it. "I like the work I do. There's a real need, Michael."

"I agree. You can't quit unless there's someone to fill the void." He rested his hands on her shoulders. "You've done so much for this town."

Jeanie shook her head with a smile. "You've done more in, what—a month?—than I did in a year."

"But what you did, giving to people, even if it was just one at a time, like with your hospice work, was the real thing. True Christian service. Pastor Bert was dead right about that." Michael rested one hand on her chest. "That's your gift. This generous heart. And I'm benefiting from it because only someone as generous as you would have forgiven me."

Michael suddenly wrapped one arm around her shoulder and practically dragged her toward their shabby old house. "Let's go home."

Jeanie raced along with him. She didn't want to give up her jobs. The truth was she got so much more than she ever gave in her work. If she helped others, that was wonderful, but those people—the elderly, the library patrons, the children in 4-H and Girl Scouts—made her feel worthwhile. She'd known since she started this whirlwind of volunteering that it was rooted in her own sense of failure and selfishness.

As if she could be good enough, generous enough, self-sacrificing enough to deserve God's love. But she knew in her heart that she couldn't earn salvation. It was a free gift, and her nearly frantic efforts to be worthy were misguided. It was time she let go of her past failure and forgave herself.

So, if Michael wanted her to quit, she should.

She would quit in an orderly way so no one was left in need, but she *would* quit and cut back on her volunteer work. She'd devote herself to her marriage and Michael's vision for Cold Creek and try, finally, to forgive herself.

It was scriptural that she'd let Michael be the head of the house. He wanted her to quit. She'd quit.

Turning to Michael as they entered the house, she opened her mouth to tell him all of this. They were new people in Christ. Their marriage was new, and it was based on complete honesty. This was something she needed to share and work through with her husband.

Before she could speak, his lips met hers, and she knew without a doubt that Michael wasn't in the mood to have a heart-to-heart talk. As she wrapped her arms around him, she decided it could wait.

Chapter 12

I want to give notice that I'm quitting." Jeanie smiled at Tim Russo, the owner of the mini-mart.

She knew she'd really helped by working two Saturdays a month. The store was family-owned, and the long hours and hectic schedule of the place was a strain. Their profit margin was slim, and they couldn't pay much. Her help had given the family their only day off twice a month.

The money wasn't good enough to tempt many people, and her boss looked at her in dismay. "I can't say I'm surprised. We really appreciate your help this last year. It's made a world of difference in our family to have that free time." Tim smiled, but he looked worried. "I feel like my kids have gotten to know me again." He squared his shoulders. "But this year, well, they've gotten older. They've started working with me on the Saturdays you don't come in. We'll get by."

"I can keep working until you find someone to take my shift." Her heart sinking, Jeanie nearly backed down and agreed to stay on, but she'd made her decision. She hadn't told Michael yet. She'd decided to surprise him instead.

"No need. We'll be fine." Tim rested one burly hand on her shoulder. "We really appreciate your help. We'll try, but we won't be able to replace you. No, your husband's back, and you two need time together. I understand that better than anybody. Consider yourself fired." He shooed her good-naturedly toward the door.

Jeanie felt bad about it, but she thanked him and left for the library.

There the mini-mart scene was repeated. The librarian, Julia Leesmith, was a retired schoolteacher, and the library was open only part-time. She insisted she didn't mind going back to her Thursday night schedule, although she'd have to give up a ladies' group that met once a month.

The nursing home was harder. She knew they were short-handed to begin with, employing lots of high schoolers who were notorious for needing time off for school events. The administrator took her up on her offer to stay until they found a replacement. She'd still be there for her hospice work and the Monday church service, but she'd grown fond of the residents of Cold Creek Manor as well as her coworkers and felt as if she was abandoning friends in need.

By evening Jeanie was near tears. Determined not to dump her emotional distress on Michael when he was still flying from the triumph of the holiday weekend, she had dinner ready by the time he got home. She remembered he'd insisted on that before.

Sliding a plate of meatloaf and mashed potatoes in front of him—it had been his favorite before, and Jeanie had carefully listened to his mother and learned to make it perfectly—she announced, "I've started simplifying my life."

Michael looked up from his plate. "What do you mean?"

Jeanie smiled and tried to make it look sincere even though her heart was breaking. "I told the mini-mart, the library, and the nursing home that I quit. The nursing home is the only place that asked me to stay on until they can find a replacement. So I'll be down to one job soon."

"Did they say how long it will take to find a replacement?" Michael tapped the white stoneware plate with his fork.

Jeanie had found the dishes and silverware used for a few dollars. Except for the bedrooms, their house was furnished out of junk stores with her meager apartment furniture. She was surprised Michael put up with it. But he'd been busy.

"They could string you along. You probably should have just given them two weeks' notice."

Jeanie gave him a saucy smile that she'd never dared give him in their earlier years. "Well, of course they're going to string me along. They're very sorry to lose me."

Michael smiled, but it didn't reach his eyes.

She hurried to reassure him. "The administrator is a good man. He'll respect my request. But the LPN program is hinged on me putting in some hours. I've been carpooling to a community college to take classes once a week. We're on break now, but classes start again in the fall, and my work counts toward course credits. If I quit completely, I'll lose the credit I've built up. I'd like to finish that. Have my license."

Michael's eyebrows lowered. "You don't need the license. You're not going to go back to that kind of work."

"I—I might someday."

"Why would you? I'm going to take care of you now."

Jeanie didn't respond. To say she wanted to be able to take care of herself seemed like she didn't trust him. "It would just give me a great feeling of accomplishment to finish what I started."

"We'll have to see if you've got time. You can try to get the hours in." Scooping meatloaf into his mouth, Michael chewed and swallowed. "This is Mom's recipe, isn't it?"

Jeanie's heart perked a bit. He'd noticed. "Yes, it was always your favorite."

"It's delicious, but it's no wonder Dad died of a heart attack, adding cheese and this sweet sauce to it. Fat and calories. Did you buy lean hamburger?"

"The local store doesn't have much of a selection." Jeanie began revamping the recipe.

"What about the senior center? When will you tell them you're quitting?"

She hadn't until this moment let herself think about Golden Days. She'd miss them so much. Tears burned as she remembered how those folks had opened their hearts to her when she arrived in Cold Creek, a new Christian. Her new baby faith had grown under their kindness. No, she didn't have a servant's heart at all, no matter what others said. Every time she helped someone, she received more than she gave.

Grateful that Michael was fixated on the meal, she fought back the tears and quickly swiped her wrist across her eyes. This wasn't his problem. She'd thought at first that they should talk it through, but now it was a gift she wanted to give him.

"I won't just quit there. I have to make sure there's someone to take over."

"Of course you do. I know it'll be hard to replace you. A lot of those ladies are pretty spry, though. Maybe they could do the cooking and cleaning."

"That's true. Some of them can work circles around me." She thought fondly of their busy hands and wisdom.

"So, they'll find someone. Maybe they could even run it as a co-op."

"Well, they already help, or I could never manage dinner for twenty-five people every day. But there's a lot more to it than just cooking and cleaning. There's fundraising and a lot of government paperwork to qualify for the financial aid we get. Some of it gets pretty complicated."

Michael waved his fork. "Maybe you could do the paperwork for a while— maybe work on that from the café. But I really need you if we're going to hope to keep the café open all day. We'll have our own family business." He set his fork aside and slid his hand across the table to clasp hers. His warmth and strength helped settle her. "I like that. Us together as a team."

The tears no longer threatened as she looked into his bright eyes. "Yes, doing the bookwork from the café could be a temporary solution."

"Good, because I'd like you to be available to work at the café right away. Two weeks' notice is all anyone can ask, and even that is more tradition than ethical. It's a dog-eat-dog world out there. Most businesses expect their employees to move on with very little notice."

"I've always thought it was common courtesy to give an employer time to make adjustments." It crossed Jeanie's mind that her new employer was, in effect, her husband. She spoke a bit sharply when she added, "Any decent *new* employer would respect that."

Displeasure cut a furrow across Michael's forehead. His hand, resting gently on the back of hers, tightened. "If you're talking about me, I'm not your *new employer*. We're *partners*. I thought that was what you wanted."

Fear twisted in Jeanie's stomach. It was mild, a reflex really, left over from the old days. When Michael first came to town, she'd have used it as an excuse to whack him with the bat. But that wasn't right for them now. She didn't fear her husband. But she did respect him, and what she'd just said was rude. Who could blame him for being annoyed?

She turned her hand over and wove her fingers through his. "It *is* what I want. I'll get it all straightened out as soon as possible."

Michael nodded, satisfied, then let go of her hand and went back to his meal.

Her food grew cold as she worried at that fear. Michael had never laid a hand on her, ever. He'd done all his damage with words, cutting insults, tiny at first, then bigger and crueler. She let that worry morph into fretting about her friends at the nursing home and the senior center. The truth was she worked dirt cheap and worked hard. And both places scraped along, just like the library and the mini-mart. It wasn't a prosperous town. They were going to have a hard time replacing her.

"Why aren't you eating?" Michael picked up his plate and carried it to the kitchen sink.

Jeanie shrugged. "It was hard today. I loved working for those people, and they need me. I feel guilty abandoning them. I guess it killed my appetite."

Michael snagged his chair, moved it next to her, and sat down. "Well, don't skip too many meals." Michael grinned at her. "If you get any skinnier, you'll blow away."

"I thought you liked me skinny."

"I like everything about you." Michael lifted her onto his lap.

She squeaked in surprise then wrapped her arms around his neck, glad he was happy with her again. Yes, he liked everything about her, except her jobs and her volunteer work—the things that gave her a feeling of self-worth. And her skinny body. He'd had a real problem with the weight she'd gained after Sally was born. So he didn't like her skinny and he didn't like her fat.

She had a split second to consider calling him on this strange, mildly hurtful conversation. He'd told her he wanted to be held accountable. But he was smiling, and she didn't want him to stop. And then he was kissing her, reassuring her with his touch that he liked her very much. And she definitely didn't want him to stop that.

He'd been so sweet about waiting until she was ready to make their marriage a real one, but she felt his frustration, and that deepened her guilt. But she still wasn't ready. Michael would just have to be patient.

One of his very worst skills.

Chapter 13

Jeanie had her hands full controlling her inner battle-ax. But she was careful not to become a nagging shrew of a wife.

Michael returned to his cheerful self. Of course, she tried hard to be loving and give him the respect due any husband.

The senior center surprised her by deciding to close when she resigned. Feeling terrible about it, they announced they'd all come to her restaurant for their noon meal, and some of them for breakfast and dinner, too. The community Meals-on-Wheels program had been attached to the senior center, so Jeanie continued providing those meals, and local volunteers delivered them just as they always had, only now they worked out of Jeanie's Café.

There was paperwork to do to transfer the government part of the subsidized program to a new address, along with the usual accounting. Michael agreed, somewhat grudgingly, to give a senior discount that equaled the very low price the Cold Creek retirees had been paying at Golden Days.

It made the café the center of the town's activities and brought attention to his rapidly expanding row of cabins. After the success of the rented Buffalo Bus on Memorial Day, Michael had found a shabby but functioning bus and bought it. He'd had signs attached to the side so they had an official Buffalo Bus and could run rides whenever a group asked for them.

Michael came into the café one hot day in the middle of June, exuberant. "We're building a golf course."

Jeanie looked up from her bookwork. She now did the books for the senior center, Meals-on-Wheels, the café, craft shop, and cabins as well. Michael had offered to do it, but she'd insisted. It had seemed like a matter of honor that she not turn over all the money to him, but she regretted taking on so much work that Michael would have done joyfully.

She really wasn't book smart. She was reminded of that daily as she struggled at her computer to make her account columns balance.

"A golf course?"

"Yeah, it was Jake Hanson's idea. There's a nice plot of land, too rough for much else, on the south side of town. He's getting a group together to do the work themselves. Did you know Jake is rich?"

"I guess I never thought about it. He doesn't live a fancy life."

"He's loaded. I'm going to encourage him to keep investing in this Cold

Creek revitalization project. He sounds willing. He's excited about the golf course."

"Can you do that? Build a golf course yourself?" Jeanie knew nothing about golf, and that was the plain truth.

"Sure you can. It's mainly working with the contours and hazards already there and planting grass. Jake has the farm equipment, and we've got lots of people who can pitch in. It'll be rough at first, but that'll make for a challenging course. And I want to open up the garage bay on this place. Make it a bait and tackle shop, maybe carry some camping equipment. You've got the back room full of crafts, and I think we need to move them to the abandoned building next to the city offices on Main Street."

"Open another business?" Jeanie glanced at her mangled efforts at book-keeping, wondering if she was up to it.

Mayor Herne rushed into the café, his face flushed pink from the summer heat. He pulled out a handkerchief and mopped his brow. "This golf course will be great. If we throw a lot of effort into it, we could seed the grass in September and possibly have it open for the late fall. There are several schoolteachers who aren't busy this summer who offered to do a lot of the heavy labor, cutting a fairway through a stand of trees here and there."

Jeanie didn't speak up about her worries over the craft shop or the bait and tackle. Heaving a sigh of relief that the golf course wasn't her problem, she went back to her figuring.

Michael and Bucky talked. A few more people came in, excited about the course. Jake came in carrying pictures of his baby, and he divided his time between fatherly pride and a long suppressed love of golf.

"I wish you'd brought Emily in, Jake. I haven't been out yet with a meal. I get lonely for her." Emily had been the best support in this last year. She was steady, sensible. Buffy was, too, but she had the same scars from her childhood that Jeanie had. And she had her hands really full. Plus Jeanie felt like such a failure around Buffy, no matter how kindly Buffy treated her.

Michael offered to design a simple clubhouse, and several of the men owned golf carts. They kept them in Hot Springs at the country club, the nearest place to play. But they offered to rent them out for people wanting to get from the cabins to the shops uptown to the golf course.

Jeanie listened with part of her attention while she did her figuring. Michael and his enthusiasm had caught fire yet again. She wanted to smile. She also had a twinge of concern that the local people were taking on too much, maybe donating more than they could afford.

With a mental shrug, Jeanie typed on until the crowd got agitated with a need to act and they all scrambled out the door, heading toward the future Cold Creek Links.

Jeanie spent another hour on her books then walked out to the nursing home to spend some time with her hospice patients. The outlook was bleak for both the patients, as was always the case, but one, Pete Hillman, had his family called in and wasn't expected to live through the night. Sadness hung heavy in the air. Jeanie spent a long while with Pete's two sons and their elderly mother as they discussed details of a funeral and all the complications involved in a loved one's death.

Her other hospice patient, Janet Lessman, was in nearly as fragile a condition, and the elderly woman had her husband sitting faithfully by her side for hours every day. They had time for a brief visit and some prayer before she left.

By the time she walked home, it was well past time for dinner.

She came inside to find Michael striding back and forth. He looked up as if he'd been afraid she was dead. "Where have you been?" He was at her side in an instant.

"I was visiting at the manor. You know I spend a few evenings a week out there. One of my clients is dying."

"I thought they were all dying. I thought that's what hospice was all about."

With a sad nod, Jeanie said, "That's right, but the time is really close for Mr. Hillman. His family had a lot of questions and just needed someone there to handle the details."

"Okay, I'm sorry." He hugged her. "You worried me."

"Did you call the nursing home or anywhere else to check on me?"

"No, I haven't been home that long. But I was late, so I knew you were late." He pulled her closer. "I'm sorry. It just. . .it reminded me of the time we spent apart. I just kind of freaked out. Panicked. I was going to call 911 in about two minutes." He laughed.

She felt him shake his head against her neck. She felt the tremors. He'd really been worried. She lifted her arms to hold him, comfort him.

"Can you just leave a note next time if you're going to be late? Something." Michael gave another shaky laugh. "I'm sorry. It's like I'm a parent worried about a kid who missed curfew. If you'd put your schedule on the refrigerator, it would give me a place to start looking."

Jeanie hugged him hard then pulled away. "Or a reminder that you don't need to start looking." She ran both hands into his hair, pushing it off his forehead. Then she pulled him down and kissed him. "Yes, I'll put the schedule up. It's a lot simpler now, without the work hours. And both the choir and my Tuesday Bible study are on summer break. Girl Scouts, too. I haven't been helping with the 4-H Club like I should, so I've kind of let others take over for the county fair, which is next week. So I'm pretty free these days, except for running the café and the bait and tackle store and the craft shop."

"I asked Bucky to find someone to take over the tackle store. I hope that's okay. I mean, how would you know what to order for tackle? Bucky knows an area fisherman or two who know just how they'd like things to be. And two of your seniors are going to run things for the craft shop."

Jeanie concealed a sigh of relief. "That's good. The café is keeping me really busy."

Feeling impish with so much weight off of her shoulders, she asked, "So, what are you making me for supper?"

Catching her face in both hands, Michael kissed her with a comic smack. "I'll be glad to make supper for my runaway bride. Let me see, what do I know how to make? Uh. . .cold cereal? No wait, do we have hot dogs?" He strode toward the kitchen. Glancing back, his eyes shone with mischief. "Do they have to be hot, or can we just eat them right out of the package?"

Jeanie caught up with him and shoved him playfully. "Forget it. I'm not trusting you within a mile of something I'm going to put in my stomach. I'll cook."

Stumbling for just a step, Michael grabbed her as if to keep his balance and began tickling her. Laughing, she tried to escape, but he pulled her back, the tickling making her squirm and laugh like a loon.

"Stop." Jeanie finally yelled through her giggling. "I give. You win."

"Just remember who's bigger next time you make me worry." Michael left the kitchen. "Call me when dinner's ready. I've got some phone calls to make."

Too tired to get fancy, Jeanie put a couple of hamburgers in the skillet and warmed a can of vegetables; then she turned her attention to writing up her schedule as Michael had asked. It was different having to consider him. She thought they'd talked about all of her commitments, and heaven knew she'd dropped a lot of them, but he didn't have it all straight. A quick thrust of impatience had her thinking of all the details he juggled with his many projects, but somehow he couldn't remember that Jeanie visited hospice patients?

As she wrote, she realized just how many things she'd dropped in the two months since he'd been back. She'd even told the hospice organizer that she didn't want to be assigned any more clients, and Michael had found someone else to clean the church and weed the flower beds.

She was left with Monday morning church services at the nursing home, two quickly failing hospice patients, and some substitute piano playing at church. Michael was wheedling for her to do that only when absolutely necessary, because he wanted her to sit with him. As it was, she'd started coming down from behind the piano between songs.

She knew he chafed at her resuming her involvement with the Girl Scouts and the 4-H Club. She'd already told the other leaders that she wouldn't be available much from now on.

She had gone from busy all day every day to working about three hours a week outside the café. She tapped the paper as she studied it. Three hours, and Michael couldn't keep that straight? Her jaw tightened. How had this happened? He'd done some pushing, but she'd mostly just assumed he'd want her to quit. Actually, he'd been quiet about it, but she'd gotten the message.

Was this something she should bring up as part of being honest in her new marriage?

God, is it?

It wasn't comfortable, this total giving up of everything she was in order to be Michael's devoted wife. But she was still busy with the café and the bookwork she did.

The Bible verse about courage she had taped on her mirror at her tiny apartment was still there. She hadn't brought it along, but she had it memorized.

"We want you to be very strong, in keeping with his glorious power. We want you to be patient. Never give up. Be joyful."

Where was her strength? All residing in Michael's hands.

Yes, she had been patient, but was it the patience of strength, or was it just the quiet nature of a quitter, a coward?

Had she given up? It didn't feel like it, but it had been so incremental.

"Be joyful." She was happy in her marriage. Michael wasn't the tyrant he'd once been. Or was he? Was he even aware that he'd taken over Jeanie's life completely? And didn't a husband have the first claim on his wife's time?

God had even been pushed out of the center of her life. They prayed together over meals, but Jeanie hadn't had her quiet time with the Lord in the early mornings for a while. After they'd moved, she'd just never gotten back in the habit.

Should I challenge Michael on this?

In prayer, she listened for the leading of God. Instead of God's voice she heard Michael talk in the room he'd converted into an office. The words weren't audible, but the rising and falling of his salesman voice was clear.

For some reason, listening to that persuasive cadence made her look around her kitchen for her bat. She hadn't seen it for a while. Odd that she suddenly wished for it.

Turning the dinner down, she hunted for her Bible and had a crushing sense of guilt that it took her many long minutes to find it, neatly tucked in a bookshelf.

She brought it with her to the kitchen and realized that the hamburgers had gotten too brown. Turning them off, she used a spatula to set them on a plate with the cold *clink* of metal on glass.

"Michael, dinner is ready." She'd read later.

"I'm almost done. I'll be right there."

Jeanie almost smiled at those familiar words. How many times had she held supper for him? He always had just one more call. She looked at the hamburger. Not burnt, but a bit crisp on one side. And the vegetables, one glance told her the green beans had cooked until they were mushy.

Michael would notice this. She almost rushed to the pantry closet for a new can of beans. If he delayed much longer, she'd be able to have a new hamburger cooked for him. She had some frozen, and with the microwave to thaw it—

She caught herself. "No. He'll eat it and be nice about it. Or he won't and I'll call him on it." Jeanie put a hamburger on Michael's plate and a serving of beans, then made a plate for herself and set it aside.

His voice continued in the background.

"It's getting cold, Mike."

"Just hang on another couple of minutes." He went on talking.

She sat down and opened her Bible. She'd marked verses about courage. She needed the kind of courage that she found only in the Lord. Because if Michael came in here and said one thing about the dinner or about her being late or too busy, she was going to stand up to him. And if he didn't take that well, she was moving out.

God, do I need to stand up for myself? Or am I just creating conflict in my home?

Prayerfully, she read her marked pages, trying to decide if she was willing to end up, before the night was over, alone in her little apartment.

Chapter 14

Michael hung up the phone, satisfied with the plans in place for the Fourth of July.

The Rapid City media was playing up the buffalo herd. Michael had placed some stories here and there about the fishing in Cold Creek and the small town charm. The cabins had been full every weekend since they'd opened, and he'd had enough weeklong reservations to make the place profitable, but it could do a lot better. They needed some hiking trails, maybe hook-ups for campers.

His mind busy, he went to the kitchen and found Jeanie reading at the table. His dinner was served and ready for him. Leaning down to kiss her cheek, he saw the Bible and his heart warmed. "You're wonderful, you know? I'm so glad we're together again."

She lifted her chin, and their lips met. She closed the Bible, set it aside, and pulled her plate into place. Michael sat next to her. Their hands clasped, then he pulled her close and they turned to God in prayer.

When they'd finished, they ate supper. Michael made no unkind mention of the pathetic meal.

Michael slid both their plates aside when they were done, and he picked up her Bible. "What were you studying when I came in for supper?" He flicked his finger over the row of bright pink sticky notes on the top of the book.

Jeanie smiled up at him, her gift of sunlight to him. Michael prayed silently as she took the Bible and flipped it open at one of the tiny stickies. "I've marked all the verses I can find about courage. It's been my one constant quest. I'm a coward. I've done terrible things out of fear." She flipped open the book to Colossians. "I've claimed this as my life verse."

Michael read. "I recognize this from our bathroom mirror at the apartment."

"Paul writing a letter of encouragement to the Colossians." Jeanie's graceful hand slid down the page to rest by the first verse. " 'We want you to be very strong, in keeping with his glorious power. We want you to be patient. Never give up. Be joyful.' All of this was missing in my life on the day I gave up Sally. I ran away, hitched a ride, and ended up in Denver. I'd stolen money from Buffy. I left feeling like. . ." Jeanie's eyes fell closed, and she shook her head.

"Like what, honey?" Michael sat around the corner from her. He scooted his chair so he was by her side and slid his arm around her shoulders, wishing his physical support could provide emotional support.

"Like I didn't deserve to live." She rested her head on his chest. "I felt so awful, just worthless. The bus station in Denver. . .I just walked out of it with no idea where to go from there."

She took a deep breath. "I saw a homeless shelter. There was a sign asking for volunteers. I still had some money but not that much. It was late, and I was in a bad neighborhood. I had no idea where to find a motel. I went in intending to help and get a meal in exchange, maybe even a place to sleep. I ended up staying for six months."

"In a homeless shelter?" Michael's skin crawled as he thought of the dangerous people who might inhabit such a place. He rubbed her shoulder as he imagined the filth and the bad food and the—

"I found God in that place. The man running the mission was a beautiful Christian. The kitchen had several people in it who had pretty much walked in off the street like I had. They were wonderful, accepting." Jeanie gave a short, humorless laugh. "They'd all done things as bad or worse than I had. They were so shorthanded and thrilled with my offer to help. They—they needed me." Her voice faded to a whisper, as if being needed was beyond her imagination. Jeanie closed the Bible gently and hugged it. "I don't know if anyone had ever needed me before."

"I need you, Jeanie." He pulled her close, hugging her, the Bible between them. It felt so right.

Please, God, create something new in me. Give me the words to encourage her.

"No, you don't."

He looked down and saw the top of her head. So familiar, so much time in her short life with her head bowed in fear or shame. So much of it his fault.

"You *want* me for whatever reason." She spoke into his chest. "Or maybe you're just *stuck* with me and trying to figure out how to make it work. But you don't need me at all."

Michael gently lifted her chin until she looked at him. Tears coursed down her cheeks. Misery etched lines into her face.

God, forgive me. Help me. I never wanted to make her cry again.

He loved her. He couldn't resist lowering his head and kissing her. Even that, in the midst of her misery, she accepted and gave without thought to herself.

When the kiss ended, Michael said, "I think we've been too busy lately, running in so many directions. We need to be spending time with the Lord. A devotion every day. Tonight we start. Let's go through these sticky notes and read your verses. And we'll make time for the Lord every morning. We've been neglecting counseling, too. Let's ask Pastor Bert if we can meet with him once a week. Maybe he'll give you a new bat."

Jeanie laughed through her tears. "I think the bat actually helped. Even just sitting in the room it was a reminder to both of us that we had a weakness in our marriage that needed our constant attention." She stretched up and kissed him. "I'll tell you something that I probably shouldn't because it will just inflate your ego."

Michael widened his eyes in mock excitement. "I could really use this. You've reminded me of how far we have to go. My ego could use some inflation."

With another laugh, she said, "I'm so proud of you."

The mock excitement died, replaced with a melting heart. "You are?"

"You have so many great qualities. I have you close, and I start depending on you and obeying you because you're so smart and so full of life and enthusiasm. It's so logical that I'd let you lead. Mostly, 90 percent of the time it would be stupid to do things any way except yours."

"Only 90 percent?"

"Okay, 99 percent." She punched his arm playfully.

"But you lose yourself." It was in his nature to take charge. He had to fight it, even if it made sense for him to run things.

"And since it's my own fault, it's even harder to talk about." She looked up, and Michael saw tears brimming in her shining eyes. "It's my problem. Taking it to you just dumps more on you and makes me a burden." Her voice broke, and she buried her face against his chest.

"You're not a burden, sweetheart. And it's not your problem. I am as much at fault in our marriage as you. More, in fact. I was the one who was—and sometimes still is—unkind. You were just too nice to start throwing coffee mugs at my head. Guess which one of those is the worst?" Aching for her, he ran a hand down her hair and held her as she cried.

After a few minutes, she shook her head and cleared her throat. "The few tiny things I'd like different are silly. I start mentally beating up on myself, and it's worse than anything you do."

Michael offered her a handkerchief. "Probably not."

Mopping her eyes, she laughed again, a husky laugh with a throat swollen from crying. "Just be patient with me, Michael. Give me a chance to figure out how to change and grow and give you what you need."

"Thank you. Thank you for trusting me enough to say that. You're such a good, sweet person." He kissed her. And her generosity was his.

After Jeanie had left him to his lonely bed, Michael took a moment to thank God then remembered they'd left the Bible in the kitchen.

He should go get Jeanie, and they should keep that commitment they'd made to have a devotional time every day. But his eyes were heavy and he was too comfortable. They'd spend time with the Lord tomorrow.

A small voice whispered inside his head not to put God off until later. His eyes popped open, and suddenly his exhaustion was lessened. He shoved the blanket back and pulled on his robe as he headed for the kitchen. He reached Jeanie's room and knocked.

"Yes?"

He heard tension in her voice. He spoke quickly before she could get the wrong idea.

"We forgot to have an evening devotion, honey. Are you too tired?"

"No, I'm not too tired. It's a good idea."

"I left my Bible in the kitchen."

Jeanie's door opened. Her face was clean scrubbed. Her hair mussed as if she'd been tossing and turning in bed. Her eyes shone with pleasure that he'd thought of this and come to her.

It was all he could do not to pull her close and kiss her. Something in her eyes told him that, right now, she'd welcome him.

"I–I'll meet you there then." She didn't move to get her own Bible.

Unable to resist, Michael grabbed a quick kiss then a slower one; then he forced himself to straighten away from her.

"Great." He moved on down the hall.

Chapter 15

Besides her normal work, Jeanie had to get a meal together for Jake and Emily, to welcome the new baby.

Their son, Logan, was beautiful. He reminded Jeanie painfully of all she'd given up. She missed confiding in Emily, but her friend was so busy, Jeanie couldn't impose.

Jake was floating around as if he'd been crowned king. He'd also found some rush of energy from fatherhood. With the help of a volunteer crew and some rented earth-moving equipment, he'd cleared the whole golf course and smoothed the rolling hills, ready to seed in the fall.

The Fourth of July celebration was coming at them like a freight train. The whole town was excited. Everyone was involved. Michael had yet to talk with Buffy and sign the adoption papers, but who could blame him?

He'd found another inflatable bat, and Jeanie kept it behind the counter at her café, but she was too much in love to use it. They'd found posters and figurines of buffalo as well as some Western décor. Michael had insisted on offering buffalo burgers on the menu, although Jeanie knew Buffy hated the idea, and he'd had a sign made naming the place the Buffalo Café.

He didn't consult Jeanie about the sign, just presented it to her as a gift. He'd been calling it Jeanie's Café up to now. She'd enjoyed having it named after her for some dumb reason. Why would her name sell food?

Michael had hinted at doing the bookwork, and though that perturbed her and she'd teased him about the bat, he'd taken it over and she didn't miss doing it.

To thank him for helping, she decided to decorate *herself* a bit and had some highlights added to her hair and started wearing a little bit of makeup again. She'd really let herself go since they'd been apart.

The café and Jeanie were both beginning to shine.

"It's this weekend." Michael came home later these days, and Jeanie had remembered some old recipes that kept well on low heat. She'd quit offering him skimpy dinners.

Smiling as he came in the kitchen, she said, "I can't wait. You've got everything ready. It's going to be huge success."

"This town is going to become a destination." He slid into his place at the table. "We're a great low-cost alternative for people wanting Mount Rushmore and the Black Hills. I've printed up some tourist information with all the places to drive in short trips. Everyone who comes to town over the Fourth will get one. We're going to have to add cabins. Maybe I could even interest a chain in selling me a franchise."

Jeanie hurried to set a platter of lean roast beef in front of him and quickly drained the new potatoes she'd cooked; then she added a plate of fresh sliced tomatoes. Michael had encouraged her to hire more help at the café, and now she got home right after lunch.

She should have dropped by the nursing home to visit with her last remaining patient, but instead, she'd driven to Rapid City to have her hair done and she'd wanted time to bake bread for supper. Tomorrow was Thursday, and the Fourth of July weekend began in earnest on Friday.

When Michael had everything in front of him, she settled into her own place on the opposite side of the rickety white Formica-top table.

After he'd eaten a few bites, he managed to look up. "I'm sorry. I'm eating like a hungry wolf, and I've barely spoken to you. I'm starving and this tastes great." Then his eyes focused. "Hey, your hair. I like it."

Her heart gave a little extra leap of pleasure. "I had it cut. Lightened a little, too."

"You look terrific. You drove into Rapid City today, didn't you?" He slid one hand over her hair and took a second to touch her dangling earrings playing peek-a-boo with her sassy, uneven cut.

She'd told him she was going to, but it must not have registered until he saw her new hairdo.

"Yeah, there's a hairdresser in the mall I'd heard a lot about. The local beautician has a tendency to burn hair to a crisp with bleach." She spent mornings at the café, but with the hired help there wasn't a lot left for her to do except greet people. Michael had hinted that she should dress a little better for the job. She'd started wearing a skirt and heels to act as hostess. The shoes killed her feet, which made it all that much easier to hand the reins over to her very competent help.

"I'd rather go with you when you drive in the city. The traffic is pretty heavy."

"I'd prefer it if you went with me, too. I haven't done much city driving. I don't need to go back for a while. Maybe after the Fourth we could visit Mount Rushmore." She'd never owned a car since she'd moved to South Dakota. Hadn't wanted one, hadn't been able to afford one. So Rapid City was intimidating.

Michael went back to his meal, filling her in on all the details of his day. When he finished eating, he headed straight for the office and his phone. He called over his shoulder as he left the room, "It was a delicious meal."

Jeanie watched him go. Their counseling sessions with Pastor Bert had been delayed for the last two weeks. They needed to get back to them. They hadn't done their daily devotions for a few days either.

She bit her bottom lip and tried to figure out how to remind Michael, but it just wasn't fair to dump this all on him when he was so busy. But how was standing here feeling drab and afraid to drive fair to her?

It wasn't. She had let things slip, and she needed to stand up for herself again.

Their marriage should come first. And it would—after the Fourth. Things would settle down then.

The time was almost up on those adoption papers, too. By the end of summer, if Michael hadn't formally protested, the adoption would go through with or without his signature. But until it was finished, Jeanie would worry. And she'd started ducking Buffy at church so she wouldn't have to see her sister fume.

As she cleaned up the kitchen, Jeanie heard Michael's voice, that rise and fall, his wheeler-dealer voice. Somehow it seemed as if he'd sold her a bill of goods, too, but wasn't that just her own sinful nature fretting, being dissatisfied?

She took her Bible and went to her room. She preferred to stay in there most evenings so she wouldn't have to see Michael and conjure up all the enthusiasm he expected for the changes he was making in Cold Creek.

Sometimes he came to her room and held her, trying to sell her on the idea that all was well and their marriage should cease to be platonic. It reminded her of when they were dating.

Hesitantly, feeling like a bother, she left her room and looked in on Michael, who was working on his computer. "Are you using the phone?"

He looked up, a trace of annoyance on his face for being disturbed. "No, but isn't it a little late to make a phone call?"

"It's just past nine. I think it's okay."

"Who are you calling?"

That bothered her. As if he was going to approve or disapprove of letting her make the call.

"Emily."

Michael nodded, which Jeanie assumed meant she had permission.

She took the handset off of its cradle. "I'll make the call out here so I won't distract you."

Settled back in her bedroom, sitting on the edge of her single bed, she dialed and Jake answered.

"Is Emily there? I mean, don't bother her if she's sleeping or got her hands full with Logan."

"No, she'll be glad to talk to an adult. She claims she's reverting to baby talk herself." Jake laughed.

Jeanie realized that Jake's little comment could have been taken as slightly insulting to Emily, but he sounded so kind. Did all husbands put their wives down? Did Jeanie just hear Michael's perfectly innocent words and twist them into something darker? Was all her unhappiness coming from her own warped mind?

"Hi, Jeanie. Thank you so much for calling. I'm desperate to talk to a grown-up." Emily laughed. Jeanie knew how happy Emily was with Jake.

"I'm coming out with dinner as soon as I can."

"Well, do it when you can stay awhile. I need to show off Logan to someone. He's so beautiful."

"I—I need to talk to someone about Michael."

There was a stretched moment of silence. "Has something happened?"

"No, well, kind of, not really. I—I drove to Rapid City today and got—got my hair colored." Jeanie waited, wondering if Emily could possibly read her mind. This would be so much easier.

"Did Michael order you to do it?"

Maybe Emily could read her mind a little.

"No, he's never said a word. It's me. I've just got this—this racket inside my head. Michael hasn't done anything wrong, but I feel like such a failure. An embarrassment."

"But he's never said a word?" Jeanie heard the doubt in Emily's voice.

"Well, nothing really critical. He wants me to dress better to hostess at the restaurant."

"Which you interpreted to mean you're a failure and an embarrassment."

"Why do I do this? It's not Michael's fault if I've got critical voices inside my head telling me I'm not good enough."

"Did you have those voices before Michael came back?"

"Well, yes, some."

"But they're a lot louder now, right?"

"A lot."

"But you don't think that's Michael's fault, right?"

"It doesn't seem fair to blame him."

"So you blame yourself." The silence stretched. At last Emily asked, "Do you want me and Jake to come in?"

"No! It's too late."

The silence returned as if Emily was trying to read the truth behind Jeanie's words.

"What you really need to do is tell Michael all of this. I think he's really trying, but if he doesn't know when his words hurt you, he can't change."

"But he's so busy."

"Too busy to be kind? Can anyone ever be that busy?"

"Things will let up after the Fourth of July."

"Don't wait until then to talk to him. Go talk to him now."

"He's doing bookwork."

"Whack his keyboard with your bat."

Jeanie pictured it then started to laugh. Just talking to Emily, speaking of her fears aloud, helped ease them. She'd be able to sleep now. "Maybe I will."

"If you're afraid to talk to Michael, that ought to tell you something."

"Yeah, it ought to. I'll be more honest with him."

"Don't twist what I've said into a criticism of your honesty, Jeanie."

"I'm not. I'm sorry."

Again there was silence. At last Emily said, "I'm going to be watching Michael. I'll give you until after the Fourth to deal with him, and then I might just show up with a *real* bat. And I promise I won't be taking my swings at you."

Jeanie laughed again. "Thanks, Em. It really helped to talk."

She didn't go talk to Michael that night. She heard him heading for bed just as she was going and decided to wait until he wasn't so tired.

Complaining always made her feel so guilty. What business did she have complaining when she was so far from perfect herself? She was lucky a man like Michael wanted her. Lucky *any* man would want her after what she'd done.

Settling into sleep, Jeanie asked God to forgive her for all her worrying when she'd made this mess out of her life. She was finally, really, fully able to love her husband.

Dear God, thank You so much for loving me. And thank You that Michael loves me.

It occurred to her to ask God to help her love herself, but she just couldn't. It was too selfish.

Chapter 16

Michael was obviously thrilled with the turnout for the Independence Day weekend.

Jeanie could see that the rest of the town was stunned. Not her, though. She'd expected Michael to make a huge success out of anything he tried.

He'd had his back slapped and his hand shaken a hundred times since the first car pulled up Friday morning.

The parade had been huge and flashy and stirring. Tourists lined the streets. The fireworks had been spectacular—Michael had seen to that. There was a hustle and bustle on Cold Creek's Main Street that added up to financial success for everyone in town.

By the time it was over, the cabins were rented for the rest of the summer and for a lot of weekends next year. A hunting and fishing magazine had sent a crew and were clearly excited about this untapped area for fall and spring outdoor sports.

The buffalo were a smash. Jeanie had seen her sister looking jubilant, because keeping the buffalo ranch financially sound was always tricky.

As the last car pulled out of Cold Creek midafternoon on Monday, the town leaders congregated in the Buffalo Café. Jeanie served coffee and donuts. Things were badly picked over thanks to hungry tourists.

Michael went from table to table, full of plans for the future. The whole café buzzed with excitement.

Jeanie brought coffee around and accepted kind words from her neighbors, too, though none of this was her doing.

"Jeanie, have we stripped all the cupboards bare in this place?" Michael smiled at her and slung an arm around her shoulder.

"I'm down to crackers and unopened cans of chili. Not exactly coffee break food."

Michael kissed her soundly.

She loved him so much when he was happy. If only she could keep him happy.

He reached for her hair and ran a gentle hand over it, tucking it behind her ears.

"I'm sorry. I've just been running all day. I must be a mess." Jeanie reached up to smooth her hair, wondering what it looked like. The pleasure of the day faded as she worried about shaming Michael. She saw that her nails were chipped. Her makeup must have melted off hours ago.

"You're fine. Stop worrying. Just go check in the mirror. Your mascara's a little smeared." Michael looked closer. "Or maybe you've got circles under your eyes. What an exhausting weekend for you."

"You, too."

"Yeah, but it's like caffeine in my blood. Being around people energizes me. You're happier when it's quiet."

"I've been happy this weekend. I've loved the activity."

Michael relaxed his hold. "Go check in the mirror, okay?"

Jeanie nodded and practically ran out of the room. There was a small restroom in the kitchen for the help. She went there and fussed with her appearance, dallying, wishing everyone outside would go away before she had to come out. She'd forgotten how much she hated crowds. When she'd been in the restroom for half an hour, she peeked out the door and saw that things had calmed down. She swung the door open and was surprised to see Buffy waiting in the kitchen, her arms crossed. Beside her stood Emily Hanson, with Logan, just a couple of weeks old, held close against her chest.

"We heard that." Buffy scowled and studied Jeanie's face as if she were a bug under a microscope.

"H–heard what?"

"What he said to you." Emily patted Logan's back. Emily had straight brown hair and sun-browned skin like Buffy. But Emily was taller. She was still rounded from having her baby. And Emily's eyes were kind, whereas Buffy glared with anger.

"Who?"

Buffy snorted. "How long did it take him to put you back in your place? He'd been here, what—two weeks, maybe a month?—before you quit all your jobs and started wearing too much makeup, trying to be good enough for that worthless Michael Davidson."

"He's not worthless. He's done so much for this town." Jeanie looked past Buffy's shoulders into the dining room, terrified Michael would overhear.

"He's gone. Relax. He won't *catch you* having an opinion. He hasn't done half for this town of what you did."

"Are you kidding? He built these cabins."

"He closed the senior center."

"They eat here now for the same price. And he brought tourists to your buffalo ranch."

"He's cut the hours the library is open."

"I didn't know about that." Jeanie rested one hand on her chest, surprised to learn of it. Keeping the library open as many hours as possible had been important to this town.

"Julia can't handle the extra hours, so she's just closing it for the evening hours."

"That's not Michael's fault." Jeanie needed to phone Julia. If there was no other way, Jeanie could go back to work. Except Michael wouldn't like it.

"The Russos are putting the mini-mart up for sale," Buffy added.

"They are?"

"Tim thinks it's too hard on their kids to work such long hours. He's hoping with the tourist rush he can unload the place on someone."

"Has he tried hiring teenagers? They usually need some spending money."

"There are three new patients at the nursing home that need hospice care. Someone is driving over from Hot Springs to take care of them."

Emily nudged Buffy, and the two of them exchanged another glance. Buffy rubbed her mouth as if she had to physically restrain the words.

Jeanie bristled. "I'm not the only person in this town who could be a hospice volunteer. Michael needs me."

Buffy's eyes narrowed, but she didn't speak.

Jeanie looked to Emily for support. Instead, she saw pity.

"Didn't you hear what he said to you, Jeanie?" Emily asked. "He's unkind."

"He told me I looked tired."

Buffy shook her head, her jaw tense. "Another way of criticizing you."

"No, a way of protecting me. He's taking care of me."

"It's not just that. I've watched him." Emily reached out and rested a hand on Jeanie's arm. "He puts one of his little barbs into you, and you start trying to fix it, make him happy. You've changed since he came back, Jeanie. You're not happy anymore."

"I wasn't happy before." Jeanie balled her fists. There was truth in what they said. And yes, Buffy had an old ax to grind, but Emily had no history with Michael.

"When you phoned me the other night, you said you'd deal with this after the holiday rush," Emily said. "Well, it's after."

Emily and Buffy exchanged a long look. Jeanie ached inside for being on the outside of whatever passed between these two. They were her best friends.

Then Buffy smiled. But the sadness in her eyes overruled the smile. "I want you to be happy, Jeanie." Buffy rested one of her work-roughened hands on Jeanie's arm.

Jeanie remembered all the times she'd sneered at Buffy for the hard, dirty work of wrangling buffalo. Jeanie patted Buffy's hand. "You know, don't you, that all those times I was such a brat to you when we were kids and after Michael left me came from jealousy?"

Buffy's forehead wrinkled. "Jealousy? You were the one who was cool. You had so many friends. You were popular."

"I was a C student, and you were a genius. I was superficial, and you had real depth."

"I was a geek, two years younger than anyone in my class. I walked the halls alone and ran out of school to work because I had no one to talk to."

"Not even me." Jeanie frowned. "Especially not me."

"I loved you, Jeanie. I understood how having your dorky, sullen, brainiac sister in class was embarrassing."

Jeanie looked at Emily. "Has she ever told you about when we first went to high school?"

"It doesn't matter now." Buffy squeezed Jeanie's arm and shook her head as if to warn her not to go on. "That's ancient history."

"We'd moved that summer. We moved around a lot."

"Don't talk about this, please." Buffy begged with her eyes as well as her words.

"I've never talked to you about it. Never apologized."

"I knew what you were going through."

Jeanie hugged Buffy. "That's perfect, trying to stop me from telling this. Just like back then. You've always tried to protect me. Even then you got it that I needed protection more—more than you did."

Jeanie's voice broke, but she steadied herself and went on, focusing on Emily. "We moved to Chicago. Dad worked for a manufacturing company that moved him around a lot. He claimed it was a promotion every time, but it wasn't. He was an accountant, but they'd transfer him from place to place because, I think, no one wanted to work with him for long."

"He'd been there long enough that they couldn't outright fire him, but I think they wanted him to quit," Buffy added.

"So we showed up at school and went our separate ways—Buffy to the gifted program, me to remedial classes."

"They weren't remedial. They were just normal courses."

"Maybe. It might have just felt remedial compared to you." Jeanie shifted away from her friends and went into the now-deserted café seating area, talking as she went. "I was, of course, immediately popular. I just knew all the moves, how to laugh, how to cozy up to the right crowd, how to dress and flirt and draw attention to myself for all the shallowest reasons."

"You were beautiful then, just like you are now." Buffy followed her.

Jeanie started wiping off the tables, and Buffy grabbed a rag while Emily bounced her sweet baby.

"So, I never acknowledged Buffy. No one knew I even had a little sister."

"And I hadn't talked to you either. We didn't run in the same circles."

"We were in the lunchroom one day. I saw her sitting by herself."

"Not even at the brainiac table. I was always antisocial." Buffy smiled at Emily. "I did homework during lunch, because after school I hung around at a wild animal park in Chicago so I could be near buffalo. I was one of those people who, if I'd snapped and done something crazy, everyone who knew me would have said, 'Yeah, we knew she was a troubled, crazed loner. Yeah, she kept to herself, too quiet.' "

Jeanie laughed. "They would not have."

"I thought you were from Oklahoma," Emily said.

Buffy shrugged. "We were from everywhere and nowhere. We came to Cold Creek from Oklahoma."

Logan started fussing. Emily settled on a chair near the center of the room as the sisters cleaned, straightened chairs, and talked.

"So this day at lunch, one of the *real* crazed loners at the school came up to the table where Buffy was sitting and started hassling her. 'You're in my seat. Beat it shrimp.' Stuff like that, shoving her."

"I *was* a shrimp. Small for my age, plus two years ahead of my grade level. I was twelve in the middle of a bunch of fourteen-year-olds, and smart as I was, I had a gift for making sure people around me knew I was smarter than they were. I was obnoxious. I didn't fit in at all. I never should have skipped those grades. It made everything harder."

"Buffy got up to move, but the guy knocked her tray as she stood, and it splattered all down her front. Milk and some kind of pudding and some gravy or something, really messy. And the whole place started to laugh."

"That guy got in big trouble. I got even."

"And she looked up, her clothes ruined, people laughing at her, and she looked right into my eyes, even though I was across the room."

"Jeanie, it's okay. It's over."

"And she needed me." Jeanie's voice broke. She breathed slowly, regaining control before she went on. "She needed help. There I sat at that table full of cheerleaders and jocks. If I'd had the guts to go to her, to bring my friends along, we could have protected her."

"You were afraid. I understood."

"You understood that you were completely alone." Jeanie stopped wiping her tears with her hand and fished a tissue out of her apron pocket to wipe her eyes. Then she tucked it away and braced both her hands flat on the table and looked squarely at Buffy. "On your own. Dad wouldn't stop hassling you for being so different."

"He hassled you, too."

"Mom wouldn't stand up for anyone against him."

"You included."

"The school kids picked on you."

"I got good at avoiding them. I always had a healthy knack for self-preservation."

"The way you looked at me, Buffy. Inside that brave, lonely shell you'd built around yourself, you needed me and you saw that I was not going to rescue you."

"You couldn't have."

"That my shallow friends were more important to me than my own sister, my own flesh and blood."

"Jeanie, don't. It's over."

"You looked at me as if I'd. . .I'd stabbed you in the heart." Jeanie's tears spilled again, and she fumbled for the tissue.

"No." Buffy set her cloth aside and came to Jeanie.

"Yes. I don't think you meant to let me see I'd hurt you. I think consciously you knew better than to expect anything of me. But you stood there dripping, being laughed at, so humiliated, and I. . .I picked up my tray, got up, and turned away. I left. I didn't even stay to see what happened next or if you had to wear those messy clothes the rest of the day."

Buffy put her arms around Jeanie, and Jeanie grabbed hold of her little sister—who was inches taller than her—and held on to her, too late, too much harm done.

"I love you, Jeanie. I do. I've forgiven you."

"I can't forgive myself."

Emily came up beside them. "You have to, Jeanie. It's so long ago. We all did stupid things at that age. And I'm sure Buffy was a major embarrassment. I can totally see pretending not to know her."

"Hey!" Buffy whacked at Emily.

Emily dodged, which wasn't hard, because Buffy wasn't trying to hit her. "Be careful of the baby!" Emily's mock offended cry calmed Jeanie's tears.

Shifting away from Buffy, Jeanie gave up on her soggy tissue and snagged a paper napkin out of the stainless steel holder on the table beside her, dabbing her eyes. She knew they were trying to lighten the mood. "Maybe if that's the only stupid thing I'd done, it wouldn't cut so deep. But I spent my whole life doing stupid things. Like abandoning Sally."

Buffy patted her, and Jeanie knew, even now, she was taking more than she was giving. Buffy had always been the strong one.

"You did the right thing for Sally. You weren't able to take care of her. Leaving and finding God, finding yourself, were things you needed to do. You're stronger now, a good Christian woman that I'm proud to have as a friend and a sister."

"Thanks. I'm trying to give enough to make up for the harm I've done."

"That's not how it works, Jeanie." Emily gave her a quick one-armed hug.

Logan cooed, and he was close enough to Jeanie's ear that she heard that perfect sweet innocence. "God forgives even though we *don't* deserve it. We forgive others, even though *they* don't deserve it. Why do you have to earn the right to receive forgiveness from yourself? I don't believe God asks that of us."

The baby whined, and Emily started a maternal bouncing that Jeanie recognized. She'd held Sally like that. And she'd given Sally up. A mother's most basic instinct is to protect her child, to fight and even die for her child, and Jeanie had walked away, just as she'd walked away from Buffy all those years ago. A coward. A weakling.

"We want you to be very strong, in keeping with his glorious power. We want you to be patient. Never give up. Be joyful."

"He asks us to start fresh." Emily pulled Jeanie out of her self-inflicted pain. "Yes, if you have wrongs you can right, I believe you should do it. But to still hate yourself for knowing you weren't able to take care of Sally? To still hate yourself for being self-centered in high school? C'mon, Jeanie, you're a decent, hardworking, generous, loving woman. Everyone who knows you loves you. It's time to learn to love yourself."

Jeanie nodded. "I know that's true. I know God washes us clean and lets us start again. But just because it's true, doesn't make it easy to accept."

The baby turned up his whine to a cry, drawing the attention of all three women. "He's hungry. I want to get him home before I feed him so he'll take a good nap." Emily smiled sheepishly. "I'm trying to get him on a schedule, but I've been running around so much, he can't settle into anything."

"Thanks for taking the time to talk, Em." Jeanie waved her off.

Buffy headed for the door behind Emily. As she left she looked back. "I don't think you see it, Jeanie, but you *are* letting Michael talk down to you, insult you. It's not much, just little things, but I'm afraid you'll let him go back to being a tyrant just because you feel like you deserve to be abused. If you can't believe you deserve better, then how about you believe *Michael* deserves better. I can tell he's a changed man, a better man, even though the big, dumb jerk has yet to sign those adoption papers. But he could backslide into the tyrant he once was if you let him, and that's bad for him as well as you."

Buffy's words hit home. "You're right. He asked me to hold him accountable. I've been failing at that." Jeanie nodded. Just another failure. "I'll talk with him about it tonight."

"Good." Buffy gave her chin a firm jerk of satisfaction and left, the doorbell jangling overhead.

Jeanie stood alone in the tidy diner and wished she had as much confidence in her entire body as Buffy showed in that single nod.

Chapter 17

That night at supper, Jeanie wanted to bring up all that Buffy had said. She couldn't.

Michael was flying from the success of the holiday weekend and bubbling over with plans for Labor Day and to make Cold Creek a year-round tourist mecca.

She did decide, though, to be brave and ask a few questions that had her worried. "You know, Mike, Cold Creek is a little town. You've been getting a lot of volunteer work out of the citizens here, and a lot of the ones who've helped most are retired. They're the ones with the spare time."

Michael cut through the savory, steaming lasagna with his fork.

Jeanie had used cottage cheese and a jar of store-bought sauce. Michael preferred ricotta and the sauce Jeanie made from scratch, but the local grocery store didn't carry the more exotic cheese and she didn't have access to fresh oregano and basil. The salad was poured out of a prepared bag of greens. The dressing was bottled. She braced herself for his cutting comments, but he ate with apparent relish.

"The community support has been terrific. I'm starting on a new cabin tomorrow. I've got room for five more cabins, and I'm building a footbridge across Cold Creek. A rope bridge I think. It'll look like something out of an old jungle movie, but it needs to be sturdy. I'll find some plans on the Internet and order the supplies. Jake Hanson said he'd—"

"My point is," Jeanie cut him off, feeling very powerful, "that you may be asking too much from these elderly people."

"Jake isn't elderly."

"Don't pretend like you don't understand what I'm saying." Jeanie refused to flinch when he narrowed his eyes at her tone. "My senior center folks are all retired. They've been working long hours every day on this project, and they've loved it. But expect them to wear out pretty soon and want their quiet life back."

Michael frowned. "I thing the town is committed to this renewal effort, Jeanie. I think they'll stick with me."

"They're excited about it, it's true. But most of your volunteers are one wrong step away from a broken hip. Oh, some of them are really spry, but a lot of them have serious health concerns. A few of them go south for the winter, and others don't get out much when the snow flies." Jeanie felt Michael's disapproval. He didn't like her contradicting him, but she remembered Buffy talking about Michael being critical and decided that if he said one wrong word, she'd hunt up her bat and have at him.

"I think you need to assess the progress and start thinking in terms of making them real paying businesses. If we hired someone and paid a living wage, the employee might relocate to Cold Creek. A young man maybe, with a wife and kids. Maybe several of them eventually. That would be *real* renewal, new families, new homes, a real estate market, a growing school system."

Michael nodded. "That will happen, but the profit margin is pretty slim right now. I want to get more of the investment recouped before I raise the operating costs."

She let out a muted sigh of relief. He wasn't going to criticize. He was listening and debating. She rested her hand on Michael's and smiled. "Just so you have it in mind and understand when your work crew starts dropping out to play cribbage."

"I stand warned." Michael nodded. "I've got rental agreements for Labor Day weekend for six cabins that don't exist. Tomorrow I start building. You're right about the volunteer help. I've been donating a lot of money to this. Several others, like Jake, have, too, but it needs to be a paying concern. And if I have to start paying for labor. . ." He tapped the table thoughtfully.

"Well, I can build these six cabins myself. Maybe a few more. They're such a simple design. I'll set up the foundations tomorrow then pour cement the next day. Then start framing." Michael finished his dinner. "This was good, honey. I haven't had a real meal in a long time. Just one more way I was an idiot."

He helped her clear the table and for once didn't have a dozen phone calls to make. He stayed and dried the dishes while she washed. He asked questions and nudged her with his elbow, grinning, if she didn't answer him quickly enough, until she got fed up with him. Still feeling the power that had come earlier when she'd disagreed with him and he'd listened, she retaliated for his next nudge by splashing dishwater on him.

"Hey!" He shoved the plate he'd just dried into the cupboard and turned on her. "Of course you know this means war!" He slung his dish towel around her waist, grabbed both ends, and pulled her close.

Giggling, Jeanie reached for the water again.

"Got to get you away from the dangerous water weapon." He dragged her a few feet from the sink.

She leaned back for the water, and he dropped the towel and put his hands on her waist to turn her fully away from her soggy arsenal. He gave her a slurpy kiss on the neck, making as much noise as possible, while she giggled and wrestled, screaming when the kiss began to tickle.

"Say you give up."

"Never!"

Michael's strong arms circled her and he lifted her off her feet. "You're helpless. Admit I'm a big, strong man and you're a helpless female."

"Give me my bat. Then we'll see who's helpless."

Michael let her go with a mock shout of fear. "Not the bat. No, I'll be good."

Jeanie leaned back against the sink, her face hurting from the laughter.

Michael sat on one of the kitchen chairs, smiling until it nearly split his face in two.

She loved him. She knew it was back, fully alive in her heart. Better this time, too. More honest, more of a partnership than their marriage had been before.

Michael looked around the shabby kitchen. "I've spent so much time focusing on work, but we need to fix this house up, too."

"We will eventually. For now, you need to finish drying these dishes."

"Yes, ma'am." His gaze settled on her as he stood and approached the sink. Nervous about the strange intent expression, she turned and pulled the plug on the sink. He finished putting the clean dishes away.

Jeanie wiped out the sink. "The house is old, but I like it. There's no rush with remodeling. Are you done with that towel? Can I use it?" Jeanie reached for the tissue-thin terrycloth in his hand, and when she pulled, he didn't let go. Instead, he let her pull him right into her arms.

She looked into his glowing eyes. He was so handsome it almost hurt. He leaned down and kissed her.

He'd been really sweet tonight. And respectful. She was figuring out how to finally be his wife. How to find from God the courage to make herself and Mike better people.

She kissed him back.

Seconds ticked by. Her arms went around his neck.

Minutes passed, he pulled her close.

"I've missed you," she whispered.

He kissed her forehead, her eyes.

He was her husband. She believed marriage vows were eternal. She'd missed him, but she hadn't realized how much until right now.

"I've missed you, too." Michael breathed the words against her neck. "And we're forever. Aren't we?" He pulled back to plead with his words and his expression.

The answer to his question was nothing more than the truth. She wouldn't deny it. "Yes, we're forever." She pulled him back into another kiss.

When it ended, Michael said, "I want this marriage to be a real one, before

God, Jeanie. I'd like to say our vows again, with Pastor Bert there. And we'll be married—and all that goes with it."

She studied his intent, sincere expression. "Yes, I think I'm ready, but I want to make our vows before God, too. First."

"We'll talk to Pastor Bert tomorrow. Maybe we can have a wedding tomorrow night."

Jeanie smiled at his usual push to get things done his way and fast.

Jeanie remembered that feeling of power she'd had earlier and wanted to have some say in this decision. She didn't want to be rushed. "How about Saturday instead? Give me one more week, Michael. One more week to be ready to truly be your wife again."

He nodded. "Saturday it is."

He pulled her close and sealed their promise with a kiss.

Chapter 18

Michael had two more cabins framed by the end of the week.

He was so happy with his life that energy poured out of him and he worked like a hyperactive dynamo. He prayed with every rip of the circular saw, praising God for the rebirth of his marriage. He'd been elated the first time Jeanie had told him she loved him. Now his feet barely touched the ground.

Saturday. Pastor Bert had agreed. Michael had spread the word around town, and a few plans were quietly being made for a simple reception for anyone who wanted to attend. He was counting the minutes.

God, thank You, praise You. I love You. Thank You for giving my wife back to me.

The visitors in his cabins were an added pleasure. He'd been trying to ask less of his volunteers, grateful to Jeanie for pointing out his insensitivity. He liked doing it himself anyway. He ordered the supplies for the footbridge and was so excited about the project he had them overnighted at a ridiculous expense.

The supplies came in, and Michael threw himself into the project. He wanted the bridge up and available for the renters now vacationing in the finished cabins. It was a pretty thing—three-inch-thick synthetic rope that looked like jungle vine and the walking surface made of treated redwood planks.

The charm of it would be a draw, and the word of mouth would bring in repeat customers. Plus, he needed to start erecting cabins across the creek, and this bridge was an essential part of that, because it was a long way to the nearest bridge a car could cross to reach cabins on the other side. But his vacationers could easily roll luggage across the footbridge.

He'd ordered a kit containing all the material, so the heavy ropes, including solid rope sides more than waist high on an adult, were easy to hang. Jake helped Michael pour a cement foundation on both sides of the creek.

Jake's help was invaluable, and Michael liked the guy, but Jake was so gaga over his new baby that it reminded Michael of all he'd given up when he'd abandoned Sally. He'd been working so hard that he'd let things slide with the adoption papers. He'd never intended to sign them, but he hadn't dared to make that clear until things were settled with him and Jeanie. He needed to get this wedding over with; then he'd deal with the legalities of regaining custody. He wanted to do it right. Give Sally a chance to get to know him and Jeanie well before they brought her permanently home.

A twinge of guilt made him wonder how Sally would handle it. Buffy was the only mother Sally had ever known, from what Jeanie had said. And Sally was five now; that was pretty old to be moved out of someone's house. But it had to be done. Sally was his. He couldn't give up his daughter.

Jeanie was threading the heavy ropes through the predrilled redwood planks as Michael had instructed her. She was always right at hand, helping wherever she could.

Michael liked having her close a lot more than Jake. And she liked being close; Michael could tell. She was as eager for Saturday's recommitment ceremony as he.

God, I was such a fool not to enjoy her as she was before. Forgive me for the way I treated her. Help me be a better person.

Michael sat side by side on the ground with his wife. "We just need to tie each plank in place. Then we pull these ropes through the holes on those pylons across the creek." He pointed to the wooden posts, nearly a foot in diameter and eight feet tall. They came predrilled with steel-reinforced holes for the top and bottom of the footbridge. "Then we tighten the rope, tie it off, and we're done."

She smiled at him as she worked, threading the rope like a pro. He marveled at what a great team they made.

"You're sure this will be safe?"

Michael nodded. "I've talked to a guy who put up suspension bridges in five different places, including one near Mount Rushmore. In fact, he's going to mail me some pamphlets on his bridges that we can give out to our tourists, to tie Cold Creek more closely to Mount Rushmore. And the State Game and Parks Department is sending out an inspector as soon as the bridge is done, so before we let a single person walk across it, we can have an expert test it for safety. Our insurance company reduced our rates when I promised we'd do that."

"I've got my last plank tied down. I'm ready."

Michael turned and grinned at her. They were sitting cross-legged on the rough, grassy ground by the edge of the chuckling creek. Towering trees shaded them. Dappled sunlight winked through on the warm July day. Birds sang and the breeze made its own music as he counted his blessings.

He leaned over and kissed her. "I'm so glad I can do that. I'm so glad we're together again."

Jeanie reached up and laid a hand on his cheek. "I thank God for you every day, every hour. He's given me a miracle."

"He's given *us* a miracle, you mean." Michael's contentment was like nothing he'd ever experienced. He marveled at the blessings of a Christian life as he quickly finished his side of the bridge.

The tied-together wood weighed a lot. He had already moved his pickup to the other side of the creek. Once he threaded the rope to the anchors on the far side of the rippling water, he'd hitch the ropes to the pickup. He'd drive slowly forward, dragging the heavy bridge across the expanse.

"Great. I'll attach the four ropes here." Michael quickly secured the near side of the bridge. "Now I'll wade across with it and thread it through the eye of the brace on the far side."

Jeanie giggled as he pulled on hip waders.

"Hey, you think these are funny-looking, but they beat being soaked to the knee."

"I'm sure they do." She fought the laughter and lost.

Her laughter sent sunshine along as he worked down the steep banks of Cold Creek, across the gently murmuring rivulet of the shallow stream, and up the far side. He'd tied narrow ropes to the heavy ones, so he didn't have to deal with all the weight as he crossed.

Climbing up the other side, he scrambled to hold all four ropes and not lose his footing. The anchoring pylon was as solid as Michael's construction experience and Jake's engineering skills could make it, which amounted to it being very solid indeed.

Michael pulled the bottom two ropes through their appointed holes easily. The top ones were just a bit over his head, but he slid one into place and secured it then started for the other. Standing on his tiptoes, he held the pylon with one hand and the rope with the other. When he got the rope threaded, he released the wooden stake to grab the rope and felt his boots slip on the dampened concrete.

"Jeanie!" Michael flailed, grabbing to stop his fall. He caught the unsecured rope and pulled it over the edge of the creek with him.

As he fell, head-over-heels down the rocky slope, he heard Jeanie scream.

—◊—

Jeanie was running before he hit the ground.

"Michael!" She splashed through the water toward his still form sprawled at the bottom of the bank. She skidded to her knees as she approached him, to hear a soft groan. He was alive!

His face was covered in blood, his right arm twisted under him.

"Michael, can you hear me?"

His eyes flickered open then fell shut.

She hated leaving him, but after a frantic moment of indecision, she got up and ran back across the creek. She screamed the whole time.

Glynna emerged from the café before Jeanie got all the way up the side. "What is it? What happened?"

"Call 911! Michael has fallen. He's unconscious. He's on the far side of the creek." She whirled and ran back. Dropping to his side, she pulled off the overshirt she wore. Wadding it, she gently but firmly pressed it to the ugly gash on Michael's temple. Thinking of spinal injuries, she kept his neck from moving.

What else? His arm was bent at an awful angle, but she didn't dare touch it.

She prayed. "Please, God, don't take him from me when I've just found him again."

Tears nearly blinded her.

Michael whispered, "Jeanie?"

"Yes, I'm here." She dashed her tears away, barely noticing her hands soaked in blood. She leaned close to his barely moving lips. "The ambulance is coming."

Even as she spoke the siren fired up only a few blocks away. "Help will be here in a few seconds."

He didn't respond.

An ambulance and a police car—Cold Creek only had one of each—pulled up as close to the far side of the creek as they could get.

Tim Russo, her boss from the mini-mart, was fire chief. He ran to the bank across from her and headed straight down. "We're bringing a stretcher across instead of going around." Tim approached her. "It will save a lot of time."

More people came dashing through the water, the first two carrying a stretcher. Behind them came someone with an armload of supplies.

Tim got there first and crouched beside Michael. "Did he fall from the top?"

"Yes." Jeanie looked up; the pylon towered overhead. It was probably twenty or thirty feet, but it seemed like hundreds from where she knelt. How bad could his internal injuries be? His spine?

"Has he been conscious?"

"He moaned, said my name." Her voice broke. "H–he opened his eyes once for a second."

The rest of the team arrived, and Jeanie was gently but firmly moved aside. The rescue squad was well trained, and Jeanie watched, crying quietly as they stabilized Michael's neck and lifted him with skilled precision onto the stretcher. Someone put arms around Jeanie's shoulders, and she was barely aware of being guided along behind the paramedics.

When she settled into a car, she realized it was the mayor's wife, Carolyn, driving. "I'll follow the ambulance to the hospital. You shouldn't drive when you're so distraught."

"Thank you."

"We're going to stop and get you some dry clothes, too."

Jeanie registered only vaguely that she was soaked nearly to the waist and shivering, though mostly from fear rather than cold. "No, I want to be with him."

"Hush, honey. We'll still be there long before they let you see him. You know how emergency wards are. They're taking him to the Hot Springs hospital, and if they're even the least bit worried about severe injuries, they'll life-flight him. If you end up in Rapid City in wet clothes, you'll be miserable."

"Life-flight?" Jeanie started crying harder.

They pulled up to the house, and Carolyn didn't even ask whether Jeanie wanted to help pick out clothes. She ran and was back with a small pile clutched in her arms within seconds. Her tires screeched as she pulled away from the curb and headed south out of town. In grim silence, broken only by Jeanie's sobs, they raced down the road. A siren sounded behind them before they'd gone a mile.

Jeanie looked up, afraid the police would pull them over, but Carolyn, in a move that would have made a NASCAR driver proud, had somehow arranged for a police escort. The police car pulled ahead of them, and Jeanie recognized Bucky driving. He wasn't on the police force. But he was mayor, and Cold Creek's police force, one full-time chief and two part-time officers, were probably all on the rescue squad, so there'd been no one to drive along with Jeanie and clear the road.

As they tore down the winding highway, weaving and twisting through the rugged hills and forests, Jeanie prayed silently until Carolyn began praying aloud. They recited the Twenty-third Psalm together. Jeanie prayed her courage verses; she'd never needed them more.

A few of the turns were nearly hairpin, and Jeanie closed her eyes, but she didn't ask Carolyn to slow down.

They pulled up to the Hot Springs hospital just as a roar overhead told them that indeed a helicopter was coming to take Michael to Rapid City.

"What did they find? What did the rescue squad learn on the drive in?" Jeanie leaped out of the car.

Carolyn was beside her, hustling her toward the helipad.

The Cold Creek ambulance sat, siren still screaming, lights strobing, near the concrete pad.

"Thank you so much," Jeanie murmured through her fog of terror. "Thank you for getting me here."

She got to the ambulance as the helicopter settled in place. Tim swung open the doors, and two other men rounded the ambulance to help ease the gurney out onto the ground. An IV bag held aloft was carried along.

"Can she ride along, Tim?" Bucky yelled over the roar of the helicopter blade, his hand blocking the bruising wind.

Two people leaped out of the helicopter and came to meet them.

Tim stepped away from the gurney as the helicopter EMTs took over carrying it. "Yes, you ride with him. We've been on the radio to them. They know you're coming along, Jeanie."

Jeanie couldn't get close to Michael, but she caught a glimpse of his blood-soaked face, his eyes closed, his body strapped down.

Her knees buckled, and Tim and Bucky caught her before she collapsed and nearly carried her along.

"Thank you. Thank you so much."

The gurney wheels folded as they slid Michael, still unconscious, into the helicopter. Jeanie's arms were steadied as she was boosted in beside him. A formidable-looking black woman, with a name tag that said Shayla, towed her to a flight seat and clicked her into a seat belt. A bundle that Jeanie thought were the clothes Carolyn had fetched was settled near Jeanie's feet. There was barely room for Jeanie in this small helicopter. The little seat she occupied was probably for one of the rescue workers.

"Stay there. Don't make me sorry we let you ride along." Shayla's compassionate eyes didn't match her no-nonsense words and brusque movements.

Jeanie decided Michael was safe in this woman's hands.

The door slammed. Shayla left Jeanie and turned to her patient before Jeanie had a chance to promise to be good.

The helicopter took off. Jeanie felt her stomach stay behind as they lifted.

Please, Lord, don't take Michael from me. We've just found each other again. We could make a life pleasing to You. Heal him, protect him, bless him.

She focused on Michael to keep her mind off the swooping of the chopper.

Two people worked over him in the cramped space. The woman talked steadily. The other emergency worker, a dark-haired man with a ponytail, leaned over Michael's head. Both of them moved constantly.

A pilot talked into his radio. Little of it made sense to Jeanie, but she was sure information was forwarded to the hospital so they'd know what to prepare for when the helicopter landed.

The part of Jeanie's mind that wasn't occupied with praying marveled at the well-oiled machine of the paramedic team.

The two people working over Michael mostly blocked him from her sight, but once in a while she'd catch a glimpse of Michael's ashen face, streaked with blood. She wanted to ask them to wipe the blood away but kept her mouth shut.

Once she saw Michael's eyes flicker open. They seemed to be clear. Shayla asked him questions, too quietly for Jeanie to hear them over the steady throb of the helicopter's rotors. Michael's deep voice added to the hum of sound and activity.

She did hear Michael say, "Jeanie," once.

The female EMT turned and smiled. "She's here. She's worried sick about you."

Michael's eyes fluttered, and Jeanie could tell he tried to turn. But his head was held steady.

"Just lie still. I told her to stay put in her seat, too. We'll be landing in a few minutes."

Shayla turned to Jeanie. "I'm feeling pretty good about spinal injuries. His fingers and toes are moving fine. We'll do a thorough exam, of course, and we won't remove his neck-stabilizing gear until we're sure. And we have to examine him for internal injuries. If he has any, that could mean surgery."

Jeanie felt tears burn her eyes at the hopeful news.

"He's definitely got a broken arm, and since he was unconscious, he's likely got a concussion. Plus the cut on his head is nasty."

The woman's voice started to sound like it was far away. The little roaring cabin seemed to get darker and her vision tunneled.

Shayla suddenly knelt at Jeanie's side, adjusting her seat belt and shoving Jeanie's head down between her waterlogged knees. Jeanie didn't know why the woman attacked her, but she was too shaky to care.

The next thing Jeanie knew, she was being helped off the air ambulance by Shayla and a stranger, and Michael was rolling away from her with two other attendants.

"What happened?"

"You fainted." Shayla kept an arm around Jeanie's waist, even though Jeanie felt much steadier now, with the helicopter on the ground and hope that Michael would be okay. "We'll leave your clothes with you. Your hands are covered in blood, so once you're steady, you'll need to wash up and change your clothes. The hospital might let you use a shower if you're going to have a long wait."

Jeanie looked and saw crimson fingers. Shayla was right. Dried blood filled every crease and crevice on the front and back of both hands.

Jeanie couldn't think clearly enough to wash up right now, so she found herself settled in a chair in the emergency ward waiting room with a clipboard in her lap and orders to fill out forms. Doing the mundane paperwork kept her from losing her mind while she sat there.

Praying steadily, an hour passed. Then another. Then she found a Bible tucked in a magazine rack. She started reading her strength verses, groping for courage.

Buffy showed up and charged her way across the waiting room to Jeanie's side. Jeanie rose to meet her, and Buffy pulled her into a hug. "Have you heard anything?"

"No, he's with the doctor now."

"Look, this might be him."

The two of them rushed toward the doctor coming from a room down a long corridor. The man glanced down at Jeanie's hands, still coated in blood. "Are you Mrs. Davidson?"

"Yes, how's Michael?"

Buffy put a supporting arm around Jeanie.

"He's going to be all right." The doctor looked exhausted. "We've admitted him for the night. His right humerus is fractured in two locations. He has a mild concussion, but an MRI shows no evidence of a subdural hematoma. The scalp laceration needed suturing. He's got multiple abrasions and contusions, but other than that, he's going to be fine. His fracture requires a pin, so we're prepping him for surgery."

"Surgery?" That was nearly the only thing the man said that made sense.

Buffy tightened her arm around Jeanie's shoulders and whispered, "Broken arm, bump on the head, cuts and bruises, stitches. Nothing serious."

The doctor gave Buffy a tired smile and nodded. "That's exactly right. Broken arm, head bump, cuts, bruises, and stitches. His arm will heal faster with surgery, and your husband assured us he preferred speed. Double fractures are difficult to set under the best circumstances."

"He talked to you?"

"Yes, he was wide awake, answering all our questions rationally. He's going to be fine." The doctor patted Jeanie's shoulder. "The surgery won't take long, but it will be several hours before you can see him. I'll send someone out to let you know when he's done. He needs a night in the hospital, mainly due to the concussion. Barring complications, you'll be able to take him home tomorrow morning."

"Thank you, Doctor."

The man left at a near run. Jeanie wondered who else was in need at this moment.

Buffy sighed. "Wow, I drove over here like a maniac. Bucky phoned and scared me to death. I thought Michael was dying."

Buffy's words were too much, the last straw. "I did, too." Jeanie broke down.

Buffy held her tight and let her cry.

When Jeanie's tears were spent, Buffy said, "We've got to get you cleaned up." Buffy went and said the right thing to the nurse at the ER desk, because she came back with permission for Jeanie to shower. She bullied Jeanie into a downstairs locker room with an unfortunately placed mirror.

Jeanie was shocked to see blood streaking her face and clothes. She'd seen her hands but never noticed the rest. She pulled herself together enough to convince Buffy she could shower and dress without collapsing.

Buffy left to phone Wyatt and let him spread the word that Michael would be okay.

When Buffy returned, Jeanie was dressed and reasonably clean.

Buffy told Jeanie she'd driven Michael's pickup to the hospital and planned to leave it. Wyatt was on his way to take Buffy home. "Now we've got plenty of time for supper. Let's go."

"Supper? What time is it?"

"About five o'clock. Sorry it took me so long to get over here."

"It was morning last time I checked."

Buffy hugged her again. "Can we leave the hospital for supper?"

"No, I want to be here when the surgery is over."

"The doctor said it might be several hours before you could see him. It hasn't been one yet. We've got plenty of time."

"Absolutely not."

"You need a good meal, Jeanie. I'll bet you haven't had a bite to eat since breakfast." Buffy gave her a one-armed hug. "Please, the cafeteria is closed and the vending machines have green sandwiches in them. I might become violent if I have to eat those."

Jeanie laughed and started to feel almost human again. "Well, I don't like getting beaten up, so let's go."

They were back in plenty of time to meet a nurse who had news that Michael was through surgery and waking from the anesthetic.

"Only one person can see him at a time." The nurse gave Buffy a glance.

"I'll go." Jeanie had a flash of irritation so strong she recognized that she was almost irrational. How dare this woman assume Buffy was Michael's wife?

The nurse smiled, the very soul of kindness.

Jeanie got hold of herself. "You might as well go on home, Buff. I'll sit with him tonight."

Buffy pulled a cell phone out of her pocket and handed it to Jeanie. "Phone me if you need anything."

Wyatt chose that moment to come into the waiting room carrying a duffel bag. "Glad Michael's gonna be okay." He gave Jeanie an awkward hug. "I brought him clothes to wear home."

Jeanie nodded and slipped the phone into her pocket. "Thanks, Wyatt. Thanks, both of you. I really appreciate you coming. It helped."

Buffy pulled her close and whispered, "You know I'm not the world's biggest Michael fan."

Jeanie wrinkled her brow in a mock frown. "No, I had no idea."

Buffy smiled. "But I'm glad he's all right."

"Thanks." Jeanie hurried away with the nurse.

At the recovery room door, the nurse turned to block Jeanie. "I heard you fainted on the chopper."

Jeanie felt her cheeks heat up. "I suppose everybody knows that."

The nurse smiled. "Sure, even your husband. I'm just warning you that there are a lot of tubes and machines, but they're just monitors mainly. We'll unhook them as he fully wakes up. He came through the surgery very well. We've got pain medicine in his IV tube, so he may not make much sense and he may not remember anything tomorrow. So don't worry—or faint—if he's a little. . .weird." The nurse waited.

Jeanie squared her shoulders. "Okay, I'm warned. I'm ready."

Chapter 19

She wasn't ready.

Michael's face was ashen. His arm was splinted, and a white bandage wrapped his head. Scratches she hadn't noticed before looked red and angry against his pallid face and arms.

She rushed past the nurse to his side.

The tubes and chirping machines seemed to hold him to life.

"Michael!" Her cry, though soft, sounded like grief.

Then his eyes flickered open. "Jeanie? You're here?" His voice was faint and slurred, but he recognized her. He was making sense.

"Of course I'm here, honey."

He fumbled for her hand, his arm held in a rigid cast, his fingers swollen until the skin was shiny.

She gingerly rested her palm under his fingers, afraid she'd hurt him.

The nurse moved to the far side of the bed and made notes on a clipboard as she checked machines. She glanced at Jeanie's nervous attempt to hold Michael's hand. "Good. Be careful. We'll leave an IV in overnight, but the rest of these monitors can come off in about an hour. Then we'll move him to another room for the night. You can come around to this side and sit down. We've got the IV in this hand, so you'll have to be careful no matter what side you're on.

Jeanie turned to focus on Michael and was delighted to see his eyes, still glazed from the sedative but open and watchful. She wondered how bad the concussion was. Maybe he was seeing three of her?

"How about a lil' kiss?"

Jeanie almost laughed. He sounded drunk. And whatever faults Michael had, drinking wasn't one of them. She kissed him. So glad he was alive and with her and in love with her.

The nurse finished her work, and Jeanie rounded the bed.

"Don't leave me!" Michael called, his voice weak but determined.

She had his other hand before he could decide to climb out of bed and come after her. "I'm staying. Don't worry. I just didn't want to bump your broken arm."

"Arm's broken?"

Jeanie ran one finger carefully down his cheek, which was scratched but not deeply. She doubted it would show once he got his color back. She realized he didn't really know much of what was going on. "Yes, you have a broken arm.

You're just out of surgery."

She spent the next hour talking with him. Anytime she stopped, he questioned her.

As he became more awake, he began fretting about his bridge, the pieces of it left on the ground. "I should've had help. I shouldn't have been doing it myself. Stupid. Careless."

She began talking again, calming him. "It was an accident. You just slipped."

Michael frowned. "You told me to leave the old people alone. I'd have had some of them there."

"They couldn't have climbed down that creek bank, Michael. You know that. Having them there wouldn't have changed a thing."

"I might not be here. Broken arm. How am I supposed to get those cabins up with a broken arm? I've got reservations for cabins I don't have built."

Jeanie wondered if she'd need to ask the doctor for something to calm him when the door opened and a different nurse bustled in.

"How are we doing?"

Jeanie didn't answer. She wasn't sure how Michael was doing right now, but she knew she felt awful.

He had a mule-stubborn look on his face, as if he were planning to get out of bed and get back to work. "I'm fine. Can I get out of here tonight?"

Jeanie moved aside as the woman studied the machines and asked Michael questions. That seemed to divert him from fretting, and Jeanie breathed a sigh of relief.

By the time the nurse was through, the doctor came by on rounds. Then they moved Michael out of recovery. It was late evening before they were alone again, and either he was exhausted or some medicine had kicked in, because Michael was smiling, heavy-lidded and sweet again.

Jeanie enjoyed the calm, but she knew the storm was coming. She'd have her hands full getting him to lie still long enough to recover.

But for now, he had a sweet, groggy smile on his face, and he whispered love to her as he fell asleep.

Jeanie sat in a recliner next to his bed and dozed fitfully all night.

Michael woke early with some help from nurses checking his blood pressure. As soon as he and Jeanie were alone, he started growling. "Let's get out of here."

"We can't leave until we see the doctor." Dark circles under his eyes worried her. "Are you in pain?"

"Of course I'm in pain," he snapped. The outburst made him drop his head back against his pillow. "My head is killing me. Can you not ask me any stupid questions for a while?"

"Do you need something for the pain?"

"Great, more questions. Go see if the doctor is around so we can get out of here."

Jeanie hesitated, but she forced herself to stand her ground. She caught Michael's uncasted hand. The one with the IV. "Michael!" She spoke sharply trying to cut through his temper and pain and the remnants of the sedative.

He froze and turned his eyes on her, but despite the rebellious look on his face, he paid attention.

"Honey, stop thrashing around. You'll hurt yourself, and if the doctor doesn't believe you're going to be careful, he might sedate you again and keep you here another day. Now control yourself while I go get the doctor." She watched carefully, afraid he might get up and dress and leave without waiting for the doctor—or her if she was slow. "I'll be back in two seconds. You'd better still be in that bed."

She left, moving at double time because she knew he'd only wait so long.

When she came back, less than a minute later, he was sitting on the side of his bed.

"Oh, Michael. You'll hurt your arm." She rushed forward.

He looked up sheepishly, with a bit of red-cheeked temper showing. "Just help me on with my clothes, okay? I can at least be ready to go when the doctor finally shows up."

"All right, honey. But we're going to go slow. Let's start with your pants. We can't do your shirt until they've taken the IV out."

A nurse came in just as Jeanie helped Michael stand.

"You should be in bed." The nurse drew Jeanie's attention.

"We're being careful."

"When's the doctor going to show up?" Michael barked the question.

Jeanie wished she had a leash—and maybe a muzzle.

The nurse scowled and hurried out.

The doctor showed up only a few minutes later. "You haven't been released yet, Mr. Davidson."

"I know. I'm just getting ready to go as soon as you do release me." But from Michael's tone, Jeanie knew he was leaving.

The doctor seemed to know it, too. He ordered the nurse to remove Michael's IV, and while the nurse worked in quiet disapproval, the doctor signed some papers and wrote out two prescriptions.

"One for pain, one an antibiotic." He issued warnings and instructions that Jeanie tried to pay attention to as Michael headed out the door. "Wait for a wheelchair and for your wife to bring the car around."

Michael was gone.

The doctor shook his head. "He's in a lot of pain, Mrs. Davidson. It's going to make him grouchy."

"You think?" Jeanie rolled her eyes. "I've got to go. He's liable to fall on his face."

She rushed after Michael, glad Buffy had managed to park the truck close to the hospital, because Michael wasn't waiting for her to drive up or for a wheelchair to roll him out.

She got to the door just in time to unlock the passenger's side for her stubborn husband.

He squinted at her.

"Don't even think about saying you'll drive."

With a huff of disgust, he climbed in and sat, leaning back against the seat as if he were in agony. He barked orders at her as she pulled out of the hospital parking lot then threw a minor fit when she pulled into a drugstore drive-through to fill his prescriptions.

"The pain pills make me dizzy. I don't want them."

"Well, what about the antibiotic? If you get an infection in those cuts or that surgical wound, you'll be twice as long healing. The doctor said you can start moving around as soon as possible. We'll hire someone to help with the cabins. You can give orders, just like when you were a contractor. You'll get everything done in time."

Michael gave her a furious look, but he didn't yell. Their gaze held, and to her surprise, Michael looked away first. "I'm sorry, Jeanie." He put his hand on his head, touching the back and grimacing. "I've got a goose egg back there. My ribs are killing me. The head and rib injuries hurt worse than the broken arm. I'm taking it all out on you. I know that's not fair. I'll probably bite your head off ten times in the next few days. I just feel like my control is really fragile right now. But I'll try and keep things together."

Jeanie's fear ebbed as he spoke. "I'll try and be patient."

"Thanks." Michael shifted to reach for his seat belt and stifled a groan of pain. Jeanie quickly gave the perscriptions to the woman at the pharmacy drive-thru window. Michael sat in a quiet, cranky pool of a sulk while she got his medicine. With some wheedling, she even managed to get him to take the pills.

He must have felt awful or he'd never have agreed to it.

With a fair amount of backseat driving, they were out of town. And soon Michael was dozing in his seat. Jeanie sighed with relief to have him unconscious.

Not a good sign.

Chapter 20

Can you get me a refill of coffee?"

Michael snapped his fingers, and Jeanie bit her bottom lip at his crankiness. Poor Michael was hurting terribly. He had insisted on coming to work today. The day after he was released from the hospital. He'd tried to come in yesterday, but Jeanie had refused to bring him, and since the day was half over, she'd prevailed—barely.

Jeanie exchanged a worried glance with Glynna who was cooking up her usual delicious lunch menu, then rushed to Michael with the coffee, afraid he'd get up, serve himself, and then collapse. It was quiet at the Buffalo Café at the moment. The breakfast rush was over; the ten o'clock coffee crowd hadn't arrived. It was one of those rare moments when the café was empty. And it wouldn't last long.

Jeanie ran one hand along Michael's shoulders. "Here you go. Can I get you a cinnamon roll or something?" Maybe a shot of sugar would give him enough energy to keep him from sliding off his chair.

Michael looked up from his laptop, where a bookkeeping program filled the screen. Dark circles underlined his eyes, his complexion too pale. "No."

"We've got plenty of people to fill in the lunch shift, and Glynna can handle things until then. Let me take you home."

"No!"

Jeanie jumped at his sharp tone. She saw Glynna lean down to look out of the kitchen window behind the counter that lined the south side of the dining room, her brow furrowed with worry.

He raised his good hand. His other was strapped to his chest with a sling. "I'm sorry. I just need to get these figures balanced before Jake comes in. He's going to help me find people to finish the work."

"Can you believe they finished the footbridge?" Jeanie looked out of the big front window and saw a beautifully framed view of the rope bridge, now in place across Cold Creek.

Michael caught her hand. "There are great people in this town. You were right about them being generous and me asking too much of them. I threatened Bucky to keep him from forming a cabin-raising party to finish the place while I'm hurt."

"I heard you threaten the man." The sound of a buzz saw droned from near the creek. "You'll notice it didn't work."

341

"He claims he just wanted to use his new saw. It's his day off, so he's cutting lumber."

"Bucky does love his power tools." Jeanie smiled, refilled Michael's cup, poured one for herself—she was exhausted from being up all night with Michael, who had awakened, moaning in pain, time after time—and then slid into the chair beside her poor battered husband.

Jeanie could hear hammering in the background, and she knew there was more going on than sawing. Michael had to know, too. It only emphasized how exhausted he must be that he didn't go out to watch the proceedings.

"I just need another couple of hours with these books. I'll set up a budget for hiring people—and I'm going to use local labor if at all possible. I'll create cabin blueprints—I was working from notes, but a crew will need the details laid out."

Jeanie sighed. "Jake can handle this. You know it. He helped with several of the other cabins. If he decides he needs a blueprint—which he won't—he can make one himself."

"Jeanie!" Michael's eyes left his spreadsheet, and he glared at her. A look that years ago would have sent her "Yes, Michael"-ing and "No, Michael"-ing.

But she was made of sterner stuff now.

She also knew he was so tired and hurt that he wasn't fully responsible for his actions.

Glynna came out of the kitchen wiping her hands, her mouth in a tight line. "Is there a problem?"

Jeanie shook her head. "We're fine." She turned back to Michael. "You need two hours, even though you're near collapse? Fine. I'm giving you two hours. That's it. No excuses. After that, if you don't let me take you home to get some rest, I'm calling the ambulance again and having you hauled home strapped to a gurney."

Michael's fury faded to a grin. "Yes, ma'am."

She leaned over and kissed him on the unbandaged side of his forehead. "Good boy."

Michael snickered as he turned back to the figures.

—∞—

"I've got to get out there, Jeanie. Don't touch my laptop. You'll mess it up. And don't even think of doing the café accounts. It'll take me longer to fix it than if I just do it myself."

"I'll leave it alone, honey." Jeanie came back to the table where Buffy sat next to Emily. Emily cradled her little son in her arms.

Through the window, Jeanie saw Michael waving his good arm. She'd kept him quiet for nearly four days, mostly because he had a wicked headache. Now he couldn't do things himself, but he could order his crew around.

Their wedding day had come and gone without notice—or a wedding. Jeanie had ached when she realized Michael had forgotten to renew their vows but found the energy to oversee the cabin construction.

As Jeanie slid into her chair, Emily looked up from Logan.

Buffy set her coffee cup aside. "What's going on with you and Michael?"

Jeanie straightened, surprised. She hadn't expected this. "Nothing. He's doing great. We're supposed to go to the hospital in Hot Springs Monday and have his stitches out. He might get his cast off, too. The pins and plates in his arm are supposed to work faster than normal healing."

"I don't mean, how is his arm? I mean, why are you letting him talk to you that way?"

"What way?"

"We've been in here for half an hour," Emily said. She had a foundation of common sense that neither Jeanie nor Buffy seemed to possess. Buffy had too many of the same old wounds Jeanie had. But Emily had a great set of parents, dead now, but they'd given her solid values, a clear understanding of God, and a plentiful supply of self-esteem. When Emily had advice, Jeanie listened.

"And?" Jeanie waited.

"And Michael has been barking at you like a junkyard dog." Emily looked at Buffy. "Is this the way he used to treat her?"

Buffy nodded. "How does he have the nerve to talk to you like that? 'Don't touch my laptop. Don't even think of doing the café accounts.' You were doing the accounts for the Golden Days Senior Center for a year before he came dragging himself in here."

"I don't even like bookkeeping." Jeanie smiled. She was so glad Michael was getting better she couldn't help the joy in her heart. She'd nearly lost him. "I know he was a little cranky this morning."

"A little cranky? Wyatt would *never* talk to me that way."

Jeanie patted Buffy's arm. "I'm handling it, okay? He's hurting and frustrated because of his arm, and he hates having to ask for help."

"No, he doesn't," Buffy interrupted. "He's asked everyone in this town to work like dogs since he moved here."

Jeanie plowed on. "Right now he's just a little out of control. But he'll stop barking when he's rested. I remember Wyatt after the buffalo stampeded his ranch. He couldn't speak without shooting fire bolts out of his eyes for weeks."

"That was different. We weren't married. He's never—"

"Buffy, will you just drop it?" Jeanie was startled by her tone. It was a whiny, querulous tone that she hadn't used for years.

Buffy fell silent, too. Their eyes met. Jeanie looked away first.

Logan chose that moment to spit up half of his breakfast.

"I'll get a rag from the kitchen." Jeanie jumped up, glad for an excuse to run.

By the time they'd cleaned things up, Jake came in. "The slave driver is giving us a fifteen-minute coffee break. I'm here to warn you about the stampede."

The coffee crowd outlasted Buffy. Jeanie breathed a sigh of relief when her little sister, who'd always been more grown-up than Jeanie, headed for home.

"Jeanie, don't make the guys wait for a refill." Michael leaned back in his chair, massaging his casted arm.

"I'm sorry." She hurried around to warm up the coffee.

"And can you reset that table Emily and Buffy used so it's ready for lunch?"

It had been thoroughly wiped after Logan's mess, but she hadn't put clean silverware out or replaced the paper placemats advertising Cold Creek. Michael had created them with his desktop publishing software.

She hustled to set the table. Yes, he was barking. But he had nearly died. Her heart still trembled with fear when she thought of his white face, so still, the blood flowing too fast. The helicopter. The long hours of waiting, praying. All she wanted now was to take care of him, make him happy, be a good wife who met her husband's needs.

The work crew cleared out with a scraping of chairs and thumping boots.

Michael heaved himself to his feet. Jeanie saw him flinch with pain. He was so determined, so strong. And all hers.

God, You gave me a miracle. You showed me how much I cared. I will insist he behave better once he's well, and I'll bet I don't have to. He's just tired and frustrated. Right now I need patience. Thank You for sparing him, Lord.

"Jeanie, stop daydreaming. We've got a lunch crowd that'll be here in a few minutes."

"I'm sorry. I was lost in thought." She considered telling him she'd been lost in prayer, but she didn't want him to think she was chastising him by sounding super religious.

"Yeah, right. You're *thinking*." He left the room, shutting the door a bit too hard.

As Jeanie watched him head for the cabins, she wished he'd let her bring him a chair outside so he could sit, but she'd offered earlier and he'd been embarrassed by it. She needed to be more sensitive to how he felt.

Glynna came out, her stout body wrapped in a white apron. A large bowl in her hands, she stirred as she talked. "He's a big grouch today."

"He's in pain. He needs time. This isn't the real Michael."

Glynna sniffed as she glared through the window at Michael's back. "A real man doesn't use hurting as an excuse to hurt others. He's from the city though. Must be in touch with his feelings or something. I like a man with a stiff upper lip myself."

Jeanie smiled as she cleared the tables. Before long the lunch crowd came in, and she hustled until nearly two o'clock.

Michael came in for lunch, but he didn't speak to her beyond an occasional sharp remark.

Wanting to insist he go home, she kept her worries to herself. He wouldn't thank her for hovering.

Chapter 21

Michael awoke alone, as usual.

Why wouldn't she stay in here with him? They were married. Yes, they'd missed that dumb recommitment ceremony. But they'd already had a wedding. Another one was just a waste of time. If she loved him, she'd stop playing these stupid games and be his wife again.

He was feeling better. She knew that. She wasn't staying away because of his injuries.

He rolled out of bed. Today he'd get this cast off. As he struggled with his clothes, he wished Jeanie would come in and help him. It stung his pride, but he did need help.

He went out into the kitchen and found her pouring eggs into a sizzling skillet.

"I heard you moving around. Breakfast will be ready in two minutes." She smiled over her shoulder at him. A perky smile that reminded him of when she was just a kid and they'd fallen in love. As she stood in the sunlight of the kitchen window, he noticed her hair glinting in the light. She'd lightened it once, but even so it was a lot darker than it had been at one time. He'd loved the shining blond hair of her youth.

"Your hair bleaches out in the summer, doesn't it?"

Jeanie shrugged. "It used to. I don't spend much time in the sun."

"Since you colored it, I see traces of the girl you used to be. You were so pretty."

"I've let it get so dark. The highlights have faded. I should get it redone."

"No, it's fine. Whatever." He kissed her head.

She used her spatula, lifting the edges of the omelet, then sprinkled cheese on the eggs.

"You used to shred fresh cheese." Michael watched her, wishing they could get this meal eaten so he could get to work. "Remember that aged cheddar you'd buy in the deli?"

Jeanie flipped the omelet, turning the circle into a half moon. She was concentrating hard, which is why she didn't answer for a few long seconds. "We use what we have, Mike. No deli in Cold Creek, so I buy shredded cheese at the grocery store. Don't you like it?"

"Hmm." Michael kissed her cheek this time and slid his good arm around her waist. "It's okay if you can't get the good stuff."

She turned before he got a solid hold.

With her hot cast-iron skillet in one hand, Michael had to step back quickly. "Be careful with that." Frowning, he went to the table.

"I'm sorry." She slid the omelet out onto his plate. "Go ahead and eat. I've already had breakfast. I'm going to wash up and walk over to the café."

She began running water in the sink. He liked her to sit down with him, but she was bustling around, ignoring him.

"I'll be done in a second. Give me a few minutes to get ready, and we can ride over together." He ate the omelet. A little dry. Too much cheese. He didn't say it though. He'd learned his lesson about finding fault with his wife.

"I'd rather walk. I like the exercise." She clanked the pan noisily and began scrubbing. Michael tried to ask her questions, but she just scrubbed and gave him noncommittal noises for answers.

"We need to go to Hot Springs this afternoon to get the cast off."

"Do you need me along?"

Of course he didn't *need* her, but he'd have liked the company. "No, I can handle it."

"If you're sure, I'll stay home." She wiped her hands and went into the bathroom, clicking the door closed.

Michael hurried, but Jeanie was already gone when he'd finished dressing. He passed her, driving, only a block from the café. She glanced up when he slowed down, but she waved him on with a smile that bothered Michael. Not a friendly smile, more polite or forced maybe. What was the matter with her today? As if he didn't have enough problems in his life, now he had a moody wife to deal with.

For a second, thinking of Jeanie as moody reminded him of the old days. She used to do this. Answer in single syllables, find countless excuses to leave the room. He didn't want the old days back.

God, I know I'm impatient. I'm sorry. Once I get this cast off and can go back to work, it'll be better. We'll have the wedding, and Jeanie and I will be together completely.

His prayer made him realize it'd been awhile since he'd prayed. And he and Jeanie hadn't been having their devotion time or counseling sessions. He needed to get back to all of that. Then he pulled up to the construction site and saw the men already hard at work. He'd hired himself a real gung-ho work crew.

They spent the morning getting the framing done for all of the remaining cabins. Michael could help one-handed now.

He didn't see more than a glimpse of Jeanie at coffee or lunch. By the afternoon break, she was gone.

He drove to his doctor's appointment and wished she'd ridden along, because he felt shaky after the cast was off. His elbow, wrist, and shoulder burned like fire. The surgical wounds were tender. His whole arm looked sickly and wrinkled and white. He'd lost muscle mass in just these few weeks, and his right arm looked almost withered in comparison to his other.

The doctor assured him it was normal and the stiffness and pain would fade and the muscles would develop again fast. Still, it would have been nice to have Jeanie fussing over him. She had a gift for comfort.

A servant's heart, Pastor Bert had said. He needed to remember that and not demand too much, because Jeanie would give until she had nothing left. He went into the house, determined to apologize for all the growling he'd been doing, and saw his wife was now almost completely blond.

Diverted from his apology, he reached out his good arm to hug her, but she picked up a stack of mail and didn't notice.

"I like your hair. It's pretty."

"I'm glad you like it. I was a little afraid to let Mamie at In-Hair-It bleach it, but I couldn't drive into Rapid City since you had the truck, so it was her or nothing." She began laying junk mail in one stack and making a pile for him and her. He noticed her mail was skimpy.

"How's your arm?" She didn't even look.

"It hurts like crazy. Stiff—the joints are used to being held still."

A furrow creased her brow, and she looked at him and laid her hand on his wrist. "I'm sorry."

She turned to him enough that he could see her face clearly. "You're wearing makeup, too."

Jeanie smiled and turned back to the mail. "I remember you used to like me to fix myself up a little. I've really let myself go in the last few years."

"Well, why wouldn't you? There was no man around to impress." He tried to flirt with her, coax a smile.

She didn't even look up. Instead, she stared at a sales flyer as if she wanted to memorize the price of sirloin steak.

He flexed his arm and nearly gasped from the pain. Why was Jeanie so moody? Why when he was the one in pain? And he'd just told her she looked nice.

A buzzer went off in the kitchen. "There's supper." She turned away from him without so much as looking in his eyes. In fact, he didn't think they'd made eye contact since he'd come in.

"It'll be ready in a minute. Come on and eat whenever you're ready." She vanished through the kitchen doorway.

His jaw set, annoyed by her strange attitude, Michael flicked through the mail, noting she'd kept several pieces for him that she knew he wouldn't want. What a waste of time to have to sort through it twice.

He went into the kitchen to find she'd grilled a steak. That meant he'd have to cut his meat and that would hurt. Like she even cared.

Chapter 22

Michael fought to keep his teeth clenched against the angry words. Three days without the cast and his whole arm still ached with every move. The August heat was oppressive. The crew worked hard and would make the deadline, but it would be close. He needed those cabins done in time for Labor Day weekend, and that was coming up fast.

God, please make this nuisance of an arm heal. It makes me feel so out of control. I know I'm being a grouch. Help me stop, Lord.

He sat down at the table and saw— "Hamburgers again?" It had been five weeks since his accident. His stitches were out, the cast was off, and his bruises were mostly gone. Only the aches and pains in his arm reminded him of his brush with death.

"Last night I made pork chops. You said a hamburger was the only thing you could eat with one hand. You said to make this."

He got so sick of her "I'm sorry." If she did things right, she wouldn't have to apologize all the time. She slid bread onto the table.

Michael stood up, too afraid to speak to ask Jeanie to get him anything. He got the ketchup and mustard out. He'd need it to choke down another dry burger. She should have known that if she was going to serve him the same garbage every night, he'd need to smother the taste.

He set the condiments on the table and noticed the loaf of bread, still in the plastic bag. Grabbing a small plate out of the cupboard, he put a few slices on and centered it. Nicer.

"Sorry, I'm in pain, okay. I don't mean to pick at you." The pain was definitely easing, but he'd figured out sweet Jeanie would put up with anything if he played the pain card. He picked up his sandwich one-handed, remembering how convenient a burger was. He straightened his silverware but carefully said nothing about the sloppy way she'd set the table.

"You yelled about the ketchup and mustard being messy the last time we had burgers." Jeanie took two slices of the bread and started her own burger.

"It's just hard to eat plain when you let the burger get cold. My fault. That call lasted a lot longer than I expected. I noticed that you left the meat on as long as you could."

Jeanie didn't look up from her plate. "A nice way of saying it's burnt."

"It's fine. Let me tell you about the call."

Jeanie listened but stayed focused on making her sandwich then picked at her food. She always picked, couldn't just sit down to a meal. It irritated him, but he said nothing. He'd found fault with her before. Those days were over. He was a new man.

God help it to become an instinct so I don't have to watch my mouth all the time.

He hit a particularly crunchy part of the burger and left the table to spit it out in the trash. Coming back, he finished telling her about the progress on the cabins.

"I've finally got the Web site done. I'm going to load it tomorrow. I'm hoping it will really bring in the customers."

Jeanie nodded, but Michael had the sense that she wasn't excited. He wanted her to be a full partner in every way. She got up and took her plate to the sink, but his frustration made him rise from the table and pull her away from the dirty dishes.

"Kiss me."

"Let me finish here first, Mike."

He turned her around and was surprised that a smile didn't break out. She was so generous with her smiles. "What is it?"

"I feel like we need to talk, but you're not going to like it. I suppose I could just let it go, but. . ."

"No, what is it? We promised we'd be honest with each other." He drew her firmly back to the table and stood over her until she sat down.

She stared at her hands, folded in her lap, and Michael had a flashback to the many times he'd stared at the top of her bowed head. Her body language reminded him of their marriage as it used to be.

Swallowing hard, he pulled his chair closer to hers and sat. "What is it? Tell me."

She spoke to her hands—an annoying habit, but he didn't mention it. He'd learned to keep all his unkind opinions to himself. He loved her for herself, quirky behavior included.

He wasn't going to pick at her to be better, stronger, a full partner. He understood that she was capable of only so much. Look at the way she'd dropped out of that LPN program. He'd expected her to quit. Jeanie had been a quitter since the time they'd met. When he offered her a way out, she'd grabbed it. Just like she'd grabbed a chance to get out of doing bookwork for the café. He'd checked her figures when she wasn't looking, and she made too many mistakes. He'd been quietly correcting them, but it took him so long that he might as well be doing the work himself.

"I'm thinking of moving out."

Michael froze. Even his thoughts quit. His mind went blank as her words hit him out of nowhere.

"I don't want to, but I don't think this is working. I spend time every day being scared of your temper."

Then his mind clicked back into place—a bad place. "My temper?" Michael slammed his fist on the table, and she jumped. Well, she ought to jump. He'd been working his heart out controlling his temper, and now she said she was scared?

"I'm not happy, Michael. Things were going pretty well before you were hurt, but even before that you were going back to the old habits of insulting me, finding fault with me. But I was handling it. I was standing up to you, and you were taking it well. But I—I guess my ability to be brave around you has wilted since you've been hurt. I've been working harder and harder to keep *you* happy, but it's *not* because I love you." She looked up, staring him straight in the eye. "I do love you. There's so much about you to love. But. . .maybe it's me. . .maybe the way you act is perfectly normal and I'm the one with the problem. But I'm afraid of you. And I hate that. I hate it that my heart races when I know the hamburgers are a little bit burnt."

"I didn't complain."

"I was already worried before you came in the room. No, you didn't complain, but you were annoyed and fighting to control it. If you think you're good at covering that up, you're not. And you did make wisecracks. You can't quite control that."

"What did I say?"

"I didn't write it down." Jeanie surged to her feet. "I hate the racing heart, the fear, the tension. I remember this from before. The feeling that I should be taking notes, detailing all your insults and slights, because they're usually small, just tiny cuts, none of them so bad by themselves, and yet, by the time you're done, I'm bleeding to death. I annoy you with supper. I annoy you when I'm not an enthusiastic partner. I just plain annoy you by existing. You think—"

"Jeanie." He stood and his height made it easy for him to look down on her. "I made a point of not saying a single thing even though the meal was cold and burnt. You can't leave me because of things I *didn't* say. The whole point of us working on this marriage is that I've got a—a control-freak problem. I know that. I like everything done just exactly to suit me. But you have your own ways. I'm respecting that. You're just. . .I don't know. . .projecting old feelings onto me. You're remembering what I'd have said before and blaming me for that now. When have I yelled? When have I done anything to scare you?"

"I'm scared of you right now." Jeanie stood and squared her shoulders. "If this were the day after you first came back, I'd call the pastor and make him throw you out."

His lips formed a tight line, and Jeanie took a step back.

That movement made his stomach dive. "Are you afraid I'll hit you?"

"No. You've never been like that. That's not where my fear is rooted. I just. . .I—" She swung her arms wide and turned her back. "It probably *is* my fault. If I had more confidence, maybe I could take your temper and your contempt and shrug it off."

"Contempt? Jeanie, I haven't treated you with contempt. I haven't."

She turned back to him, her arms crossed tight over her chest, her whole body wrapped around itself, cutting him out, saying, "Stay back." She looked up, and he saw the fear, the unhappiness.

"Wh—" Her voice broke. "What are we going to do?"

God, please don't let this dream slip away from me. Help me. Open my eyes to what she needs to get over this baseless fear.

The prayer helped. Michael pulled in a deep breath, letting go of the anger and, yes, his own fear. He had fears, too, that their marriage would be ruined a second time. He reached out his good hand. "Let's pray together."

Their eyes held. The distrust in Jeanie's expression broke his heart. Finally, that kindness, that generosity of spirit he craved and loved and needed as much as he needed air overcame the distrust. She gave him the very best part of herself. The part he'd taken advantage of since the day they'd met.

She took his hand. "Yes, you're right. Instead of saying I was leaving, I should have said, 'We need to pray together.'"

At the end of their prayer, Michael leaned down to kiss her, to really get the marriage back to the footing they'd been on before he'd fallen.

She turned away. "No, Michael. I'm not ready for that yet." She left him to go to her solitary room.

Left him. She hadn't moved out, but hadn't she really left him in her own way?

God, change her heart.

Michael caught himself. He raised both hands to his face, wishing he could wipe the anger and impatience from his mind. That wasn't the right prayer. Or at least not the only prayer he needed.

God, change my *heart.*

Chapter 23

I can't change him. I have to accept that. God, help me love him for exactly who he is. Heal this fear in me. Give me courage, strength, wisdom.

He'd been trying; Jeanie had to admit that. But watching Michael try to control his temper was almost as bad as the temper itself, because he was terrible at pretending. Jeanie's heart raced when he walked around with the black cloud overhead.

Buffy came in to have coffee at the café almost every day. Jeanie felt a new closeness to her little sister, but the fly in the ointment was the way Buffy scowled at Michael and Michael's refusal to sign those papers. The time was nearly gone; Sally would be Buffy's soon.

"I don't know why you have to hassle Michael. He just hates the thought of signing his name to that paper, but he's not going to do anything to stop the adoption."

"You don't know that. You said he refuses to talk about it."

Jeanie had said that. And it was probably true. But honestly, she'd never pushed him, never even brought it up. She dreaded imagining how he'd fly off the handle, maybe do something rash like protest the adoption.

If they were just quiet and let the deadline come and go, everything would be fine.

Michael brought the men in as he always did for morning coffee break, and Jeanie spent the fifteen minutes jumping and waiting on them all before Michael could snap at her. He was trying. Since she'd threatened to leave him, she could tell he was trying.

When they left, Jeanie sank back down beside Buffy at the table nearest the front window. They could look out at the trees lining the creek and the mountain peaks that soared behind them. The neat cabins were nearly done. Tourists were staying in nearly all of the finished buildings.

The café phone rang, and Jeanie went to get it just as Emily came into view through the window. Stephie was with her, but the little girl ran off. She had a lot of friends in town, so she was no doubt going visiting.

Jeanie listened, tears burning her eyes. Grieving, she hung up the phone.

Emily looked up and was on her feet immediately. "What's wrong?"

Buffy came to Jeanie's side right behind Emily.

"The nursing home patient called. Janet Lessman died."

Buffy rubbed Jeanie's back. "She'd been doing badly for a while, hadn't she?"

"She was my last remaining hospice patient. I hadn't realized the end was so imminent. I failed that sweet lady and the whole Lessman family when they needed me most."

Emily and Buffy hugged her.

Jeanie dabbed at her eyes and looked up to catch a strange, serious look pass between her sister and her best friend.

"And why do you think you failed them?" Emily guided Jeanie toward the table.

"Because I did. I haven't really been in to see her since. . ." Jeanie couldn't say it.

Buffy had no trouble. "Since Michael came back."

Emily said, "Jeanie, we have to talk."

—

"Mike, we have to talk."

Michael looked away from the door he'd just finished hanging on the last cabin. "Sure, Jake, what is it?"

"Take a walk, okay?" Jake's eyes went to the other men working nearby. "Its private."

Wondering what was up, Michael swung the door shut and heard the latch click shut solidly. Perfect. With a satisfied smile, he turned and walked along with Jake. "What's up?"

Jake didn't speak until they'd put quite a bit of distance between themselves and the carpenters. Some problem must have come up on the cabins. Michael was a great problem solver, so he prepared to hear about it and fix it.

As they reached the far side of the café that contained the bait and tackle shop, which didn't open for a while yet, Jake stopped, his arms crossed. "What's going on with you and Jeanie?"

That came out of left field. Michael shook his head a little to shift gears from work. "Nothing's going on. Why?"

"Emily and Buffy are in the café right now talking to her. We're really worried. She's changed. When you first came back, after the rugged beginning you two had, it looked like things were going well. But not anymore. She's not happy. And neither are you, Mike."

Michael had focused on Jake. Now he saw Pastor Bert had joined them. From the serious expression on both men's faces, Michael knew they'd planned this.

Chapter 24

We've barely spoken in the last weeks, Jeanie." Emily patted Logan on the back. "We used to talk all the time. Now we barely say hello at church."

"You've been busy."

"I've been almost housebound with a new baby and an overprotective husband. Why haven't you come out to visit?"

"I—I was going to. Then Michael got hurt and—"

"And the gift you sent—you ordered it online, didn't you?"

Jeanie shook her head to clear it. "You didn't like the gift Michael and I gave you?"

"I loved it. That's not the point. You didn't go shopping. You didn't come to visit."

"And you didn't help the Lessman family," Buffy added.

"I feel terrible about that." Hurt crept up along with anger at this strange conversation. "And shopping isn't worth the effort when Michael's so busy."

"What does that have to do with anything? You don't need Michael to buy a present."

"It's not worth—" Jeanie stopped before she admitted it wasn't worth putting up with Michael's scorn if she went to the city alone. Or putting up with his scorn if he had to drive her. She'd had the present overnighted, and she'd put up with his scorn for how much shipping cost.

Jeanie's jaw tightened.

"The thing is—," Buffy began.

Jeanie put up her hand. "I get it now. This is about Michael."

"This is about us loving you, Jeanie." Buffy said. "And we want you and Michael to be happy. And you're not." Silence stretched between the three women.

Jeanie thought of a dozen things to say, all full of defending herself and excusing Michael. Finally, she thought it through to the end and knew. "You're right." Why had Jeanie let it happen? Because she had. Michael had been a tyrant, but Jeanie had put up with it, almost without a whimper. "All the little cuts. Even if every little insult is true and he acts like he's trying to protect me and help poor, dumb little me, it's still wrong."

"Jeanie, you're not dumb. Stop." Emily rested her hand on Jeanie's arm, and

Jeanie realized that the two of them were facing her, almost as if they intended to hold her prisoner here until she admitted they were right.

Well, they wouldn't have long to wait. "You're right. I'm not dumb. I can drive in Rapid City. I was getting top grades in my LPN class. I'm not incompetent. He's not protecting me. He's cutting me off from my friends and my family and making me dependent on only him."

Some of the creases eased from Buffy's face, worry replaced by hope. "How can we help you?"

Jeanie ran her hand through her ridiculously blond hair. She realized she had heavy makeup on and a dress and high heels. And her heart was a mess—soiled, angry, and afraid all the time. All the surface changes had changed her inside for the worse. But no more. "Maybe you could help me find my bat."

Chapter 25

What's this about?"

The look in Pastor Bert's eyes sent an odd chill of fear up Michael's spine.

"This is about the pathetic mess you are making of your marriage." Pastor Bert squared off in front of Michael, Jake at his side. "You need to come to grips with what you're doing to Jeanie."

"Is this some kind of. . .joke?" Michael asked, thrown by this sudden confrontational situation.

"No." Jake's eyes warmed with concern. "We care about you and Jeanie. We want you to be happy. At first you seemed to be working things out, but lately things have gone wrong."

Pastor Bert nodded. "I watched Jeanie change since you've been back."

"And I've worked with you enough to know all the gifts you have. I respect your talents and intelligence. Your faith, too," Jake added.

"We're just fine. I appreciate your concern." Michael shook his head. The word *denial* crept into his thoughts.

"I've seen you change just in the few months since you've been in Cold Creek." Jake stood shoulder-to-shoulder with the pastor, his expression grim. "Not so much at work as with Jeanie. You've started being unkind, hurting her."

"No, I haven't. We've worked through our problems. We're happy now. We're in counseling and—"

Pastor Bert cut him off. "You're not in counseling to my knowledge."

"We meet weekly with you."

"Past tense. I haven't seen you for far too long. But I have seen Jeanie give up all her work of service to Cold Creek."

"She was doing too much. She isn't available for everyone to take advantage of anymore." Michael had saved her from that life of endless demands.

"That work meant a lot to her." Pastor Bert looked straight into Michael's eyes. "And you've cut her off from that and made her into a quiet, isolated shadow of her former self."

Michael's heart sank at the pastor's unflinching stare. This was a man he respected, and he'd thought Bert respected him. Bristling, Michael scowled, ready to throw this all back at them. He'd go somewhere else then, to a town that would appreciate all he could do for them. There were people who'd be grateful.

The door to the café slammed open, and Jeanie came out flanked by Buffy and Emily. From the intent look on his wife's face, Michael knew she'd been getting this same kind of scolding he had.

Jeanie moved so she stood between the other men and Michael. She'd tell them. She'd make sure they knew this wasn't appreciated. She'd take his side and—

She turned to face him. Somehow she was standing with them, against him. Emily and Buffy added themselves to the lineup confronting him.

Except Jeanie's expression wasn't confrontational; it was kind. She reached forward and took his hands. Her eyes, so blue, so sweet, were looking at him like. . .like she felt sorry for him.

"When you first came back, we heard what Pastor Bert had to say, and we made a commitment to change, but we're not living up to our commitment. And that's my fault."

Feeling a little less stunned, Michael tried to listen, tried to ignore this ridiculous business and just give Jeanie all the help she needed.

"It's my fault because I've been letting you hurt me, Mike."

"Hurt you?"

"Yes, and whether that's my problem, left over from childhood, or your problem because you need to control me, I still shouldn't have put up with it. I've swallowed all the little cuts, the slights, the insults."

"Like what? What have I ever said to you that wasn't kind?"

Jeanie glanced over her shoulder at Pastor Bert, who now stood behind her in a row with Buffy, Emily, and Jake, standing like guard dogs protecting her from the man who was supposed to love her as Christ loved the church.

Michael felt deeply and shockingly and painfully alone.

Jeanie reached into her pocket. "This isn't scriptural. What's the verse, Pastor Bert? About not keeping track of when people sin against you."

Bert smiled. "It's from the Love Chapter, 1 Corinthians 13. '[Love] does not keep track of other people's wrongs.'"

Jeanie held up a roll of paper that looked like it had been torn off a cash register receipt roll, and shook it.

Michael's eyes followed it as it unrolled two feet.

"Then I haven't been loving you biblically, Mike. Because I've been keeping a record of your wrongs—the things you say that make me feel bad."

Michael felt his ears heat up. This was humiliating. He hated this. The heat in his ears turned to heat in his temper.

"Stop." Pastor Bert stepped up beside Jeanie.

"Good. I'm glad you stopped her. She shouldn't discuss something private in front of a group." Michael truly respected and cared for this man. He had a fatherly way about him that Michael never had from his own dad. His dad was a tyrant who could wound everyone with a single word. Michael mentally stumbled over that thought. A tyrant? Was that what these people were accusing him of being?

Bert rested one large hand on Michael's shoulder. "I'm not stopping *her*. I'm stopping *you*. I can see you growing angry. The whole purpose of this gathering is that we all love you."

Michael looked from face to face. He wondered about it.

Pastor Bert might love him; he was a man of God.

Jeanie's eyes said that she loved him, even though she stood there holding a list of his sins.

Emily and Jake, maybe—sure, why not? Jake had worked beside Michael a lot. They were good friends.

Buffy, well, she'd always been a woman of faith. If anyone could love an undeserving brother, it was Buffy.

Michael noticed Wyatt wasn't here. Possibly the man had to work. But Wyatt was the one who'd done the most scowling over those adoption papers. More likely, Wyatt was forbidden to be here because, when they'd planned this, Wyatt had voted to round up a posse, a noose, and a lone oak tree. But these folks mostly did love him—in Christian brotherhood. Yes, even Wyatt might claim that, under threat of torture.

Michael could say that, too. He loved them all right back. And he *was* a tyrant. He could take this intervention like a man. He needed it. He needed them all, a lot more than they needed him.

Nodding, he looked at Jeanie. "Tell me. I'm ready to listen. But before you start, I want you to know you're right. I knew when I first got back here that I was the one with the problems, not you. But I let that get away from me." Michael took her hands. "I need help to change. I let the counseling slide and the daily devotions. I'm sorry."

Jeanie crushed the list in one hand and wrapped her arms around him. "I love you. And you're not the only one who went wrong."

Brushing her hair back off of her forehead, Michael noticed it was white blond. Her makeup was heavy. Her clothes were too tight. This was his fault. "You've gone wrong by putting away that bat."

Jeanie lifted her chin and smiled. "I've gone wrong because I kept everything inside. You asked me from the start to make you accountable. I failed. I was doing okay until you got hurt, and then I was just so glad you were alive." She hugged him so hard it hurt.

The best hurt Michael had ever felt.

"I was so glad I had you in my life. You were hurt and understandably grouchy, and I wanted to make your life as comfortable as possible. I started saying yes to every demand and. . .I just let it get away from me. It's so much easier to keep quiet, to avoid confrontation, to take all the blame and try to change myself."

"Twist yourself into a pretzel, you mean."

Jeanie shrugged.

"The accident made it worse, Jeanie," Emily said. "But you remember the day Buffy and I heard Michael putting you down. You were already making excuses for him."

Michael realized he couldn't even remember a time he'd insulted Jeanie in front of Emily. It was too easy to let emotionally abusive language slip free. "I think you'd better read me that list."

"I will, but later. When we're alone. And I'll get another bat."

Pastor Bert produced one from the inside pocket of his suit jacket, and Jeanie let go of Michael to take possession.

"Thanks a lot," Michael said dryly.

"And your counseling resumes tomorrow morning. We'll meet faithfully once a week, and you'd better not make me hunt you down." Pastor Bert sounded kind and unmovable. "You've made promises before, Michael. I really don't know if you can control yourself without someone a little tougher than Jeanie watching you."

"I've stayed too far back from this, too, Michael. I'm not leaving Jeanie to handle you alone." Buffy put an arm across Jeanie's shoulders. "And I tried to talk to you a couple of times about the way Michael treated you, Jeanie, but I let you persuade me to drop it. I won't do that again. If that makes me a meddling little sister, too bad."

They were right. Michael had learned it all at his father's knee, and being a tyrant wasn't something he could change in a day no matter how completely he admitted he had a problem.

Michael looked at the people in front of him, willing to confront him in Christian love, and it struck him that this was what a family meant. This support, this intermingling of lives. And when he thought of it like that, he also knew his whole definition of family had been warped.

He remembered Jeanie's life verse: *"We want you to be very strong, in keeping with his glorious power. We want you to be patient. Never give up. Be joyful."* Jeanie had said she clung to the part about strength but couldn't ever find the joy. He knew now how she felt.

"I want to take my wife home and talk things out." He looked from face to face, until finally he got to the only one that mattered.

Jeanie, her eyes spilling over with tears of pain and love, nodded. "Let's go home."

"Thank you all. I'm going to be a better man."

Jeanie swiped her wrist across her eyes. "I'm going to make sure you are."

"Stop." Buffy's sharp command stopped Michael in his tracks. "Before you walk away, we're going to talk about Sally. I've let that slide, too. I've talked with

Jeanie, but I've never faced you with this. Are you planning to sign those papers or not?"

Jeanie's arm tightened around Michael.

Silence reigned.

Buffy didn't budge. Neither did the pastor or Jake or Emily.

As the silence stretched, Michael felt pain growing until it ached like a broken arm. He heard echoes from his past. Jeanie scared of him. A baby crying. His own cruelty.

God, I was so steeped in sin. I still am.

The pain deepened as Michael faced all that his choices had cost Jeanie, Sally, and himself. And all the pain the wrong choice now could bring.

"I. . .I don't know if I can, Buffy." The least he could do was be completely honest. It was long past the time for not being completely honest. "I haven't signed them because. . .because I would have to admit I'd failed. To sign my daughter away is—" Michael's voice broke. He whirled away, shocked and humiliated by his lack of control.

Jeanie wrapped her arms tightly around him, and he pulled her hard against him, feeling like a fool for crying. A lifetime of sin crushed him. He'd never taken the time to love Sally as she deserved. He'd given no thought to Jeanie when he'd stormed out of her life.

Michael thought of the Love Chapter. Love is patient, and he was terribly impatient.

Love is kind, and he'd been so unkind to Jeanie and his little girl.

It does not envy. Michael never stopped wanting more, wanting what someone else had.

It does not boast, is not proud. Michael wore his pride like a royal robe, and he never stopped boasting about his success.

It is not rude. It is not self-seeking. It is not easily angered. It keeps no record of wrongs.

Michael looked at that list crumpled in Jeanie's hands. But wasn't he the one who had always kept a record of wrongs? Wasn't he the one who had always found fault, never let a chance slip by to criticize?

But he remembered more than the list that convicted him.

He looked into Jeanie's kind eyes, so much more than he deserved. "Love always protects, always trusts, always hopes. It never gives up."

"The Love Chapter," Pastor Bert said quietly.

"I've failed in all of that, Jeanie." Michael's eyes fell shut. It was almost more than he could do to speak the words aloud. "But I'm not going to fail Sally now."

"Michael, please." Fear widened Jeanie's eyes. "You've got to—"

"I mean," he cut her off—and promised himself and God it was for the last time. But this once, because she misunderstood, he stopped her before her hurt could go any deeper. "I mean I'm going to let her go."

Tears burned at his eyes again. But this time he didn't even feel embarrassed. If a man couldn't cry when he gave his child away, then God had no reason to invent tears.

Jeanie threw herself hard against him, buried her face against his chest, and together, for all the failure, all their rugged past, they cried.

A quick signature. Painful as the slash of a knife, but Michael didn't know if it would ever heal. Then he pulled Jeanie close and they turned to go.

Buffy rushed past them to plant herself in their path. "I'm going to be watching you." Her words were tough, but there was kindness in her eyes along with hope. She wanted her sister to be happy. Her expression said she thought that maybe Michael was up to being part of that happiness.

Michael realized he had a real family—a sister, a brother in Wyatt, nieces, nephews. . .a wife. True friends, friends who cared enough to stand in his path when he was heading down the wrong one, in Jake and Emily. He ran a quick hand across his eyes to wipe away the tears then leaned down and kissed Buffy on the cheek. "I'm counting on it."

Buffy stepped aside, and Michael and Jeanie headed for home to begin again for the last time.

Epilogue

Pastor Bert refused to perform the wedding ceremony until Jeanie and Michael went through intensive counseling.

Even Jeanie was impatient by the time the stubborn man finally agreed, declaring the counseling would continue whether they wanted it or not. Jeanie wanted it. She was delighted that Michael agreed with her.

Impatience aside, Jeanie loved every minute of those months. She and Michael were talking as they never had before. Michael wasn't always perfect, but he'd learned to catch his temper, recognize it, and calm down, usually before she threatened him with her support system. The bat sat as a reminder, but Jeanie knew they couldn't rely on that alone again.

She went back to her job at the library. Michael now ran the cash register at the mini-mart every other Saturday. The new cabins lined the creek, the restaurant hummed with activity, and Michael agreed it was enough. No more grand plans—just a lovely little vacation spot.

Jeanie dragged Michael into every volunteer project that came her way. They were so busy they had to schedule the wedding on a weekday night, right after choir practice.

It didn't matter; the wedding was small. Buffy and Emily as bridesmaids. Wyatt and Jake as groomsmen. Their children and a very few others as guests—unless they counted that the whole town of Cold Creek came.

But it wasn't as if they were invited. Having a wedding under the beautiful fall foliage out in front of a row of cabins—well, that was public land. Anyone who wanted could stop and stare. Even a few renters quit their vacationing and attended.

Even knowing it was a huge mistake, Pastor Bert insisted Jeanie use the bat as a ring pillow. With Colt and Cody as ring bearers, the rings had no chance of survival. Jeanie suggested tying fake rings on the bat. Michael agreed and kept the real ones in his pocket.

Sally was the flower girl. As she stood beside the pastor, Jeanie realized they hadn't lost their baby. They could love her wholeheartedly without tearing her secure life apart. And wasn't that *real* love?

"Dearly beloved"—Pastor Bert ducked a line drive like he'd played in the majors—"we are gathered here today. . ."

Wyatt had even warmed up to Michael enough that he acted as best man—and referee. When his Stetson went flying off of his head, Wyatt finally grabbed the bat away from both boys then growled under his breath at the pastor, "I can keep 'em occupied, but I can't keep 'em quiet. Hurry it up."

The vows were spoken quickly. But Jeanie heard the sincerity in every word Michael spoke, and she poured all her love into her own promises.

As the pastor pronounced them man and wife, he closed with an unlikely wedding scripture: " 'We want you to be very strong, in keeping with his glorious power. We want you to be patient. Never give up. Be joyful.' "

It was finally, completely true. Jeanie smiled at Michael and knew joy. A joy that hadn't been there when they'd married the first time. And it hadn't been there when he came back. It had been a rocky road, but God knew they'd needed to walk such a broken path to learn true strength, to find abiding patience, to experience great joy, to know true love.

As the scripture said, they'd never given up. And they'd made it.

Smiling, Jeanie stood on her tiptoes, eager to obey the pastor when he told her bossy bridegroom to kiss the bride.

A Letter to Our Readers

Dear Readers:

In order that we might better contribute to your reading enjoyment, we would appreciate you taking a few minutes to respond to the following questions. When completed, please return to the following: Fiction Editor, Barbour Publishing, Inc., P.O. Box 719, Uhrichsville, OH 44683.

1. Did you enjoy reading *Black Hills Blessing* by Mary Connealy?
   ❑ Very much. I would like to see more books like this.
   ❑ Moderately—I would have enjoyed it more if _____
   _____
   _____

2. What influenced your decision to purchase this book?
   (Check those that apply.)
   ❑ Cover   ❑ Back cover copy   ❑ Title   ❑ Price
   ❑ Friends   ❑ Publicity   ❑ Other

3. Which story was your favorite?
   ❑ *Buffalo Gal*   ❑ *The Bossy Bridegroom*
   ❑ *The Clueless Cowboy*

4. Please check your age range:
   ❑ Under 18   ❑ 18–24   ❑ 25–34
   ❑ 35–45   ❑ 46–55   ❑ Over 55

5. How many hours per week do you read? _____

Name _____

Occupation _____

Address _____

City_____ State_____ Zip_____

E-mail _____

RODEO HEARTS

Love is a rodeo in modern-day Nebraska. A contemporary romance three-in-one collection.

ISBN 978-1-60260-797-2

Contemporary, paperback, 352 pages, 5¾" x 8"